THE LAST CHIEF

The Divalian Chronicles

Book 2

S. T. Hobbs

Table of Contents

Chapter 1

L EADING THE SMALL BLACK MARE out of the paddock, Sasha made his way to the front of the barn. His brows knit together in frustration as he stopped to catch his breath. This was getting old, very old. Taliea had warned him not to push himself too hard. She said it would only make it worse. But Sasha was sick of just hanging around the house, watching everyone else go about their work. He dropped the mare's rope as he came to the saddle. It was disappointing how much effort it took him to lift it and carry it out here. Bracing himself for another round of exertion, he bent and scooped it up off the ground, laying it heavily on the horse's back. Someone cleared their throat behind him, and Sasha turned to find Hamo waiting.

"Sasha, can I talk to you?"

Sasha's throat constricted at the somber strain in Hamo's tone. Everything was fine. At least, Sasha thought it was. Now, trying to read the expression on Hamo's face, Sasha wasn't as sure.

"It's not something to be worried about." Hamo smiled a little, picking up on Sasha's anxiety, "It's just, there's something you need to know. Wait for me a minute, alright?"

"Alright." Sasha turned back to tightening his horse's girth. It took him several tries before he was convinced he'd secured it tight enough.

Hamo came out of the barn a few minutes later, leading his own saddled horse.

"Come on. You can ride with me to the forge," he said as he started off, leading the way.

Sasha hurried to catch up with him. He had known Hamo often worked at the forge but had never been to the place. Unfamiliar with most trades, curiosity tangled with anxiety as they rode. Thoughts strayed to his recent conversation with Ophelia at Aldrid and Taliea's wedding. So far, he had just been focused on regaining his strength and health. But she was right. He knew she was right. If he was going to find Mother and Agathe, he would need some means of making money. Maybe it was time to turn some serious thought in that direction.

"You know, I spoke with King Darien during the union meetings," Hamo started.

"I know." Sasha looked over at him, confusion stamped on his features. What Hamo was saying was no secret. He'd been gone for days at the meetings, leaving Sasha home with the family to recover. He'd also secured what Sasha considered to be his two most precious possessions at those meetings. "Thank you, by the way. I forgot to tell you when you came back."

Hamo brushed his thanks aside, his face still perturbed. "It was nothing, and I owed it to you. To be honest, I think King Darien likes writing those things. Sasha, what did you say your brother's name was?"

"Which one? I sort of have a lot."

"The one you were telling me about. When you first woke up, you told me one of your brothers was there, and that he was going to kill you, but didn't. What was his name?"

"You mean Boris?" Sasha's confusion deepened.

Hamo nodded thoughtfully.

"What is it?" Sasha couldn't even begin to think why Boris' name was of the least importance now. No doubt he was gone, either dead or returned home - which might be the same as dead, Sasha realized. Father would hardly be in the mood to welcome back an already disgraced son after such a devastating defeat.

"He's alive."

The words struck Sasha with an almost physical force. He stiffened in his saddle, his face paling several shades. The full meaning of Hamo's words took a moment to fully register. If Boris was truly alive, then he could take word of Sasha's betrayal to Father. It might even be enough to earn his way back into Father's favor.

"What? How? I mean, how would you know?"

"He was taken prisoner after the battle." Sasha's face flooded with relief. "I don't know the details. All I know is he was being held in Dorsten by Lord Bayner when the lord was removed from his position and King Darien took over."

"Did the lord do the same things to him that he did to me?" Sasha's face clouded with the memory of his time in Lord Bayner's hands. "Did he torture him too?"

"Yes. Worse, I think. As badly as everything worked out for him, I would imagine the lord took out a lot of his anger for you on him."

Sasha shut his eyes, trying to push away the images that rose in his mind. His own imprisonment and torture. His own hand wielding the whip that tore into Boris' back. Boris raising his sword to deliver Sasha's death.

"There were other prisoners taken, not many, but some. Boris is the only one of any significance as far as we can tell. King Darien had him brought here."

"He's here?"

"Well, in Bren. In the castle, that is. They're holding him there for now. The truth is, Sasha, the king doesn't really know what to do with him. We can't just turn him loose, but he also doesn't want to just leave him locked up. You know better than anyone, is there any chance your father would make some sort of deal to get him back?"

Sasha shook his head. "Not a chance. He sent Boris in the front ranks because he wanted him to die. It was part of his punishment."

"That's what I thought. It's what I told King Darien. I think he still plans on trying though."

For several minutes the only sound was that of the woods around them. The trees, heavy with their summer foliage, rustled gently in the breeze. The sound of small animals skittering and scampering mingled with the sharp staccato of a nearby woodpecker. Sasha looked around at the peaceful scene. Peace. Until these last few weeks, he had no idea what a wonderful word that was. Having it was the best thing in the world. Sasha sighed. The troubling memories of the battle surfaced uninvited, pushing away the sense of peace and tranquility. Boris' face, all his rage, all his hate channeled into the words he screamed at Sasha.

But Boris hadn't killed Sasha.

Whatever was going through his brother's head in that moment was a mystery to Sasha.

"Can I see him? Would you take me?"

"No."

Sasha's face fell.

"I'm not going anywhere. Not for as long as I can possibly help it. I'm getting a little sick of being away from my family. However, you are free to go and see him if you like."

"I can do that?"

"As much as anyone else in this country. Didn't Stephan give you those papers?" Hamo laughed.

"You know he did. I just...," Sasha paused. "You know, I've never actually been allowed to just go and do things that I wanted to. It's really strange."

"Having a hard time getting used to the idea? Actually, that was sort of the whole point of my telling you all this. King Darien wanted me to ask you if you'd be willing to help him. I already figured you'd want to see him so..."

"You knew I'd want to see him?"

"It's been bothering you ever since you came out of your fever. Now's your chance to ask him. Besides, he's your brother."

"Doesn't mean much. What does King Darien want my help for?"

"Apparently, either he's incredibly stubborn or he truly doesn't understand anything that's been said to him."

"He doesn't. Father only had me learn your language, I don't know why." Actually, when Sasha took the time to think about it, there was a lot Father required of him that he did not make Boris do. "King Darien wants me to talk to him? Does he trust me to do that?"

"If you're willing to. I just told him I'd ask. I think everyone would understand if you didn't want to be put in that position, though."

Sasha pulled his horse up as they approached the forge. Just the short ride had tired him out, and his leg ached deep in the bone. He debated riding straight back or staying for a while. Curiosity won out, and he slid down, careful to place most of his weight on his good leg. Letting the reins drop to the ground in the signal that any well-trained Aruuken horse would recognize as a command to stay, he followed Hamo inside.

"I don't know if I'm up to riding that far at the moment," Sasha said, settling onto a stool and letting his head lean back against a wall.

Hamo was too busy starting a fire to respond. Sasha watched him, marveling at how easy he made it look. His own attempts had been frustrating, to say the least. Suddenly, Sasha sat forward.

"Show me."

Hamo's head snapped up and he cast a questioning glance in Sasha's direction.

"Show me how you do it. I want to learn." Sasha remembered Ophelia's suggestion that he learn a trade and make his own living. Since he had little idea about any trade, one seemed as good as another, and he didn't think he'd mind Hamo as a teacher.

"You want to learn how to start a fire? Or all of it?"

"We can just start with making a fire, but all of it eventually."

"I don't know that you're quite up to learning something like this yet. It's not that fun in the first place, and it's horrible if you're not fully recovered."

"You say that like it happened to you."

"It did." Hamo's tone left Sasha in no doubt that the conversation wasn't going any further in that direction.

Sasha picked up a tool and fiddled with it in his hands, his thoughts turning once more to Boris. It would be a while before he would feel up to the task of traveling all day. It would be a while before he could fully accept that he was allowed to. The idea was so foreign, so beyond the strict control that he had spent his entire life under that it was almost frightening.

Chapter 2

BORIS STARED IDLY AT THE ceiling. At this point, he'd memorized just about every crack and crevice. With a sigh, he rolled over onto his stomach, staring now at the wall. Now that he was no longer in constant, debilitating pain there was nothing to occupy his thoughts.

This boredom would drive him mad. He could feel it already, gnawing away at his sanity. If only they would do something with him. If he had a certain fate, a sentence, he might be able to hold the madness at bay. But there was nothing, nothing but interminable separation and confinement. At least, there was nothing that they were telling him. Not that they could tell him. Since he'd been brought here from Dorsten, not a single person said something in a language he understood. He'd never realized the depth of loneliness that accompanied being unable to communicate with anyone.

Shutting his eyes, he conjured up a picture that was etched deeply in his memory. Sasha. Sasha was the reason he was here. If he'd just killed him and moved on, or even left him to die on his own and escaped while he had the chance, he wouldn't have ended up here. As badly as Sasha was wounded,

Boris doubted he survived. The fact that he didn't know for sure bothered him.

Laying on his cot with his eyes shut, Boris began to doze. Sleep was the only way he had to make the time go by faster.

A rattling of keys outside his cell awoke him and drew his gaze to the heavy door. Not bothering to get up, he watched the door swing out. Expecting to see only his jailer bringing his daily fare, Boris started to turn back to the wall. It was always just the jailer, and he only ever came to set the tray of food down or take it away again. Boris ignored the man.

The sound of more than one pair of feet stepping into the room caused Boris' head to whip around again. Three men, the jailer and two guards, entered the room.

Boris tensed on his bed.

Whatever they were coming to do, he would fight them, just like he'd fought the guards in Dorsten. It was exhausting and inevitably ended in great pain for him. But it gave him the sense of control he so desperately needed. Besides, it irritated the men who had to do anything with him. And that annoyance, that knowledge that he was causing them more trouble than they cared for, was sweet satisfaction.

It was his only satisfaction.

The jailer, an older man who looked strangely out of place for his task and whose breathing made an annoying wheezing sound, motioned for Boris to get up. Boris didn't move, glaring at the man. The jailer gave vent to a heavy sigh, and Boris smiled internally. A handful of strange words were exchanged between the trio.

Boris watched with a wary eye as the jailer waved a frustrated hand in the air and the two guards stepped forward. Laying on his stomach on the cot probably wasn't the best position to be caught in, Boris decided when he was almost immediately pinned down. His face was shoved into the pillow, smothering any protests he might have made. Not that they would have understood him anyway. His arms were pulled behind him, and he felt the cool clasp of metal locking around his wrists.

Not much of a fight, Boris acknowledged as they pulled him up from the bed. He let his legs go limp beneath him, forcing the men to bear his entire weight. Blood filled his mouth and pain spread across his jaw as one of the men struck his face. Compared to his time in Dorsten, the blow was relatively harmless, but it set off alarm bells in Boris' head that were hard to ignore. Punishments could get worse, a lot worse.

Without consciously deciding to, Boris found his legs cooperating with the guards. He found himself taking a step with them, moving toward the door. And Boris began to fight in earnest. Every single time he had left his cell in Dorsten had been a nightmare of agony. The thought of it starting all over again spurred him to desperation.

With his arms secured behind him, there was only so much Boris could do. He twisted in his captors' hands, tried to throw himself to the floor to break their grasp, and all the while the doorway grew closer. He sank to the ground once more, allowing all his weight to fall on the men. This time, they didn't even bother to hit him. Keeping a firm hold on his arms, they continued pulling. Boris bit down a scream as his arms were wrenched forward, threatening to come out of joint. He scrambled to get his feet under him, anything to take away the burning, tearing pain that erupted through his arms and shoulders.

They were standing outside his cell now. Boris panted, his breath coming in hot, heavy gasps that betrayed the defiance he tried to maintain on his face. The jailer met his eyes and Boris was surprised to find that the man's face didn't convey anger, but pity. The jailer shook his head sadly before turning to lead the way down.

Rather than being put in the dungeon here, he was in a tower cell. The spiraling flight of stairs stretched down in front of them and held firmly between the two guards, Boris began his descent.

Reaching the bottom, he was surprised and dismayed to find a hall with more than a few people milling about it. Servants scurried about, busy with their work. Here and there, groups of what he assumed were noblemen and women stood in groups talking. Members of the castle guard, apparently off duty, stood in a cluster not far from the foot of the staircase. They collectively looked up at Boris' arrival. One of the uniformed men called out to the guards holding Boris, and everyone in the group began laughing. Quite sure that the laughter was directed at him, Boris lowered his head as blood rushed to his face. His ears burned at the sound of their mockery.

Fortunately, his walk down that hall was short. They had only gone a little way before the jailer pulled open an unmarked door and ushered the group inside. There wasn't much in the room and no other people that Boris could see. He was led, dragging his feet, to a chair that sat by itself in the center of the room. Undoing the shackles that held his arms, they pushed him into it and quickly secured him to the arms of the chair before Boris had a chance to fight them.

Without another word, Boris was left alone.

His efforts to break free of the straps that held him down proved futile. At last, Boris gave up exhausted and sank back against the chair, resigning himself to whatever was to come. His mind wandered in the quiet emptiness, dragging him back to the dungeons of Dorsten and reminding him of the torment that most surely awaited him. His body was only just now healing from all of that.

The silent emptiness of the room grew tangible with the passing of time. Boris' defiance drained away. There was no one to see it here anyway and he lacked the strength to maintain it. He needed his strength for what was to come. He needed his mind in control.

Boris took a deep breath, trying to still the tremors that rose up inside him. The sound of a door creaking open behind him brought them rushing back. To his dismay, it took longer than usual for Boris to hide his despair.

Chapter 3

SASHA STARED AT THE HANDFUL of coins in his palm.

In his entire life, he'd never given two thoughts to money, or how he would make it. He never needed to. Everything was always provided for him when he was in Aruuk. Now, staring at them, Sasha realized how unprepared he was for any life other than the one Father had chosen for him. Knowing Father, that was probably exactly what he intended.

Stephan had given him these coins, in return for promised work as soon as he felt well enough. Sasha was a little uneasy about working with Stephan, but he knew he couldn't go somewhere on his own without any money at all. Stephan might not have been his first choice of an employer, but Sasha wasn't in a position to be picky.

Shoving the coins into his pocket, he spurred his horse into a trot. Sasha let his gaze wander over the countryside he was riding through, trying to convince himself that what he was doing was really acceptable. Hamo had reassured him, probably more times than he really cared to, that Sasha was perfectly fine traveling on his own.

It was a strange sensation to be out on the open road, not hiding from anyone, and not with the threat of discovery and death breathing down his neck. With Father thoroughly defeated, the lump of worry and fear had finally been able to dissipate fully. Knowing that Boris was safely locked away and unable to take word of his treachery to Father removed the last piece of apprehension from his mind. Sasha was the safest he'd ever been in his short life, and it was wonderful.

By late afternoon, Bren was visible on the horizon. The sharp salty scent of the sea was carried in by a gentle breeze. It had taken Sasha a while to place the odor, having never been to the sea before. He mentally added that to the list of things he wanted to see or do.

Nervousness resurfaced as he rode under the stone archway of the castle. He relinquished his horse to the hands of a stable hand and allowed himself to be led inside by a tall, rigid man to whom he had first stated his business. The interior of the castle was just as surprising as the first time, but he wasn't given a chance to gawk. The man led him further into the castle than he had come with Hamo, and Sasha wondered if he would even be able to find his way out again. Stopping in front of an unmarked door near the end of one spacious corridor, his guide turned to him.

"Wait out here."

Sasha watched the man's stiff figure disappear into another door and sat down on a bench to wait. Twiddling his fingers as he waited, his thoughts strayed willfully, reminding him of why he was here. He was going to see Boris. And he had no idea if Boris wanted to see him. If the look on his face in the battle was anything to go off of, Boris hated him. For the last three weeks, since Hamo first disclosed Boris' survival to him, Sasha had thought about what he would say. Now, twisting his fingers together, the words frayed apart in his mind and evaporated into nothing.

"Thank you, Sasha, for coming. I hope the trip was not too much for you. Hamo told me the extent of your injuries and I think it's safe to say you are a very lucky young man."

Sasha jumped to his feet at King Darien's words, unsure of what his own behavior was supposed to be. Everything was so different from the last time he'd met the monarch. And King Darien was so different from any other leader he'd ever met.

"I'm going to be very honest with you," King Darien continued without giving Sasha adequate time to make any sort of obeisance, "this brother of yours is very uncooperative. He's done his best to give us trouble at every turn."

Sasha's heart sank with the words. Boris' face had said everything on the battlefield. He'd called Sasha a traitor then. Sasha could only imagine what his brother would think if he saw Sasha now, working with King Darien. Despite that, there was one question that ate away at Sasha, one he had to ask his brother. His curiosity overrode his apprehension.

"Can I see him alone first?"

King Darien hesitated. He exchanged a glance with the man who stood a few paces behind him. The man frowned and shook his head slightly. King Darien sighed.

"I'll give you five minutes with him alone," King Darien said while the frown on the other man's face deepened. "He's just in there. And Sasha, you won't be doing any favors for him if you try to help him escape."

"I'm not going to do that." Sasha poorly concealed the hurt of distrust in his voice. "To be honest, he probably hates me. There's every chance in the world that he won't speak to me."

"Five minutes then. If he will talk to you at all, I'd like to ask him some questions. If you are willing, of course."

Sasha nodded, moving toward the door. He preferred not to be drawn into questioning Boris at all, but King Darien was being generous, and Sasha felt compelled to repay that generosity. Besides, if Boris already hated him, what did it matter?

The door opened on squeaky hinges and Sasha stepped into the room. There were no windows in this room allowing the warm summer sun to flood it with its light. It was lit up by a small fire, and a number of torches mounted to the wall, giving the entire room a soft orange glow and a drowsy feel.

Sasha's eyes fell immediately on the centerpiece of the room, a chair with a figure seated in it, facing away from him. Without seeing his face, Sasha knew it was Boris. The sag in his shoulders was painfully familiar, awakening an old ache inside Sasha for what they had shared when they were younger. In the fraction of a second it took for Boris to register that he was being watched, Sasha saw the despair and fear that hung over his brother.

Boris' head snapped up and his entire body went rigid as he became aware of another presence in the room. The fear morphed into defiance. He twisted around in his seat and turned his head as far as he could, and Sasha watched the tumult of emotions battling for supremacy on his face. Clearly, Sasha was the last person he had expected to see. Even so, it only took him a moment to recover, a moment for his features to harden, for his eyes to grow cold and distant. He faced the front of the room, away from Sasha, and stared straight ahead.

"What are you doing here?" Boris' words cut through the air like a whip, loud and echoing in the near-empty room. "Come to watch them torture me?"

"No. I wouldn't do that," Sasha began.

Boris snorted. "You're going to be the one carrying it out, just like you did for Father? It'd be just like old times."

Sasha tried to swallow the lump of guilt away. Of the many moments in his life Sasha wished he could take back, that one ranked among the chief. He crossed the room to the space in front of Boris, his footsteps reverberating off the walls.

"You know, I saved your worthless life, and this is what happens to me. And you just can't miss being a part of it." Boris's voice rose with each word, and he gave a savage yank against his bindings. Sasha retreated a safe distance, leaning against a heavy oak table behind him, glad that his brother had been restrained. "You traitor. I hate you. I should have killed you. I should..."

"Why didn't you?" Sasha interrupted.

Boris froze. His head hung down, refusing to meet Sasha's gaze.

"You had me there, laying on the ground. I couldn't have stopped you if I wanted to. So why didn't you do it? Why didn't you kill me?"

"I couldn't," he whispered after a long moment. Regaining his composure, he glared up at Sasha, allowing a sneer to spread across his face. "You were so scared watching me, thinking I was going to kill you. I could see it all over your face. I drove my sword six inches into the ground next to your head, but I couldn't put it through it. And now I'm here. So, whatever you've come to do to keep your new friends happy, do it. I don't care."

Sasha lowered his gaze to the floor. Boris couldn't miss the pained look on his face as the door opened again and two men entered the room. In an instant, Boris' demeanor changed yet again. His face went gray. His breath came heavy and fast, and Sasha watched his fingers curl around the arms of the chair, his knuckles turning white with the strength of his grip. Again, Boris' fear was on full display for Sasha, and Sasha hated it. He knew where it came from and wished there was time to ask how badly Lord Bayner had hurt Boris. It was too late.

"You're a liar. You did come here to help them," cried Boris, his face a mask of horror and desperation. "What are you going to do to me?"

"They just want to ask you some questions. I'm not going to hurt you, Boris. I wouldn't do that."

"Except when Father told you to." Boris' voice carried with it all the bitterness of that awful day, and Sasha didn't have a good response. "Or have you conveniently forgotten that part?"

"Just tell them what they want to know."

"Traitor," Boris hissed as the men sat down at the table.

Sasha ignored his brother's last word and turned to King Darien and the man accompanying him. He recognized him as being one of the men at the war council, although he didn't know his name.

"Well, judging from the look on your face, I'd say you were correct in assuming he hates you?" King Darien offered a sympathetic smile as Sasha nodded glumly, "At least he is talking to you. Perhaps he'll be more willing to cooperate."

"I don't know about that."

"Perhaps you can inform him that his life is entirely in our hands at the moment, and as we have reason to believe he participated in the raid against Dorsten some months ago, we have grounds to hang him. He should consider that possibility before behaving the way he does," the councilman said.

"Baron, please." King Darien held up a placating hand to stop his companion. "Sasha, I know I'm asking a lot of you here, but please tell your brother that we have made an offer of exchange to the Chief of Aruuk. Should that offer be declined, and I'm guessing it will be, he will remain here as our prisoner. If he does not want to spend the rest of his time alone, I would suggest he at least stop fighting with whoever we confine him with. He is only succeeding in making his own time here harder."

"That's what he's been doing?"

"We've tried three times to put him with others, each time has ended in a fight that he was the cause of."

"He doesn't even understand what anybody's saying. How can he be starting anything?" Sasha wasn't sure why he was even trying to defend Boris. Boris could have cared less. But his own experience in prison had been ghastly. He couldn't imagine how much worse it would have been to not understand anyone.

"Sasha, we put him in with his own people. That wasn't the problem, I'm afraid."

Sasha turned to his brother and relayed King Darien's words. Boris, his face once more shielded by the stony mask of defiance, refused to acknowledge him at all.

"Ask him if the Chief is planning any more attacks of this nature," the baron spoke up, and since King Darien didn't contradict him, Sasha did so.

Boris actually looked up at him then. And laughed. A bitter, hollow laugh that echoed off the walls of the near-empty room.

"Really, Sasha? Isn't that a question you should be answering? Aren't you the one Father invited to all the meetings? I wouldn't know because you whipped me, and Father banished me."

"Boris, stop," Sasha finally snapped. "None of this is my fault. You're just making things worse for yourself."

"Not your fault? You say that a lot for someone who has taken matters into his own hands repeatedly."

"Just answer their question."

"No."

Sasha decided to take the no as Boris not knowing anything and that was what he told King Darien and the councilman. A few more questions later, it became obvious that no was the only answer Boris was willing to give. Sasha didn't blame him, but he felt the baron's distrust growing by the minute. At last, King Darien pushed his chair away from the table and stood up.

"Thank you again, Sasha. I'm sorry things had to be this way," he said as he started to leave the room. Sasha ran after him.

"Your Majesty, wait. Please. What are you going to do to him? My father's not going to agree to any exchange. He sent Boris to die in the first place. So, what happens to him?"

"Honestly, I don't know. I can't simply turn him loose. He's proven he can't be trusted to stay out of trouble, and he was taken in battle against us. At the same time, I can't really stand the idea of keeping him locked up forever. I'll bring it before the council and let them decide if it comes to it."

Sasha accepted the answer and stood out of King Darien's way. He watched two guards come in and remove the restraints that held Boris to his chair. Boris fought them as soon as the restraints came loose. He managed to push one man to the ground and dodge the grasping hand of the other. He sprinted toward the door, freezing when he caught sight of Sasha still standing there. Boris' eyes went wide, an unasked question in them. Sasha hesitated. If he stopped his brother now, there was no chance of him ever regaining the friend he'd lost. But if he let him go, no one here would trust him anymore.

Sasha stepped in front of Boris' path.

Chapter 4

BORIS DIDN'T EVEN BOTHER TO climb onto his cot. He sat where the guards had deposited him on the floor in the middle of his cell, his mind replaying the scene from an hour before over and over. His body hurt all over. The guards, already more than frustrated with his past behavior, had been thorough in their punishment of him.

None of it hurt as much as the knowledge that Sasha was the one to stop him. It didn't matter that he couldn't have actually run very far. It didn't matter that there were at least a dozen other guards milling around outside who would have stopped him the second he stepped foot outside that door. It didn't matter that he had no real plan for escaping and nowhere to go.

All that mattered was that Sasha had looked him in the eye, had seen his unspoken plea, and ignored it. Sasha had brought his bid for freedom to a halt. The worst of it was that Boris could have gotten past him. He was bigger than Sasha and certainly desperate enough. It was the shock of seeing his brother act against him personally that froze him in his tracks. It was the betrayal that stopped him.

The door groaned on its hinges, alerting Boris to someone's entrance. He didn't bother to turn and see who it was. He couldn't bring himself to care. He heard the wheezing breath of the jailer coming in behind him. His ears strained to catch the presence of anyone else as his body tensed. He'd been expecting them to start torturing and questioning him any day, just like they had in Dorsten. Since he refused to answer any questions earlier today, the torture was no doubt on its way.

There was only one set of footsteps in the room, and they came closer. The jailer came into Boris' peripheral, the tray of food balanced carefully in his hands. He set it down on the small table that was bolted against the far wall. Boris' eyes followed his movements dully. The jailer, having deposited the tray as required, turned to go. He paused, looking at Boris, sympathy written all over his face.

Boris hated him for it.

He hated everyone here.

He hated the hours and hours and hours of being alone. He hated that no one understood anything he said. He hated his brother for turning on him. As one hatred piled on top of another, Boris' rage boiled over.

He waited until he heard the lock click back into place before grabbing the tray in both hands and flinging it, and all of its contents, into the wall. Food splattered against the stone and slid down it, leaving colored streaks behind it. Boris stared at it for a moment before beating his fists against the same wall, a horrible, primal yell tearing from his throat.

As the wall turned red with his blood and his voice grew hoarse from yelling, the door flew open and a guard entered, shouting over him. The string of foreign words did little to assuage the rage that coursed through Boris. Even if he'd wanted to, Boris could no longer control himself.

He turned on the guard.

He had as much chance of tackling the guard as he had running away earlier. The man saw him coming and before Boris could lay a hand on him, the guard stepped to the side and tripped him, sending him sprawling across the hard stone floor. His head bounced off of it. Blackness closed in on his vision. Hands pinned him to the ground. He pushed against them. His eyes blinked open long enough to see the fist coming. Pain exploded across his face. His ears rang. His vision clouded over completely.

Chapter 5

SASHA ENTERED THE INN TRYING to maintain a casual, nonchalant look. He didn't want anyone here guessing that he had never done anything like this before. The tavern that took up the lower level was boisterous and crowded. Sasha shrank back at first.

There were times when he missed the rigid order of Father's house. He didn't have any idea how to act in the face of such informality and freedom. Skirting past a group of men, he made his way up to the counter. The young woman tending it looked no more than a few years older than himself, but she was efficiently managing her job. A polite smile that lingered a little longer than necessary as if it was plastered on and couldn't be peeled off again graced her face when she caught sight of him.

"What can I do for you?" The smile finally faded as she spoke.

"I, um...do you have a room? That I could use. Tonight."

"Certainly. Do you want supper as well?"

Sasha glanced around the room. He couldn't imagine trying to eat down here. "Can I eat it in my room?"

"Yes."

"Good." Sasha couldn't hide his relief. He pulled out his entire handful of coins and held them out.

"Not much of a partier?" The woman counted a few out of the palm of his hand and handed him a key. "Up the stairs, three doors down, on the left. What name shall I put down for it?"

"Sasha Gundarson."

"That's a funny name. Don't think I've heard it before."

Sasha decided it was time to leave before she could keep the conversation going any longer. Talking face to face with women was still something he was adjusting to. He did alright when it was one of Hamo's daughters or Edith or Taliea. Beyond that, he couldn't shake the wrongness of it.

Climbing the stairs, Sasha counted down to his door and unlocked it. Aside from the sounds of the tavern that drifted up through the floorboards, the room was quiet. Sasha lay back on his bed, hands crossed over his stomach, and stared at the wooden beams above his head.

The silence wasn't what he wanted right now either, he realized. His thoughts clamored for his attention and shutting his eyes, all he could see was Boris. Boris had silently pleaded for Sasha to let him go. But Sasha hadn't. He'd watched the aftermath with a pang of guilt that grew heavier by the minute. The guards, already tired of Boris' behavior, unleashed their anger on his brother's body.

Sasha must have drifted off. A persistent knocking on the door made him sit up, blinking with sleep. The knocking grew louder. Sasha hurried to the door and opened it. Another young woman, this one wearing a wide apron over her clothes, held a tray.

"Your supper, sir." She held it out to him.

"Thanks."

The smell of the food reminded Sasha how hungry he was. Once again, he thought of Boris. He had been starving during his imprisonment in Dorsten. He wondered if Boris was now. King Darien didn't seem like the kind of person who would do that to anyone else, but the guards might.

He was halfway through the savory stew when another knock sounded on his door. Expecting to open it and find one of the serving women, Sasha's mouth dropped open at the sight of a castle courier.

"Sasha Gundarson?"

"Yes?"

"King Darien sent me to get you. He needs to see you."

Sasha's face underwent a quick transformation from confusion to concern. He had only been there two or three hours ago. What had happened since then? Knowing he could not simply refuse the king, he followed the courier out into the hallway, locking the door carefully behind him.

"What does he want to see me about?"

"Not my place to tell you," the man said shortly, then, noticing Sasha's trepidation for the first time, added. "If you were in trouble, though, he wouldn't have sent me to come and get you."

"Good to know."

It was well after dark when Sasha followed the courier into the same library he and Hamo had first met with King Darien. The king looked up from what he was doing when they came in and rubbed a hand across his forehead.

"Thank you, Colin. Just wait outside a minute, would you? Sasha, come in." King Darien motioned him to a seat. "I'm afraid I've some bad news for you."

A cold premonition came over Sasha. "What happened to him?"

"According to the guard who first entered the room, he'd gone mad. I understand his feelings toward you, but I thought you should know. He was injured when they restrained him."

"Can I see him?"

"Do you think that would be a wise idea? Perhaps it was seeing you this afternoon that caused this. I mean, he's given us trouble from the time we brought him here, but nothing like today."

Sasha thought about the way Boris sat slumped in the chair before he knew someone was there to see him. The bravado, the defiance, it was all an act. "He's scared, that's all. He thinks he's going to be tortured again. He doesn't understand anyone but me. He doesn't know what's going to happen to him. I think that has more to do with it."

King Darien nodded his understanding. "Colin can take you to him."

Following Colin up the winding staircase of the tower gave Sasha at least a minute or two to wonder just how badly his brother was injured. A guard stood outside a heavy wooden door that was bolted shut.

"He's here to see the prisoner. King said he could," Colin said to the man, signaling him to open the door and step aside.

Sasha took one step into the room and his eyes widened. Evidence of Boris' mad tantrum remained, plastered and drying to the walls. Boris himself lay on the narrow cot; his eyes shut. Sasha stepped toward him. Even in the dancing light of a torch, Sasha could make out the jagged gash on his brother's face and the bruised skin around it. The top of his head was wrapped in a bandage. A glance over the rest of him revealed heavy iron chains holding his neck, wrists, and ankles to the cot. Clearly, they weren't taking any more chances with him.

Sasha sat down on the floor next to his brother's bed, conscious of the fact that both Colin and the guard were still standing there watching him. It occurred to him that they probably had no idea why Sasha was even here. King Darien had made it a point to keep his identity secret, a choice Sasha thought it wise not to argue with. A surreptitious glance at the two men showed he was correct. They were curious.

"Are you planning on spending the night in there?" Colin finally asked.

Sasha nodded, realizing that was exactly what he intended now that it had been put into words. He wondered if they were going to try intervening. King Darien had not really specified how long he could see his brother. He watched them as they fell into a brief discussion. The guard shrugged at whatever Colin said.

"I have to lock the door back up. If you're wanting to stay with him, you'll be locked in too."

Sasha considered the man's words for a moment. Being locked in a room was reminiscent of his own time in prison, a time he would have preferred to forget. He almost stood up and walked out, conscious of the claustrophobia he knew would descend on him as soon as the lock fell into place. A look at Boris' pale, still face refrained him. Boris would wake up eventually, and find himself chained to a bed, unable to move and no one but Sasha could even tell him why. No matter how Boris hated him, Sasha owed him at least this much.

"That's fine."

The guard surveyed him with raised eyebrows. "If you change your mind, I'm just outside."

Sasha nodded and tried to ignore the knot in his stomach that formed the second the door shut. He let out a long, shaky breath. He could let the guard know he wanted out, he told himself. He only had to stay as long as he wanted to. Forcing himself to relax, he looked over at Boris again. His brother was stirring, a low, strained moan coming from him.

Boris' eyes flew open, and he jerked against the chain holding his right hand to the side of the bed. Sasha watched as panic spread across his brother's features as his efforts to bring his hand up failed. His body trembled and his breathing hitched as he grew more frantic. Sasha rose to his knees alongside the narrow cot so that Boris could see him. Boris' eyes reminded Sasha of the look a wounded animal gave when he came up to finish them off. They burned into him, begging for pity.

"Boris, stop. They're chains, you can't break them."

"Sasha? What are you going to do to me?" Boris' wild eyes met his, all the anger in them replaced by fear. He continued pulling against his restraints, this time trying to sit up. "Don't hurt me. Don't let them torture me. Please."

"I'm not going to do anything to you."

"Why can't I move?"

"You sort of went crazy, they said. You were hurting yourself. And you went after one of the guards. They're not going to let you up for now."

Boris sank back, panting heavily, surrendering to the confines of his restraints. His face contorted in pain.

"My head," he moaned. "What happened to it?"

"You just hurt it a bit. It's nothing serious. They've already taken care of it. You should try to go back to sleep."

"I can't." Boris pulled spasmodically against the chains once more. "They're going to hurt me. They're going to start again."

Sasha sighed, knowing nothing he said would convince his brother otherwise. He leaned back against the wall again, his face troubled. Hamo said Lord Bayner had done worse to Boris. Looking at his brother, he knew it was true. His own time in Lord Bayner's hands had been barely a week. Boris had spent more than a month in his power. No doubt that was the cause of much of Boris' fear now. Hatred for what the lord had done both to him and Boris weighed down on him, accompanied by the certain guilt that Lord Bayner had unleashed the wrath he intended for Sasha onto Boris.

The door swung out slowly, and an older man, his breath wheezing loudly, entered. The guard followed with a chair in his hands. A tray balanced precariously in the jailer's hands and when he saw Sasha sitting there, he started, causing the contents of the tray to rattle. Boris struggled to turn his head enough to see the jailer. His eyes darted from Sasha to the jailer to the tray in his hands. The guard set the chair down and left the room, closing the door behind him.

"Please, don't do this to me, Sasha. Don't help him hurt me," Boris whispered in horror as he watched the jailer. "Sasha?"

"What are you doing in here?" the jailer asked Sasha. "He's not safe for anyone to be around by themselves."

"The king said I could be. How isn't he safe? He can't move." And you came in here by yourself, Sasha wanted to add but decided against it. The jailer looked kind, and the last thing Sasha wanted to do was anger the man in charge of his brother's care.

"I suppose that's true. You don't happen to understand what he's saying, do you?"

"I do. What are you going to do to him?"

Sasha's eyes traveled over the tray that the jailer set on the small table. There was a pitcher, a small tin basin, a cup, a roll of white cloth, and a few other items that Sasha could not immediately identify on it. They didn't look like torture tools.

"Move out of the way." The jailer ignored Sasha's question and made a shooing motion with his hands. Sasha reluctantly got to his feet and moved off to the side, conscious of his brother's pleading eyes following his every move. The jailer pulled the chair up next to the bed and sat down. "Pour some of that water into the basin, will you?"

Sasha did as he was told. The jailer took a washcloth, dipped it in the water, and wrung the excess out. He undid the bandage from Boris' head that Sasha could see was now soaked with blood and began cleaning the wound that lay beneath the bloody mat of dark hair. Boris tensed at his touch but had no choice other than to submit. The man worked quickly, finishing up with a tincture of herbs that smelled vaguely familiar to Sasha. A fresh bandage was bound in place.

"You said you can talk to him?"

"Yes."

"Good. Tell him I'm going to let one hand at a time go so I can take care of them. If he gives me any trouble, I will not help him."

Sasha translated quickly, adding his own warning and plea for Boris' cooperation. The words had their desired effect. Boris lay still and quiet while the jailer tended to his shredded knuckles, one hand at a time. By the time the jailer was done, Sasha was half asleep leaning against the wall. He watched through heavy eyes as the jailer offered his brother a drink of water from the cup he brought in.

"If you're planning on staying in here all night, I'll leave this for you," the jailer gestured toward the chair. "If he wants any more water, feel free to give it to him. Despite what he seems to think, we're not actually trying to hurt him. Maybe you could tell him that."

"I tried. Believe me."

The jailer studied Sasha for a moment. "Who are you to him?" When Sasha didn't answer him, a new understanding filled his eyes. "You're the one everyone's been talking about, aren't you? The one who brought word of the attack?"

Sasha nodded.

"You're related to him, aren't you?"

Again, Sasha nodded. "He's my half-brother. But don't say anything to anyone. King Darien doesn't want everyone knowing."

"That would be for the best, wouldn't it?"

The jailer shook his head a little, looking down at Boris, whose face still held traces of fear. Sasha saw the pity in the older man's eyes and was glad Boris had been brought here.

"Thank you," Sasha said as the man turned to leave.

"For what?"

"For taking care of him and being kind to him."

"Just doing my job. There's no rule that says kindness can't go along with it."

With the room empty again aside from the two brothers, Boris twisted his head around to see Sasha.

"Are you going to leave me?" he asked, his voice breaking over the words. "Please don't, Sasha. Please, don't leave me alone."

"I'm not going anywhere tonight."

Sasha watched as some of the tension leached out of Boris' body, and his breathing finally relaxed. Sasha made himself as comfortable as he could in the chair and fell asleep.

Sleeping in a chair was miserable, Sasha decided when he woke yet again from nearly falling out of it. He rubbed a weary hand across his eyes. Leaning forward enough to get a look at his brother's face, he was startled to see Boris wide awake, staring at the ceiling. Sasha wondered how long he had been awake, or if he had ever gone to sleep. Judging by his wide-open eyes, Sasha thought it was the latter. He couldn't blame him. Immobile against the bed and haunted by what must have been frightful memories of abuse, Sasha didn't think he would have been able to sleep either.

"Do you want some water?" he offered.

Boris jumped a little at his voice. Without moving his head, he looked at Sasha. From underneath the bandage, his eyebrows came together in confusion.

"Why did you do it?" Some of the old bitterness crept into Boris' voice. Sasha sighed a little. Keeping up with his brother's erratic moods was impossible.

"That question could mean a lot of things. Why did I betray Father, or why did I come here to see you, or why did I stop you from running? Which one are you asking?"

Boris' confusion wrinkled up his forehead even more as he thought about Sasha's words. Absently, he tugged at his wrist restraints.

"All of them," he said at last.

"That's not an easy answer."

"Give me water first."

Sasha acquiesced, ignoring the sullen command in Boris' tone. As he set the emptied cup back on the table and leaned back into his chair, he began.

"I wanted out. Only, when I first left home, I didn't know that I did. I just wanted something different, I guess. When I was captured, they hurt me. They hurt me whenever and however they liked, and I couldn't do anything to stop them. I hated it. I hated it so much. They sentenced me to die, you know. I was supposed to be hanged, but the night before that was supposed to happen, I was rescued - sort of. And the men who rescued me weren't like everyone else. They took care of me. And even after they found out what I'd done, they let me go."

"They're the ones who found you after the battle, aren't they?" Boris interrupted.

"Yes. But, how do you know about that?"

"I saw them. They came looking for you hours after it ended."

It was Sasha's turn to look puzzled. Hamo already told him about how he and Aldrid found him hours after the battle, but he never made any mention of anyone else being around. Realization dawned on Sasha's face as the pieces of his survival fell into place.

"You saved me," he whispered. "You didn't just not kill me, you're the one who stopped the bleeding. You saved my life. Why?"

"You're supposed to be answering my question." Boris went through the uncomfortable effort to turn his head away from Sasha and toward the wall, his voice gruff.

Sasha swallowed his own questions and continued on.

"When I came home, I wanted Father to care. The way I'd seen other people care about their children. And he didn't. He just made me punish you. No matter how much I tried after that, nothing seemed right. When he gave Dagmar to me, she was terrified of me. No one had ever been terrified of me like that before. And I thought that's what I wanted, but it really just reminded me of when I was in prison. And then there was the war he planned. It wasn't like planning a raid on people you'd never met. The men who were kind to me, they were in danger of Father's war. I just couldn't live with myself knowing that I would help destroy them. That's why I left. That's why I told them what Father was planning."

"And you still want to say none of this is your fault?" Boris kept his face to the wall.

"I never meant for this to happen," Sasha said, unable to keep his frustration out of his voice. His petulant brother had to see that Sasha never intended him harm. "I never meant for you to be hurt or end up like this. I just wanted something different."

"What are they going to do with me?" Boris' tone changed as abruptly as the direction of the conversation.

"They sent Father an offer..."

"He doesn't want me back, you know that. He wanted me dead. So, what are they going to do with me when he refuses? Are they going to kill me?"

"I don't think so," Sasha said, concealing his own concern over the matter. The baron was on the council, and he clearly thought hanging Boris was a well-deserved punishment. Hamo was on the council, too. Sasha was pretty sure Hamo wouldn't vote to hang his brother. Either way, he didn't want to talk about it. "You should try to sleep."

"I can't. Not chained down like this. It's too much like..." Boris' voice trailed off, his eyes growing haunted at the memories, leaving Sasha in little doubt of what he was reminded of.

An overwhelming urge to protect this perverse brother of his who was trying so hard to masquerade his terror beneath a cloak of anger came over him.

"No one's going to hurt you here. I promise. They're not like that. They're probably not even going to keep you chained up like this for very long. They just have to know you won't go crazy again."

Boris didn't answer and after a few minutes, his even breathing told Sasha he was asleep.

Chapter 6

S O, WHAT EXACTLY DO I HAVE to do?" Sasha stood in the dirt outside Stephan's barn, hands deep in his pockets, trying to look indifferent and casual.

"What do you know how to do?"

"Well," Sasha bit his lip, his self-assured nonchalance disappearing rapidly under Stephan's scrutiny, "I can saddle them."

"And?"

"That's about it. You know I never had to actually take care of them before," Sasha admitted. One look at Stephan's face told him Stephan was already well aware of the fact and was asking only to tease.

"Come on. Today, I'll teach you. Tomorrow, you'll actually earn what I lent you."

Sasha followed him into the barn. The pungent, yet comfortingly familiar smell of horses filled his nose. Sasha ran an appreciative eye over the many fine animals. Stephan had good taste in horses, he admitted to himself. Father had always been picky about the quality of the horses in their stable, and Sasha couldn't quite shake the passed-down trait. Stephan stopped in front of a long-handled shovel.

"This is a shovel." Stephan grinned wickedly.

"I know what it is." Sasha rolled his eyes, then allowed himself a reluctant half-smile.

"Good. Do you know how to use it?"

Sasha grabbed the shovel, unwilling to admit that he'd never once used one. The weight of it felt odd in his hands. He followed Stephan to an empty stall.

"Clean this out and then I'll show you the next thing."

"I thought you were teaching me. This is just telling me what to do. How does this not count as work?"

"I am teaching you. Tomorrow you'll be even faster and be able to get more done because you'll have had a chance to practice. I'll be outside if you need me."

It was on the tip of Sasha's tongue to say that Stephan wasn't being fair, but he reconsidered. Stephan would just make fun of him. Shaking his head, he bent to his task. Despite having slaves to do all the mundane tasks of living, Father had never allowed his sons to be lazy. Far from it. They spent their days learning and practicing and training. But after weeks of doing almost nothing while he recovered, Sasha was surprised by how difficult the task proved to be. More than once, he was tempted to quit and take at least a short break. Knowing that Stephan could come in at any time to check on him, he pushed through.

"That took you forever," Stephan commented when Sasha came out to find him. "See, that's why I'm having you practice."

Sasha suppressed a retort. He was out of breath and lightheaded from his exertion. Hopefully, whatever else Stephan had in mind for him wouldn't be as demanding. He followed Stephan behind the house.

"Ever chopped wood before?"

Sasha pressed his lips into a thin line as he shook his head. He took in the ax embedded in a thick tree stump and a large stack of unsplit wood. He chewed

36

on his lower lip, considering telling Stephan that he didn't think he was quite up to such a task. He shook the thought away. Stephan didn't strike him as the type of person to accept even valid excuses. He gripped the ax handle and pulled it free.

"Do you want me to show you first?" Stephan held out his hand for the tool.

"I guess so."

Sasha watched as Stephan neatly split several logs with single strokes. Each time the ax fell, Sasha grew more apprehensive of his own ability to replicate the smooth, swift motion of the older man.

"So, what happens if I can't do something?" Sasha kept his voice light.

"You don't think you can chop wood?"

"I wasn't necessarily talking about that, but sure. What happens if I can't chop the wood?"

"You can practice more. That's what today is for."

"No. I mean, I'm not that strong again yet. Is there going to be some kind of punishment if I can't finish it?"

Stephan stopped what he was doing and studied Sasha. He took in Sasha's labored breathing and his nervous eyes. Whatever Stephan was going to say died on his lips.

"Tell you what, for today you'll just stack it after I chop it. Think you can do that?"

Sasha nodded, relief flooding his face. He moved to pick up the ones Stephan had already split. After several minutes of working in silence, aside from the ringing thud of the ax, Stephan paused, wiping a hand across his forehead.

"Hamo told me you went to see your brother. How'd that go?"

"I don't know."

"You don't know? You were the one there. How do you not know?"

"Sometimes he was so angry I'm pretty sure he would have killed me if he had the chance, and then the next minute he'd be so scared he didn't want me to leave him. I think they hurt him a lot worse than they did me in Dorsten. He wouldn't tell me about it. He just...he wasn't himself. Except, he sort of was. King Darien says he's started all kinds of fights, and he's caused trouble every chance he gets."

Sasha picked up another load of wood and carried it toward the woodpile. He hoped Stephan wouldn't pursue the subject any further. Boris had gone back to being angry on Sasha's last day in Bren. He told Sasha he never wanted to see him again and Sasha didn't want to admit to anyone how much he hated hearing those words.

If Stephan noticed his attempt to end the conversation, he didn't comment on it. When Sasha returned empty-handed and stood waiting for another load, he remained quiet for a while.

"So, aside from giving me a hand around here, do you have any other plans?" Stephan seemed determined to bring up all the things Sasha didn't really want to talk about. He thought back to his conversation with Ophelia at the wedding. Apparently, Ophelia hadn't already told everyone. He appreciated that.

"Not anything definite. I don't know how to do much."

"So I've noticed."

"Hamo says I haven't got enough strength back for him to teach me anything at the forge. If I did, I'd probably just do that."

"You probably couldn't do any better. I don't have much experience with that sort of thing, but I've been told he is one of the most skilled ironworkers in Dival."

"Really? He never mentioned anything like that. He just said it was hard, and that I shouldn't try it until I was fully recovered."

"I don't imagine that is something he'd mention. He hates doing it, though not as much now as he did. It's what he had to do when he was a slave. Probably why he told you to wait too. They didn't with him.

They threw him into it when he was barely on his feet again from being wounded, and it nearly killed him. He'd feel awful if the same thing happened to you."

"I didn't know all that. I don't mind waiting, though. Besides, there's something I have to take care of before I start anything like that."

"What's that?"

Sasha paused, his hand hovering over a split log, wondering what Stephan would say about his idea.

"I'm going to find the rest of my family."

Chapter 7

THE LONG, HOT DAYS OF SUMMER were nearing their end and Sasha wasn't even a little sad about it. The heat down here off the mountains was far more intense than what he'd grown up with. Wiping the back of one hand against his sweaty forehead, Sasha set his bow down and moved to retrieve his arrows. When he wasn't helping Stephan, Hamo, or even Aldrid occasionally, he had been trying to get some practice in. Having spent almost every day of his life practicing archery since he was old enough to draw a bowstring back, he was disappointed to find how badly his skill had dropped in the months it had taken him to recover. Three weeks of daily practice, and it was just now coming back to what it should be. Sasha was determined to not let the skill slip again.

Sliding his arrows into his quiver, he started back for the house. It was late evening, yet the sun was not quite setting. Its brilliant orange reached even beneath the dark green leaves of the trees. Sasha didn't usually come out to practice after supper, but he wanted out of the house tonight. He was restless. With little reminder of his injuries save the scars that would never go away, he was ready to put his plan in action. And tonight, he had decided to tell Hamo.

Sasha stashed his bow and arrows in the barn before heading into the house. Even though it was still light out, the younger girls and baby Drogo were being put to bed. Sasha sat down to wait in the sitting room. Ophelia was the only other occupant, and she was reading. Sasha sometimes wondered if she ever put her book down.

"Where's Meredith?"

"Uncle Al's gone overnight, so Meri and Dagmar are staying with Aunt Taliea," Ophelia answered without ever looking up.

"You didn't want to go too?"

"Not really. Dagmar will spend all night playing with her puppy and Meredith and Aunt Taliea will talk about all sorts of medicine things. Neither of those are things I feel like doing."

Sasha's leg bounced up and down as he sat, waiting. He stood up and paced back and forth, chewing on his lip.

"You don't have to tell me if you don't want to, but is something going on?" Ophelia finally glanced up from her reading, her eyes following him as he went from one end of the room to the other and back again.

"No, nothing," Sasha said too quickly.

"So, you're just making me nervous doing all that for no reason. Could you stop?"

"Sorry, yes." Sasha sat down again but couldn't hold still. What he was about to start could end so badly. What was he thinking? Why did ideas have to take hold of him like this? Once he thought of something, he just couldn't let it go.

"You're still doing that thing with your leg." Ophelia closed her book and peered at him. "You're going to do it, aren't you? You're planning on going back home to start looking for them."

"No, of course not." Sasha let out a nervous laugh. "Why would you think that?"

"You're really bad at lying, you know. Besides, it wasn't that hard to figure out. I've seen you practicing. It makes sense you'd want to get good at it again before going."

Sasha's face fell. "I didn't think I was so obvious."

"You did sort of tell me what your plan was, remember?" She started to open her book back up, and then closed it again, "Besides going back home, do you actually have a plan?"

"Sure. Go home, break into wherever Father keeps the auction records, and find their names and who they were sold to, then leave. I'll be gone before anyone even knows I was there."

"That is a terrible plan."

"What's a terrible plan?" Edith came into the room and sat down, taking up the knitting that almost never seemed to leave her hands.

Ophelia waited for Sasha to speak, which he had no intention of doing. He really only wanted to talk to Hamo about it. As the silence grew awkward and Edith looked from one to the other, Sasha gave in.

"It's just an idea I had."

"What idea did you have?" Hamo came in and sat down next to Edith. Sasha resigned himself to telling all three of them.

"I want to find my mother and my sister. I want to help them if I can."

"Well, that's not a terrible idea at all," Edith said, looking at Ophelia in bewilderment. "I think it's a very good one. I'm sure his mother and sister would appreciate it."

"Just wait 'til you hear how he's doing it."

"How are you planning on going about that? Do you have any idea where they are or where to start?" Hamo said.

"I don't have any idea where they are, but I do know where to start. My father keeps meticulous records of everything and everyone that is sold. They would be in those records, and it would give me something to start with."

"And where are these records kept?" Hamo asked.

"This is where it gets to be a bad idea," Ophelia said quietly, pretending to read her book again. Sasha shot her a look of exasperation.

"You're planning on going back to get them, aren't you?" Hamo said.

"It's the only way. There's nothing else to go off of, and they could be anywhere. There are a lot of people from a lot of countries that come to buy and sell in the Spring Market."

"What happens if he catches you?"

"He won't. I know how to sneak in and out. Boris and I used to do it all the time."

"But if he does?"

"He'll kill me in the most excruciating way he can think of," Sasha said quietly.

"And that's why it's a bad idea," Ophelia whispered loud enough to make sure everyone could hear her. Sasha wanted to be annoyed with her, but she was right. Going home could be a really bad idea.

"I think I agree with Phelie. Sasha, we didn't go through all the trouble of saving your life just so you could throw it away."

"Hamo, if you tell me I shouldn't go, I won't. But I want to get them back. I want to help them. And the only way I can do that is to find out where they went in the first place." Sasha turned toward Hamo, trying to read his face, trying to ignore the tiny part of him that wished Hamo would tell him not to go.

"I can't tell you not to go. You know that. You're free to do whatever you want. I can't even tell you that you shouldn't go. Or I would have to say you shouldn't have come here. You risked a lot doing that too. When are you planning on leaving?"

"Soon. I'd have to make it there and back before winter sets in."

"Do you have any money for that kind of trip?"

"I've been saving everything Stephan and Al have paid me. I honestly have no idea if it's enough or not."

"Well, I'm not going to stop you."

"I think I'll start in a week if I can. I really don't want to get stuck snowed in somewhere."

"Somehow I don't think the snow's going to be your biggest problem," Ophelia said.

Sasha let out another nervous little laugh, knowing full well that she was right.

Chapter 8

SASHA RECHECKED HIS GIRTH one last time before leading the black mare out of the barn. The sky was still a deep blue with only a thin line of golden light on the eastern horizon. The packhorse he had first brought with him was already standing patiently outside, loaded with his gear and held by Hamo.

"You're sure you want to do this?"

"Not really. But I think I have to try." Sasha tried to ignore the nausea in his stomach. It had made it almost impossible to eat earlier, and now it threatened to make him sick entirely. What was he thinking, throwing away his safe life here?

"As long as the weather doesn't get in the way, you should be back in around a month. I guess we'll look for you then."

"I guess so. You know, I've never really said goodbye like this before." He smiled ruefully.

"Good luck."

Sasha stepped into his stirrup and pulled himself up. Taking the lead rope from Hamo, he prodded his horse forward. Edith was standing in the darkened doorway, and one of the twins - he couldn't tell which. He raised his hand to wave.

"Don't get caught." Sasha smiled as Ophelia's unnecessary warning reached his ears.

Days of riding alone stretched out before him, and Sasha had more than enough time to think about how he was going to sneak into Aruuk, and more importantly Illsen and Father's house. Just thinking about slipping in unseen reminded him of the times he and Boris had done it. After their first, unsuccessful wolf hunt they had done it several other times. He should have remembered to ask Hamo what the council was planning on doing with his brother. Not that he should care. Boris certainly didn't.

It took him only a day to reach the old border forts of Dival. No longer needed, they stood like silent sentinels as a testament to the war that was no more. Staring at them as he rode through, Sasha found their emptiness eerie. They reminded him somewhat of his night alone at the stockade.

As the days slipped away, and the miles with them, Sasha decided that traveling alone was no fun. Of course, none of the trips he had taken so far had been fun. But the tedium of riding for hours at a time, with no one but his horse to talk to wore on him. He was relieved to see the former border forest of Dorsten darken the far horizon on his fifth day. Guards no longer stopped travelers on the road entering the thick, overgrown woods.

Despite the union and his King's Pardon, Sasha had no desire to stay in the town. The thought of running into Lord Bayner, even if he wasn't still in charge here, was something he wished to avoid.

Pushing past it into the familiar terrain of the mountains, Sasha took in a deep breath of the mountain air. He liked his life back in Dival, but there was something about the mountains that felt comfortable. Autumn wasn't as distinct in the mostly evergreen forests that covered the lower halves of the slopes, but a bright splash of red, orange, or gold added a beauty that was unmatched.

"You like it too, don't you?" He reached down to pat his mare's neck as her ears twitched forward. He had taken to talking to her a lot more than usual on this trip since there was no one else to talk to. "Not too much farther and we'll stop for the night."

The cabin buried between the trees was hard to find. Sasha passed by it the first time, and it was only the howling bark of Drogo's pet wolf that helped him spot it. He turned his horse's head toward it. By the time he reached the door, Drogo was already standing in it, watching his approach with curiosity.

"Sasha?" He squinted at him. In the months since Sasha had last seen Drogo, the man had aged greatly.

"Yes, it's me." Sasha dismounted. "I was passing through, and I'd rather stay here than in town, if that's alright?"

"Where did you come from?"

"From Hamo's. I've been staying with him and his family."

"So, you made it all the way. I thought you did." Drogo smiled slowly as stepped aside, allowing Sasha to enter. "He was not angry with you then?"

"I don't know about at first. But he's not now."

"And what brings you here? You are not thinking of going back, are you?" Drogo regarded him closely. "It would be a mistake, boy. You are happy there."

"I have to go back. I need to find my mother and sister, and Illsen is where Father keeps all the auction records. It's the only thing I have to go off of."

"You are crazy," Drogo stated simply. "I hope you can manage it."

"Uh...Thanks, I think. I hope I can manage it too." There was something unsettling about the way Drogo just said things. Ophelia was like that a lot. "I have to at least try."

"You do know what Gundar will do to you if he catches you?"

"Something I'll hate, I'm sure." Sasha brushed it off. Having other people worry about him almost made it easier not to worry about himself.

"Something that will end with you dead. And probably hours after you have wished to be dead."

"Yes, something like that. But he won't catch me. I can sneak in and out easily. I did it with one of my brothers. Besides, no one actually knows what happened to me. They won't be looking for me." Sasha had thought it through carefully during his long hours alone. "For all they know, I was one of the many soldiers trapped on a sinking ship and drowned. The only one who knows what I did, is locked up in Dival."

Drogo settled into the chair across from him.

"Do you know where he keeps the records?"

"No, I still have to figure that part out."

"They'll be in his personal quarters if he's like any other Chief. There's a room built for it in the house, not far from where he sleeps. I suppose, being Chief, they tend to like to keep their profits and records of profits close."

"I guess that's where I'll look then."

Chapter 9

BORIS DIDN'T ACKNOWLEDGE the jailer standing in the open door less than ten feet in front of him. Staring at the wall, his fingers mindlessly fumbling with thread that had come unraveled from his shirt, he was lost in some world of his mind's making. When the man set his tray of food on the table, Boris made no move to get it or even look at it.

Days, weeks, years for all Boris cared, had gone by since he had yelled at Sasha that he never wanted to see him again. So far, Sasha had taken him at his word and kept his distance. Boris hadn't seen him again and time itself ceased to have any meaning to Boris.

He almost never moved and when he did it was only when an uncontrollable rage filled him. He'd already broken one hand from pounding against the stone walls of his prison. The jailer and guards were used to his fits by now. No one ever came to check on him when he caused a ruckus. The only one who ever entered now was the jailer. He came in twice a day with his maddening sameness. The same wheezing sound as he walked, the same creak of the door as it opened, the same smell of food, the same silent, sympathetic shake of his head.

The door shut behind him again. The smell of food drifted towards him. Boris' impassive face changed ever so slightly as a new smell reached his nose. Something different, something new.

Tantalized by its sweetness as much as by its variance from the norm, Boris got up and took the tray in his shaking hands. Boris stared down at the rattling tray, trying to will the tremors to stop. They wouldn't and he knew they wouldn't. The only reason they were there was because of his time in Dorsten.

Aside from the thick stew and piece of bread that was his daily fare, there was a cloth napkin tied up around something. Boris slowly loosed the napkin, eyes widening in disbelief as he took in the warm, sweet pastry laying inside. Boris picked it up, savoring the scent of it while puzzling over who would have done such a thing. Perhaps it was given to him by mistake. Perhaps it was meant for another prisoner, who had behaved themselves enough to earn a reward of sorts. Surely, no one would even think of such a kindness for him. Not after the way he had acted. The only thing he had earned was rough treatment and the disdain of those who had to take care of him.

The gesture, whether intentional or not, broke through the mindless, numb daze that took hold of him most of the time. If it was an accident, it was a pleasant accident. If it was intentional, it meant that someone, somewhere cared.

Boris settled himself on his cot, resting his back against the wall with his legs stretched out before him. He carefully wrapped the pastry back up in its napkin, saving it until he had eaten everything else. Most days he could only bring himself to down a few mouthfuls - if that. Today, however, he was going to make himself eat it all. At last, he finished the contents of the wooden bowl. Taking the smallest nibble at a time, and chewing it slowly, allowing all of the sweet goodness to fill his mouth, he ate the pastry.

Whatever comfort the treat gave him was lost again when the door opened and, instead of the jailer coming to collect his tray, two guards came in. Boris, caught off guard, tensed, ready to fight them. He hadn't been removed from his cell since Sasha was here. If they were coming for him now, it could only mean torture. The guards never gave him a chance. Used to his outbursts at this point, he was quickly overpowered, and his hands were secured behind him. No matter how hard Boris tried to stop it, the tremors took over his entire body, crippling him. He wanted nothing more than to beg for them to leave him alone, but they wouldn't understand him.

He allowed himself to be led down the staircase, and into a very different sort of room. It was a spacious room, with five large windows spaced along the outer wall, allowing the morning light to shine in. Long tables, pushed together to form a horseshoe and lined with chairs on the outside, were the central focus of the room. Boris was brought to a single chair that sat in the middle of it. As the guards secured him to the chair, Boris craned his neck trying to look at each table. Despite his worst fears, no torture instruments, such as he had seen in Dorsten, were visible.

Once again, he was left alone for some time. Here in this room, he could hear things. In his cell, the walls and door were too thick, the room too far removed from everything else. But here, voices drifted in from other rooms and from the hallway outside, indistinct but human. Boris fought against the urge to slump down in his chair. He strained to catch the sounds of other people, aching with the loneliness that was his life now.

When the doors opened this time, he was prepared - although for what, he wasn't sure. Sitting stiffly in his chair, his face hardened to hide his fear.

The only clue anyone would have been able to see was the slight trembling of his hands gripping the arms of the chair. To his surprise, though he worked hard to hide it, it was not a single person who entered the room, but many. Boris stared at the floor in front of him.

Lifting his eyes without moving his head, he saw that the King was there. So was the other man who had been with the King and Sasha when they questioned him.

Sasha was not.

Boris couldn't decide if he was angry about that, or hurt, just like he couldn't make up his mind about whether he really wanted to see his brother again or not. It was out of his hands anyway. If Sasha didn't wish to see him again, there was nothing Boris could do about it.

The men in the room had a lot to say, Boris decided, as he sat in a chair that grew more uncomfortable with every passing minute. He squirmed a little in it. If he could only understand what they were saying. He was sure it had something to do with him, or he wouldn't have been brought here.

A hush fell on the room and a single man rose to his feet. Carefully pronouncing each word as though he had to think about it, he addressed Boris in Aruuken. Before he could stop himself, Boris' head snapped up and he paid attention to the man, drawn irresistibly to the familiar language that he had not heard in ages.

"Boris Gundarson, King Darien wishes for me to inform you that the offer made to Chief Gundar of Aruuk for your exchange was declined. It is now up to the council to decide your fate. It is in your best interest to answer any questions the council members have truthfully."

Boris heard his own mad laughter ringing through the room. He was going crazy; he was sure of it. Of course, Father didn't want him. He'd always known that. But hearing it, having it definitely confirmed, snapped something inside him that he hadn't even known was there. He shouldn't be laughing, not now. But he couldn't stop himself. The hours of staring at the same four walls, with no one around, no one to talk to or to hear him were driving him mad. He saw the way some of the men were looking at him. They thought him insane as well. His laughter was horribly, dangerously close to hysteria. And it was utterly, frighteningly beyond his control.

"Boris Gundarson," the interpreter tried to cut him off, his voice chiding, "such behavior is hardly going to be well received by the council."

Boris found his voice, only it didn't sound like his. It was reckless and high-pitched. "Just kill me and be done with it. It's what you want to do anyway."

Boris couldn't believe the words coming out of his mouth, but he could feel the fit of rage welling up inside him, a monster buried within him threatening to overwhelm him yet again. He had to stop. He had to get control again, but it was already too late. The anger overflowed once again as he threw himself against the chains that held him in place. He was screaming at the man, saying things that he couldn't even comprehend.

He wore himself out quickly, and sagged, panting heavily against the seat. He barely saw the way the men were looking at each other or him.

"Kill me. Please. Just end this," he murmured. "I want to die."

"That will be for the council to decide," the translator heard him and answered.

That was when Boris noticed the shaking of his shoulders, and the great heaving sobs coming from deep inside him - the other half to his madness. He couldn't break down and cry. Not in front of these men. His outburst was already bad enough. He could see in their faces what they thought of him because of it. But to cry? To do something so weak he hadn't done it since he was a child. He hadn't even cried when they tortured him in Dorsten. He'd screamed, yelled, cursed until his throat was raw and his voice cracking, but he never cried. His fingers closed tightly into fists, his nails digging painfully into the palms of his hands. He squeezed his eyes shut, trying to hold it back, but it was useless. As useless as his efforts to quell his mad laughter had been. There was an uneasy stirring among the men in the room as they became aware of what was going on. Through tear blurred eyes, Boris saw the interpreter opening his mouth to address him again, but King Darien lifted a hand to stop him and shook his head slightly.

Aside from the horrible, heaving sobs that were wrenched out of him, the room was silent for a long minute. Boris couldn't even bring his hands to his face to hide it. The best he could do was to keep his head lowered.

As he struggled to regain some sort of control over himself, the others in the room broke into conversation. The deliberate attempt to ignore him helped more than he could have hoped for. Although he had no way of telling time, he thought only a few minutes had passed before his breathing steadied and tears stopped forcing their way to his eyes. In their place, an emptiness consumed him. He wanted to sleep and never awaken to the misery and madness of his current life.

The casual tone of conversation in the room defied the turmoil inside Boris, but he was getting quiet again. And with the quietness came an overwhelming exhaustion. Even after he had stopped, they ignored him for several more minutes.

"Are you ready to answer our questions?" the interpreter finally said.

Boris nodded meekly, wishing he could at least wipe his face clean. He didn't trust himself to speak yet.

"Very good," the man said. "Did you take part in the recent raid on Dorsten?"

Boris nodded again.

"Tell us about it."

With all the fight gone out of him for the moment, Boris did as he was told. In as few words as possible, he explained his own part in it and then sat quietly while his words were translated. He stared down at his lap as the room broke out into conversation again. Boris wished again that he knew what they were saying. It was an argument of some sort, an argument that centered around him and doubtless discussed what was to be done with him.

He didn't bother to look at any of them until only one man was speaking. Boris turned slightly to see him and stared in shock. He forgot for a moment where he was and what was happening.

He knew the man.

Well, not really knew him, but he had seen him before. He was one of the ones who came looking for Sasha on the battlefield. He was one of Sasha's friends. Since everyone had stopped talking and was listening to this man, Boris allowed himself to stare at him as well until he was finished.

The argument dragged on and on. Boris shifted again in his chair. At last, the room fell silent again, and the interpreter stood up. Boris turned despairing eyes toward the man, his heart leaping to his throat.

"The council has reached a decision regarding your sentence, Boris Gundarson. While they recognize that your crimes in the form of kidnapping with the intent to own or sell are worthy of death, it has decided that a lighter sentence would be appropriate. You will serve six months of indenture on a work gang. That sentence will be reviewed at the end of your six months and extended should your behavior prove as troublesome as it has in the past." The man started to sit again.

"What does that mean? What will I have to do?" Boris blurted out before he could stop himself.

"It means that you will have to work very hard, do as you're told, and behave yourself. If you can manage that for six months without causing trouble, you will most likely be freed."

Boris sank against the hard wooden back of the chair, taking in the man's words. They were making a slave of him. After everything else that had happened, it was the final insult, but he was too worn now to feel anything at all. He didn't look up as the shuffling of chairs marked the movement of the council members.

The room emptied quickly until only three men remained. They stood near Boris, and Boris was sure they were talking about him. He looked up long enough to see who it was. King Darien, the man who came for Sasha on the battlefield, and the interpreter. None of them seemed to be in a hurry to leave.

A guard came in and unlocked the shackles that held him to the chair. Lacking both the will and energy to put up a fight, he allowed himself to be lifted up and led, shuffling, from the room. King Darien remained behind, but the other two men followed.

The fresh air struck Boris in the face. Aside from when he was brought to Dival, he hadn't been outside since his capture. He forgot about making any attempts to escape. It didn't matter anyway. Something had died inside of him while he was in that room. His will to fight had shriveled up beneath the weight of his madness. Taking deep breaths of the clean, crisp air he simply followed his escort's guiding hand. The smell of smoke and hot metal mingled with the air and Boris found himself standing in an open-air smithy. He balked against the guard's grasp, eyes widening in horror.

The fire, the heat, the scorching pain, it all came rushing back to him. Hours of fiery torment.

Chained down, unable to get away from the flames searing his skin. Red hot metal pressed into his flesh by an indifferent tormenter while he screamed himself hoarse. They hadn't said anything about that in his sentence.

At the first sign of resistance, a second man joined the first guard in restraining him. They pulled him to a tall wooden table, and stretched his right arm out across it, pushing his sleeve up to his elbow.

"This will go quicker if you don't try to fight it," The interpreter said from the side. Boris ignored him and fought with a wildness he hadn't thought he could muster again, jerking his arm against the grip of the two grown men.

The blacksmith approached, a strip of metal still glowing with heat held in his tongs. Boris bit down on his lip hard enough to make it bleed as he watched the man bring the metal, soft enough to bend but not quite liquid, towards his arm. Biting his lip wasn't enough to stop the scream that came from deep within him, triggered as much by memory as by the intense pain. The metal was bent around his wrist, fitted to it, and the ends melded together. Still screaming, still struggling, his arm was plunged with a steaming hiss into the barrel of cool water sitting next to the worktable.

His eyes watered as the cool water alleviated the worst of the pain. Before he was nearly ready to take it out again, the guard was tugging on it, pulling him away from the comforting moisture. Another hand on his arm stopped the guard, and Boris looked up to find the man who saved Sasha moving his arm back into the water, saying something to the guard. The guard shrugged and released his grip on Boris' limb. Whoever this man was, Boris was very glad he was standing there just now. He let his arm rest in the water for as long as it helped.

Having soaked up all the relief the water could give him, Boris was taken into a large, windowless room built off the side of the castle. Straw mattresses marked the spaces of multiple occupants, although none were in the room for now.

"You will stay here with the others. The rules are very simple. If you fight, your sentence gets longer, so do yourself a favor and figure out how to get along. Try to run away, and you'll hang. Do as you're told and don't argue. Here." The interpreter held out an entirely gray outfit. "Put this on."

Boris considered refusing, but his arm hurt, and he was tired, and his head was beginning to ache from the ordeal of the day. Besides, he'd made enough of a scene earlier. Stripping off his old clothes, he hastily complied, getting the new ones on as fast as he could before any of the accompanying men had a chance to see the scars that now covered his body. The material was itchy, ill-fitting, and hardly warm, but they were clean, which was more than he could say for his other clothes.

"You will start tomorrow. I'd suggest you get some rest now," the interpreter said, not unkindly, pointing to an unused mattress in the corner. "You'll need it."

Drained of anything but his pain, Boris stumbled to the corner and sank down, no longer caring that the men were still watching him. He flinched and looked up through dull eyes at the touch of a hand on his arm. The man who had put his arm back in the water was kneeling down next to him, something in his hands. Shifting the newly fitted band as much as he could, the man rubbed a cooling ointment on the burn beneath. Boris let out a gasp of relief. The pain shrunk until it was bearable. When the men left him, he could rest at least a little.

Chapter 10

SASHA ALMOST SMILED AT THE futility of the border guard between Dorsten and Aruuk. With the redrawn boundaries, King Darien had set to work right away, establishing a form of security along the northernmost border. Given the difficult terrain, there was only so much that could be done. The large pass, the only one an entire army could fit through, was well secured. The same could not be said for the dozens of little trails and defiles that stood between the two countries. Sasha slipped easily from one to the other, without ever confronting a border guard.

Now that he was in Aruuk, Sasha couldn't ignore his misgivings any longer. His worst fear, when he really considered it, was not so much that Father would kill him. It was that no one would know for sure what happened to him. They would expect him back and he would never come. That bothered him more than he ever imagined it would. He hadn't come all this way just to give up though, so he kept his horse moving forward, drawing closer to Illsen every day.

By the third afternoon, he knew he was close. He passed the entrance to the old stockade.

Remembering his nightmarish stay there, he almost bypassed it entirely. But the sun was getting low in the sky, and he would have to find another place to camp if he didn't use the buildings there. Reluctantly, he turned into the mouth of the rocky enclosure.

There was little left of the men who had died there. No one had bothered to come out and bury them, so they lay where they fell still. Months of lying out in the open available first to the wolves, and then to every other scavenger, had reduced them to piles of bones. Sasha swallowed down the nausea that filled him at the sight.

Once again deciding that it would be best to bring the horses in with him, he made himself as comfortable in the guard hut as it was possible for him to do.

After taking care of the horses, Sasha sat lost in thought. He was less than a day away from Illsen, and still only had the barest skeleton of a plan. He would have had less of one if Drogo hadn't been so informative. He absently stroked the black mare's head when she nuzzled his shoulder. As the hut grew dark, Sasha's eyelids grew heavy and no matter how much he wanted to stay awake and try to piece together a sure plan, he couldn't. Pulling his blankets over himself, he finally gave up and went to sleep.

Morning brought some clarity as to his course of action. Without bothering with either of his horses, Sasha collected the few items he thought would be necessary in the next two days and set off on foot. Even walking, he was sure he would reach Illsen by nightfall, which was the soonest he could hope to sneak in anyway. Leaving the horses behind seemed logical since he had nowhere to hide them and couldn't just ride into town.

Rather than heading straight for Illsen, he made his way eventually up the sloping side of the mountain as the shadows grew long in the early evening. He found his old hunting spot and made himself as comfortable as he could to wait for complete darkness. He and Boris had spent so many hours in this very spot. Sasha shook away the memories that wanted to crowd their way into his mind. He needed to focus. Boris was nothing more than a distraction. It would be better if he could just forget about him altogether. Boris certainly had.

Searching for something to distract him, Sasha turned his gaze on the town below him. There was something different about the place, something out of the ordinary he couldn't quite identify. The same smudges of gray smoke rose from chimneys, the same wooden palisade surrounded it protectively. Sasha squinted, his eyes traveling more carefully over the wooden fence that was meant both to keep intruders out as well as the townspeople in.

It took several seconds of careful scrutiny for him to spot it first. Along the wall in a handful of places, the wooden wall was broken down. And the ever-present gate sentries were either extremely well hidden from view or non-existent. A twinge of uneasiness crept over Sasha. In his entire life in Illsen, the gate was never left unguarded or the walls in disrepair. For the first time since the battle, he wondered just how much damage Aruuk's defeat had cost them.

Hours after darkness had fallen, Sasha crept forward from his hiding spot. Still uneasy by the change in Illsen, he decided to sneak in at the same place Boris and he had. The palisade created a long, jagged, black line against the night as Sasha stole softly closer. Reaching it, he paused in its protective shadow, listening and trying to still the hammering of his own heart.

Silence met his ears.

Reaching for a handhold in the rough wood, Sasha almost gave himself away when the entire thing sagged against his weight. The damage to the other parts of the wall clearly affected the stability of this part. He needed a different way in.

Keeping close to the wall and pausing every few feet to listen for sounds of alarm, Sasha made his way to the nearest breakthrough. The smell of scorched wood surprised him. Reaching the broken-down gap, he laid a tentative hand on the rubble. Charred wood met his touch. Sasha frowned. Broken walls were troublesome, burned ones were disturbing. It wasn't just disrepair. Someone had attacked Illsen. His blood ran cold at the thought. He was too late. If Illsen was overrun by some enemy, no doubt the records he sought were gone.

Scrambling over the pile of broken, scorched wood as quietly as he could, Sasha stepped inside his hometown for the first time in months. No foreign army patrolled the streets. No hidden voice shouted out an alarm at his intrusion. The entire town lay peacefully quiet. Sasha let out a breath. The quiet defied his own anxiety. He crouched down, hidden from any casual view, and tried to collect himself. The worst was over, he told himself. He was in. Now he just needed to find what he needed. Steeling himself against the nerves that threatened to keep him frozen in place, he moved forward.

Slipping in and out of the shadows of the houses, some of which were in as much disrepair as the wall, Sasha's steps brought him within the yard of the Chief's house.

Home.

His home.

Only the word didn't fit, not anymore. Avoiding the slaves' quarters and the main door, he slunk around the side to his old room. The window was low enough to the ground that he could easily reach it and the shutters on it hadn't latched properly in years. Unless Father had been overcome by a sudden urge to improve his son's quarters, the latch would still be faulty, and Sasha knew exactly how to undo it.

Pushing one shutter up while pulling the other down, Sasha heard the familiar click of it coming undone. The room stood empty of all but the bed, just like it had when he returned from captivity. Father thought him dead again. He was curious as to how many other son's rooms had been cleaned out after the battle. If he was not in so much danger of being caught, he might have explored a little to satisfy his curiosity.

He ran into no one as he made his way down the maze of hallways that led to Father's personal quarters. Father's room was dark. Sasha moved past it and began testing the doors to the other rooms.

For all of his worry about it, the record room was surprisingly easy to find and even easier to enter. No lock prevented him. Apparently, Father, although paranoid about an attack from the outside, did not share the same level of concern for the inside. Pulling off his cloak and stuffing it along the bottom edge of the door to hide any light that might seep out, Sasha felt around and found a candle and lit it. The soft glow of the flame illuminated a rather dusty, crowded room.

Stacks and stacks of parchment faced him. Mounds of paperwork shoved into shelves in apparent disregard for any order met his searching eyes and Sasha groaned internally. It would take him hours to search through. That was time he didn't have before the sun came up. With the sinking weight of despair pressing down on him, Sasha started.

The sheer number of people who had passed through the hands of the auctioneers at the Spring Market was sickening. The longer Sasha stared at name upon name, the worse it got. These weren't just names. They were people. People like Dagmar - snatched from their lives and sold like animals to the highest bidder. Sasha's eyes swam with the rows of names and numbers, the money brought in from the sale of human beings. The hours wore on. Sleepiness threatened to overwhelm his efforts.

Sasha blinked, rubbing his eyes, forcing them open. He pulled yet another paper out of the stack he was working through. The words blurred as his eyelids grew heavy and slid shut against his will. His head dropped forward. Jerking back up, he saw it. Halfway down the page, the name Denise screamed up at him. Eyes wide open again, he ran his finger across the page, connecting his mother's name to the man who bought her and his location. Wasil, Karu. Sasha had never heard of the place. Never mind, though. He could find it when he was somewhere safe. Folding the paper up, he put it in his pocket and with renewed energy began searching for his sister's name.

Another hour and he had it. Rising stiffly and massaging the tightened muscles in his neck with one hand, Sasha got ready to leave. Blowing out the candle and putting his cloak back on, he eased the door open an inch at a time, scanning the hallway outside for any sign of another person. Finding the hall still empty, Sasha crept out of the room.

A dim light shone under the door to Father's room and a murmur of voices reached his ears. Sasha hesitated. Father's voice was distinct. The same note of arrogant command it had always carried was still there, sharper now that Sasha understood it. Whoever he was with answered him, and Sasha found the voice strangely familiar. He cocked his head, bending his ear closer to the door. It was thin, proud, and... Sasha tried to remember where he'd heard it from. Staying up all night didn't put him in the best position to think clearly about anything though, and the identity of that voice remained a mystery. Sasha considered trying to get closer to understand what was being said, but since it likely had nothing to with him and the dark was beginning to turn gray, he decided it was time to leave.

Chapter 11

BORIS TUGGED AT THE IRON BAND on his wrist, his sleep-starved eyes following the movements of the man speaking to him but not really registering them. He was the one in charge, Boris assumed. But Boris couldn't understand anything that came out of his mouth. His gaze wandered over to the other men, already at work. He stared at them, ignoring the senseless sounds coming from his overseer.

He tugged at the iron band some more and grimaced. The skin underneath was an angry red, and blisters had formed. His wrist hurt. It was hurting the worst that it had since the man had put the ointment on. The pain distracted him from everything else.

A pair of hands grabbing the front of his shirt and shaking him roughly brought his wandering attention back to the speaking man. The overseer's face was turning red with frustration and without warning Boris' indifference gave way to quaking. The blood drained from his face and all he could see was the face of his tormenter in Dorsten. Boris lifted his hands to shield his face as the overseer's irritation increased. Rather than beating Boris, though, he took him by the arm, thrust a shovel into his unresisting hands, and pointed him toward the other workers. With more effort than it should have taken, Boris understood that the overseer simply wanted him to do the same thing as everyone else.

Since his outburst in the council room yesterday, Boris had been uncharacteristically docile. His anger and hate were spent in that room, and now he was empty. He didn't even look at his roommates when they were brought in last evening. He'd sat on his mat, in his corner, content to ignore and be ignored. Doubtless, that was a relief to the men guarding them.

The ditch they were digging made no sense to Boris, but since he couldn't work up the energy to refuse, he buried his shovel into the hard dirt and started digging. Half an hour into it, Boris decided it was going to be a very long six months. His body protested against the grueling task, and it was hard to ignore the deep residual pain of his time in the Dorsten dungeon. He'd never really healed from that, and it flared to the surface now, making every movement with the shovel misery. His lack of sleep and appetite did little to help him, either.

By the end of the day, Boris was too tired to cause trouble even if he wanted to. He fell in line to get food and then retreated to his mat, avoiding eye contact with anyone else in the room. The prison created by the language barrier shut firmly around him as conversations between the other men picked up. Boris was as isolated in this group as he had been in his cell. Staring down at the food in his hands, similar to what he was fed before in his cell, Boris thought about the sweet pastry someone had slipped in to him just the day before. It seemed like an eternity ago. Picking at his supper, he wondered who had done such a thing. He hadn't made any friends here.

Sleep ought to have been a relief. But when Boris woke up screaming and thrashing against the torments of his nightmare, there was nothing refreshing about it either for him or for the men locked up with him. Clenching his thin blanket in his sweaty hands, he saw and heard the others stirring, looking at him. At least alone in a cell he didn't need to worry about anyone else seeing the terror that descended on him in his sleep. Even awake, it took him forever to break out of the paralyzing fright. One of the other men was approaching him, saying something.

Boris scooted back away from him as far as he could get, the terrible quaking beginning all over again. The man's nearness threatened Boris. He cried out in alarm, his words futile and meaningless to those around him. Realizing that he wasn't going to do any good, the man retreated again, and within a few minutes, the others in the room went back to sleep. They were far too tired to stay up needlessly.

Boris rocked back and forth where he sat, hands clamped over his mouth to keep any sound from coming out. He couldn't sleep. Not now, not with his heart hammering its way out of his chest. Morning found him still, rocking in his spot, the blanket lying on the floor around him, eyes glazed with exhaustion.

He didn't sleep the following night or the night after that. When, on the third night, he finally succumbed, it was brief and troubled, forcing him awake again. With the sleeplessness came the madness. Boris felt himself slipping into it but could do nothing to stop it.

Chapter 12

SASHA PRESSED HIS HORSE INTO a canter, pulling the packhorse along with him. The dirt drive flew quickly by, bringing the familiar house into view. It was funny, Sasha thought, how a place he had spent less than a year in felt more like home than the place he'd grown up in.

Pulling his horses to a stop just outside the barn, he started to lead them in.

"Sasha's back!" a little girl's voice called out and Sasha glanced over his shoulder to find Adelaide in the window waving at him. He smiled and returned her greeting before disappearing into the barn.

Putting his saddle away he heard footsteps coming up behind him.

"Didn't get caught, I see," Hamo said.

"No one even knew I was there."

"Did you find what you were looking for?"

In response, Sasha pulled out the two pieces of paper that bore record to his mother and Agathe's sales. Hamo took them quietly and looked them over.

"Which ones are they?"

"Denise, there." Sasha showed him. "That's my mother. But I've never heard of the place her buyer was from. And Agathe, there. I think that's the same place Taliea and Dagmar come from."

They started toward the house together.

"I meant to ask you before I left. About Boris. What did the council decide to do with him?"

"He's in trouble," Hamo said quietly.

"Well, that's why King Darien was going to have the council decide what to do with him, wasn't it?"

"No. I mean, something's wrong with him." Hamo stopped walking. "I don't know what Lord Bayner did to him, but he's pretty messed up."

"Still? I thought that was just with me because he was angry with me."

"Right now, he's angry at everyone. And scared." Hamo went on to briefly explain Boris' display in the council room.

"So, what are they doing with him?"

"They banded him. He has to serve six months on a work gang."

"What does that mean?"

"They put a metal band on his arm so if he tries to run, he's easily identified and then he has to work for six months. It's pretty much what happens to anyone who gets sentenced."

"They did that to him?"

"There were those on the council that thought he should hang. This was the better option, trust me, Sasha. In six months, they'll turn him loose and he'll be free to go wherever he wants. It's not as bad as it seems." Hamo paused, sensing the disagreement in Sasha. "He didn't come the way you did. When you came here, you were ready to put all that behind you and start over. You came of your own free will and offered us help. He was captured fighting against us. They have to do something with him."

"They couldn't have just counted what Lord Bayner did to him as enough punishment? You said yourself he hurt Boris worse than he ever hurt me. And he hurt me a lot."

"That's not how it works."

Sasha nodded reluctantly and started back toward the house. He could not even explain why he was bothered by what the council did to his brother. Boris hated him, and the sooner Sasha could accept that, the better it would be.

"I think you should try to see him again. They'll let you, you know," Hamo called after him.

"He doesn't want to see me."

"He doesn't know what he wants. I think you should try. He needs it."

"I'll think about it," Sasha promised as they entered the house.

Sasha put his things away and sat down on his bed, spreading the two pieces of paper out and reading them again. Thirty slaves were listed on each. Thirty people. His eyes returned to the two names that meant something to him. Just reading their names was a success. It made them seem like they were already within his reach. Sasha pulled out a map that he had bought in Dorsten on his way back through and laid it next to the papers. Running his finger along the different names written in on the map, he searched for Karu. A light knock on his door interrupted his search.

"Come in."

"Mother wanted me to tell you supper's ready." Ophelia stuck her head in. "And since you're still alive and in one piece, I take it you were successful."

Sasha nodded, still looking at the map.

"What are those?"

"What I went for. Sales records. And a map. I've never even heard of this place." He leaned back, frowning. "And I can't find it on the map, either."

Ophelia stepped into the room. "What's the name of it?"

"Karu. Wasil, Karu is where my mother's buyer was from."

Ophelia bent forward, scanning the map.

"It's there." She finally put a finger on a small dot. "It's an island, and I don't think it's very big."

Sasha picked the map up and held it close. There was only one way to get to an island. He scanned the map again, this time looking for Sondaru. This was easier to find. It lay across the sea, just to the south of Dival. He wasn't going to get to Agathe without sailing either. He sighed, grimacing at the thought.

"So, what's your plan? I hope it's not as terrible as your last one."

"My last one worked. I'm here, and I have what I wanted."

"You were lucky."

"It was a good plan. Anyway, I can't do anything until the spring. Nobody's going to try sailing across the open sea in the winter. Besides, I need more money."

"A lucky plan. You and Meri will be leaving around the same time if you go in the spring."

"Oh? Where's she going?"

"Nothing for sure, but she's trying to talk Father and Mother into letting her study with an apothecary in Bren."

"I see."

Ophelia picked up the two lists of names that he'd taken.

"Which ones are yours?"

"Denise and Agathe." He pointed them out to her.

"Your sister sold for a lot."

"She was really pretty, just like Mother, and only fourteen."

Ophelia shook her head in disgust. "That's so wrong."

Sasha nodded.

"Well, sit in here and pour over your map. I'm going to go get supper."

Sasha waited, lost in thought, for another minute before following her out to the kitchen. Everyone was already there, and more than a little anxious for him to share the details of his trip.

Chapter 13

BORIS LOOKED UP FROM HIS work long enough to watch the passing wagon, loaded down with goods for market, drive by. The snow from winter was melting and the spring rains had been falling off and on for the last week, forming puddles of muddy water that filled the ruts in the road. The wagon wheels bounced through the deep puddles, sending a wall of brown water all over Boris, soaking the lower half of his trousers.

Boris muttered under his breath, but the driver never even looked back. It was like that all the time. The iron band on his arm and gray suit of clothes he wore marked him as a criminal to these people. And being a criminal meant he was worthless, and apparently, invisible.

A shout from their overseer sent him back to work. In the long winter months, Boris had picked up enough of the language that he could understand most of what was said to him, as long as it was said slowly. Despite that knowledge, he had yet to say a single word to anyone.

What he had not managed to do throughout the winter was get past his nightmares. They came every time he fell asleep, and so he slept as little as possible, going two or three days at a time before his body simply collapsed.

At the end of the workday, shivering because of his wet clothing, Boris followed the overseer and the rest of his group back to their quarters. He barely picked at the food he was given, mostly just pushing it back and forth in his bowl. As the rest of the men settled in for the night, either talking amongst themselves or laying down to sleep, Boris huddled up in his corner. No one tried to approach him or speak to him. They avoided him. They had since that first night.

He needed sleep. His body ached with his need for it, his eyes burned with it. The temptation to curl up and give in to it was overwhelming. But he fought it. He hated what happened when he slept enough to fight it. He sat up, forcing his eyes to stay open so that he wouldn't have to relive the horrors of his time in Dorsten.

When the room was finally quiet, Boris stood and paced. He could only take three steps in each direction before running into the next man, but he would do it for hours. Three steps forward, turn around, three steps back. He would do it until his legs felt like they were going to fall off and then he'd sit until his eyes grew too heavy for him to keep them open, then he'd get back up and pace some more.

When the first sliver of daylight showed through the crack beneath the door, Boris looked up with bleary, red-rimmed eyes. Another night, and he'd managed to stay awake. Another night, and he'd managed to delay the nightmares again. Rising stiffly, he moved trancelike when the door was flung open, and they all stepped outside to assemble.

Despite the coming of spring, the morning was still chilly, and Boris shivered as they stood waiting. His left hand traveled to the band on his right arm and fingered it, twisting it about absently.

A hand clapped on his shoulder, and Boris sank to the ground in a whimpering heap with his arms shielding his head.

"Get up. Nobody's going to hurt you, boy." The man's voice was gruff and impatient, but not cruel, as he pulled Boris up. Boris took a minute to recover himself as his heart raced inside his chest. "Come on. It's your day to see the Magistrate."

Boris stumbled unresisting behind the man. The Magistrate's office was not large, and the enormous desk in the center made it seem even less so. Every inch of that desk was covered in paper. The Magistrate himself was a younger man in his thirties and new to the job according to some of the other men imprisoned with Boris. He glanced up at the sound of them coming in and waved Boris toward the desk. Sifting through one of the mounds of papers on his desk, he pulled out one sheet and held it up. His eyes narrowed as he read it, then he looked back up at Boris.

"Boris Gundarson?"

Boris acknowledged his name with a slight nod.

"You do understand what I'm saying, don't you?" Again, a wary nod from Boris. "Very good. Your six months is up. Now, it was subject to review based on your behavior. It says here," the Magistrate perused the paper in his hand, "You've only had to be separated from the others three times in the last six months. Based on your previous encounters, I'd say that's an improvement, wouldn't you?"

Boris' forehead wrinkled with endeavor as he struggled to process the man's words. The Magistrate spoke quickly and left little time for Boris to comprehend what he was saying. He could have done better if he'd slept in the last three days. Steadying himself with a few deep breaths, Boris cleared his throat. He blinked several times trying to force the haze of exhaustion away. His face contorted with the effort he had to put into it.

And for the first time in six months, Boris spoke to another person.

"What does that mean?" His voice was husky, having only been used to cry out during his nightmares, and his words were slow and heavy with accent.

"It means," the Magistrate gave the papers a little flourish, and smiled. Boris stared at his smile, disbelieving. He couldn't imagine having anything to smile about, but it softened his own uncertainty and soothed his fears. "That you are free to go. You will be provided with a change of clothes and enough money to see you through two or three days. And, if you know where you might want to go, we will attempt to find arrangements to get you there."

"I can go home?"

"If that is what you wish." The Magistrate regarded him with an odd expression. "Are you sure that's where you'd like to go?"

Boris stared at the ground, his face blank. He could go anywhere. But there was nowhere that Boris wanted to go. There was nowhere he could go. Home wasn't an option. Even the Magistrate knew that, judging by the way he'd asked his last question. And he didn't have anyone here. At least, not anymore. Sasha never came back. Not since Boris told him he didn't want to see his brother anymore. For all he knew, Sasha had forgotten all about him. His brother had new friends here, people who liked him enough to search for his body on a battlefield.

Boris had no one.

Boris was no one.

"I don't think so," he finally answered, his voice faltering over the admission.

"Do you need a little time to think about it?" the Magistrate prodded, leaning forward to rest his elbows on the edge of the desk.

Boris nodded.

"I'll make your release date tomorrow, and you can spend the day thinking about it. If you have someplace in mind in the morning, we'll try to help you out."

"Do I have to work? Today?"

"No. Your work is done." The Magistrate smiled again. "I'll send for you in the morning."

It took his escort's hand on his arm to propel Boris out of his dazed stupor. If he hadn't stayed up the last three nights, he might have handled the news better. He shuffled along, his left hand tugging aimlessly at the iron band that had become an extension of himself in the last six months, as the man led him back to their quarters.

Without windows, it was still dark inside. Dark and quiet and empty. Boris made his way over to his corner and sank down, burying his head in his hands. The old, now-familiar panic was rising, and Boris was too tired to push it back down.

Free.

That was what the Magistrate said. Boris could go anywhere he wanted. Free. He could do whatever he wanted. Boris had never been free his entire life, and the idea of being thrown out into the world without being told what to do was overwhelming. And he didn't have a clue where to go. He curled up, his body demanding sleep. In the quiet, empty room with no one around to hear his screams when the nightmares came, Boris gave in.

Morning found him just as lost. He stood in front of the Magistrate again, unable to come up with a single idea of where he should go. The Magistrate was sympathetic.

"No friends you could stay with for a while? Maybe a family member? Anyone at all?"

"My brother doesn't want to see me."

"You could try. If it doesn't work out, at least it gives you a place to start. Where is he?"

"I don't know."

"Well, what's his name?"

"Sasha," Boris whispered, his voice catching slightly over his brother's name. "His name's Sasha."

The Magistrate smiled, a broad, pleased smile that extended all the way to his eyes and Boris found himself staring at that smile again. He couldn't remember the last time he'd smiled. "That has become a familiar name around here. I know where to find him. Would you like for me to arrange for you to go there?"

Without any other ideas, Boris shrugged. Just the way the Magistrate spoke of his brother was another stark reminder of how different their lives were now. Sasha had truly made a new life here. Boris was just a worthless criminal who wouldn't be missed if he simply dropped dead. Sometimes he wished he would just die. What his life was now wasn't worth living. He didn't even have a firm grip on his own sanity. The Magistrate was clearly trying, though, and Boris couldn't bring himself to reject the help.

Early the next morning, dressed in the new clothes he had been given, Boris watched while the Magistrate handed over some of his money to the driver before giving what was left to Boris. Boris stared down at the coins. He'd never had or needed money before. They're weight was unfamiliar in his hands.

"It's less than a day, and you still have a bit left over," the Magistrate's voice tugged on him, drawing his eyes up to the man's face and propelling him into action.

Shoving the coins into his new pocket, Boris settled into the back of the wagon, unwilling to join the driver up on the seat, and watched as the town dropped away, opening up to the broad expanse of the country. Spring was turning the entire countryside a fresh, bright green. Hills dotted with cattle, horses, and sheep glided by exuding the peace that settled over the entire country.

Leaning against the side of the wagon, watching the landscape slide by, Boris tried to muddle through his own thoughts. Less than a day, and he would know for sure if Sasha would even want to see him. Boris couldn't decide if he wanted the day to pass by quickly or drag.

Chapter 14

IT'LL BE FINE. HONESTLY. I know what I'm doing now, and if something goes wrong, I can just get Al or Stephan," Sasha said.

Hamo, standing next to the wagon, didn't look quite as sure. It was still early morning, but everyone was up and dressed, and waiting now in the wagon. Sasha had helped load Meredith's things into the back of it the night before.

"Don't hesitate to get them if something happens," Hamo said. "We'll only be gone a week, just long enough to get Meri settled in."

Meredith, perched on top of her trunk, was smiling with excitement. She was finally getting to do what she'd wanted to do ever since she met Taliea. She was going to learn medicine.

When the wagon started off, and they waved to Sasha, Sasha couldn't return it. His hands were full, holding Zade, a monstrous black and white dog that never left Dagmar's side.

"She'll be back, Zade." Sasha dragged the dog back to the house and brought it inside. The animal, its shaggy fur hanging over its face, ran to the door, clawing and whining. "So much for it being quiet while they're gone."

Sasha went through all the morning chores. It was harder doing them alone and doing all of them, but with no one else around, he didn't have any plans for the day. Sitting by himself at the table, eating breakfast, Sasha couldn't keep his disgust off his face. He'd never cooked anything. Not really. His first attempt was less than palatable. He left it half-eaten and, collecting his bow and arrows, left the house and Zade behind him, disappearing into the woods.

The silence didn't seem quite so stifling out in the woods. Sasha hadn't realized how much he had gotten used to being with these people. He missed the constant noise and business. He was lost without it now. The day inched by. Having wasted most of it wandering around the woods, making a pretense at hunting, he decided it was time to head back and take care of the animals before it got dark. He'd have to attempt cooking for himself again, too.

Sasha filled the last bucket with water for the horses and started back toward the house. It was dusk and the shadows were lengthening toward night. Sasha frowned as he heard Zade's frantic barking from the house. After all this time, he thought, the dog should have gotten quiet. He sighed. The dog was going to make the week unbearable. Maybe he should have convinced Dagmar to take the dog. It probably wouldn't have taken much.

The person sitting on the front steps made Sasha freeze.

"Hello?" Sasha called out, hoping his voice conveyed more certainty than he felt. If it was Stephan or Aldrid, they wouldn't just be sitting there. "Can I help you?"

"You won't want to." The voice that answered him was dull, hopeless, and most definitely Aruuken.

"Boris?" Sasha took a step back, a knot twisting in his stomach at his brother's proximity. Boris had tried too many times to break free and come after

Sasha when he visited him months ago. In all those months, Sasha hadn't been able to bring himself to go and see his mad brother. Now he winced at the accusation and hostility in Boris' voice. "What are you doing here?"

"I'm free." Sasha couldn't see Boris' face in the deepening shadows of dusk, but he could hear the bitter twist in his voice as he said the word.

"Free? Your sentence is up?"

"Yes, it's up. You don't have to worry about turning me back in for escaping."

"I wouldn't do that."

"Like you wouldn't stop me. Or hurt me. Or help them hurt me."

"I had to do that, Boris. If I didn't stop you, they would have thought I was trying to help you escape. Besides, you wouldn't have been able to get out anyway."

"And that would have been a horrible thing? Helping your brother?"

Sasha bit his lip. Boris hadn't changed much since he'd seen him months ago. All the anger was still there. Sasha thought back to what Hamo had told him of his brother. The fear was probably still there too.

"What do you want?"

Boris didn't answer. Inside the house just behind him, Zade still barked wildly, and Sasha thought if they waited too much longer, the dog might claw its way through the door. The seconds slid by in awkward silence until Sasha decided to move towards the door and Boris sitting in front of it. He couldn't just stand out here all night waiting for his brother to talk.

"Come on. Let's go inside."

Boris rose and shuffled into the house after him. Sasha pulled Zade out of the way and watched out of the corner of his eye as his brother sat down along the wall next to the door. His face turned into a puzzled frown. With no one else in the house, seats were plentiful. Boris didn't seem to see them, nor did he seem interested in keeping their conversation going. In fact, after casting a wary glance around the entire house, Boris shrank into himself, making himself as small and unobtrusive as possible.

By the smell of it cooking, Sasha suspected supper would be no more appetizing than his breakfast. How did people ever learn to be good at things like this? Sasha left it to cook and went into the sitting room to stoke up the fire. Despite the warm spring days, the nights were still quite cool, and tonight was no exception.

"What are you doing?" Boris called from across the room, his voice holding a hint of panic.

"Building the fire. What does it look like I'm doing?"

"What for?"

Sasha turned to his brother in bewildered frustration. Whatever retort he was planning on making never came out. Fear etched his brother's gaunt face as Boris stared, his eyes fixed on the growing fire.

"It's cold out this evening," Sasha said carefully. "You'd be warmer if you sat closer."

Boris didn't move or even look in Sasha's direction at the sound of his voice. He remained transfixed by the fire.

Sasha shrugged and went to the kitchen. He made two plates of food and brought one out to Boris. Boris took it without a word but didn't start eating. As thin as he was, Sasha was surprised his brother did not immediately devour the food. Instead, Boris stared at it almost as if he didn't know what it was and pushed it around with his spoon.

"Aren't you hungry?"

Boris' head jerked up, his eyes blinking rapidly as he stared at Sasha.

"Whatever," Sasha muttered to himself. Boris went back to staring at the plate. "So, what exactly are you wanting?"

82

"It wasn't my idea to come." Boris snapped out of whatever reverie he'd been trapped in, and anger filled his previously blank face. "They brought me here."

"I see."

After a few seconds of awkward silence, Boris' shoulders slumped forward, and his anger vanished. It was exhausting just trying to keep track of his mood, Sasha thought, shaking his head.

"I don't know where else to go. They said I could go anywhere. They said I was free. But I don't have anywhere to go. I didn't know where else to go."

"Were you planning on living here with me?" Sasha couldn't quite keep the alarm out of his voice.

Boris looked up at him, his eyebrows drawn together in a deep furrow. "I didn't plan anything."

Sasha swallowed the last mouthful of his food, grimacing at the flavor. He took the dishes into the kitchen, buying himself some time to think. Boris couldn't stay. Hamo would never let him. He'd said himself that Boris was different from Sasha. Even if he wanted to help, there simply wasn't room for him here.

Besides, Sasha had his own plans for the spring and summer. When Hamo and the family came back, he was leaving in search of his own family. He'd just have to tell Boris that he couldn't stay. It was better that they parted ways anyway, as much as Boris hated him. Sasha stepped out of the kitchen, determined to break the news to him right away.

Boris wasn't looking at him. He sat, huddled against the wall with his arms wrapped tightly around himself, and when Sasha had watched him for a moment, he realized his brother was quaking. Sasha's words died before they even began. He couldn't throw his brother out right now, not when the sole reason for all his torture was Sasha's own actions.

"Look, I don't know what to do. You can stay here for now, I guess. There's no one here but me for a few days."

Boris didn't acknowledge him.

Sasha sat down near the fire, studying Boris. He was thin, almost emaciated, filthy, and unkempt, his hair formed in a matted tangle. As Sasha's eyes traveled over his brother, he noticed the iron band around his right wrist. The sight of it was startling. There was only one way it could have been put on. He hadn't given it that much thought when Hamo told him about it. Now he couldn't tear his eyes off of it.

"Did it hurt?" Sasha broke the silence.

"Did what hurt?"

"When they put that on," Sasha gestured toward the band.

Boris glanced down at it as if seeing it for the first time. His fingers tugged at it. He didn't answer and Sasha gave up waiting for one. With a sigh of exasperation, Sasha got up and went in search of extra blankets. Carrying an armful of them out to the sitting room he dropped them next to Boris, making his brother flinch.

"Here. I'm going to bed. You can sleep on the couch if you want."

Sasha retreated to his room, puzzling over what exactly he was supposed to do with this brother of his. Boris still clearly disliked and distrusted him. And Sasha had no idea what Hamo would say when they returned from Bren.

For some time, Sasha lay awake, staring at the dark ceiling. He could always go to Aldrid or Stephan and ask for advice. Aldrid would be the one to ask, he thought, remembering his own experiences coming to Dival. Yes, he could go to Aldrid and talk to him about it, first thing in the morning. Perhaps he would have some idea of what to do. The decision made, Sasha finally fell asleep.

A scream yanked Sasha out of his sleep. Throwing off his covers, he dashed out of the room, fully expecting his eyes to be greeted by some terrible sight. Instead, he found Boris, crying out in his sleep, his arms shielding his face from some unseen horror.

"Boris, wake up!" Sasha put his hand on his brother's shoulder, intending to shake him awake. He never had the chance before Boris' eyes flew open and his brother shoved him away. Sasha stumbled back a step.

"Leave me alone," Boris said, dragging himself closer to the wall and away from Sasha. "Get away from me."

"Boris, you were just having a dream. It wasn't real. No one's going to hurt you here." As Sasha spoke, he saw the terror drain from Boris' face only to tense and go red with anger.

Boris struggled to his feet and turned away from Sasha. "Get away from me. I don't need your help."

Sasha watched as he disappeared out the door. A small part of him hoped it was for good. If Boris left on his own and never came back, Sasha wouldn't have to feel guilty about not taking care of him. He waited for at least half an hour, and when Boris still hadn't reentered, decided to go back to bed.

The light of morning found Sasha on his way out the door. He nearly tripped over his brother sitting on the front step. So much for him leaving, Sasha sighed. Sasha moved around him, ignoring him, and started towards the barn to do chores. Boris stared after him with vacant eyes.

"Are you planning on just sitting there all day?" Sasha asked when he'd taken care of the animals. He continued when Boris didn't respond. "I'm going over to a friend's. Do you want to come or stay here?"

Boris looked confused at the choice. Sasha shrugged and started to walk away, a little surprised when he heard his brother stand and follow him.

"What's going on?" Aldrid asked when Sasha caught up with him as he checked his traps. Aldrid looked over Sasha's shoulder, taking in the sight of Boris hanging back well behind his brother and looking uncomfortable. "Who's that?"

"My brother, Boris. He's why I'm here," Sasha went on to explain how Boris came to be there, keeping his voice low enough that Boris couldn't hear. "I don't know what to do."

"I don't know that there's a lot you can do."

"What do you mean?"

"Well, you have two options, right? You can either tell him to go find someplace else, or you can figure out a way for him to stay with you."

"I don't think he'd make it on his own. He's messed up."

"Guess you only have one choice then."

"But how? Hamo won't let him live with us. I can't ask him to do that, anyway. And besides, I have plans for this summer."

Aldrid stood up from resetting a trap, his face thoughtful. "They're coming back in a week?"

"Yes."

Aldrid nodded. "Why don't you come and see me again in a couple of days. I might have an idea that could work."

"Really?"

"Might."

Sasha anxiously awaited the passing of two days. By the end of that time, he was beginning to rethink his conviction that Boris couldn't make it on his own. The thought of living with him was burdensome. The only times he could coax Boris into a conversation ended with Boris lashing out at him. Otherwise, his brother would sit for hours on end, staring at nothing at all. It was that vacant staring that bothered Sasha most. Watching Boris sink into the dark recesses of his mind with no way for Sasha to pull him back out again was unnerving. It was more than unnerving; it was a stark reminder that something was very wrong with him.

"So, what was your idea?" Sasha had left Boris behind this time when he came to visit Aldrid, mostly because Boris was staring unresponsively at the wall and hadn't so much as blinked when Sasha tried to talk to him.

"Come on, I'll show you."

Sasha followed Aldrid deep into the woods past a creek, mud brown and swollen with melting snow and spring rains. Sasha had never been this far in the woods. He was surprised when Aldrid stopped in front of a small wooden structure. Stepping inside, the air was musty and thick with the scent of leather. It was a single room, furnished sparsely.

"Whose is this?"

"Mine. Before getting married, this was where I lived. It's deep enough in the woods that I didn't have to go far for my work. Taliea and I decided hers was the better place for us both. I still come out here to tan hides and such, but I could make that work at home."

"You're saying Boris could stay here?"

"I'm saying both of you could."

"No," Sasha said, shaking his head. "No. I don't want to. I like where I'm at. If it's just me and Boris here, it'll drive me crazy. He just gets angry at me or says nothing at all for hours at a time. I'm not giving everything up just to take care of him. No."

Aldrid ran a finger across the stovetop and made a face of disgust when he brought it away dusty.

"Sasha, he's your brother."

"That doesn't mean anything."

"Maybe not where you came from, but you're not there anymore and neither is he. You said yourself he can't make it on his own, and you're right. He needs help." Sasha hung his head a little, remembering when Aldrid had said the same thing about him, defending him to Hamo and Stephan. He'd appreciated those words then, but now they were like an anchor weighing him down. "You're the only one who can really give him that."

"But," Sasha began weakly, not ready to admit that Aldrid was right, "I can't help him. I don't know how. He hates me. And I'm leaving."

"No. He doesn't hate you. He's lost. And you could take him with you. It might be good for him. Look, Sasha, I do know a little bit of what I'm talking about here. You know, when we brought Hamo back after being a slave for nine years, he was a lot like Boris, scared of every shadow, not sure what to do with himself without being told."

"He was?" Sasha couldn't picture it.

"He was, and he's not anymore. Since you're a big part of the reason Boris was tortured so much, don't you think you sort of owe it to him?"

Sasha had nothing to say. It was true. All of it was true, and he knew it. But to move out here, away from everything that was just starting to feel normal, to give all of that up after having gone through so much to get it, that was too much to ask. Especially when he would be giving it up for someone who spent so much of his time angry at Sasha.

"I'll think about it," he finally conceded.

Before he even reached home, Sasha knew what he was going to do, even if he wasn't happy about it. Maybe he should have gone to Stephan instead. He would have received a different answer to his dilemma for sure. Stephan wasn't quite as quick to see things the way Aldrid did.

Throwing open the door to the house, Sasha was surprised to find Zade wasn't there waiting to knock him over in his excitement. Since Dagmar left with the rest of them, that had been the dog's response every time he came through the door. Instead, the house was silent. Sasha glanced in the kitchen and found it empty. So was the sitting room.

"Boris?" Sasha noticed his bedroom door ajar and made his way over, pushing it all the way open. There, curled up on the floor in the farthest corner with Zade lying next to him, was Boris. It was the first time since the night Boris showed up that Sasha had seen him asleep.

Sitting carefully on the edge of the bed, he watched the two. With a sinking heart, he pulled out the sales records and stared at the two names on them that he had set his heart on finding. Sasha ran a hand through his black hair, leaving strands of it sticking up wildly. Even if Boris would come with him, was it safe? Boris clearly wasn't in control of himself. His presence might jeopardize everything Sasha wanted to do. At least he had a couple of weeks to figure it out.

Chapter 15

SASHA STRAIGHTENED AND wiped his hands on his trousers. He'd spent the last three days getting the hunting cabin ready to live in again. Surveying his work now, he was satisfied. All that remained was to move his few possessions over. It might not be as comfortable as Hamo's house, but it would work.

The more time he had to think about it, the more convinced he became that Boris shouldn't come with him when he went on his search. He just wasn't stable enough. Remembering all the things they had done together, Sasha couldn't decide who he hated more - Lord Bayner for driving his brother mad or Boris for succumbing to the madness. At least he would never have to see Lord Bayner again.

He lingered in the woods, reluctant to return straight home to Boris, and found himself wandering along the creek. The mad rush caused by spring was still there, causing the water to roar as it cascaded over the rocks. There was something soothing about the sound. Sasha had the feeling he would be spending a lot of time here.

"We're going somewhere else to stay tomorrow," Sasha said as he sat down to pull his boots off. Boris had been pacing restlessly when he came in today. Now he paused and looked at Sasha.

"Why?"

"Because you can't stay here. When they come back, there won't be room. I don't even know what they'll say when they find out you've been staying with me."

Boris couldn't hide the hurt Sasha's words had caused, although he tried to cover it as fast as he could with feigned indifference. Sasha was relieved that he at least wasn't in some trance or rage. Boris was having one of his rare lucid moments. Sasha wasn't sure how long it would last, but he was glad he'd been able to break the news to him before it was dispelled. Seeing what his brother could be changed Sasha's annoyance to pity for the moment.

"It won't be so bad. You'll be safe there and no one will bother us."

"I thought you were leaving. You're not planning on leaving me behind again, are you? You're not going to leave me alone?"

"I haven't thought about it yet," Sasha lied.

"Yes, you have. And you are planning on leaving me. What's wrong with you? I saved your life, and you still don't trust me?"

"It's not that. It's just..."

"I'm not safe." Boris let his head hang. "It's alright, Sasha. I know it already. It's been like that ever since...ever since Dorsten. I try. And sometimes, like right now, I'm alright. But I can't control it. It just happens."

"What did they do to you?"

"Nothing." Boris stiffened and Sasha regretted asking. He was ruining the few minutes of sanity his brother had to enjoy just to satisfy his own curiosity.

"I'm not leaving yet, so I really haven't decided." Sasha tried to steer the conversation back to safer waters, realizing as he spoke that he did, in fact, mean it. "Either way, we're moving tomorrow. It really will be for the best."

"You don't want me around your new friends."
Boris became petulant again and Sasha knew that if
they kept talking about it, his brother would lose
himself in anger.

"You'll meet them, I promise. I'm going to make
us something to eat."

"You shouldn't. You're not very good at it."

Sasha actually smiled. That sounded like the old
Boris. "Want to try instead?"

"No."

Boris was right, Sasha thought as he bit into the
tough piece of meat. Blackened on the outside, and
leathery on the inside, it took several minutes to
chew just a bite of it. Boris gave up after the first bite
and now sat staring absently out the darkening
window. He was slipping away again, Sasha realized
with a pang of regret. Sasha wondered if he was
going to sleep at all tonight. Most nights he didn't,
and Sasha had given up trying to coax him into it.

In the morning, Sasha hurried through chores
and breakfast. Hamo and the family would be back
either today or tomorrow. Boris needed to be out of
the house before then.

"Come on. It's time to go," Sasha said when he
had cleaned up breakfast, hoping that Boris wouldn't
argue.

When they walked out the door, the only one to
argue was Zade. Having apparently decided that
Boris was a more acceptable replacement than Sasha
during Dagmar's absence, the dog now refused to
stay inside the house when Sasha tried to shut him
in.

"Let him come," Boris said.

"I can't. He can't stay with us, he's Dagmar's."

"But I like him."

"Doesn't mean you can just take him. Fine,"
Sasha threw his hands up as the dog lunged toward
the open door again, "He can come with us for now,
but he has to go back when they get here."

Sasha led the way, and it took them little time to reach the small, one-room cabin. Sasha ushered them in. Boris eyed the single room warily. Sasha could see him tense as he took it in but couldn't discover why. Other than being small, it looked ordinary and at least moderately comfortable. Sasha shrugged and set his things down and went outside to get some firewood.

It was a dwindling pile. Sasha allowed himself a grimace as he thought of the hours of wood chopping he would be doing. The few times he'd done it at Stephan's had left him sore and frustrated. It was a task he had yet to develop the necessary skill to be considered competent. Maybe he could convince Boris to do it from time to time. After all, Boris would have to help with something.

When he came back in with the wood under his arm, Boris had retreated to the farthest corner from the fireplace and sat down with Zade lying next to him. Leaving them behind, Sasha returned to Hamo's.

Sasha lingered in the barn. They would be back this evening, and Sasha wanted to be there to explain right away. The sound of the wagon wheels coming down the drive let him know that he didn't have to wait much longer. He stepped outside and watched as they came to a stop in front of the house.

"Sasa!" Little Drogo called out, waving a chubby hand, "Sasa here."

Sasha smiled at the toddler's mispronunciation as he grabbed the horses' heads. He still wasn't used to people being excited to see him. No sooner did the little boy get down from the wagon than he ran over and wrapped his arms around Sasha's leg.

"Someone missed you." Ophelia came around to grab him. She met Sasha's eyes and cocked her head. "What's wrong?"

"Nothing." Sometimes it was annoying to be around people who could read everything he was thinking, Sasha thought.

"So, something you're not going to tell me." She laughed a little as she pried Drogo free and carried him into the house.

"Where's Zade?" Dagmar said from the house.

"He's fine. I'll explain in a minute."

Sasha followed Hamo into the barn with the horses.

"I need to talk to you."

"Did something happen?"

"Sort of. Boris is here. His sentence is up, and he came here."

"Here? In the house, here?"

"No." Sasha hurried to explain the arrangement Aldrid had offered. "I don't know what else to do. He's really messed up like you said. Most of the time he just sits there and stares at nothing. Or he's really angry."

"Not much has changed then."

"I don't know that it ever will. And I really don't know what to do about him when I leave. I don't think it's a good idea for him to come with me."

"Still set on going? If so, I think your best choice is to take him with you. It might help, give him something to do and think about other than this."

"I guess. I just don't know. Anyway, Zade's over there with him now. He wouldn't stay back here when we left. I don't think he'll come back unless Dagmar comes to get him."

"Do you think it's safe to have Dagmar go?"

"I don't think he'd do anything to her if that's what you mean."

Back inside the house, Sasha sought Dagmar out. She was helping Edith in the kitchen.

"Did everything go well?" Edith looked up when he came in.

"Mostly." Sasha thought it best to let Hamo explain the details. "Dagmar, do you want to come and get Zade with me?"

"Where is he?"

"I'll have to show you."

Dagmar looked at him for a second, her face drawn into perplexed lines, then decided that going along would be the only way to find answers. She pulled a shawl over her shoulders and followed him out the door.

Since he'd brought her here and set her free, Sasha had never been alone with Dagmar. She had eventually stopped tensing up every time he walked into the same room, but otherwise she kept her distance. Walking alone with her out in the woods, Sasha noted some of the old tension returned. He couldn't very well blame her. The longer he'd lived away from home, the worse their practices seemed to him.

"He is alright?" Dagmar broke the silence.

"He's fine. He, um, found someone else he liked better than me while you were gone."

"Someone else? Who else?"

"My brother."

Dagmar froze, the blood draining from her face.

"It's alright. He won't hurt you. He doesn't even know who you are," Sasha hurried on to reassure her.

"You're sure?" Her face remained doubtful, but she started forward again to Sasha's relief.

"I'm sure. Even if he did, there's nothing he could do about it. He can't go home any more than I can."

"Why not?"

"Father would kill both of us."

"I'm sorry. I can't imagine having a Father I was afraid of."

"It's just the way it is in Aruuk." A thought came to Sasha as he spoke. For a moment he debated dismissing it entirely. "Dagmar, do you want to go back to your family? Because, if you did, I could take you. I'm planning on going there this summer and you could come too, and maybe help me out a little with the language and such."

Dagmar slowed down, her head bent so that Sasha couldn't see her face. She was quiet long enough that Sasha regretted asking.

"Sasha, I don't have any family left," she said at last. "The only one who might still be alive is my sister and your father chose her for himself."

It was Sasha's turn to stop short.

"My father picked her?"

"He picked both of us, but then he changed his mind and decided to give me to you," Dagmar's voice was barely a whisper.

"I'm so sorry, Dagmar. I didn't know."

"Why are you sorry? You didn't do anything."

"I shouldn't have asked. I shouldn't have brought it up at all." Sasha bit his lip. All the female slaves his father had kept came back to mind. None of them lasted long. Perhaps there was a measure of mercy in that. Whatever Dagmar's sister suffered at Father's hands, her suffering was probably over by now. He wasn't sure if there was any comfort in telling Dagmar that now. She probably already knew, he decided and kept quiet.

"I will come with you though, if you want, and help," Dagmar said suddenly several minutes later.

"You would? Why? I mean, I'd be glad for the help, but there's no reason for you to help me."

"Sasha," she stopped walking and turned to face him, "you gave me my freedom and my life and a new family and... you never took nothing from me. I can at least help you give your mother and sister the same."

Sasha stood dumbfounded by Dagmar's words.

"Thank you," he said at last, but the words were weak and inadequate compared to Dagmar's generosity. "Come on, we'd better hurry if we're going to get back before dark."

No light showed out of the single window of the cabin as they approached it. Sasha made an exasperated sound in his throat as he pushed the door open to find the fire he'd started just that morning completely gone out. The last bit of daylight was enough to reveal that Boris hadn't moved.

While Dagmar allowed Zade to jump up on her, placing his massive paws on her shoulder and nearly knocking her down, Sasha knelt by the hearth and restarted the fire. Aside from shrinking into a smaller heap on the floor in his corner, Boris did nothing.

When Zade's enthusiasm dissipated some, Dagmar cast an uncertain glance toward Boris. She moved closer to Sasha.

"Is he alright?" she whispered.

Sasha shrugged. "I guess not. I'll tell you about it when we head back." He finished with the fire, and turned to Boris, "We have to take Zade with us. I'll be back in a bit."

Boris' face scrunched up with effort as he processed Sasha's words. After a long moment, he nodded, and Sasha breathed a sigh of relief. At least he wasn't going to argue about Zade leaving.

"Is he always like that?" Dagmar asked when they were once again outside.

"He didn't used to be. He was captured after the battle. And Lord Bayner tortured him, I think. Now, he's pretty much always like this." Sasha turned away, troubled. "I really don't know what I'm going to do with him when I go."

"Take him with you."

"No. He can't control himself. There's no way I'm going to drag him around half the world with me."

"But he needs you."

"You think so?"

"You're his brother. You know better than anyone what he's gone through, don't you? Lord Bayner did the same to you, didn't he? If anyone can help him, it's you. I'd do it for my sister," Dagmar said softly.

Knowing what he knew now of her sister's fate, Sasha wondered at the words. If only helping his brother didn't mean being tied down to one place because he couldn't trust Boris outside of the confines of their cabin. If Boris could just see how much he was giving up to take care of him maybe he would put some effort into it himself.

"I don't know," Sasha answered, hoping to end the conversation. He couldn't understand why everyone thought it was such a good idea to take Boris anywhere. It was a terrible idea. But so was the alternative. Sasha hated the idea of spending the rest of his life stuck taking care of a brother who was only ever sometimes there.

Chapter 16

SITTING PERCHED ON THE VERY edge of his bed, Boris watched with anxious eyes as Sasha packed. Sasha hadn't said anything. In fact, he was doing everything in his power to ignore Boris and avoid his pleading eyes. For two weeks, very few words passed between the brothers.

Now, as Boris watched Sasha moving about the small cabin collecting all the things he had set aside for his trip, Boris tried to work up the courage to speak. His hands tightened into fists, his nails digging into the calloused skin on his palms. It had never been so hard to just talk to people, especially his brother.

For a fleeting moment, he remembered the way things used to be, before Sasha fell down the ravine, before Sasha turned up alive, before Sasha beat him, before Sasha betrayed them. The effort of remembering was too painful and taxing. Boris gave it up. He took a deep, shaky breath and swallowed down the sick lump of nervousness that rose up in his throat.

"I'm coming with you." Boris rushed through the words, anxious to get them out before his courage forsook him entirely.

Sasha, his back to him, stiffened and put down whatever he had in his hands. He turned slowly around and met Boris' eyes, his lips pressed into a thin, tight line. Boris could see the refusal in his face already. Tremors that he had been fighting back came, and Boris cursed inwardly. The last thing he needed was to start trembling in front of his brother. He shifted his hands to the bedding beneath him and gripped it with all his might. Sasha would never agree to take him when he was so weak.

"Sasha, you can't leave me here alone. Not again."

"You won't be alone. You've met my friends and they will come check on you. They'll take good care of you."

Boris shook his head, catching the placating tone in Sasha's voice. He had met Hamo, once. As for the rest of the family, Sasha had been very careful and not very subtle in keeping him away from them. Boris was just glad he could finally meet the man who had shown him kindness the day of his sentencing. Hamo probably would come and look in on him regularly. Boris didn't doubt it.

What he did doubt was the hours and hours of being alone. The four walls of the cabin crowded in on him in a way that was terrifyingly reminiscent of the cells he had occupied. The long stretches of silence were undoing him. He hated when Sasha left for even just a few hours.

"Please." Boris tried to force his voice to be more than a whisper, but he couldn't manage it. "Please, I'll stay out of the way."

Sasha sat down on his bed, staring at his hands in his lap. He chewed on his lower lip, lost in thought.

"I'm not leaving yet," Sasha started.

"Stop lying to me," Boris said, his voice thick with despair. "You are going. I'm not that crazy, Sasha. I know what you're doing."

Sasha's face went red, and his hands tightened into fists. Boris fought back the urge to crawl into a corner to escape the anger he was sure was coming.

This was Sasha, he told himself. He shouldn't be scared of Sasha. Reason told him Sasha wouldn't hurt him. But Sasha had hurt him once, and there was no reasoning that away. The urge became more powerful when Sasha threw his hands up in the air and Boris squeezed his eyes shut.

"Fine. Come with me."

Boris opened his eyes and stared at his brother, trying to comprehend his words.

"You'll let me?"

"Everyone seems to think it's such a great idea, so why not?" Sasha's tone left Boris in little doubt as to how he felt about it.

Boris watched as Sasha finished packing, with a lot more intensity than he had been earlier. Retreating to his corner, as far from the fire as he could possibly get, Boris tried to maintain his grip on saneness for just a few minutes longer. It was so maddening to feel himself slipping away and not being able to stop it. Sasha didn't understand, couldn't understand.

"I'm going out for a bit. I'll be back," Sasha said over his shoulder as he left the cabin. Boris made no response.

Chapter 17

SASHA DIDN'T HAVE A destination in mind, he just needed to get away. He needed to be out of sight of Boris' pleading eyes. Boris was scared of him. In the face of that fear every resolve Sasha had just crumbled. He needed to not think about what he'd just agreed to.

Breaking into a jog, then into a run, Sasha allowed himself to be lost in the mindless effort of exerting himself. The air whipping past his ears was perfect for drowning out his thoughts. The pounding of his heart and lungs drove away the worry that nagged him about the trip.

Coming to a breathless stop beside the creek, Sasha bent over for air. The dull ache in his chest reminded him that he should be more careful. Even after a year, too much stress on his lungs caused the old wound to flare up. Sasha grimaced, placing a protective hand over the spot. He could feel the raised bump of the scar beneath his shirt. Taliea said it would fade with time, Sasha just wasn't sure how much time she was talking about. A year seemed like a very long time, and it was as vivid as ever.

Scooping up a handful of cool water from the flowing creek, he splashed it across his now hot, sweaty face and gasped at the coldness of it. The warmer days of late spring hadn't reached the water yet. Wiping the excess off with his sleeve, he took several deep breaths trying to calm the pain that his exertion had awakened.

"Aside from trying to freeze yourself, what are you doing?"

The voice behind him made Sasha jump and spin around. Ophelia stood several feet back, her dark eyes the only evidence that she was trying hard not to laugh.

"How long have you been there?"

"Long enough. I didn't know it still hurt." She raised an eyebrow as she glanced down to where he was still holding his chest.

"Just when I try to do too much."

"Like running madly through the woods as if wild animals were chasing you. I can see why that would hurt."

"That's not what I was doing." Sasha pulled his hand away but stayed bent over slightly. "It felt good."

"I can tell."

"Well, it did, before this started hurting again," he motioned toward his wound, "I just needed to get away."

Ophelia came up next to him, facing the creek. She stooped down and picked up a rock to throw in the water.

"From your brother?"

Sasha nodded and Ophelia laughed a little, though it lacked her usual enthusiasm.

"You're here because you can't figure out how to live with your sibling, and I'm here because I can't figure out how to live without mine." She brought her arm up and cast the stone into the water. It hit with a PLOP and ripples creased the surface.

"Do you really miss Meredith that badly already?"

"We're twins. A matched set, right?" Ophelia glanced over, mischief on her face.

Sasha threw his hands up as he rolled his eyes. "Am I ever going to live that down?"

"No. Definitely not. Why would I let you live that down?" A shadow fell over Ophelia's face. "I do really miss her. I mean, she's never not been there. We've always been together. It's strange, and kind of lonely, not having her around. Although," she smiled a bit, "I'll probably get into a lot less trouble with her gone."

Sasha kicked a rock loose and sent it spinning into the water as he shoved his hands down into his pockets. Even at their best times, Boris and he had spent every waking minute trying to outdo the other and vying for Father's hard-won attention. It was a game that had no ending, and no winners. He couldn't even fathom missing Boris quite the same as Ophelia was describing. At the moment, he was missing his life without him. It had been as close to perfect as Sasha thought possible. Boris' presence was ruining everything.

"Come on." Ophelia turned away and started walking.

"Where?"

"I want to show you Meri and I's favorite place. We weren't supposed to come up here when we were little, but Meri talked me into doing it a lot anyway."

Sasha followed her deeper into the woods. The ground became rougher and sloped up a bit. After hiking for almost ten minutes, the trees thinned out slightly, exposing a small, cascading waterfall. The water, swollen with melted snow and spring rains, gurgled and sang as it rushed over the rocks and fell with a splash into itself below. The sunlight that managed to filter in between the trees caught the spray of water and turned it into a thousand miniature rainbows.

"This is your favorite spot?" Sasha could see why.

Ophelia nodded, stepping out onto a large, moss-covered rock that jutted out above the falls. Sasha followed her.

"You know, in the mountains, there are waterfalls that fall fifty, a hundred feet. The water comes down so hard it wears away the bottom into a giant bowl."

"I bet they're beautiful to watch."

"They're loud, really loud. You can't hear yourself think if you're standing next to one. And they're dangerous. I knew someone who fell down one once. There wasn't much left of them by the time they were pulled out of the water."

"Ugh...why would you ruin a perfectly good picture in my mind? Now every time I think about them, I'll imagine someone falling down and dying." Ophelia sat down, letting her feet dangle just above the water's reach.

"Sorry." Sasha sat as well, letting the white mist of water reach him. "I guess I didn't really think of it that way."

"So, what happened with your brother that made you come out here?"

"We argued." Sasha shut his eyes, thinking about the way Boris had trembled when he thought Sasha was angry with him. Sasha had been angry with him. "I made him afraid when I got angry, so I felt bad and told him he can come with me."

"You're going to take him?"

"I told him I would. I'll probably change my mind when we leave tomorrow, though."

"You can't. He's your brother."

"You know, that's what everyone has said to me. We're not like that though." Sasha felt the heat rising to his face. He leaned back, his hands behind him on the rock. "When I fell down that ravine, you saw. He never even came to look for me. He didn't care. When we were growing up, we never stopped trying to get the better of each other. We're not like you and Meri."

"But you could be, at least a little." Ophelia stared down at the water, her face drawn into a concerned frown. "Sasha, you're all he has."

"But he's so hard to take care of and be around. He doesn't do anything for himself. He can't even keep the fire going while I'm away."

Ophelia remained quiet for some time, staring down into the swirling flow of water, a thoughtful frown caressing her features.

"When Father brought you back and you were dying, you were really hard to take care of too. But people still did it because they thought you were worth saving."

Caught completely off guard by the bluntness of her words, Sasha gripped the edge of the rock beneath him, his mind reeling with the revelation in Ophelia's speech. He'd been so busy fighting to live and recover that he never gave a thought to the difficulties faced by those who nursed and coaxed him back to life. It must have been exhausting, and inconvenient on everyone in the family. Yet, they did it. He'd been attended to night and day until his strength returned, and even after that, he'd been offered a home that was made possible only by the rearranging of the family. And all because, according to Ophelia, they had thought him worth saving.

"You know, I hate when you do that," Sasha mumbled.

"Do what?"

"When you just say things."

"That's called talking. You hate when I talk? That's not very nice." Ophelia cocked her head to look at him, her face a puzzle.

"No. When you say things so bluntly. It's annoying."

Ophelia laughed. "Why? Because you know I'm right? Admit it, Sasha. That's the only reason it bothers you so much."

Sasha found himself smiling in spite of his frustration and he shook his head, throwing his hands in the air.

"Fine. I won't change my mind. He can come with me and if it all ends terribly, and I'm sure it will, I can come back and blame it on you and everyone else who has this crazy idea that I should."

Ophelia stood up and jumped lightly down from the rock and Sasha followed.

"I should get home before Mother starts worrying. You're stopping by to say goodbye tomorrow, aren't you?"

"Have to. Dagmar's coming with me."

"Oh, that's right. I should really be mad at you. You're taking away the last of my company."

"You have your other sisters."

"Eh," Ophelia shrugged, "They're not the same."

"But they're your sisters," Sasha mimicked her tone from earlier.

"Not fair, Sasha. It's nowhere close to the same thing."

Walking through the woods at a leisurely pace rather than sprinting, it took Ophelia and Sasha several minutes longer to reach the split in the path.

"See you tomorrow," Ophelia called out as she headed for home. Sasha waved briefly and started for his.

Pausing outside the door, Sasha rested his hand on the latch. As much as he said he hated when Ophelia spoke so bluntly, her words had cleared his own mind in a way that he was unable to, even with running. Pushing open the door, he didn't need to bother to look for Boris. He was huddled in the corner. His eyes widened a little when he caught sight of Sasha. He was still afraid that Sasha was angry.

Sasha sat down on the floor next to Boris, who shrank away from him.

"I'm sorry about earlier. I shouldn't have been angry with you." He didn't dare look at Boris for fear of making things worse, but he could sense his brother's eyes watching him. "If you're coming with me, I guess we'd better get some things ready for you. Come on, let's eat and then we'll pack."

He got to his feet and held out a hand to help Boris up. Boris was staring at him still, but the fear was gone. He took Sasha's hand and stood.

Chapter 18

WITH THE DIRT ROAD SLIDING away beneath them, Sasha settled back against the side of the wagon. Stephan had agreed to take them to Bren so that Sasha could find a ship willing to take them across to their southern neighbors. Boris was sitting so that he faced away from the wagon, staring out at the passing landscape. Dagmar shared the seat with Stephan. The woods gradually gave way to grassy rolling hills, most of them dotted with cows or sheep.

Sasha shut his eyes. It had been harder to say goodbye this time, and he wasn't even sure why. There was a lump in his throat that didn't want to go away no matter how many times he swallowed. There had been no such thing when he left home behind for good.

The hours dragged by, and Sasha managed to doze a little, the mild spring sun warming him comfortably. Considering how little he'd slept the night before, he needed the rest. He couldn't stay asleep long, though. The reality of what he was attempting bore down on him. Waking up from another short nap, Sasha realized Bren was in the distance, the castle towers cutting their jagged scar into the skyline ahead. His fingers reached into his pocket of their own accord, feeling the folded papers that he'd stuffed in there. Whispering a silent promise to Mother and Agathe, he pulled his hand free.

Reaching Bren an hour or so before dark, Stephan stopped at an inn within sight of the castle. Boris, having stayed quiet and docile for the entire day, now stiffened at the sight of the place. Sasha watched as his face turned gray and he froze in place.

"Boris," it was Dagmar's voice that broke through Boris' spell of fear, "Let's go inside."

Dagmar led the way in with a confidence Sasha had yet to feel walking into public establishments like this. He and Stephan followed with their luggage. After securing their rooms for the night, they went upstairs to drop off their things.

Sasha lay back on his bed, running over the list of things he needed to do in order to reach Sondaru. He'd go out by himself tomorrow to find a ship that they could buy passage on, and if it was too much, he'd offer to work in exchange for the ride. And then he'd go see Meredith, not because he was anxious to see her, but because he'd had an idea and needed to ask her about it. Then he'd have to find a few changes of clothes for Boris. He'd come from imprisonment with nothing but the ones he was wearing. Sasha's eyes slid shut, and before he could piece together any more of a plan, he was asleep.

Bright sunlight streaming in through the window forced him awake. Sasha sat up, rubbing eyes still bleary with sleep and yawning. The height of the sun in the sky told him he'd slept a lot later than he intended. Groaning, he ran a hand through his disheveled hair and got all the way up. Splashing enough water on his face, and the washstand as well, to finally start feeling awake, he ran through the list of things he had to get done today. Sasha glanced around the room and found Boris, wide awake, sitting in the corner. He hadn't slept. Sasha had stayed with him long enough to know that any night that was quiet was a night Boris didn't sleep.

"I'm going to head down to the docks and see about getting passage," Sasha said as he headed for the door. To his surprise, Boris stood up and followed him. "Are you sure you want to come?"

"I'm sure. I don't want to be left alone."

"Alright."

Despite having been in Bren before, Sasha had never made it down to the docks and consequently had never seen the sea. When the last row of wooden houses ended and the wharfs opened up in front of him, Sasha stopped and gawked at the endless expanse of water. The tangy saltiness that hovered in the air was thicker and mingled with another scent Sasha couldn't place. As they made their way down the wharfs, he guessed this other, more unpleasant odor belonged to the multitudes of fish. He scrunched his face up in disgust. Fish wasn't something anyone ate in Aruuk, and smelling them now, Sasha was sure he would never willingly consume them.

Finding a ship's captain who was heading to Sondaru and willing to take passengers was easy. Securing passage with one after they caught sight of the iron band on Boris' arm proved far more difficult. As one captain after another turned them down with either a pointed glance at the offending accessory or with an offhand comment about how they didn't need thieves aboard their vessels, Sasha's frustration deepened. He should have insisted Boris stay at the inn with Dagmar.

Approaching yet another captain, Sasha already had a fair idea of how the conversation would go. The captain couldn't have been described as young or old, but somewhere in between. He had the weathered face that was standard of anyone who spent their lives out at sea. As Sasha and Boris approached his boat, a medium sized vessel that was as weathered as her captain, the man was shouting down to someone below deck. Sasha waited until he was done and had noticed them.

"What can I do for you?" The man stepped down off the boat and stood on the pier with them.

"We're looking for passage to Sondaru. Are you headed that way?"

"Might stop in if I have good reason to. Who's we?"

"My brother and I," Sasha gestured toward Boris, "And a young lady."

"It'll cost you more to bring a lady. Have to give up my own cabin for them and sleep with the crew."

"You'd be willing to take us, though?"

"Might be. What's your business in Sondaru?" The man leaned against a mooring pillar.

"I'm going there to find some family." Sasha really didn't think it necessary to share the details of why any of his family was there.

"You aware of the fact that there's a civil war going on in Sondaru right now?"

Sasha shook his head.

"Not a safe place to be. Not a safe place to put a ship in, either." The captain looked up at the sky, thinking. "Unless, of course, the captain knows what he's doing."

"I don't know how safe it is or isn't, but my sister's a slave there, and I want to get her back," Sasha blurted out.

"Is that right? Well, let's see." The captain's eyes wandered for the first time over Boris. Jerking his chin toward the band on Boris' wrist, he asked, "What'd you do to get that?"

Sasha's heart sank. The man was mere moments away from refusing them entirely. And Boris wasn't making it better, either, by just staring blankly at the man and tugging at the band with his free hand. Out of any other ideas, Sasha began explaining.

"He got it because he was captured in battle after accompanying a raiding party into Dorsten more than a year ago."

The captain pursed his lips, considering Sasha's explanation. He shook his head. "No. I think you owe me more than that, if I'm going to let you on my ship for a few weeks."

"We're from Aruuk." Sasha cringed inwardly as he saw the effect the name had on the captain, "I'm the one who came and brought warning of the attack. He's my brother. He was captured during the battle they fought in the mountains and was sentenced to a work gang. That's the only reason he has the band. He's not a thief. And he won't cause any trouble. I'll make sure of it."

"I've heard of you. Everybody around here says you saved the country by coming and telling the king. They call you a hero." The captain's eyes narrowed as he studied Sasha's face. Sasha felt blood rushing to it as a hot wave of embarrassment washed over him. He hadn't heard anyone talking about him, but then, he had been completely out of it for the weeks following the event. The captain, apparently satisfied with his scrutiny, leaned back again. "Alright, I'll take you. But I can't make any promises about hanging around for you to come back. Like I said, there's a civil war on, and there's no telling who holds what these days down there."

"Since you're the first person we've talked to that was willing to take us, I'll take it," Sasha said with relief. "When will you leave?"

"Morning after next. Lawrence, by the way," the captain said as he extended his hand.

Sasha introduced both his brother and himself before arranging a price for their trip. For all his talk about it being more expensive with a girl, the price wasn't nearly as much as Sasha imagined it would be. He kept his thoughts to himself, afraid that voicing them would lead to an increase in expense.

Leaving the docks behind them, Sasha started back toward the inn. The streets were crowded and noisy in the late afternoon. As they neared the inn, a chill went down Sasha's spine accompanied by the distinct sense that someone was watching him. A cursory glance around them as he stopped to open the inn's door showed no one in particular staring at them. Sasha shrugged the feeling away. In a town this size, it was quite possible someone had been staring, probably at Boris since he had the iron band that these people treated like the plague. Still, he didn't like the uneasiness that it caused.

"Do you want to come with me to see Meri?" Sasha asked Dagmar when she stuck her head out of her room at his knock.

"Yes!" Dagmar came out of the room a moment later and followed them back out into the street. "I can take you right to where she's working."

Dagmar hurried through the streets as they followed and stopped in front of a squat wooden building, stuck between two much taller ones. The only thing visible through the windows were rows upon rows of jars filled with many colored substances. A bell jangled as Dagmar pushed the door open.

"Meri?" She stepped into the shop and glanced around.

Sasha almost didn't recognize Meredith with her hair done up and completely hidden beneath the white cap and standing behind the counter talking to another man. It wasn't until she looked in their direction and smiled at Dagmar that he realized it was her.

"Dagmar, Sasha what are you doing here?" She moved from behind the counter and embraced Dagmar enthusiastically.

"We're going to Sondaru to look for Sasha's sister."

"Still going to try?" Meredith said to Sasha.

"I have to. Dagmar's coming along to help me. And so is he." Sasha glanced toward Boris, hanging back as far as he could get.

"Is that...?" Meredith stiffened and pressed her lips together tightly as she recognized him. Sasha grimaced and cursed his own stupidity. He'd forgotten that Meredith knew nothing about Boris. The last time she'd seen him was when he and Sasha kidnapped the girls.

"My brother. He's actually the reason I'm here," Sasha lowered his voice. When Meredith looked at him curiously, he continued. "He was captured after the battle and tortured by Lord Bayner. He's been messed up ever since."

"Serves him right." The man Meredith had been talking to turned around and leaned back, resting his elbows on the counter. Sasha almost choked.

"Oh, I forgot. This is Karl. Although," Meredith glanced between the two of them, "I guess technically you two already met."

"I wouldn't have called that a meeting," Karl said. "My sister still has nightmares from what you and your people did to her. Never understood why they just let you go."

"Karl. Stop," Meredith said.

"Your sister might still have nightmares, but at least you and her are still alive. Which is a lot more than you would be if they hadn't let me go."

"What are you trying to say?"

"Karl, he's the one who brought word of what Aruuk was planning. He really is the only reason we're all still alive," Meredith spoke up before Sasha had a chance to. Karl's eyes narrowed in suspicion as he continued to stare at Sasha. Before anyone else had a chance to continue the argument Meredith turned to Sasha. "What is it you wanted from me?"

Sasha took a moment to collect his wits. "I wanted to see if you knew of any kind of medicine that might help him. He can't focus on anything, he barely sleeps or eats, and he spends most of the time just sitting and staring at nothing at all."

"I'm sorry, Sasha. I've never heard of anything that would help with that. Is he really that bad?"

"Just look at him now. He's afraid to come any closer because he doesn't know you. It never changes."

"I'm sorry," Meredith repeated. "I don't think there's anything I can do for him."

After Meredith and Dagmar chatted for a few minutes and Sasha endured Karl's glare for an equal amount of time, they left the apothecary behind them. Sasha's own mood was considerably fouler after his exchange with Karl, and he paid little attention to anything around him until he heard Dagmar call his name from behind him. She and Boris were standing in front of a shop window. Sasha backtracked to them and saw that it was a bakery. And visible in the window was an assortment of baked goods that Sasha had never seen.

"Can we go in and get one?" Dagmar asked. "I have a little money from Taliea. And they are so good."

"They are good," Boris spoke for the first time since leaving the inn that morning.

"When did you have one?"

"In prison, here." Boris' face scrunched up with the effort it took him to remember. "The day they sentenced me. I don't know who gave it to me. Or why. It was just there. And it was good."

After that Sasha didn't have the heart to refuse. A few minutes later, he was introduced to the sweet, light bread filled with fruit cream and decided he didn't regret being talked into the purchase. Watching Boris actually eat and savor anything made it worth the few minutes and coins, Sasha thought.

Chapter 19

T HE COAST OF DIVAL WAS NOTHING more
than a thin dark line on the misty horizon and
Sasha was already regretting his haste in
setting sail. His stomach churned at the gentle,
rocking motion of the ship and it was taking all of his
will power not to be sick. Boris and he shared a very
tiny cabin that was barely enough room to stand up
and turn around in. Boris, bothered by the close
space, spent most of his time out on the deck
wherever he was most out of the way. Sasha didn't
try to coax him back inside. As cramped as it was,
and as sick as he felt, he appreciated being alone for
once.

Sasha sat on the edge of his narrow bunk,
gripping the sides of it until his knuckles turned
white. The seasickness didn't appear to bother his
brother at all. Sasha was a little jealous of the fact
until he thought about how much just about
everything else bothered Boris. Maybe it was only
fair that he escape this calamity.

When, after three days of misery and keeping to
his bed, Sasha was finally able to get up and walk
around without the threat of his stomach heaving, he

sought out Lawrence. He found him standing at the helm, eyes intent on the course before them.

"I almost forgot we had you on here." Lawrence laughed as Sasha staggered over, gripping the deck railings the entire way.

"How do you just stand there?"

"Oh, you get used to it after a while. When you've done it your whole life, there's nothing much to it."

"I can't imagine ever being used to this." Sasha attempted to relax his grip on the railing. The ship dipped forward, and his hands clenched it tightly once more. "How long is it until we reach Sondaru?"

Lawrence studied the sky for a few seconds before answering. "If the weather holds, no more than ten days. Speaking of which, I'm not planning to put you ashore at a harbor."

"What do you mean? That was the deal. That's what I'm paying you for."

"The deal's still on. But, like I said before, there's a civil war going on and I'm not going to risk putting into harbor and being caught between the two sides. We'll row you in at night, somewhere a little less visible."

"I guess that makes sense. How bad is this war?"

"Oh, nothing too serious in the way of wars. It's more of a spat, from what I've heard. Sondaru has two types of people. Very rich and very poor. For whatever reason those two can't seem to get along for more than a few years at a time. I guess they're not too different from us." Lawrence laughed a little and Sasha remembered the war between Dorsten and Dival that had only recently been put to rest.

"They do this often?"

"Every ten, twenty years. Sometimes a little longer."

Dagmar came up just then, and Sasha watched with a little twinge of jealousy as she walked easily across the deck without a handhold.

"This isn't the first time you've sailed, is it?"

Dagmar shook her head, a wistful look filling her eyes as she stared out at the sea. "No, my father was a fisherman. I grew up on boats."

"See? What'd I tell you? Spend your whole life doing it and it's as easy as riding a horse."

"That wasn't very easy," Dagmar whispered, her voice barely reaching Sasha's ears.

The weather remained fair and the wind steady, pushing them farther and farther south. By the tenth day, Sasha decided he could never make his home here in the south. The heat shimmered in the air and hung heavy even through the night hours. Early in the morning on the eleventh day, pale brown merged with the blue expanse of the sea on the horizon. Boris joined Dagmar and Sasha at the railing to watch it.

"That's it." Lawrence pointed the subtle change in color out to them.

"We'll land tonight?" Sasha couldn't hide his eagerness to return to solid ground again.

"Tonight, it is. Although, I figured you'd be getting used to sailing at this point," Lawrence said, a teasing smile pulling the corners of his mouth up.

"I don't think that's possible, ever."

Sasha spent most of the day either standing in the bow of the ship watching the thin line of land grow larger or in the tiny cabin checking and rechecking that all of their things were ready to go. Anticipating getting back on land made the hot hours of the day drag sluggishly by. The sun was a sphere of flaming orange that barely touched the distant western edge of the water before the landscape became distinct.

"It's so brown," he commented to Boris who had once again roused himself enough to join Sasha in his watch.

"It is a desert. Didn't Dagmar tell you that?"

"No, she never mentioned it. When did she tell you?"

"The other night."

Sasha frowned. He didn't remember any such conversation. Boris noticed his expression.

"You weren't there."

"Oh." Sasha did a poor job of hiding his surprise.

"What? Is she not allowed to or something? Or am I not? You're not afraid I would hurt her, are you?" Boris turned sullen instantly, and Sasha wished he could have kept his expression to himself for once.

"No. She's allowed to talk to you. She's free to do whatever she wants now. Both of you are."

"You don't want her to, though."

"It's fine, Boris. I don't care. It just surprised me." Sasha regretted ever starting the conversation and sought for a way to end it. "It'll be interesting seeing a desert, I think."

"You probably won't like it very much." Dagmar came up behind them. "It takes a long time to get used to the heat and dust and sand."

"That's encouraging." Sasha's face fell.

Even after the sun set, Lawrence waited, insisting that the best time to go ashore would be in the darkest hours just after midnight.

"You should get some sleep while you can," he suggested when Sasha expressed his impatience, "You have no idea what you're going to face out there."

Although he laid down, Sasha couldn't sleep. The rocking and pitching of the ship that others found restful was still foreign enough to him that it couldn't lull him. Getting up, he slipped outside onto the deck. Boris sat in a corner, staring vacantly out at the sea. Sasha, their brief argument from earlier still weighing on him, went and sat down next to him. To his surprise, Boris actually broke off his staring and acknowledged his presence.

"You should try to sleep," Sasha whispered.

"Can't."

"No one's going to mind if you have nightmares. You need sleep."

"I mind." Boris turned back out to the sea. "Sasha, what if something goes wrong?"

"Nothing's going to go wrong. We're going to go, find the man who bought Agathe, find her and rescue her. We'll be in and out before anyone even knows we're there."

"If your plan works. If it doesn't...if something bad happens there, with the war and all, don't leave me, please?"

"I'm not leaving you anywhere. Why would you think that?"

"I know I'm not worth keeping around," Boris said quietly. "And don't say you haven't thought that, because I know you have. Sometimes, I wish they'd just killed me. I think it would have been easier."

Sasha remained silent, turning Boris' words over in his mind.

"What happened to you?" he finally asked.

Boris laughed, the bitter, mirthless laugh that was his now. "You want to know what happened? What happened was you. Everything they did to me was because of you. They tortured me for hours. And do you know what he did while I lay there screaming my lungs out? When I begged for him to kill me? He laughed. He laughed as if it was the greatest joke in the world. The more pain he put me through the funnier he thought it was. And every day he would tell me that it should have been you there, that if it were you there, he wouldn't have to hurt me."

Sasha didn't have to ask who Boris was talking about. His own experiences with Lord Bayner had proven him to be such a man. He hated that man, now more than ever. It was a good thing he'd never have to see him again. If he did, there was no telling what Sasha might do.

An hour or so after midnight, the sweltering heat of the day had finally dissipated, leaving the night air cool and chilling. Sasha carried his things ashore off the small boat that Lawrence and two of his sailors had rowed them to shore in. His feet sank in the sand of the beach and Sasha stooped down to run his hands through the strange substance. The grains slipped through his fingers and blew away in the light breeze coming off the water. If it weren't for the importance of his task, the prospect of exploring would have been delightful.

"Sasha," Lawrence's voice in the dark pulled him back, "I'm sailing further south to trade, but I'll be back this way in a month or so. If you finish what you've come to do by that time, wait for me here. I'll hang around out there for a few days. Light a fire, and I'll know to come get you."

"Thank you. I appreciate it."

Watching the boat drift slowly away until it was nothing more than a black spot in the darkness, Sasha almost wanted to call it back. The sand, the heat, even the smell of this place was so unfamiliar.

"Do you have any idea where we are?" he finally turned away from watching the now empty black sea and asked Dagmar.

"Yes. Where do you want to go?"

"Her buyer was from Kaldura. Do you know where that is?"

"The capitol. I know where it is." Dagmar shouldered one of the packs. "It's going to be a long walk."

"Great. Might as well get started."

"We'll want to avoid people too, which will make it longer."

When the sun first sent its scorching fingers of heat over the eastern edge of the sand filled world, they were still within sight of the sea. After walking for some minutes in the light, Sasha noticed that they were keeping parallel to the sea rather than moving away from it.

"Is Kaldura further up the coast?" e asked Dagmar.

"No."

"Then where are we going?"

"Pinjaru."

"That's where you're from, isn't it?" When Dagmar nodded, Sasha continued, "Why are we going there? I thought there was nothing left of it."

"There's an oasis. If we're going to trek across the desert, we'll need water."

At the mention of water, Sasha realized just how parched his throat was. It didn't help that he couldn't breathe without sucking in and swallowing the particles of sand that were ever present in the air.

It was nearing midday when the first sign of civilization showed itself in the form of a red stone wall, crumbled and half buried in drifts of sand. Much of what remained of the village was buried out of sight by the sand, but beyond the few visible ruins lay what Sasha assumed was the oasis Dagmar spoke of. A few trees, quite different from anything he had ever seen, spread out across a patch of ground. The large, sweeping leaves of the trees grew only near the tops and had a thick, waxy sheen. Scattered between and around these trees were several stalky shrubs, their leaves equally thick. Pools of water shimmered in the bright sunlight.

"It's three days to the next oasis. We'll have to carry enough water with us to make it there," Dagmar said, kneeling next to the nearest pool and scooping water into her hand to drink. "We should probably just stay here for a few hours until the heat passes."

Sasha, already soaked with sweat, couldn't argue with her. He and Boris joined her at the pool and drank their fill of water before filling their water skins. Sasha tried to estimate just how much water three people would need crossing a desert. As hot and dry as it was, the best he could figure was a lot.

"When we get to the first big town, we're going to need different clothes," Dagmar said.

"Why?" Boris beat Sasha to the question they were both thinking.

"You have too much skin exposed. Your arms and face are going to burn in the sun. Besides, we should blend in if we can."

Sasha glanced down at the already red skin on his arms while Boris leaned back against the trunk of one of the odd-looking trees and closed his eyes. Sasha, watching him, tried to push away the nagging worry that this would prove to be too much for Boris. He looked exhausted, and they'd only traveled half a day. Of course, he hadn't slept in the last three, so that didn't help. And his eating was so sporadic that he never regained any of his lost weight. Sasha sighed and tried to make himself comfortable against a tree as well.

"You should sleep too," Dagmar said, staring out toward where the village used to be.

As much as he did not want to admit it, Sasha was drowsy. The heat was oppressive, and sleep was a reprieve. He let his eyes shut.

It was the vague sense that something was off that woke him up some time later. For a terrifying second his eyelids, full of sand and burnt already from the sun, refused to open. When they did, Sasha winced at the dry burning in his eyes. Without looking at the others he cupped fresh water in his hands and flushed his eyes out until the stinging faded. Only then did he look around and find that he was alone. Jumping to his feet, he scanned the area for any sign of his brother or Dagmar. Their things were still sitting here, untouched, but they were nowhere in sight. For a moment Sasha was torn between leaving their things and going in search of the two or waiting for them to return on their own. Impatience made him choose the first.

Leaving the scant shade of the trees, Sasha headed toward the remains of the old village. Wandering across the hot sand and trying not to trip over the rubble hidden beneath the sand, Sasha made his way back to the sea. A wooden pier, rickety with age and neglect, stretched out across the water.

And to Sasha's relief, and annoyance, both Dagmar and Boris were sitting on it, their feet dangling out over the sparkling blue water.

"What are you doing?" Sasha called out as he picked his way across the rickety pier. "You left me."

The way both of them jumped at the anger in his voice stopped him from saying anything else. Boris went blank and shrank away from him, and even Dagmar took a moment to compose herself. Sasha took a deep breath. That was the unfortunate thing about traveling with these two, he realized. Dagmar had spent so long conditioned to fear him that even a hint of anger from him made her tense. He forgot about that most of the time, until something like this happened. And Boris, well, Boris couldn't handle anger from anyone.

"We didn't mean to," Dagmar said quietly. "I came out here to...," she faltered over the thought, "to sit. And Boris couldn't sleep."

Sasha quelled whatever frustration he was feeling. Of course, Dagmar had come out here by herself. This was her home they were sitting in. Empty. Desolate. Dead. And all because of his people.

"Sorry. It just scared me to wake up all by myself." He sat down next to Boris and let his own legs hang over the side.

"We really didn't mean to," Dagmar said. "We should probably get going soon, though. The hottest part of the day is over."

"It's over? I feel like I'm burning up right now."

"Because you are. Your skin's burnt."

"That's nice to know." Sasha grimaced as he stared down at his arm again. "Come on, Boris."

Chapter 20

SASHA SHIFTED HIS PACK AGAIN, pulling the damp, sticky cloth of his shirt away from his shoulders for a moment. If there was just a tiny breath of wind, the heat would be more bearable, he thought. For two days, they had been trekking through the endless sea of sand. The only landmarks that Sasha could tell were a handful of jagged red rocks reaching to touch the sky, and some strange and very thorny plants that were nothing more than thick round stalks growing ten to twenty feet high.

On their first full night in the desert, Dagmar found a small plant whose leaves were filled with a sticky, slimy substance that she insisted would help their sunburnt skin. Despite his qualms with the texture of it, Sasha had to admit it worked well.

Now, towards the end of the third day, the monotony of the desert was broken up in the distance by a series of unidentifiable shapes. The oasis, Sasha guessed. It lay a little to the left in front of them, and when Dagmar turned toward it, he was certain he was right.

"I don't know if we should go in there right now." Dagmar stopped abruptly, raising a hand to shield her eyes from the blinding sun and squinting at the watering hole.

"Are there people there?"

"It's a traveling town, I think."

"What's that?" Boris surprised Sasha when he spoke up.

"A group of people. They live in tents, and they don't stay in one place long. Some of them are really nice, but most of them are just gangs of thieves and outcasts."

"We need water," Sasha said.

"And different clothes. And some sort of tent would be nice." Dagmar bit her lip, worry etching her face. "I still think we should wait, at least until after dark."

"Dagmar's right," Boris said, surprising Sasha for the second time in the last few minutes.

"Really?" Sasha held Boris' gaze for a moment and realized that for now at least his brother was in his right mind. For some inexplicable reason the fact that he was siding with Dagmar annoyed Sasha. "They don't own the water there, do they?"

"Well, no. But that doesn't mean it's a good idea for us to all go in there," Dagmar answered. "Technically, everyone has an equal right to any oasis. But they outnumber us, and there's no one to enforce that right."

"Maybe just one of us should go, in case something happens," Sasha suggested.

"I'm not going by myself." Dagmar's face mirrored the horror that was in her voice.

Of course, she wouldn't risk something happening to her, Sasha thought. Even without Boris responding, Sasha knew he couldn't do it either. Sasha wished he hadn't made the suggestion. But since he had, he didn't see any way out except by admitting that Dagmar and Boris were right, and however illogical it was, he just couldn't bring himself to do that. Picking up their empty water skins, he got to his feet.

"You're really going to go now?" Dagmar looked up at him, her eyes still worried. "We could just wait and see if they leave soon."

"Might as well. Neither of you are going to, and I don't think waiting until dark is going to do us any good if they really are a bunch of thieves. They'll probably have someone up all night keeping watch. Besides, I'm thirsty and we've no water left."

Without waiting for an answer, Sasha started off. Walking away alone, he couldn't help but feel a little put out that neither of the other two even offered to come with him. The sand sucked his feet down with every step, making his progress slow. He hated the desert. Who would choose to live in such a place? By the time he got within hearing distance, he was completely out of sorts.

People, only men from what Sasha could see, milled about the place. From the shouts and stares of the nearest people, Sasha assumed he'd been spotted. Suddenly, he was acutely conscious of just how out of place he looked. Everyone there was dressed in long, loose fitting clothing, with their heads and most of their faces covered. Keeping his head down and avoiding the stares of the natives, Sasha made his way to the nearest pool of water. No sooner had he knelt to fill the first water skin, then he sensed someone standing just behind him.

Despite knowing someone was just over his shoulder, the voice coming from so near startled him. And the words meant absolutely nothing to him. Turning to look at the man, there was nothing visible on the man's face except for his eyes. Sasha found himself staring at the man's eyes. Outlined in some sort of black paint, they reminded him a little of a racoon's. Sasha shook his head and held his hands out with a shrug to indicate that he didn't understand the man's speech. Again, the man spoke, only this time he placed his hand on Sasha's arm and lifted him up.

Sasha grimaced as the man threw his arm around his shoulder with a little more force than friendliness. Whether he wanted to or not, Sasha was going with this man. He found himself led away from the pool of water and toward a group of men sitting in a loose circle. Their eyes were similarly outlined in the heavy black that made them stand out sharply. Unable to understand their words, Sasha couldn't mistake the fact that he became the center of their loud conversation. The man who had brought him over gestured for him to sit and he knew he had no choice but to do so.

A pair of hands pushed a handful of small, round pieces of fruit into Sasha's hands and when he met the giver's eyes, the man indicated he should eat them. Relaxing a little at the open friendliness, Sasha put one in his mouth. It had a tart, almost sour flavor and was comprised almost entirely of juice. Sasha ate the whole handful and the man nodded approvingly.

As the conversation flowed around him, Sasha tried to interpret the meaning of their words by their numerous and exaggerated gestures. He'd never seen people use their hands so much when they spoke. Whatever they were saying, they referred to him frequently, making his uneasiness return. This must have been what it was like for Boris all those months, Sasha thought, remembering how his brother had no knowledge of the language spoken by his captors. Sasha had never fully understood or appreciated the fear or isolation that accompanied that. These men could be planning his murder, and he would have no clue about it.

To Sasha's relief, their interest in him slowly faded. As long as he sat quietly and did nothing to renew their attention, he was beginning to think nothing bad would happen. There was only one problem with that. Dagmar and Boris were waiting for him. They were probably getting worried. Although he doubted either would have the nerve, the idea of them coming to look for him and being found by these men was more disturbing than it should have been considering the fact that they hadn't done anything to him but give him food.

Sasha cast surreptitious eyes about the oasis, taking in the tents, and the strange animals at the far end of it, as well as the pool of water where his own water skins still sat untouched. No one was paying attention to him now, he didn't think, although it was hard to tell when so much of their face was hidden. Now that the sun was getting low in the sky, perhaps he could just slip away. After all, Sasha told himself, they hadn't made any indication that he couldn't leave.

Grayness spread over the desert, and the shadows in the oasis grew long. Several times, Sasha almost convinced himself to just stand up and walk away. But each time, he lost his nerve and remained still. A few of the men wandered off from the circle, and the conversation died down. They appeared to have lost all interest in Sasha. It was now or never, he thought.

Easing himself up off the sand as slowly as he could, Sasha got to his feet. No one made any move to stop him, and Sasha let out a tense breath. He turned away and started walking toward the pool he'd first stopped at. Bending down to pick up the water skins, he wondered if he should risk taking the time to refill them. Before he could decide, a heavy hand fell on his shoulder and Sasha was thrown to the ground.

Chapter 21

"HE SHOULD HAVE BEEN BACK by now," Dagmar said, staring at the now darkening horizon.

The oasis was no longer visible in the gathering gloom of night, but neither Dagmar nor Boris had stopped watching in that direction. Boris looked away now, staring down at the sand by his feet. He ran his hand through the stuff, letting the coarse grains run through his fingers. He was on the verge of losing his grip again, his mind dangerously close to the abyss that held it captive so often. Boris shut his eyes, not even bothering to fight it. He'd spent days, weeks, even months fighting. He was too tired to do it now.

"Do you think we should go look for him?" Dagmar's voice jolted him back at least temporarily. He looked up at her, his eyes heavy with confusion, her previous words already forgotten. Dagmar sighed but continued, "For Sasha. Do you think we should go find him, see if he's in trouble?"

Boris shook his head. "He shouldn't have gone."

He was right, he knew. Sasha had only gone out of his own ridiculous need to be in control. If he'd bothered to listen to them at all, they would have nothing to worry about.

"But if something happened, we can't just leave him."

Boris shrugged and continued running his fingers through the sand, the motion now more of a nervous gesture than anything else. Dagmar turned her attention away from the invisible oasis and watched him for a few minutes without a word. Finally, she reached out her own hand and stopped his. Boris, startled by her touch, looked up.

"Boris, I think we should go see what happened. I'm going." Dagmar got to her feet and started walking away.

After watching her for a moment, Boris rose as well and followed at a distance. Neither spoke as they approached the now dark oasis.

It was hard to make anything out at all now that the sun was gone. Laying down on their stomachs, just on the other side of a small rise in the sand, all they could see were shadows. The sound of voices drifted up toward them.

"I'm going to try to get closer. Stay here," Dagmar whispered.

Boris watched her disappear. Left completely alone in the middle of an unknown desert sent a wave of anxiety through him. This was exactly what he had tried to warn Sasha about, but Sasha didn't take anything he said seriously anymore. He sat up, drawing his knees up to his chest and wrapped his arms tightly around them. He couldn't slip away now. He couldn't just let go of his sanity and drift away. Not while he was alone and unguarded.

The moon rose, a mere sliver of pale light in the otherwise dark sky. A slight breeze sent a thin layer of silver sand swirling around. A shadow passed over him, startling him, but it was only a large bird gliding overhead in search of food. He hunched down further, trying to calm his own ragged breathing, shutting out the sights and sounds of the desert, retreating to the safe quiet of mindlessness.

"Boris," Dagmar's voice whispered out of the darkness behind him, and he turned to find her sitting only a foot or two away. "I didn't see him, but I heard them talking. They're a scouting party for the insurrectionists. They think Sasha is some sort of spy for the imperialists and they're planning on taking him to their commander."

"He shouldn't have gone."

"Probably not, but we have to figure out a way to get him back. We can't just leave him."

"How?"

"I don't know," Dagmar admitted. "We probably have a few days before they are ready to move again. Let's just rest for now and try to think of something in the morning. Come on, we've left our stuff long enough."

Retracing their steps, they came upon their own packs, left haphazardly in the sand and half buried by the stuff. Without the heat of the sun, the night air was cold. Dagmar dug out their blankets and passed one to Boris before laying down herself. Boris didn't even bother to lay down. He wasn't going to sleep, he couldn't sleep.

The light of morning brought a dismaying sight to their eyes. The oasis stood empty. No sign remained of the group that had occupied it just the night before. Dagmar gave a little cry as she took in the sight.

"No! They must have left during the night. Didn't you hear anything?"

Boris, his eyes red with exhaustion, simply stared at her. Realizing he wasn't going to answer her, Dagmar got up and shouldered her own pack.

"Come on, Boris. We have to try to catch up with them." She reached down and grabbed him by the arm, pulling him into action.

Reaching the now abandoned watering hole, Dagmar spotted the still empty water skins lying where Sasha left them. At least they hadn't taken those with them. Dagmar filled them. It was easy to see which direction they moved off in. It was a fairly large party and they had made no effort to cover their tracks.

"We're not going to catch up with them," Boris said, staring at the tracks that led away. "Why didn't he just listen to us?"

"It doesn't matter. We just need to find him."

By mid-morning, it was clear that Boris was right. They weren't catching up. In fact, they were falling further and further behind. Dagmar glanced behind her at Boris and her face fell. He was keeping up with her, but he wasn't with her, not really. It was more like watching someone sleepwalk. He mumbled to himself every now and then, but otherwise kept quiet. No wonder Sasha lost his patience with him sometimes.

Dagmar paused long enough to scan the horizon. The sun glinting off the sand creating a mirage in the distance, but there was nothing else to see. Dagmar didn't even know where they were at this point. They weren't moving toward Kaldura, that much was sure. Even if they found Sasha again, she had no way of knowing how to get back on the right path.

Chapter 22

WITH AN EFFORT, SASHA OPENED his eyes to the noise around him. Even with his eyes closed, sand managed to find a way in, making them smart and sting and blurring his vision. Sasha tried to bring a hand up to rub the sand away but found he could not. With the discovery came the memory of last night. Sasha stifled a groan as he leaned back against the tree he'd been tied to. The last thing he wanted was for anyone to know he was awake. How he managed to fall asleep in the first place, sitting up against a tree, was beyond him.

He tugged at the rough rope that held his hands together behind the narrow trunk of the tree, testing the strength of the knot. It was no use. His fingers tingled painfully from the lack of blood flowing to them, but the knot didn't give.

Sasha fought down the panic that was rising in his chest. He couldn't panic. Not now. Not when his only hope of getting away rested entirely on himself. Dagmar and Boris might want to rescue him, but he doubted they would have the nerve, or the ability in Boris' case.

Giving up any pretense of sleeping, Sasha opened his eyes fully and looked around. He realized he had not imagined the commotion that awakened him. There were around twenty men that he could see and every one of them was busy in spite of the darkness that had not lifted yet. Even without understanding their shouts and calls, Sasha understood what was going on and his heart sank. They were preparing to leave, and something told Sasha that they were planning on taking him with them. It didn't make sense. If, like Dagmar had said, they were just thieves then they had nothing to gain by dragging him along.

The smell of food drifted across the air, but none was offered to Sasha. Neither was water. Sasha ran a swollen tongue over his lips, realizing how parched and cracked they were. He hadn't had anything to drink since the afternoon before, and in this heat, he felt its effects acutely. His mouth tasted of sand.

There was still another hour before dawn, Sasha guessed, when two of the men came over and untied him from the tree. Knowing that nothing he said would be understood anyway, Sasha kept his mouth closed. He was shoved forward in the direction of the now assembled group of men. Two or three of them rode strange beasts. Sasha had never seen their like. Much taller than a horse, with two large humps on their backs, they walked with an awkward, swaying motion. Everyone else, including him, followed on foot.

Walking through the desert with Dagmar and Boris hadn't been fun. But struggling to stay on his feet with his hands secured behind him and the ground constantly shifting and sinking beneath him was not only difficult but exhausting. More than once he lost his balance entirely and had to be pulled back up to his feet. His captors, although negligent in providing him with food and water, were hardly malicious, though and did not seem inclined to hurt him.

Sasha fought back the temptation to keep glancing over his shoulder. Dagmar and Boris' existence was still a secret to these men, and he certainly didn't want to arouse their suspicions by constantly looking for his companions. Still, there were times when the temptation grew too strong and he just had to see if they were back there somewhere, following. The handful of times he looked were disappointing. Aside from the mirages the sun cast across the distant sand, there was nothing. Nothing but sand, sand, and more sand.

Sasha was sick of the sand, sick of the grit it left in his eyes, nose and mouth, sick of the way it gave beneath his feet. As the heat of the day set in, Sasha couldn't think of a place he hated more. He tried to imagine what it was like back home in the mountains, wading through the cool spring water. Anywhere, but here.

He was more than ready when the group stopped for the hottest hours of the day. Letting himself slump to the ground, Sasha tried to rest. Thirst made it impossible. His tongue tasted and felt like sand. A dull ache seized his head. Swallowing hurt. And still no one in the group thought to offer him water. Sasha was beginning to rethink his initial opinion regarding these men. They didn't need to handle him roughly out here, all they had to do was deny him water.

When they moved on again in the late afternoon, Sasha could think of nothing but his overwhelming thirst. He'd never been this thirsty in his life. He ran a dry tongue over equally dry lips. The ache in his head swelled to a sharp pain and he found it harder with each step to keep his feet beneath him. The world spun and his eyes refused to focus.

The setting of the sun ought to have been a relief from the burning heat of the day, but Sasha was in no shape to appreciate it. The company pressed onward, apparently determined to cover the ground they lost during their midday stop. It wasn't until the sky was full of stars and the moon had risen turning the sand from brown to silver with its light that they finally stopped.

Sasha lay where he fell. Exhausted as he was, his thirst made sleep elusive. He watched with dull, glazed eyes as the men set up a camp of sorts. Again, the aroma of food reached his nose and again no offer of that food or water was made to him. Sasha decided they must be trying to kill him.

Still tormented by thirst, Sasha eventually managed to drift off to sleep.

Morning came and the previous day's routine was followed again. Sasha lacked the fortitude to prevent himself from looking over his shoulder often. There was never anyone there.

They were only a few hours into their trek for the day when Sasha looked behind him yet again. A thick cloud of brown hung over the horizon off to the side, and Sasha stared at it. By the shouts of the men, they had seen it too. Sasha squinted against the bright sun, trying to discern what it was that made the cloud. A hand on his arm dragged him down a steep sand dune and out of sight of the cloud. Sasha glanced around at the other men in earnest now. Whatever it was, they were alarmed.

Sasha sat down and watched as the others crouched together as close to the sheltering side of the dune as they could get, pulling the covers they wore over their nose and mouths up over their eyes as well. His mind and senses too dulled by thirst to fully comprehend his own danger, Sasha made no effort to shield himself against whatever was coming.

The first swirls of tan above blotted out the bright sunlight. Moments later, Sasha could see nothing at all. Squeezing his eyes shut in a desperate attempt to prevent the blowing sand from destroying them altogether, Sasha struggled to breath. Stinging grains of sand whipped through the air, cutting into his bare skin on his face and arms. Tied so that he could not bring his hands up to shield his face made it worse. He couldn't draw breath. Not without sucking in whole mouthfuls of sand into his lungs. He wanted to scream but his lungs had no air in them.

He barely felt the fingers that worked at the knot binding his wrists. Without consciously recognizing that they were free, his body moved of its own will and brought his hands over his nose and mouth, blocking out at least a fraction of the sand that he was inhaling. It wasn't until he felt the same hands tugging on him to get him to stand that he realized he was not alone.

The blinding whirl of sand settled once more to the surface of the desert, but Sasha could no longer open his eyes to see it. Grit sealed his eyes shut. It was the absence of the needles of pain that made him first aware of the change. The wind no longer drove thousands of grains of sand into his skin. The hands that had guided him away from his captors were gone now, and Sasha sank down into the yielding sand. A hoarse, dry cough wracked his body as his lungs tried to expel the sand from them, each cough producing an excruciating throb in his head.

"Here, drink this." The female voice came from far away, and Sasha realized his head was pounding and a low roar filled his ears. Something touched his cracked lips and a moment later tepid water filled his mouth, running over and moistening his swollen tongue. He swallowed quickly, guzzling the life-giving liquid until it was pulled away. He reached feeble hands up to bring it back, but the voice chided him gently, "You can't drink that fast, Sasha. You'll make yourself sick."

Sasha lay back against the hot ground, the rays of the blazing sun searing his face. His eyes still refused to open. A shadow moved over his face, blocking the heat of the sun. Water trickled over his eyelids and a soft cloth wiped away the sand that held them closed. The process was repeated several times before Sasha blinked painfully. Even with his eyes open, the world was blurry. Lines lost their usual sharpness and grew fuzzy as if he were looking through a haze of smoke. It took a moment for him to recognize the shadow leaning over him.

"Dagmar?" Sasha's voice croaked and he started coughing again.

"Yes, it's me," she answered as she held the water for him to drink again.

"What was that?"

"A sandstorm. They're dangerous."

Sasha tried to laugh but his throat was still too dry. It seemed a little late for Dagmar to be telling him that sandstorms were dangerous. He drank more water, sipping it slowly so that Dagmar wouldn't take it away again.

"Where's Boris?"

"He's right behind you. You shouldn't try to talk right now." Dagmar sat back watching him, her face troubled. "How long has it been since you've had any water?"

"Two days." Sasha squinted and turned his head to the side, trying to avoid the sun that Dagmar was no longer shielding him from.

"You're lucky to be alive."

"I guess that makes us even." Sasha tried to push himself up on his elbow and failed. He lay back down, grimacing at the renewed pain in his head, and shut his eyes.

"What do you mean?" Dagmar asked.

"I saved your life when you were freezing to death, and now you've saved mine."

"I'm not sure I've saved it just yet," Dagmar said quietly.

Sasha's eyes opened again, and he squinted up at Dagmar's face. "What do you mean?"

"I don't know where we are, Sasha. I'm sorry." The tremor in her voice was all too familiar. "We were trying to catch up to them and get you back. And now we're lost. And I don't know how long our water will last. You need more because you've been without, and we already drank more than we ought to because we kept going through the hottest part of the day."

Sasha let her words sink in. Lost. Despite the thick fog that hung over his mind the word was terrifying. He'd never been lost before, not really. Especially not in a place as deadly and dangerous as the desert. Even with the water Dagmar was letting him sip, his tongue was still thick and swollen with thirst, his throat still parched. The cold realization that he could die out here settled over him.

"Can you walk?" Dagmar's voice broke through his dark thoughts. "Because, if you can, I think the best thing we could do is keep moving."

Movement shot pain through his head as if all the blood in his body was cramming its way into that single entity. Sasha forced himself up to a sitting position before the pain was simply too much to fight against.

"It's no use." Sasha gripped his head between his hands. "I don't think I can."

Dagmar was incapable of arguing with him. In spite of all the time that had passed, she couldn't bring herself to contradict him. It was Boris, who had been silent up to this point, who prodded Sasha into further effort.

"You have to," he said simply as his hand tugged on Sasha's arm, propelling him to his feet.

Sasha groaned as Boris pulled him up. He swayed a little but found that he could in fact stand. Walking was another matter entirely. The world tilted precariously beneath his feet, and he would have fallen on his face with his first step if Boris did not still have his own hand on Sasha's arm. Without a word, his brother slid a supporting arm beneath Sasha's. Sasha leaned against him, willingly accepting the help as they started off.

"Won't they be looking for me?"

"No," Dagmar said. "They won't waste the water. Besides, there's no point. They'll think you ran off and assume you'll die out here."

"They might not be wrong," Sasha muttered under his breath.

"We'll keep heading south. We'll run into something eventually." Dagmar's voice failed to convey the confidence her words held.

Pausing only often and long enough to drink, they pressed on through the day. More than once Sasha's hopes were raised as his eyes played cruel tricks on him. A mirage, Dagmar called it, created by the glaring rays of the sun against the sand. Each false image of water in the distance drove Sasha mad with thirst. But already, even though they had only been moving for a few hours, he saw how depleted their store of water was. Once again, icy fingers of fear clutched at his heart. The possibility of dying out here was becoming more real with every step.

When the setting sun brought some relief to the heat of the day, they were still surrounded by nothing but dry, endless desert. For the last several hours, none of them had spoken a word. It was too much trouble and effort to speak. It wasn't until the night fell fully and darkness swallowed up the vast sea of sand that a glowing light in the distance became visible. At first, Sasha thought he was imagining it, like he had imagined water throughout the day. But when both Boris and Dagmar stopped to look in the same direction, he decided it was real.

"What is it?" Sasha's voice sounded strange to his own ears after so many hours of silence.

Dagmar shrugged, her eyes still staring at the faint glow. When she did finally speak, her voice was hoarse, "It's south."

"What if it's the same group that had me?"

"They weren't going south."

Sasha let himself sink down, too tired and thirsty to keep going. Neither Dagmar nor Boris protested.

In fact, they joined him after only a few seconds hesitation.

With a start, Sasha realized he was almost asleep. Jerking his head up to find Dagmar already curled up, her eyes shut, and her breathing even, he was reminded a bit of their journey from Aruuk, plagued by cold rather than heat.

"It never stops, does it?" Boris' voice, no more than a husky whisper, startled Sasha from behind.

Sasha turned his head. Boris was half sitting, his back resting against one of their packs, wide awake and aware. Despite not wanting to admit that everyone else may have been right, Sasha couldn't help but notice that Boris had been lucid far more in the last few days than he had been in the weeks when he and Sasha shared the close little cabin. Maybe getting away from everything familiar was good for him.

"What are you talking about?"

"Us." Boris turned his gaze out to the open desert, away from Sasha, his fingers playing with the sand beside him. "We're hundreds of miles from home with no one around to see but her," he glanced toward Dagmar, "And you're still trying to be better than me."

"I'm not trying to be better than you. I haven't been."

"Yes, you are. That's why you just had to go down to that oasis in the first place. I said you shouldn't, and you just had to prove you were smarter than me."

Sasha's silence was answer enough. He looked down, not wanting Boris to see the effect of his words. So much for being different, Sasha thought, but didn't he have every reason to think he knew better than Boris? After all, Boris was the one who spent most of the time with his mind wandering, staring listlessly out at nothing and ignoring everything real around him. How was Sasha to know when he was being reasonable and in his right mind?

It made sense for Sasha to make his own decisions, without Boris' input.

"Maybe if you didn't spend so much time acting crazy, I would actually listen to you," Sasha finally said.

Boris laughed. "Not your fault again, is it? Nothing ever is. You decide, but then it's someone else's fault when everything goes wrong."

"Well, if I listened to everything you said, I wouldn't have ever taken you in and given up my nice life just to take care of you. You're the one who said you never wanted to see me again," Sasha's voice rose with anger.

Boris fell silent and, after a long moment, Sasha turned to see why. Boris was no longer looking out at the desert. He had his face in his hands. With a sinking heart, Sasha realized he'd done it again. His temper had robbed Boris of his sanity in a moment. Still angry, Sasha couldn't quite work up whatever it was he needed to reach out to Boris now. He followed Dagmar's example and laid down to sleep. When, a few hours later, he was awakened by Boris' nightmare induced cries, Sasha rolled over and ignored him.

Chapter 23

SASHA HAD NO SOONER FALLEN back asleep after Boris' disturbance than he heard Dagmar softly calling his name. Sitting up slowly and rubbing a hand over his eyes, he looked around for her.

"I think we should try to get closer to the light," Dagmar said. "I don't think it's the same group as before. It might even be a town of sorts."

Still half asleep, Sasha tried to sort through her words. After his previous encounter he was wary of running into anyone else. If he'd listened to Dagmar before, though, he wouldn't have been caught, he reminded himself. With a sigh, he started to get up. Maybe Boris wasn't entirely wrong. Maybe he should try listening to them this time and things would work out better.

"Alright. We might as well." The headache that had plagued him for the last couple of days had receded to a dull ache that only came if he moved too quickly. He bent down carefully and shouldered his pack. He looked to where Boris had retreated several feet away from them and with his back to them. "Come on, Boris."

Sasha started off. The absence of any sound behind him alerted him to the fact that neither of his companions were following. Sasha stopped and turned, searching for the reason. His eyes widened in surprise when he saw Dagmar kneeling next to Boris. It was obvious he hadn't moved when Sasha said they were leaving, and it was equally obvious that Dagmar was talking to him. He watched as she reached out and pulled on Boris' arm, guiding him to his feet. As much as he didn't want to, Sasha couldn't help but feel a little ashamed that Dagmar took more time to reach out to his brother than he did.

In silence, they made their way closer to the glowing light. It had grown fainter through the night and Sasha wondered if whatever it was had moved. They walked for some time before their progress was even noticeable, but at last, it was clear that they were getting close. A pink line across the eastern horizon promised that the sun wasn't far away either. Dagmar came up next to Sasha.

"I think it might be a town," she said.

"That's a good thing, right?"

"It should be. We should still be careful, though." Dagmar didn't say it, wouldn't say it, but her word of warning was a direct result of his own previous actions, Sasha was sure of it. "If it is really a town, it might be best if I go in alone."

"Are you sure? What if something bad happens?"

Even in the darkness, Sasha could see Dagmar's face was troubled. "I might just have to risk that," she answered quietly. "Most likely, it'll be fine."

Sasha glanced behind them where Boris was following at a distance. Every now and then he caught the sound of his brother's muttering to himself.

"It's nice he actually listens to you," Sasha said to Dagmar.

Dagmar hesitated before answering him, "I think he would to you too."

146

"No. He hates me. Thinks I'm the reason for everything bad that has ever happened."

"I don't think he hates you. You just don't give him a chance."

They came up a slight rise in the sand and stopped. A small village, the low buildings scattered between pools of water and trees, lay before their eyes. Sasha heard Dagmar's faint sigh of relief. A village meant they weren't wandering around hopelessly lost without water. Although she hid it well, she had to have been just as afraid of dying out here as he was.

"We should wait a bit here," Dagmar said, letting her pack slide off her shoulders and hit the ground before sitting down next to it. "People will be up and moving about soon."

"Then what?"

"Then you should give me some money and the water skins. I'll get us some food and water and new clothes if I can. And find out where exactly we are."

"We should come with you; in case something happens."

"I really don't think that's a good idea. You two don't speak the language. You'd just stick out."

Sasha looked over at Boris, wondering if he would speak up this time or not. Boris wasn't even paying attention to them. Sasha shrugged.

"We'll wait here. If you're not back in a couple hours though, we'll come look for you." Sasha rummaged around in his pack until he found his money and counted out some of it to hand to Dagmar.

Midmorning found Sasha and Boris alone. Sasha mostly watched the village but couldn't help but glance at his brother from time to time. The thought nagged at him to speak to Boris, but he pushed the idea aside. It wouldn't do any good. Boris was lost in a trance. He probably wouldn't even acknowledge Sasha if he spoke. Sasha sipped on the last bit of their water and lay back, letting his eyes close for a while to pass the time.

He dozed lightly until he became aware of the approach of another person. Sitting up, he watched their approach for a few seconds before recognizing Dagmar. Dressed already in the loose, colorful garments that were native to Sondaru, she looked completely different. Most of her face was covered, leaving only her eyes visible.

"Did you get everything?"

"Everything. And if you don't feel like sleeping out here tonight, there's a small inn, although I think we should probably keep moving." Dagmar sat down and opened one of the parcels she'd been carrying. "Here," she tossed a bundle first to him and then another to Boris, "put these on over your other clothes."

Sasha held them up. Compared to the dull browns and grays that he was used to wearing in Aruuk, and had continued to wear in Dival, they looked absurd.

"This is supposed to make us blend in?" he asked.

"It's what everyone else is wearing."

"It's not what those men were wearing at the oasis."

"Because they were a militant group. They weren't trying to blend in with the people, just the desert."

Sasha examined them for a few more seconds before conceding. Aside from the flamboyant colors that screamed for attention, they felt oddly light. Sasha decided he preferred the tighter fitting clothing he'd grown up wearing. The sleeves hung down from his arms like wings and made his movements clumsier than normal. He tried imagining trying to draw back his bow with them. That would take some practice. At least he could hide his bow and quiver of arrows easily beneath the loose robe-like outfit. A soft giggle brought him out of his reverie. He glanced over to find Dagmar, one hand clasped over her mouth and trying hard not to laugh loudly.

"What?"

"It's just funny." She quickly brought her face under control. "We should get going."

"I don't know if I'm in a hurry to go anywhere people can see me. I feel ridiculous."

"But you look normal to everyone here. That's the point. Besides, I wasn't actually thinking we should head down to the town. The people there said Kaldura is only four days away."

"That's not so bad."

"No. Except we only had a month or so before Lawrence was coming back. We've already used up a week of that time. Even if we find your sister right away, it'll be hard getting back to the coast in time."

Sasha hated to admit that he'd completely forgotten about Lawrence's promise. He'd been too busy worrying about how to escape, and then how they were going to survive lost in the middle of the desert. Dagmar's words stirred a sense of urgency, and he collected their things.

"Are you ready, Boris?" He turned to his brother. Boris hesitated then got to his feet without a word. "Do we have enough water for four days?"

"As long as nothing goes wrong. But we won't need it as much when we get closer," Dagmar answered.

"What do you mean?"

"Kaldura's not in the desert. They built the capitol in the river valley. You'll see."

By the second day, the desert was changing noticeably. Where there had been only a handful of cacti, as Dagmar called them, scattered here and there, now the vegetation grew less sparse. The plants were still brittle, stalky specimens clearly used to surviving on very little water, but their population increased with every hour. Thickets of spindly bushes and patches of colorful wildflowers now graced the landscape adding a much-appreciated touch of color to the travelers' eyes. A rugged line of mountains cut across the southern horizon. Sand gave way to rock and gritty soil.

Late in the afternoon of the third day, the mountains were fully visible. Disappointingly unlike the mountains of Aruuk that were thickly covered with evergreens and dark foliage with snowy caps reaching above the clouds, these mountains were mostly red rock with only a smattering of greenery growing on their sides. With the foremost mountains close enough to become their own distinct shape, Dagmar changed directions slightly.

"What's that sound?" Boris broke his four-day silence abruptly, causing both Sasha and Dagmar to stop and turn to him. Sasha strained his ears trying to catch the noise. After a moment a faint gurgling reached him.

"It's the river," Dagmar answered. "Or, at least, it becomes a river. It's more like an almost dried up stream here."

The closer they got to the source of the sound the more distinct it became, separating from the sounds of the desert behind them. Rounding the last bit of the foot of the mountain, the creek finally came into view. Little more than a trickle that wound its way through a bed of red rock, it snaked like a blue ribbon up between two mountains, growing wider as it went up. Sasha's eyes followed it.

"Here it is. The river valley." Dagmar threw her hands out with a flourish. "We don't have to worry about dying of thirst until the return trip. And there," she extended a finger up the mountain, "is Kaldura."

Sasha's eyes reached it just before she said it and his mouth fell open in shock. Gleaming white against the red of the mountains, the city looked like an upside-down cone built between three mountains. Even from this distance, it was enormous. Bigger than Illsen, or Bren by far. The sun, breaking through the easternmost mountains, glinted off the white making it look like the entire city had been chiseled from a giant pearl.

"Don't be too impressed." Dagmar noticed both Sasha and Boris gawking up at the city. "You're only seeing the upper levels, where the richest live. You can't see the lower city from here because it doesn't have quite the same glow."

"It's still bigger than any city I've ever been to," Sasha said as they left off gawking and started forward again. "It'll take us ages to find anyone in there."

"Not quite. Let me see your sister's sales receipt."

Sasha had to reach beneath layers of fabric to get to the pocket where he kept the two slips of paper that bore Mother and Agathe's names. Pulling them out and shaking the sand out of the folds where it had accumulated over the last week and a half, he handed Agathe's to Dagmar. Dagmar traced a finger from Agathe's name to the amount she was sold for.

"As much as Master Josef Zbreck paid for her, he must be close to the top of the city. Especially since she was only fourteen and pretty. He wasn't buying her for labor. He paid that much just for fun which means he has a lot to spend."

"I guess that makes sense." Although he had never had any doubts as to what Agathe's use as a slave had been, Sasha winced at the way Dagmar said it. He exhaled loudly. "It's still going to take us a while."

Dagmar simply nodded.

By the time they reached the city gates on the morning of the fourth day, Sasha was beginning to see what Dagmar meant. The lower levels of the city, invisible from a great distance, were crowded, dingy, and reeked of poverty and want. A thick wall built of the same white rock that shone in the sunlight surrounded the approach and the only way in was across a bridge spanning the now wide river that came through and around the city, and then on through the gate. The gate itself was an impressive structure, too large to be budged by any single person, it was opened and shut using a series of levers and pulleys such as Sasha had never seen. The road leading through it, although wide enough to allow at least eight horses riding abreast of each other, was still crowded with people going both in and out.

"You should stop staring like you've never been here," Dagmar whispered next to him.

"But I haven't ever been here."

"You don't want everyone knowing that. You're supposed to be blending in. And everyone your age would have seen Kaldura by now."

He glanced down at her and noticed that she'd taken a hold of Boris' hand, guiding him through the thickening crowd of people. He should have thought of that first, he realized guiltily, but since he'd been pretty much ignoring his brother's presence for the last four days it just hadn't occurred to him.

"And don't talk if you can help it," Dagmar added as they allowed the press of the crowd to push them along.

Although there were guards, dressed in lavish uniforms of burgundy and silver that Sasha thought would likely be more of an impediment than an asset should they be required to do any fighting, no one was stopped as they entered or left. The purpose of the men at their posts was entirely lost on Sasha. For all of its grandeur and pomp, Kaldura was an easy city to infiltrate, he thought. It was likely only due to the fact that the wealthy capitol was situated between a rugged mountain range and a desert that had ensured its survival up to this point.

The thickness of the outer walls muffled much of the noise of the city so that it was quite startling to step beneath the archway into the city itself. Dagmar, still holding onto Boris by the arm, led them to a relatively quiet corner several streets down from the entrance.

"I don't think we even need to start looking for the first three or four tiers. No one down here would be rich enough to spend that much money," she said. "Sasha, what's wrong?"

Her question was posed when she noticed Sasha craning his neck to look around. He gave their surroundings a final scan before turning to her.

"Nothing. I just felt like someone was staring at me. So, how do we get to the upper tiers?"

"The Emperor's Highway we came in on goes all the way up," Dagmar said.

"The what?"

"This road, it's called the Emperor's Highway because it was built to go all the way up to the palace." Dagmar looked down at her own clothes and frowned. "We'll need different clothes if we have to go too high."

"This is a complicated city," Sasha muttered, glancing once more around. The uneasy sensation that he was being watched refused to go away. "We should get going."

Compared to the dazzling impression of the city at a distance, Sasha found himself grimacing at the squalor of the lowest level. Even on the main road, where there was a better mix of both wealthy and poor, it looked and smelled little better than a pigsty. Beggars, dressed in rags and often missing parts of their bodies, held filthy hands up in search of generosity. Wild cats and dogs rummaged through the heaps of garbage and refuse, slinking away only when threatened. Sasha was glad for the first time that he was wearing the customary sand cloth over his mouth and nose. Dagmar had told him everyone wore them to keep from breathing in so much sand, but here, he thought everyone wore them just so they wouldn't have to smell the stench.

The road spiraled around the city, working its way slowly up. It was the sight of the second, smaller gate that truly confirmed Sasha's deteriorating opinion of Kaldura.

"What is that for?" he asked Dagmar as they joined the throng of people queuing to go through.

"It's how they maintain order. Keep the riffraff out of the upper levels."

"What an awful lot of trouble to go through."

"Shhh...," Dagmar turned horrified eyes toward him. "Don't talk about it. You'll get us in trouble."

"It's not that different from home," Boris said, and Sasha, turning to look at him, could see that his face was thoughtful. "It's just another way to control people."

"I guess so."

Dagmar shot them both another frightened look, this time jerking her head toward the men manning the gate. These men, although dressed in the same colors of burgundy and silver, looked far more serious about their task.

Moving slowly forward, Sasha tried to suppress the shiver of doubt that came over him. Something was not right. Some sixth sense screamed a silent warning to him, and Sasha was suddenly very grateful for the headdress Dagmar insisted was the normal clothing here. It gave him anonymity that felt very important at the moment. Without turning his head, he peered around at the people milling about him, but couldn't find the source of his alarm. What he did see was Boris watching him, and in the second it took for their eyes to meet, Sasha recognized the same uneasiness in his brother. The fact that Boris was completely himself at the moment merely drove the point home.

Something was wrong.

Sasha let Dagmar do all the talking when it was their turn to pass through the gate. He let out a breath he'd been holding when they were waved through. Before Dagmar could lead them anywhere, Sasha grabbed her arm and pulled her off the main road into the first narrow street he could see.

"What are you doing?" Dagmar recoiled from him, her eyes widening with fright.

"I don't know. I think we should get off the road for a bit." He held up a hand to stop her questions. "I can't explain it. I just feel like something's not right. Like someone's following us or something."

"Do you want to find a place to stay for the night? It's still early but..." Her eyes remained fearful, but Sasha was relieved to see it was no longer directed toward him. There were just some things he was never quite going to live down, he supposed, but he did think they'd been through enough for Dagmar to trust that he wasn't going to hurt her.

"No. I guess not. It's probably nothing. Let's just stay off the main road for a bit."

"I don't really know my way around except for the Emperor's Highway. We might get lost."

Sasha let out a sigh. Back here away from everyone, he was beginning to think he'd imagined the whole thing. No, he was sure he was just imagining it. He was just nervous being in such a new, big, different place.

"It's fine. We'll just keep going like we were." When neither Boris nor Dagmar appeared to mirror his confidence, he tried a weak smile. "Come on. We should make it as far into the city as we can today."

Dagmar finally shrugged and started back toward the main road with Sasha right behind her. A hand on Sasha's arm sent a spasm of fear through him until he turned and realized it was only Boris.

"There is someone following us," Boris said softly. "I saw him."

"Who? We're nobody here. No one knows us."

"I couldn't see his face. It's covered up just like us."

"We'll be careful. It's probably just a thief or someone like that looking for a target."

Boris didn't look convinced but didn't say anything more as they made it back onto the Emperor's Highway. Sasha glanced around, and, seeing no one watching them, began climbing up the road again.

By the time they reached the fourth tier, their mysterious follower was no longer just a figment of Boris or Sasha's imagination. Trying to maintain an appearance of nonchalance was difficult in the face of this unknown individual. Although there were long stretches of their walk that were apparently free of his presence, just when they were beginning to think they had shaken him entirely, he showed up again. Always at a distance. Always in a crowd.

The fourth tier was as different from the first as it was possible to be and it was here if Sasha could have pulled his attention away from their stalker, that the wealth of Kaldura was first truly seen. Instead of twisting alleys and narrow dirt lanes that formed an impenetrable maze, the roads here, branching gracefully off of the highway, were wide and paved in red brick. Palm trees, much taller than the ones in the desert, grew in rows down the centers of the widest roads. The houses, each several times larger than several of the first-tier huts put together, were made almost entirely out of white and tan stone. The tiled roofs reflected the bright sunlight beating down between the mountains. The crowd had thinned out quite a bit as well, leaving Sasha more nervous than ever.

"I think we should find a place to stay for the night." Dagmar's voice carried her own worry clearly. "I don't want to be out here after dark with...him."

"Good idea." Sasha had been on the verge of making the same suggestion himself. "Someplace that has locks on their doors, preferably."

Dagmar led them off the highway and down one of the spacious roads adorned with stately palms. The buildings along this stretch were places of business rather than houses and it wasn't long before Dagmar stopped beneath the sign of one such place. Its entrance was near the wall that separated the fourth tier from the third. Although the wall had been at least twenty feet tall from the third tier, it barely came up to their waists on this side. Sasha wandered over to it and looked down on the city below. The sun, halfway beneath the westernmost mountain, cast a brilliant orange down the levels. Sasha realized for the first time just how high they had climbed.

Scrutinizing the people milling about outside the inn one last time and catching no sight of the man who'd been following them, Sasha followed Dagmar and Boris inside. Sasha and Boris both hung back, allowing Dagmar to make the arrangements for their stay. When she returned with only one key in her hands, Sasha shot her a quizzical look.

"Don't you want your own room?"

"There's no way I'm staying all by myself all night after being followed by some stranger all day today. Besides, it's not like I had my own room when we were out in the dessert," she whispered, her eyes darting around the room as if she expected the stranger to materialize before them. "Come on. They'll bring us supper in our room."

The window of the room overlooked the wide street beneath. Sasha stood to the side of it, watching the people walking below. He half hoped to catch sight of their elusive follower, but the man was nowhere in sight. After a final perusal of the scene before him, Sasha pulled the slatted wooden shutters closed and latched them shut.

"Who do you suppose it is?" Dagmar asked, staying far back from the window.

Sasha shrugged. "Never got a look at his face. You don't suppose it was one of those men from the desert, do you?"

"It's not likely. They weren't interested enough in you to go through all the trouble."

"I don't think it was them, either," Boris said. He lowered himself onto the edge of one bed. "I think it's someone who knows us."

"What makes you say that?"

"It wouldn't make sense for it to be anyone else."

"A thief?" Sasha suggested.

"Wouldn't have followed us through the tiers," Dagmar said.

Resigning himself to the mystery, Sasha joined Boris on the bed, his legs stretched out on the mattress. It was a welcome relief after the many days spent sleeping out in the desert. Lacing his fingers together behind his head and leaning back on a pillow, he dragged his thoughts away from their follower and back to why they were even in this place.

"We're in the fourth tier now. How should we start looking? Do we just start asking people if they know Josef Zbreck?"

"I guess so." Dagmar shrugged. "If he's very wealthy, people will most likely have heard of him at least."

A light rap on the door interrupted them and Sasha pulled himself off the comfortable bed to open it. The tray of food that was put into his hands by a serving girl gave off an assortment of smells, most of them unfamiliar. Several small, silver dishes sat on the tray. Setting it down on the small trestle table in the room, Sasha lifted the lid off of one of them. His face wrinkled up in disgust as he recognized the distinct aroma of fish. Further investigation revealed a variety of fruits and vegetables that he'd never seen. Picking one up and popping into his mouth, Sasha turned to the others.

"I have to say, I like the food where I come from better," he said.

Dagmar shook her head as she picked up a piece of thin bread and scooped a bit out of several dishes and then spread a sauce over the whole thing. Sasha watched her with curiosity and tried to mimic the way she put it together. It still wasn't enough to hide the flavor of the fish, he thought as he bit into it.

Falling asleep after their scare was easier than Sasha imagined it would be. Their trek through the desert and subsequent journey through the city left all three exhausted. Even Boris managed to lay down and sleep for a few short hours. Sasha heard him wake up again, gasping quietly and moving away from the others, but he was used to it by now and it did little to disturb his own rest.

He'd gone back to sleep when a whisper worked its way into his consciousness. His eyes flew open to find Boris leaning over him. Boris had laid a finger on his lips and Sasha tensed at the seriousness of his brother's face.

"Someone's outside," Boris' voice was barely loud enough for Sasha to hear him.

Sasha was wide awake now. Easing himself up into a sitting position, he followed Boris' gaze to the latched door that stood between them and the hallway. A faint light showed beneath the door, but that wasn't any cause for alarm. Sconces lined the hallway outside and the candles in them were kept burning through the night. What was disturbing was the shadowy outline breaking up the line of light. Boris was right. Someone was outside their door. Without moving, Sasha glanced at the other bed and saw Dagmar was already sitting up, her back pressed against the headboard, her wide eyes staring at the door.

Sasha inched forward, wincing at the slight creaking the bed made as it shifted beneath his weight. Hopefully, to whoever was waiting outside their door, it would simply sound like someone turning over in bed. He made his way over to the window and peeked through the wooden slats. The street below, although well-lit with streetlamps, was deserted. Sasha studied the few shadows and finally convinced himself that no one lurked in them, watching their window.

Turning back toward the room, he saw both Boris and Dagmar watching him. He made up his mind quickly and picked up his own pack, motioning for the others to do the same. The drop from the window to the street was at least twelve feet, but a ledge jutted out several feet beneath them which would make their descent easier. Climbing out the window and taking off in the middle of the night seemed like a reckless and ill-conceived plan, even to Sasha. But it beat the alternative of waiting, trapped, in their room for some stranger to make the first move.

Sasha lifted the latch a little at a time and pulled the shutters open, praying that their hinges were well oiled and silent. He climbed through first, hanging off the window sashing until his feet found the ledge beneath him. Dagmar leaned out of the window.

"Come on," Sasha whispered.

"It's so far." Dagmar hesitated a moment longer before climbing out as well.

Sasha watched anxiously as Boris leaned out the window. It would be just like his crazy brother to freeze up now and endanger them all. It was what Sasha had been afraid of before starting out. Boris, however, had never been afraid of heights. Sasha remembered the fact with relief as he watched his brother join them.

"Where are we going to go now?" Dagmar asked when they were safely on the ground.

"As far from here as we can get."

"We'll stand out. No one else is walking around."

"Let's just get away from here for now, and then we'll figure it out." Sasha started off down one of the streets branching off. "Maybe this time, we'll really be rid of him."

"Whoever he is," Boris added under his breath.

Chapter 24

DAYLIGHT FOUND THEM NEARING the gate to the fifth tier. As they joined the line of people waiting to go through, Sasha looked over his shoulder one last time. Their midnight escape from the inn had been successful, so far. The entire morning slipped away without any sign of their pursuer - and without a clue as to who it might be. Sasha massaged a stiff, sore neck with one hand. It came from watching behind his back so much.

"I think we're safe to start looking," he said to Dagmar as they passed through the gate.

Dagmar nodded.

Moving away from the gate and working their way further into the tier until they reached a large square. Vendors, with a variety of goods Sasha had never even seen before, lined the square. At the far end of it, dominating the entire scene was a magnificent building.

"Wait here," Dagmar said. "I'll ask around and see what I can find out."

"Don't go too far. If he shows up again, we shouldn't be separated."

"I'll stay within sight but try to look like you're doing something other than just watching me. The last thing we want to do is attract attention."

Sasha nodded his understanding and watched as Dagmar melted into the crowd. Despite the exotic wares and strange language, the vendors hawking their goods carried a sense of familiarity reminding Sasha of the Spring Market. Thanks to most of his face being covered, it was easy to watch Dagmar without arousing suspicion from anyone around them. Sasha's eyes wandered over the booths of the nearest vendors.

One stall in particular caught his attention and Sasha moved a few steps closer to it. Beaded jewelry lay scattered about a table, while the more expensive looking pieces hung in an orderly manner from a row of small hooks in the back. Sasha glanced at the merchant. It was a woman and even though he could not understand her words, he knew exactly what she was doing. The quick exchange between her and a customer was nothing more than a haggle about the price.

"Sasha." Dagmar's voice startled him, and he turned to find her standing just behind him. "I found him."

"That fast?"

"Come on." Dagmar started walking away from the booth and into a less crowded spot. "He's not actually here. And it's not going to be easy getting anywhere close to him, either."

"What do you mean?"

"He's a guild master. That's why I could find out about him so fast. Everyone knows who he is."

"I don't understand. What's a guild master?"

Dagmar sighed. She opened her mouth to answer him. She stopped, her eyes looking past him.

"Where's Boris?"

"He's right behind me, isn't he?" Sasha turned his head and searched the sea of half covered faces behind them.

"Maybe he's just wandered off somewhere. Come on, we have to find him."

Sasha gave vent to a growl of frustration. Here they were, on the verge of finding Agathe, and Boris was nowhere to be found. He followed Dagmar as she moved forward through a group of people. What could have possessed his mad brother to go off on his own? Now he would have to waste precious time in search of Boris. There was a tiny part of Sasha that considered the benefits of not having Boris along anymore. If they failed to find him, if he was simply gone and lost forever, Sasha wasn't sure he would actually be sorry.

"What are we going to do?" Dagmar asked after an hour of walking around the market square found them back where they started.

Sasha shrugged. "Tell me about this man. What is a guild master? Why does that make him so hard to get to?"

"But what about Boris?"

"What about him? We can't find him. We tried."

"You're just going to leave without him?"

Sasha tried to ignore the accusation in Dagmar's eyes. "It's what he did. Look, Dagmar, he's the one who left when he shouldn't have. He knew to stay close to us and he didn't. It's his fault. Come on. Let's just see if we can get to this man's house."

Sasha started off toward the entrance of the market square without looking back. He pushed away the guilt that kept stealing over his mind. It was Boris' fault. And Boris had left him, once.

He reached the stone archway that marked the entrance of the market. Pausing beneath its shadow, Sasha realized Dagmar was not behind him. A quick glance around and his eyes fell on her, standing exactly where he had left her.

"What are you doing?" he asked, approaching her again. He made no effort to conceal his growing anger. "We're leaving."

"I'm not," Dagmar said in a whisper.

"What? What do you mean you're not? That's the whole reason you came. To find Agathe, not to watch out for Boris."

"I'm sorry, Sasha. I'm not going with you now."

Sasha stared at her in disbelief. Aside from her rapid breath, there was no other outward sign of Dagmar's fear and that almost made Sasha more upset than Boris' absence. Dagmar, who had never once so much as hinted at contradicting him, was flatly refusing to do what he said. The temptation to reach out and grab her by the arm and drag her away with him flitted across his mind. His hands clenched into tight fists at his side.

"I'm not saying I won't still help you," Dagmar said, as if reading his thoughts. "I will. Just not now. Not until we find him."

"Why? You know this would be easier if we didn't have him to drag around."

Sasha watched as his words registered on Dagmar's face. "How can you say that? You've traveled half the world on the chance that your sister will be here, but you won't spend a few hours looking for him when you *know* he's here somewhere?"

"He shouldn't have wandered off."

"I'm not going," Dagmar said again, her chin tilting up in defiance. "We didn't leave you when you shouldn't have gone off. It's not right that we leave him. Besides, what if something happened? What if he didn't just wander off? Someone was following us, just yesterday."

Sasha could not deny that Dagmar was right, although he wished he could. He gave a weak nod, acknowledging her words.

"And what if we can't find him? We just stay here forever, looking?"

"It's been barely more than an hour."

The day marched on without a sign of Boris. Leaving the market square behind them, Sasha and Dagmar ventured into the streets beyond. The patchwork of alleys and nooks that existed in the bottom tiers were missing here. With its broad streets and spacious setting there were few places outside to hide.

Returning to the market square in defeat as evening came on, Sasha rubbed a weary hand over his face. If they ever did find Boris, there was a lot Sasha wanted to say to him.

"Sasha, isn't that him?" Dagmar said, stopping, her head turned toward a retreating figure.

"That's not him."

"No. I don't mean Boris. I meant the man following us the other day."

Sasha studied the man more. There was a familiarity to his stride and bearing.

"It is him. Come on." Sasha started off in the stranger's direction.

"What about Boris?"

"This might have something to do with him."

Sasha glanced over his shoulder long enough to know that Dagmar was coming. After their altercation earlier, he wasn't sure she would.

Despite the lateness of the day, there were still quite a few people strolling through the market square. Sasha weaved in and out of them, hoping Dagmar would keep up, hoping he wouldn't lose sight of the man. The stranger, his steps purposeful and quick, was heading toward the magnificent building at the far ending of the square. Sasha watched in frustration as he melted into a crowd moving up the steps and between the marble columns.

"We've lost him," he said, as they stopped at the foot of the steps.

"We could wait and see if he comes out again?"

With the sun going down and no better ideas, Sasha led them off to the side where the shadows were growing deeper. He settled back against a stone wall that allowed him to still watch the doorway of the building. Minutes went by and as the sun got lower the crowds finally began to disperse. A gnawing sensation reminded Sasha of how hungry he was.

"I haven't seen him come out and we can't just stay here all night," Dagmar said at last. "The city watch won't let us."

"So, what? We just find a place to stay for the night and come back and look for him again tomorrow?"

"I guess." Dagmar stood up.

Sasha joined her and in the deepening gloom they started across the now nearly empty square. Knowing the man who had followed them was still in the area left Sasha uneasy. More than once he turned to study the shadows behind them but found nothing. As they neared the entrance of the market square, Sasha turned once more and cast a final searching glance at the place. Dagmar's fingers dug into his arm a moment later. He followed her eyes to an alcove between two pillared columns. It took a second for him to see what she was seeing, but when he did a wave of mixed relief and annoyance washed over him.

"Boris?"

The shadow huddled inside the dark recess made no move. He gave no indication that he'd heard anything. And yet, Sasha was more than certain that it was his brother. Everything about him reminded Sasha of the first time he'd seen Boris in Bren. It reminded him of just how far Boris had come, and now gone back again.

"Boris?" he repeated, stepping into the alcove.

Still no reaction to his voice, Sasha noted with growing concern. Now was a terrible time for Boris to go back to the way he'd been in Bren.

"What happened to him?" Dagmar said, still standing out in the open looking around as if expecting someone else to be hiding nearby.

Sasha shrugged and approached Boris. He crouched down in front of his brother and laid a tentative hand on his shoulder. The touch elicited a spasm from Boris, and he finally lifted his head, his vacant eyes meeting Sasha's through the gloom.

"He's here," Boris whispered. Then he shrank down even further, pulling away from Sasha.

"Who?" Sasha fought back the urge to take his brother by the shoulders and shake him back to reality. He knew it would never work. He turned to Dagmar instead. "Let's find somewhere to stay for now."

Tugging on Boris' arm finally brought his brother to his feet. Although Boris walked along at Sasha's leading it was more like watching someone walk in their sleep. His eyes remained blank. His movements were dazed. He kept his arms wrapped about himself as if cold despite the sultry night air. Sasha was at a loss. He could only hope Boris could pull himself out of it. One thing was sure. They couldn't drag him around like this while they searched for Agathe.

Once inside a room for the night, Sasha lowered himself onto the edge of the bed and watched Boris sitting in the darkest corner. He'd retreated there the second Sasha's guiding hand left his arm. Aside from his cryptic words when they found him, he hadn't made a sound. The bed shifted as Dagmar sat next to him.

"What do you think happened?" she whispered.

"Don't know. He hasn't been this bad since...well, never, that I've seen." Sasha gestured helplessly. "I mean, he stares at nothing all the time. But not the same. The other times, it's like he doesn't want to deal with anything so he just sort of shuts down. Right now, he's more..."

"Scared," Dagmar finished. "Something scared him so much he can't handle it."

"Exactly. But what? Or who?" Sasha added, remembering Boris' only words.

"You think it was whoever was following us?"

Sasha shrugged and leaned forward burying his face in his hands. "I have no idea. There's just so much that doesn't add up. The man. The fact that Boris definitely wasn't there when we searched earlier today. The way he," Sasha gestured toward Boris, "is now. There's only one person I can imagine him being that afraid of."

"Who?"

"Lord Bayner. He's the one who made him like this in the first place, but him being here is impossible. It just doesn't make sense. We might as well give up looking for Agathe at this point. We can't take him back out into the city like this."

"He'll get better. Won't he?"

"I don't know."

"You can't just give up."

"I mean, I actually can. Look at him. What are we going to accomplish dragging that around?"

"We've made it this far. Let's just see what happens tomorrow."

Tomorrow was every bit as disappointing as Sasha thought it would be. Boris was unchanged. Sasha shook his head in both frustration and despair. They weren't going anywhere today. The long hours of the day stretched before them. Sasha switched between pacing restlessly and sitting drumming his fingers impatiently on his leg.

"So, tell me what you found out about Josef Zbreck?" He finally asked Dagmar, more to alleviate his own boredom than to formulate an actual plan. All thoughts of planning were gone now, ruined by Boris' regression.

Dagmar's face was drawn into thoughtful lines. "He's a guild master. Merchants' guild, I think. That means he controls the sect of merchants who operate in the city, making him both very rich and very powerful."

"I thought you had an emperor here."

"We do. The emperor rules the people, but the guild masters rule the emperor."

"I guess that would put him in one of the top tiers."

"Second to top. The top one is the imperial tier."

"We're only one tier from it," Sasha said, lost in thought. The beginning of an idea was forming. "Would it be fairly easy to recognize his home?"

"It'd be a palace pretty much. But so would all the other guild masters'."

"So, nothing about it that I could recognize it by if, for instance, I went by myself?"

It was Dagmar's turn to grow thoughtful as she considered his words. For several moments, she didn't speak. Then her face lit up.

"I know. Each guild has its own crest. It would be displayed somewhere on the house. But do you think it's really a good idea to go alone?"

"If we're going to do anything, I think it's the only idea. Whoever was following us is clearly still around. But he's watching for us to be a group of three, not just one person. When I leave, you can lock the door and let no one in until I come back. And, we won't have to worry about him." Sasha motioned to where Boris still sat in the corner. "I'll just go in, find his house and find a good spot to watch it from. It might take a couple days, but if she is there, I'll probably see her at some point."

"There are a lot of holes in that plan."

"Stop. Now you sound like Phelie. It's the best I've got."

"Phelie's right," Dagmar said quietly. "Besides, since when do you care what Phelie thinks of your plans?"

"I don't. You're just sounding a lot like her when you say things like that. Either way, it's what I'm doing. If that's alright?" Sasha added as he watched Dagmar frown.

"I guess. You know, we're not making it back in time to catch Lawrence."

"I know. We'll figure something else out. What's the symbol?"

"What symbol?"

"The one for his guild. I have to know what it is if I'm going to find it."

"Oh, that symbol. It's a picture of a merchant ship."

Sasha's pacing took on a little more purpose through the afternoon as he tried to sort through the holes in his plan. Much as he hated to admit it, Dagmar was right. It was a poor plan. But maybe, just maybe, he could get lucky. After all, his plans so far in life had not been the best, and yet, they had all worked out more or less. He elected to ignore how close to death some of his plans had left him.

"You know, Sasha. There's just one problem with your plan," Dagmar said much later in the evening. "How are you going to get into the tier?"

Sasha's face fell. "I hadn't thought of it. Can the walls be climbed?"

"I wouldn't know. I've never tried. But they have guards. They're meant to stop people from doing that. I don't know what they'd do if they caught you."

"Well, I don't have a better idea, and we can't just stay here forever waiting for one to come."

Dagmar fell silent again, although her face remained serious. As the sun set and shadows spread across the room, Sasha lay back on his bed. Tomorrow he would find Agathe. He would rescue her and bring her back to Dival where she never had to belong to another man.

Chapter 25

A N HOUR OR SO BEFORE THE sun glinted off
the eastern slopes of the roofs in the city,
Sasha slipped over the wall into the sixth tier
of Kaldura. Going through the gate without Dagmar
was out of the question. The wall had been his only
option, and if it weren't for the fact that the guards
making their rounds were quite predictable, even
that would have been impossible.

Near the top of the conical city, it was noticeably
smaller than the other tiers, but no less spacious.
According to Dagmar, only the guild master's
inhabited this tier. Rather than demeaning their tier
by having their own marketplace, they sent people
down to do it in the lower tiers. Sasha tried to blend
in but for the first time he felt underdressed. His
clothing was closer to that of the household slaves he
saw in the streets. Unlike in Aruuk where the female
slaves were required to keep their faces covered,
here the slaves were the only ones with their faces
uncovered.

Calling the living space of the guild masters
houses was an understatement, Sasha thought as he
made his way through the tier. Walls, only slightly
shorter than the ones that separated the tiers,

surrounded each cluster of buildings. Wrought iron gates barred the only entrances into these walled off estates. Dagmar was right about the guild symbols, Sasha noticed. Each was prominently displayed by the gates of their respective master.

A loud commotion coming from down the street took Sasha's attention off of the estates. As Sasha watched, a large group rounded the corner and came into view. A man, his bare face marking him as a slave, walked in front of the procession calling out the same phrase over and over. Judging by the reaction of everyone else in the street, Sasha assumed he was telling everyone to get out of the way. He moved back against the wall. Curiosity kept his eyes trained on the group as they drew closer. Aside from the slave leading the way, there were a group of four carrying an ornate chair, and several more, both men and women, following behind. Sasha studied the man in the chair. Little of his face was visible, only his eyes and those seemed to ignore everything around him. He was grossly overweight and the loose-fitting clothes of the country ballooned around him ridiculously.

Sasha was so intent on looking at the man who was so obviously one of the guild masters' that Dagmar had spoken of that he very nearly missed seeing anyone else. It wasn't until the man was carried past him that Sasha gave a passing glance to the slaves who followed.

Sasha let out an audible gasp when he saw her. He clapped a hand over his mouth to stifle any further sound. He couldn't believe his luck. Sasha smiled to himself as he thought of the word but there really wasn't any other word for it. After all these years, he didn't think it would be possible to recognize Agathe so quickly. They had both been children when she was sold. Staring at her now, though, was like staring at Mother. Her face, unhindered by a veil, was identical to Mother's. By the time he regained his own composure they were past him, but that didn't matter. Just knowing that she was here was enough for the moment. And the procession wasn't hard to follow. Sasha waited until they were a safe distance beyond him to move on.

They came to a stop before a gate and disappeared inside it. To avoid any suspicion, Sasha continued past it, marking the merchant ship crest emblazoned above the iron gates. Now he just had to figure out how to get in. Sasha debated going back to Boris and Dagmar for the night, but excitement overrode the idea. He couldn't leave, not now, not when she was so close to him. He just needed to talk to her, tell her that he was here. Perhaps, if he could get a chance to speak with her, she would already know of a way to escape.

Sasha spent the rest of the day trying to remain inconspicuous while still attempting to scout out the estate. There was no way he could go through the gates. Those were guarded. The walls were possible. The stone used to build them left plenty of hand and foot holds to climb with. But then there was the question of what to do once he was inside. The gate was the only view he had into the place and although there were lots of buildings there was little about them to indicate their purpose. Sasha really hated the idea of going from building to building hoping to find the one that housed the Josef Zbreck's female slaves. That is, of course, assuming that they were housed separately. There was every chance that they stayed in the main house which, as Dagmar said, was more of a palace. It was the centerpiece of the entire estate, rising well above the other buildings. If Agathe was in there, Sasha knew his chance of reaching her was almost nonexistent.

By the time night fell, Sasha had made up his mind. It was a horrible plan as plans go, but he couldn't think of anything better. At this point, he'd gone all the way around the tier and worked his way back to Josef Zbreck's mansion. Settling back into a hiding spot he'd picked out earlier in the day, Sasha waited.

A full moon and a cloudless sky took away from the concealment of darkness, but Sasha didn't worry too much. After all, no one was expecting him to climb the wall, so probably no one was looking for it. The city watch made their rounds like Dagmar said they would but after the first two hours watching them, Sasha knew they weren't worth worrying about either. They stuck to their schedule and route with great persistence. Their predictability made them useless.

When the moon began its descent, Sasha made his move. The watch had just gone by only a few minutes before, leaving him almost an entire hour to climb over the wall and conceal himself on the other side.

Dropping lightly to the ground on the other side, Sasha was amazed by the sight that met his eyes. The terraced gardens, with a fountain at their center, had not been visible from the front gate. It was like stepping into an entirely different world. The brown of the rest of the city fell away to rich green and colorful flowers that were just visible in the bright moonlight. Finding a spot that he hoped was out of the way, Sasha hid himself until morning.

The first people began moving about more than an hour before sunrise. That was no surprise really. In Aruuk, the slaves were always up that early starting their work. Since no one suspected an intrusion, though, no one searched for an intruder and the first few hours of the day passed by without incident. They also passed by without sight of Agathe. Sasha was beginning to despair of seeing her at all when a door opened from one of the outer buildings and she emerged.

Luck was with Sasha for Agathe not only came out but now was moving toward his own place of concealment in the garden. He crouched behind a hedge of bushes with the wall to his back, waiting as she got closer. She was less than a few feet from him, close enough that he could see the thin golden circlet that rested on her black hair. Stepping out from beneath the hedge just enough for her to catch sight of him, Sasha whispered her name. Agathe jumped and gasped, her eyes widening as she saw him. In another second she would scream, Sasha realized with horror.

"Shhh, it's alright. I won't hurt you," he hastened to tell her, holding his hand out in a placating gesture. "I'm your brother, Sasha, remember?"

Slowly, her eyes still wide with alarm, Agathe nodded. Sasha let out a sigh of relief. At least she wasn't on the verge of giving him away completely.

"I need to talk to you." He motioned for her to come behind the hedge with him.

Casting a nervous look over the yard and garden and seeing no one around, Agathe took a tentative step toward him.

"I can't believe I actually found you." Sasha was almost giddy with his success. It was so easy.

"What are you doing here?" Even her voice sounded like Mother's, Sasha thought, although she now spoke Aruuken with an accent that hadn't been there all those years ago.

"I came to see you, and to help you escape."

Sasha watched as his words registered on her face. If he was expecting her to share his own excitement, he was sadly disappointed. Confusion clouded her delicate features. Stepping away from him a bit, she shook her head.

"No. It can't be. It's a trick. You're going to get me in trouble. Father sent you, didn't he?"

"No. It's no trick, Agathe. Father has no idea I'm here."

"That's not my name. Not now."

Sasha recoiled a little at the bitterness that edged her voice with the words.

"Alright. But it's still not a trick. I ran away from Father more than a year ago. I don't live there anymore. I came here looking for you. I want to help you get away, and you can come with me and live somewhere safe. You won't ever have to belong to anyone else ever again."

Agathe's face became unreadable and for several moments she said nothing.

"I can't go with you," Agathe said at last.

"What? Of course, you can. Look, I know you're afraid. I get it. But you don't have to live like this. I can take you from it. I can..."

"I can't go," she repeated.

"But you can. We'll plan a..."

"I have a son, Sasha. His son."

Sasha stopped talking and stared at her for a full second before her words sunk in. "Your master's son?"

Agathe nodded. "He let him live. I can't go. I can't risk that."

"We can figure out how to get your son, too. Trust me."

Agathe was shaking her head before he finished speaking, a single tear running down her cheek. "No. If we get caught, he'll... he'll kill him. I can't let that happen. You don't understand. Melish is all I have."

Sasha swallowed back the lump of disappointment that threatened to choke him. How could Agathe refuse a chance at freedom? From the tears that were sliding down her face, he could see it wasn't easy. Laying his hand on her arm, he managed a sad half smile, even as he felt his dream slipping away.

"Is he good to you, at least?"

"He let Melish live. I suppose that makes him better than some."

"I guess it does." Sasha remembered about Father's own rule about slave born children. He was glad he'd never been in a position to follow through with it. "Do you get to see him? Your son, I mean."

"Sometimes."

"And there's no way I can change your mind? I came all this way planning on bringing you back. You'd love it where I live now. It's so different."

Agathe shook her head once more.

"You should go. Before someone catches you." She started to pull away from him, glancing over her shoulder to make sure they still weren't watched.

Sasha held onto her arm, unwilling to watch her walk away after all that he'd hoped and gone through. "I'm sorry, Agathe. I'm sorry for not trying to help you that day. I should have done something."

"You were a child, Sasha. There was nothing you could have done." Agathe brought a hand up and swiped away the tears that were falling faster now. "Now go. Go, before someone sees you. And, Sasha, thank you."

Agathe lifted his hand off her arm and turned away. Sasha watched as she moved through the garden, back toward the cluster of buildings. There was no amount of swallowing that could dislodge the lump constricting his throat. This wasn't supposed to be how it went. This wasn't supposed to end in failure. How could she refuse her one chance of freedom?

Sasha sank back against the wall, staring at the now empty garden, his thoughts in chaos. He didn't move for hours as the sun continued its march across the sky. At last, as darkness came, he rose to his feet and found a spot on the wall that was climbable.

As he dropped to the ground on the other side, he gave one final look at the place.

He did not look back again.

Chapter 26

A SOFT KNOCKING ON THE DOOR made Dagmar sit up. In the two days Sasha had been gone, no one had disturbed her and Boris. Tiptoeing across the room to the door, Dagmar hesitated with her hand resting on the latch.

"It's just me, Dagmar," Sasha's voice came through the door and Dagmar let out a little sigh of relief as she lifted the latch to let him in.

"You're back."

Sasha didn't answer but went straight to the bed and sank down on it, burying his face in his hands. Dagmar waited for several minutes but still he didn't speak.

"Did you find her?" she ventured at last.

"She wouldn't come." Sasha's voice, muffled by his hands, was broken. "She's not coming."

"I'm sorry," Dagmar whispered, gingerly sitting on the other side of the bed. "Why not?"

Sasha finally straightened, running both hands through his hair before spreading them out in a defeated gesture.

"She has a son. She won't risk something happening to him. Which is ridiculous, because she barely even sees him and really he belongs to her master, and he'll do whatever he wants with him. He's not worth giving up her chance of freedom, but I couldn't make her see that."

"I'm sorry," Dagmar repeated. "So, what now?"

"Now? We leave. There's no reason to stay. We still have my mother to find."

Dagmar nodded. "What are we going to do about him?"

Sasha followed her gaze to Boris. He ran his eyes over his brother. Nothing had changed with him in the last two days.

"Has he said anything else yet?"

"Nothing. And he hasn't slept or eaten. When I've tried to talk to him, it's like I'm not even there."

"Now you know what it feels like for me all the time," Sasha muttered, doing little to conceal the bitterness in his voice. Nothing was going his way. He didn't have the patience to spend on Boris now. "We'll just have to drag him along and hope he doesn't make a scene or get us into trouble."

Later, Sasha lay on his back, his eyes staring up at the ceiling above his head. Sleep refused to come.

He'd failed.

The task he'd given himself, the dream he'd held onto achieving, was over. Even if he found Mother, it would be incomplete. He'd return home and everyone would want to know what had happened. His thoughts drifted to home and those waiting for him. For a moment, he wished himself back by the little waterfall with Ophelia saying things that made everything make sense. He wondered what she would say about this. Not that it really mattered. He knew he failed, whatever anyone else said.

Morning's light found the trio leaving the inn behind them. As usual, Dagmar's hand guided Boris while Sasha led the way. Sasha was too wrapped up in his own misery and thoughts to notice the now familiar man standing in the shadows of a nearby doorway. And even if he had noticed, he would not have been able to see the smile on the man's face.

It took them a day and a half to leave the city, with its tiers of wealth, behind them. Rather than heading back out into the desert, Dagmar led them to a different road. This one skirted the foot of the red mountains.

"There's a port city only a few days from here. We should be able to find a ship there," she said in explanation.

Sasha, having been almost as silent as Boris for the last two days, nodded.

"Were you planning on sailing straight to Karu?"

Again, Sasha nodded.

"I won't be much help to you there."

"Do you want to go home?"

"No. I just won't be able to really help you there like I did here. But we should be really careful going there."

"I thought you didn't know anything about them?"

"Father knew about them. He said they were mostly pirates."

"Well, this has already turned out to be a disaster, so it can't be much worse."

"I hope not."

Three days of walking brought them to the port city. Securing passage here was a lot easier than in Dival, Sasha noted wryly. Nobody here cared about the band on Boris' wrist.

Although he hated the idea of being back on a ship, Sasha could not wait to leave Sondaru, with its deserts and its disappointments, behind. He heartily wished to never see the place again. As the brown strip of land receded from sight and gave way to the endless blue of the sea, Sasha could only hope that the rest of their venture proved more successful.

He glanced over at where Boris crouched against the bulwark of the ship. For once, Dagmar wasn't at his side. Sasha walked over and sat down next to him.

"We're gone now. You can't even see the land. So, whoever it was back there that scared you, he's gone too." Sasha waited a moment, but there was no reaction from Boris. He started to get up again when Boris reached out suddenly and put his hand on Sasha's arm.

"He's coming," Boris whispered, his eyes coming alive with fear.

"Who? Tell me, and we'll stay away from him."

"He knows."

Sasha shook his head and rolled his eyes. A lot of good his brother's cryptic warnings were going to do if he wouldn't say who he was talking about. Sasha didn't even have a guess.

"Whoever he is, there's no way he can know anything about us or where we're going."

"He knows," Boris repeated, only this time it was more than just fear in his eyes, there was an unspoken plea in them for Sasha to understand what he incapable of putting into words.

Chapter 27

WASIL, KARU CAME INTO SIGHT through a blinding sheet of rain, it's rocky crags rising sheer and black out of the churning sea, wreathed in mist and fog. For three days, a storm had driven the ship forward. Sasha had spent the entirety of those three days in his cabin more seasick than his first trip with Lawrence.

Even when the ship was safely moored to the dock, his stomach refused to cooperate. It was about all he could manage to make it from his cabin down the ramp onto solid ground. Boris and Dagmar were already there, waiting for him.

Sasha noticed that Boris was no longer staring straight ahead, but rather his eyes were darting around as if searching for something. Remembering Boris' only communication on the ship, Sasha gave the wharfs a cursory glance himself. No one within sight was someone he recognized and the chill of premonition he felt faded away. A further relief came when Sasha found he was able to understand most of what everyone around him was saying. Although the dialect was quite different, the language was the same as in Aruuk.

"So, do you have a plan for finding her?" Dagmar asked.

"Not really," Sasha admitted. He'd spent most of the trip still reeling from his disappointment as well as being seasick. He had given very little thought as to what they would do once they reached Karu.

"Maybe we should find a place to stay first?"

Sasha nodded, looking around. Although he could not have said exactly why, there was a definite air of rowdiness and roughness radiating from the entire place. He could well believe that the island, for that was what Karu was, was inhabited by pirates and thugs.

"Come on, Boris," Dagmar said, as she laid a hand on his arm. Boris, his eyes still nervously scanning their surroundings, allowed himself to be guided forward.

The rain poured down on them and they were soaked to the skin by the time Sasha recognized the wooden sign swinging wildly in the wind above a doorway. Pushing the door open, he led the way into the inn. The room they stepped into served as a tavern and was full to bursting. A man stood behind the counter, a tumbler in one hand and a cloth in the other. Sasha pushed his way through the crowd up to him.

"What do you want?" The man barely spared him a glance as he set the cup down and filled it for another customer.

"A room for the night."

"Here for the auction tomorrow? Heard it's going to be a big one. Lots of slaves and livestock."

"Yes," Sasha said, thankful for the man handing him a perfectly good reason to here.

Sasha, key in hand, started toward the stairs when a man stepped in his path. He heard Dagmar's sharp intake behind him and glanced back to see another man gripping her wrist, his eyes taking in the brand on her forearm. His free hand grabbed her by the chin and jerked her head up to inspect her face.

"How much for your girl?" the first man asked.

"What?"

"How much do you want for the girl?"

Sasha stared at him for a moment. "No. She's not for sale."

"Oh, come on. Name your price. It's not often we get such a pretty face come through here."

"She's really not for sale." Sasha turned to the man holding Dagmar and yanked his hand off of her. "Let go of her."

"What about a loan for a few hours? Come on, what have you got to lose?" The man reached past Sasha and ran a rough hand over Dagmar's hair. Dagmar's face was white, and Sasha noticed a slight trembling taking hold of her.

"She's not for sale," Sasha said again.

Behind Dagmar, Boris' face hardened. Before anyone could say anything else he shoved Dagmar forward away from the men and toward the staircase and she yielded instantly. The man stumbled out of the way and let them pass.

As Sasha locked the door behind them, he heard Dagmar's sniffling. She was sitting with her back against the headboard of the bed, her face hidden by her arms. Sasha looked from her to Boris, unsure of what to do. In the almost two years that he'd known Dagmar, he'd never seen her cry, not even when he hit her, not even when she thought he might rape her.

"Are you alright?" he ventured at last.

"I'm fine." Dagmar pushed the words out between hiccups. "I hate being pretty."

Sasha did not know what to say to that. He had the vague idea that telling her she wasn't that pretty wouldn't help. Neither would telling her that lots of other girls might wish they were as pretty as she was. Instead, he stood awkwardly by the door sliding his hands in and out of his pockets.

"They don't do it because you're pretty, they do it because they're bad," Boris said.

Sasha wasn't sure what startled him the most - the fact that Boris put together a coherent sentence for the first time in two weeks or that what he said actually seemed to help. Dagmar rubbed her face on her sleeve and both she and Sasha turned to stare at Boris.

"What?" Boris noticed their gaze and asked.

"We've barely gotten two words out of you since Kaldura and now you're going to say something like that?"

At Sasha's mention of Kaldura, Boris' face darkened, and he looked away, but Sasha wasn't ready to let it go.

"What happened there? You disappeared for hours and hours and when we found you, you wouldn't even speak."

"Nothing," Boris said.

"Nothing? Really? How can you say that when we all know something *did* happen?"

"I can't tell you." Boris met Sasha's eyes for a brief moment - long enough for Sasha to read the deep pain, and guilt, in them. "If I did, you would just hate me more."

Sasha opened his mouth to argue but the words refused to come. The memory of how close he came to simply abandoning his brother in the foreign city was too close. The one thing Boris had pleaded with him to not do, and that Sasha had assured him would never happen, was the one thing Sasha had done almost without hesitation. It was Dagmar who held him back, not himself. If he'd had his way, Boris would still be lost in Kaldura.

For once, Sasha tried to imagine what that would have been like for Boris - lost, alone in a strange city, abandoned by the only person he knew. That he'd nearly done that to his brother was awful.

S. T. Hobbs

"This isn't really going to help us find your mother, Sasha, is it?" Dagmar, once more in control of herself, said. "We need some sort of plan."

"There's an auction tomorrow. Maybe we should go to it?" Sasha suggested.

Dagmar's face went a shade paler, but she didn't disagree.

"She won't necessarily be there, but people will think we're just here to buy slaves so they won't get suspicious, and it might give us an idea. If you don't want to go," Sasha said to Dagmar, "you could stay here and wait for us."

"No. I'm not staying anywhere by myself here. But I don't really want to go, either. What if those men are there too?"

"I imagine they would be."

"I could wear some of your clothes so people will think I'm a boy?" Dagmar said hopefully.

"You've worn my clothes before, and it didn't make you look like a boy. Sorry."

Dagmar frowned. "Even if I cut my hair?"

Both Boris and Sasha shook their heads and Dagmar's frown grew deeper and more thoughtful.

"I guess I'll just go like this."

"I won't let anything happen to you, and we'll stay away from those men if we see them. Get up from the bed for a minute."

"What are you doing?" Dagmar looked suitably puzzled as she got to her feet.

"I want to actually sleep tonight, and the only way that's going to happen is if I know no one can sneak in on us," Sasha said as he shoved and maneuvered the heavy bed frame in front of their door.

"Why didn't we just do that in Kaldura?"

"Didn't think of it then. Besides, it was more exciting to climb out of the window." Sasha grinned.

Chapter 28

NEVER THOUGHT I'D SEE ONE of these again, Sasha thought with a grim smile as the three of them reached the auction sight. Beyond the wooden platform that stood several feet above the ground were the slave and livestock pens. It was still early morning, but a crowd was gathering already in anticipation of the day's events.

Sasha turned away from the pens and scanned the crowd. He didn't catch any sight of the two men who had accosted them the day before. Not that it made Dagmar feel any better. She was holding onto Boris' arm as usual, only this time it appeared to be as much for herself as for Boris.

"Let's walk around," Sasha suggested and started for the area behind the platform.

It was customary, he knew, for people to view what was being sold for the day so that they would have an idea of what they wanted to bid on. To join the people already appraising the day's merchandise would only help them blend in. Sasha couldn't help the twinge of disdain he felt as he looked inside the cages. Father would never have allowed most of these into his market. Although there were a fair number of younger ones in the pen, none stood out as being particularly attractive or strong. Most of those being sold were well past their prime and usefulness.

"Do you have any money?" Boris asked suddenly from beside him.

"Some, yes. Why?"

"Because that's your mother, isn't it?" Boris jerked his chin toward a woman near the back. "And it looks like you'll have to buy her if you want her back."

Sasha followed Boris' direction and he took in the woman. Her face was painted in an effort to hide her age, the jewels Sasha had grown up seeing on her were gone but even so Sasha knew her. After the weeks it had taken them to find Agathe, it seemed laughably easy. No searching, no asking around, no clandestine meetings in the garden of her master. She was just there, within his reach.

"Mother," he whispered, his fingers grazing the wooden bars that separated them.

As if drawn to his inaudible word, she looked up and for a second their eyes met. It was only a second, and she dropped her gaze, staring instead at the ground. However repulsive the idea of buying his own mother was, and it was very repulsive, Sasha's fingers reached into his money pouch and absently counted the coins that remained. He would buy her. He wouldn't give her a chance to refuse him the way Agathe had. He wouldn't fail.

The auctioneer's voice rang out, pulling the crowds away from their spectating to the empty space in front of the platform. Sasha heard little of the man's introduction. He couldn't tear his eyes off of the sight of his mother.

"If you don't at least try to act like you're interested in this, someone is going to guess something's up," Boris jabbed him in the side with his elbow and hissed in his ear.

Sasha gave a startled jerk and turned his head enough to see what Boris was talking about. Not far from them, and openly watching them with suspicion, were the two men who had confronted them the night before. Out of the corner of his eye he saw Dagmar stiffen. Her face was almost entirely concealed by the hood of her cloak that she'd insisted on wearing despite the warmth of the weather.

With a sigh, Sasha resigned himself to taking a greater interest in the proceedings. They needed to think he was here to buy any slave that took his fancy. He did not want them knowing that there was only one he would even bid on. Only one that he cared about.

To his relief, none of the bidding came anywhere close to what it would have in Illsen. One after another was sold in quick succession. A young boy had just been paid for by one of the men from the inn and Sasha took his eyes off the platform long enough to watch as the man inspected him in the same way one would an animal.

He turned back to the platform sickened and just in time. His mother was brought up now and Sasha silently prayed that no one else would bid high for her. The auctioneer went through his spiel that Sasha mostly ignored. He didn't really care how old she was or useful or what lot number she was in their sale.

"Don't you think it's funny," Boris whispered to him as the auctioneer neared the end, "How they speak the same language as us, but we never knew this place existed?"

"Shhh," Sasha hissed as he lifted his hand to bid. After two weeks of silence, now Boris couldn't shut up, Sasha thought with annoyance. "Not now."

He only had to bid once more before the auctioneer cried, "Sold."

"Come on, let's pay for her and get out of here," Sasha said and moved toward the money keeper's table around the side of the platform.

"Number twelve?" The man at the table asked without looking up from his book.

"Yes," Sasha said as he started counting out the coins. His hands were sweaty, and his fingers didn't want to work all of a sudden. He fumbled the coins nervously before setting them on the table in front of the man. Now that she was being led over to him, Sasha couldn't bring himself to look at her. This was his own mother that he'd just bought.

"She's a bit old for you, don't you think?" The bookkeeper finally looked up as he recounted the coins, a smile that reminded Sasha a little of a wolf on his face. Sasha felt the blood rush to his face and had the almost unstoppable urge to hit the man.

"Come on," he said to his mother, turning away before the man could say anything else and heading away from the whole thing.

"How much money do you have left?" Boris asked behind him.

Too angry to answer, Sasha tossed the pouch back to him and kept walking. It wasn't until they were free of the gathered crowd that he realized Boris was no longer with them.

"Where did he go?" he asked Dagmar, who was looking around with equal confusion. She shrugged. Sasha let out a growl of exasperation. "Why does he do this?"

For several minutes they waited without a sign of him. Sasha, acutely conscious of his mother's gaze, could not bring himself to meet it and instead stood stiffly ignoring her. He hadn't planned on finding her this quickly, or on having to buy her. All the things he wanted to say to her, he knew he never could. Especially not here. It would be a very bad idea to let anyone know that she was more than just a slave to him.

"I suppose we should look for him," Sasha said at last.

"Isn't that him over there?"

Dagmar pointed and Sasha looked. As much as Sasha did not want to believe it, it was indeed his brother, standing in front of the money keeper's and counting out what appeared to be the rest of Sasha's money. Frozen in shock, Sasha just watched.

"He didn't just...," Dagmar didn't finish.

"I think he did."

When he started toward them, followed closely by a girl, Sasha's worry was confirmed.

"What," he started when Boris was close enough to hear him, but Boris held up a hand to stop him.

"You're welcome. Now they're not watching you like hawks," he whispered.

"Who?"

"Who do you think? They saw you staring at her, and noticed she was the only one you bid on. You made yourself suspicious."

Sasha bit back his retort. This wasn't the place. If any of what Boris was saying was true, the last thing they needed was to have an argument out here in front of everyone. He turned to walk away.

"Wait." He turned back again, "How much money is left?"

In answer, Boris held the money pouch out. Sasha snatched it out of his hand. Two coins clinked together inside it. Two, and they still had to get home. Sasha groaned and ran a helpless hand through his hair. Of the many moments on this trip that Boris had left him frustrated and upset, this one had to be one of the worst. Finally, throwing his hands up in resignation, Sasha started back toward the inn.

The inn was deserted at that early hour of the day, most of its occupants attending the auction, and they made it up to their room without incident. Five people in one room was a little crowded, but there was nothing that could be done about it.

"How could you do that?" Sasha nearly yelled when the door was safely locked behind him. Boris flinched. Sasha lowered his voice and fought to keep his anger out of it. However upset he was, he hated when Boris was afraid of him, especially when he knew, even if he did not wish to admit it, that Boris had acted to help him. "That was *my* money. That was what was going to get us home. We're stuck here without it."

"He already told you why," Dagmar spoke up. "Yelling isn't going to change anything."

This wasn't how any of this was supposed to go. This wasn't what he wanted Mother to see. He glanced now at where she and the girl were standing together. While Mother's face remained mostly impassive, the girl was clearly terrified and looked on the verge of tears. She wasn't beautiful the way Dagmar was, and she was too thin like someone who missed more meals than they ate. Although her face had been washed for the auction, her brown hair was in a matted braid and her clothes carried the filth of the streets on them.

"I just don't know how we're going to get home now."

"Let's worry about that tomorrow. Something might come up," Dagmar said quietly.

Sasha gave a glum, tired nod. He went over to the basin of water sitting on a small trestle table against the wall. Wringing out the excess of water from a washcloth, he carried it over to where Mother and the girl sat.

"Here. You can wash all that off your face." He handed it stiffly to Mother. She looked from the cloth to him and for a moment Sasha thought he saw a flicker of recognition in her eyes. She took the cloth and began to clean the paint from her face. "Do you know...Hey!" Sasha yelled as the girl's hand darted forward and pulled his knife free of its sheath at his side. His own hand clamped over her wrist just as she was swinging the blade toward his chest. The girl squealed and let the knife fall to the ground with a clatter. "You're trying to kill me? What is wrong with you?"

The girl's face went a sickly white as she looked from Sasha to the fallen knife and then back up at Sasha. With more speed than Sasha could have guessed possible, her free hand scooped up the knife. Instead of going for Sasha again, she brought it to her own throat. Sasha's other hand closed around her wrist again, pulling both it and the weapon away from her.

"Drop it," he ordered. She shook her head. Sasha squeezed her wrist harder until, with a yelp, she finally released it. Ready this time, Sasha picked it up and returned it safely to his side before she had the chance to recover. He stepped back watching as she hunched over, nursing her hurt wrist. "Do you understand what I'm saying?"

With obvious reluctance, the girl nodded. Her eyes glared up at Sasha.

"Good. If you try something like that again, you'll regret it. Understand? Now get away from me."

Again, she nodded. Her eyes dropped and she scooted back against the wall away from him.

Sasha turned his attention back to his mother. Her face, now clean from its adornment, bore evidence to the years of use. Although she was still recognizable, Sasha couldn't miss the lines that creased her once smooth skin nor could he ignore the sunken hollows in her cheeks or the dark circles that hung beneath her eyes or the deathly pallor that clung to her complexion. And she was thin. Not just the thin of someone who'd gone without food too often, but the sort of thin that came from wasting away.

"Are you hungry?" It seemed like a silly question to ask, but Sasha couldn't think of anything better. He was inexplicably shy and awkward with her, unsure of how to proceed. "You don't have to be afraid of me. You know who I am, don't you?"

Mother shook her head quickly. "You're my master."

"I'm your son," Sasha cried. "Don't you remember me? I'm Sasha." Mother's face clouded over with bewilderment and Sasha continued, "I came here to take you back with me. You'll be free there. You won't belong to anyone but yourself. You won't have to do anything for anyone else ever again. You'll be safe."

"Sasha," she whispered his name slowly, letting it linger on her thin, cracked lips. "Sasha?"

"Yes, it's me. I'm going to take you home and take care of you. Everything will be better."

Chapter 29

SASHA STARED OUT THE WINDOW at the streets below. Muddy puddles, remnants from yesterday's storm, dotted the road. After the wealth and order of Kaldura, this town appeared shabby and unkempt. Below the window, the last stragglers from the day's auction were making their way home.

Home.

Just watching everyone disperse reminded Sasha of the fact that they had no way home now. He wished he could take Dagmar's advice and worry about it tomorrow, but it nagged at him no matter how much he tried to push it away. There was something about Karu that made him want to get away as fast as he could. It was too much like home. And too much like Kaldura.

With a sigh, he turned back to the rest of the room. Mother lay asleep on the bed. It had taken him several minutes to convince her that he did, in fact, want her to rest on the bed. Even from across the room, he could hear her breathing. It was louder, more labored than it should have been, he thought. Most likely, that was the reason she'd been put up for sale. It wasn't uncommon for masters to sell off

weak or sickly slaves that could no longer maintain
their usefulness. Whatever the reason, her presence
at the auction was the only good thing that had
happened here. That, and Boris now seemed more
like himself, although, at the moment, Sasha was
having a hard time admitting that was a good thing.

"She's so thin," Dagmar broke the comfortable
silence. She was sitting on the bed next to Denise,
her hand absently stroking the older woman's hair.

"I know," Sasha said. "I couldn't get any more
food, though."

The last of his money had been parted with an
hour before in exchange for food.

"Something will work out."

"I don't know." Sasha sighed, turning to look out
the window one last time before joining Dagmar on
the bed. The brilliant pink and orange of the sunset
were fading into deep purple. "I'm going to go down
to the docks tomorrow morning and see if there's
anyone who'd be willing to let me work our way
across."

"You're going to work on a ship?" From anyone
else Sasha would have thought the question derisive,
but Dagmar asked it sincerely.

"I don't know what else to do. We can't stay here.
Even if I work here, staying in the inn like this, we'll
be spending the money as soon as it's made."

"But how are you going to work on a ship when
you get so seasick?"

"Maybe I won't this time. Look, I know it's not
the best idea, but I don't want to stay here."

"I know."

"It's not just those men and they're reason
enough to want to leave." Sasha hesitated. "You
know how, in Kaldura, we thought we were being
followed?"

"We were being followed."

"Before we knew. When Boris and I just
suspected it. I don't know why, but this place feels

the same way. Like there's something or someone watching us, waiting for us."

Boris, sitting behind Sasha's back, turned gray and shrank into himself, staring once more at nothing.

Dagmar was still thinking about Sasha's words when a girl's scream followed by a man's raucous laughter punctuated the air, coming through the wall from another room. Dagmar froze, the blood draining from her face.

"Sasha?" she whispered, then clamped a hand over her mouth as if she were going to be sick.

Sasha didn't say anything. There really wasn't anything to say. He shut his eyes, wishing he could shut out the sounds as the night around them descended into the after-auction orgy he'd forgotten all about. The noise was enough to rouse even Boris. Denise was the only one who remained undisturbed. Sasha stared at her while she slept through the chaos.

"Guess we're not getting any sleep tonight," he muttered, more to himself than anyone else.

Not that he was going to sleep anyway, after the girl Boris bought had tried to stab him. Remembering her now, he looked in her direction and found her sitting still against the wall, her face as pale as Dagmar's and her hands gripping the seams of the loose, tattered trousers she was wearing. Witnessing her fear made Sasha's anger at her attempt on his life dissipate some. He spoke to her, "What's your name?"

Face still ashen, she pressed her lips together and shook her head, her eyes fixed resolutely on the floor in front of her. Sasha gave up.

Sleepless hours went by, reminding Sasha a little of the night he'd spent listening to a wolf pack devour the bodies of his raiding party. As the night finally quieted, Sasha's eyes grew heavy. A single candle still burned on the small table and by its light Sasha could see Dagmar had finally fallen asleep, sitting up with her hand still resting on Denise's head. Even the nameless slave girl appeared to be sleeping. Boris was not, but that didn't exactly come as a surprise to Sasha. Sasha, sitting on the floor now near the door, leaned his head back against the wall and let his eyes close for just a second.

A soft creak in the floorboards dragged him out of his doze. For one drowsy moment, Sasha couldn't connect the sound with the motion. His brain came fully awake as another board groaned beneath the weight of someone. The candlelight was gone now, having burned completely down, but Sasha's eyes were accustomed to the dark. Without moving his head, he looked toward the source of the sound. The figure moving across the room was definitely not Boris.

"I couldn't care less if you ran out that door, but like it or not, you're safer in here than out there," Sasha whispered when the girl was near enough to reach the latch on the door.

She jumped and let out a tiny yelp of surprise. "And why should I care what you think?"

"So, you can talk. I was beginning to wonder," he answered wryly. "Well, to start with, I haven't torn your clothes off yet, so I'd say that counts for something."

"And I'm supposed to thank you for that?" This girl could have rivaled Boris for bitterness, Sasha thought as she spoke. Her words dripped with it.

"Like I said, I don't care if you run. I won't come after you. So, if you think your chances are better out there with men who haven't practiced a moment's worth of restraint all night, then be my guest."

"What do you want with me?"

"Nothing."

"You're making a game of me. Why?"

Sasha shook his head, although in the darkness the gesture was missed by the girl who still stood poised to run.

"Look, I didn't want you. I came here for one reason, and you weren't it. The only reason you're here is because my brother thought people were too suspicious and decided to buy you. So go, run. Then I can sleep without worrying about being stabbed."

He could see her hand hovering over the latch, undecided. A girl's muffled voice from beyond the wall, inarticulate and pleading, filled the silence. Her hand moved away from the latch, and she took a tentative step backward then another. Sasha could hear her breathing grow heavier and hitched.

Great, he thought, now she's going to start crying. It had been bad enough when Dagmar had cried earlier. Sasha didn't know what to do when a girl started crying. And despite her bitterness and the fact that she'd tried to stab him, Sasha couldn't help but feel a little sorry for her.

The girl sat down where she was and put her face in her hands, but no sound came from her. Sasha decided to try one more time.

"What's your name?"

"Kezi," her voice was muffled by her hands.

"How'd you end up there, in the auction?"

For a moment she didn't answer, and Sasha almost gave up waiting for one.

"I got caught," she whispered at last.

"Caught?"

"Out on the streets. If they catch you, they sell you."

"I don't understand. You're not allowed out?" Sasha was on the verge of deciding that this place had far stranger rules than any other.

"Not like that. I...my parents, they're not here...anymore," Kezi stumbled over her words with reluctance.

"So, you've been living out on the streets." Understanding dawned on Sasha. "What happened to your parents?"

"Sick. Died. Last year."

Sasha wasn't sure what to say to her and so he said nothing. He settled back against the wall again watching her.

"If you're not going to run, you might as well go back and try to get some sleep," he said at last. "Nothing's going to happen to you as long as you stay in here."

Chapter 30

IT WOULD TAKE A MIRACLE TO get us out of here, Sasha thought, scuffing his foot against the wooden pier beneath him and stifling a yawn. The sun was just rising, showering the docks, ships, and water in soft yellow hues. The pungent odor of fish mingled with the saltiness of the sea. The docks weren't as big as the ones in Bren and the ships that were moored there were crowded close to each. Sasha took his time walking. He was almost certain his request would be met with a no from everyone down here, but since he lacked any other ideas, he was determined to try.

Sasha paused, frowning. A feeling that was all too familiar, and that he had hoped he'd left behind, crept over him. Someone was staring at him. He started forward again, less certain this time. It had been bad enough when it happened in Kaldura, and he'd had Boris and Dagmar with him. Alone, he was a lot more vulnerable. Footsteps started on the wooden planks of the pier far behind him. They quickened, closing in on him. Trying to remain casual, Sasha slid his hand down to his knife, resting it on the hilt. He wasn't great when it came to using one, but he certainly intended to try.

"Sasha?" A voice from behind him called out and Sasha stiffened. "I thought that was you."

With relief, Sasha placed the voice and turned around. "Lawrence? What are you doing here?"

"I could ask you the same. You weren't there when we came by."

Sasha shook his head. "We didn't find her in time."

"But you did find her?"

"It's a long story."

Lawrence narrowed his eyes, studying Sasha, before glancing past him over his shoulder.

"You're in trouble, aren't you?"

"No. Yes. It's nothing." Pride forbade Sasha from asking this man what he'd come down here to ask.

"You know someone's watching you, right?" Lawrence's voice dropped.

"Huh?"

"Don't look, but he's standing back there. Has been since you showed up. He was coming towards you when I called out."

"I thought that was you." Sasha resisted the overwhelming urge to disregard Lawrence and look.

"So, what's the trouble?"

Sasha considered how much to tell Lawrence. Aside from his taking them to Sondaru, he didn't really know the captain. But he was being followed, again. And he had no money. Throwing aside caution, he explained in as few words as possible the situation they now found themselves in. Lawrence listened without interruption, every now and then looking over Sasha's shoulder.

"I came down here to find someone who would let me work our way across," he finished.

"You? Work on a ship?" Lawrence chuckled, shaking his head. "That might be hard to do when you're vomiting every time the ship hits a wave."

"Trust me, I know. I'll figure something else out."

"Or you could just ask for help? Maybe some generous soul will give it to you."

"I can't ask you..."

"We're loading supplies now. Planning to set sail in a couple hours when the tide comes in."

"You don't have to..."

"No, I don't. But I don't like the look of that man and I'd never forgive myself if I didn't."

"I'll pay you, when we get back."

Lawrence clapped his hand on Sasha's shoulder and, with a final glance behind them, started walking. "Come on. I'll help you get the others. We'll figure out the money once we're under way."

Grateful for the presence of someone else, Sasha led the way back to the inn. Everyone but Boris had been asleep when he left and, since it was still very early morning, he imagined they still were.

Reaching the door, Sasha unlocked the door and stepped inside. Boris, sitting in the far corner, looked up quickly at his entrance, a strange look passing over his face. Before Sasha could fully register it, the expression was gone, replaced by his vacant one. Sasha pushed it out of his mind. They had a way home, and even better, they were leaving within two hours. He hurried to where Dagmar was still sleeping.

"Dagmar, wake up."

She blinked and rubbed her eyes before sitting up. "What's going on?"

"We're leaving. Hurry!" Sasha ignored Dagmar's bewilderment and moved from her to Mother. Laying a gentle hand on her shoulder, he nudged her awake. "Mother, wake up."

Her blue eyes opened, and she stared at him. "Sasha?"

"Yes, it's me. Wake up now. We're going to leave. I'm going to take you to my home."

He slid his arm under her shoulders, noting once again how thin and bony they were, and helped her sit up. Then, pouring water from the pitcher into a cup, he helped her drink. A full night's sleep had done nothing to touch the dark shadows around her eyes.

"We'll get something to eat soon, but we need to go now."

As Sasha took care of his mother, Dagmar moved around the room, hurriedly repacking their things. The flurry of movements woke Kezi from where she had eventually fallen asleep in the corner. Sasha noticed her sitting up and realized he had no idea what he was going to do with her.

"We're leaving, Kezi," he started, unsure of how to go on. "I guess, if you want to, you can stay here or come. I don't care."

Kezi scowled, although the effect was somewhat lost by her sleepiness. "Is it where you are taking her? The place where you said she'll be free?"

"Yes."

Kezi didn't say anything more, but when they moved out of the room she followed.

It took them longer to reach the docks than it had taken Sasha that morning. Sasha kept his arm around his mother's shoulders, letting her lean against him. Too busy trying to keep her from collapsing, he missed when they passed the man who'd been following him. He missed Boris' eyes darting to the man's face and away again. He missed the sick fear in his brother's face.

The ship stood waiting near the end of the wharf, her brown hull bobbing gently in the green sea water.

"We'll get everything sorted when we've put to sea." Lawrence's normally easy-going tone was gone when he spoke quietly to Sasha as they boarded the ship. "I think we need to leave as quickly as possible."

Sasha nodded, helping his mother to a spot where she could sit out of the way while Lawrence and his crew cast off. He lowered her to the deck and sat down beside her. Her head rested against his shoulder and her labored breathing steadied a little. Sasha guessed that she was asleep again and that could only be a good thing.

"How is she?" Dagmar asked, coming up on the other side.

"She's alright. Tired and hungry, but alright."

"Sasha," Dagmar looked away, refusing to look Sasha in the eyes, "I don't have any idea why you didn't, and it really doesn't matter, but I just wanted you to know, especially after last night, that I am so thankful you didn't do that to me. You could have done whatever you liked with me, and you didn't. Thank you."

For several minutes, Denise's loud, ragged breathing was the only sound. Sasha couldn't come up with a suitable response for Dagmar, and she didn't seem to be looking for one. He couldn't explain everything that held him back. He let his own head rest against Mother's, the long night catching up with him.

"I'm going to go help Lawrence get something set up for her." Dagmar finally got to her feet. Before walking away, she turned and looked down at him, frowning. "Sasha, do you think Boris has been acting strange?"

"Ever since he showed up in Dival."

"No. There's something more, something he's hiding."

"Like what actually happened in Kaldura?"

Dagmar nodded. "He won't hardly talk to me anymore, but not because he can't. Because he won't. It's like he's choosing to hide."

Many hours later, Sasha emerged from the cabin his mother and the girls were sharing onto a darkened deck. He wasn't the only one plagued by seasickness. Mother refused to touch her food despite his pleading with her.

Swallowing down his own queasiness, Sasha made his way to the helm where Lawrence stood, his hands gripping whatever solid surface they could reach along the way.

"Ready to work?" Lawrence asked, a teasing smile tugging at the corners of his mouth.

"Just as soon as I can get my legs under me."

"I'm not holding out much hope for that. There are some people who aren't made to sail. You, my friend, are lucky enough to be one of those people."

"Thank you. I don't know what we would have done if you hadn't been there."

"You were lucky to see us there. I don't generally put in at Karu. Can't say I care much for the place. We wouldn't have been there at all if we hadn't needed to make repairs from a storm."

Sasha stared out over the dark gray water. The gentle lapping of the waves against the wooden sides as the ship glided through the water created an ambience of peace that was hard to ignore. They were going home. In only a couple of weeks he would be back in the now familiar woods. He would be telling everyone about their adventures, skimming over the bad parts of course. Ophelia would call him lucky and tell him his plans had been bad from the beginning, and he would laugh and argue that they had all worked out in the end.

"How is your mother? Did she get settled in alright?"

"She's seasick, but she'll be alright."

"Just seasick?"

"And she's worn out from everything. But honestly, she'll be fine."

"I hope so, Sasha. For your sake, I hope so," Lawrence spoke quietly, almost as if he did not wish to be heard.

"Why do you say that?" Sasha looked at him in alarm.

"It's hard to make a person live when they've given up wanting to."

Sasha recoiled, shaking his head in disbelief and denial. "No. No. That's not what it is. She's just tired and half starved. She'll get better. I'll make her better. She has to."

The next morning, when Sasha made his way to his mother's side, he was surprised to find her not only sitting up but eating.

"How are you feeling?" he asked, sitting down on the narrow cot next to her.

She shrank away from him for a moment while she studied him.

"Sasha?"

"Yes, it's me. You're better this morning, aren't you?"

"Sasha," she murmured his name again and he laid his arm over her shoulders and pulled her close to him, letting her lean her head against his shoulder. She'd held him the same way when he was little, and the gesture was familiar and comforting.

"She's eaten well this morning," Dagmar said when she came in. "I think she likes it here with us."

Sasha smiled. "I think so. Now we just have to get home. She'll like that even more."

Chapter 31

"SASHA? CAN YOU HEAR ME? Dagmar told me to tell you she needs you." Kezi's voice carried into the tiny cabin Sasha and Boris shared once again.

Sasha sat up and swung his feet onto the floor. His hands gripped the sides of the hammock.

"Tell her I'm coming," he said through a stifled yawn. He heard her feet moving away from the door and made himself stand up.

He crossed the swaying deck a little more easily now that they had been to sea for a few days. Yawning again and rubbing the sleep from his eyes, he pushed open the door to the girls' cabin, letting a rectangle of yellow lamplight escape out onto the dark deck.

"What is it?"

"I don't know, but something's wrong," Dagmar said.

Sasha moved across the narrow space to the bunk his mother lay on. Dagmar was sitting on the edge of it, a cup in her hands. He crouched down, taking one of Mother's hands in his own. They were cold. Deathly cold. And her breathing, always harder than it should be, rattled in her chest as she gasped for each breath. The thin skin of her eyelids was blue, the rest of her face a ghastly white.

"Mother?"

Denise's eyes fluttered open and shut several times before opening fully and coming to rest at last on Sasha. He tried to smile reassuringly, but that was hard to do over the lump of worry in his throat. Lawrence's words reverberated in his mind. He'd forgotten all about them in the last few days. Mother had eaten, she'd slept deeply, she'd started to look better, more alive. Until now. Until tonight.

"Sasha?" Mother's voice was a feeble whisper.

Her sunken chest fought to rise and fall with every breath. Her free hand reached for his face but flopped back on the bed before she could manage it.

"I'm here. I'm here, and I'm going to take care of you." He brought her hand up so that she could touch his face and she relaxed a little. He took the cup from Dagmar's hands and held it to her lips, "Here, try to drink something. You need it."

She drank a few sips but mostly it just spilled down her chin. Sasha set the cup aside and leaned back, watching her. Mother's eyes closed again, and her breathing took on a slow, shallow rhythm. It occurred to Sasha that she looked exactly the same sleeping as she did awake. Her face never changed. It wasn't like Boris who went through spells of listlessness that were interrupted by both moments of lucidity and anger. For Mother, there was nothing. No anger. No fear. No life. She wasn't anything more than a breathing shell of a human.

"How much longer 'til we get home?" Dagmar asked.

"A week, if we don't run into bad weather."

"That's a long time for her."

"I know, but she'll make it. She was getting better, she'll be alright. When we get there, I'll find a doctor in Bren. I'll stay there with her if I have to until she gets better."

Dagmar leaned forward, cupping her chin in her hands. "Have you talked to Boris at all?"

Sasha considered for a moment and then shook his head. "I haven't hardly even seen him since we came on board."

"I'm going to go out on the deck for a bit, if that's alright?"

"Of course, that's fine. Thank you for helping with her."

Dagmar's absence left him alone with Mother and Kezi, who had made herself as small as possible on her own bed. Sasha shifted to Mother's bed, letting her head lay on his lap, and watched her sleep, feeling the coldness that seeped from her body.

The long hours of night drug by. Sasha dozed off again, only to be awakened by Mother's stirring. He reached for the cup of water Dagmar had set down and, lifting her head up, held it to her mouth to drink. Mother turned away, letting the water spill and drinking none of it.

"Please drink it, Mother. You need it." Sasha found his voice breaking over the words but to no avail. At last, he gave up. His hand held hers as she grew restless.

"Sasha?" She murmured.

"It's me." The sound of his voice seemed to soothe her and so he kept talking. "You're going to be alright, you know. We're going to get to my new home, and I'll take care of you. You'll love living there. It's nothing like Aruuk. And I have friends there that you'll get to meet. I'm sure you'll like them. They're very kind. You know, I never thought I'd end up living somewhere away from Father. It's kind of a long story."

Her eyes shut again, and he kept talking, piecing together the course of his life since her absence. At first, he was conscious of the slight rise and fall of her chest with each breath, but soon he stopped paying attention to that. It wasn't until he finally reached the end of what he had to tell that he noticed the total silence, the stillness, in the room.

"Mother?" Sasha leaned forward, his hand tightening around her cold, limp one. "Mother?" No voice answered him, no weary eyes opened to meet his plea. "No. No, no, no. Mother, wake up. Wake up, please. You can't...you can't go. I only just got you back."

Chapter 32

*T*HE ROOM WAS HOT. *And dim. And stifling. Boris struggled to draw a single breath in. A thick cloth resting between his teeth and tied in place at the back of his head, prevented the panicked shout that welled up inside of him from escaping. He was on his knees, his hands secured behind him.*

And he wasn't alone.

"You know, I've missed our times together, Boris Gundarson. Haven't you?" The familiar voice came from behind him, and the sound of it set Boris' heart to pounding. He pulled against the rough rope binding his arms. "Now, I know you can't answer me just yet, but we'll get to that. First, allow me to explain where we are and then, perhaps, you'll give up your very futile efforts to escape. Kaldura is such an interesting city, isn't it? So full of secrets. But it's greatest secret is this. Did you have any idea that beneath this entire city runs an entire labyrinth. No? It's really quite impressive. From inside these tunnels and hidden rooms you can get anywhere in the city. You see, we are currently several stories beneath the surface, and

consequently, there is no one who will be able to hear anything that happens down here."

Although his eyes had adjusted to the darkness, Boris could not see the speaker. The man stood behind him. But Boris did not need to see to know. He continued to struggle against his bonds, his efforts growing more desperate as memories washed over him.

"Now, now. There really is nothing to be gained by all that," the thin voice continued. The sound of something rubbing against another surface came to Boris' ears and he cried into his gag as his arms were pulled up behind his back a little. "I want to talk to you, that's all." Again, the rope tightened, pulling his arms even higher, threatening the joints in his shoulders and elbows. Boris blinked back tears and bit down on the cloth in his mouth. "You know things that I and someone else you know would be very interested in hearing. So, what do you think? Are you ready to start?"

Boris stopped fighting. His teeth ground against his gag. His breath came heavily. How did he end up here? He tensed when a pair of hands touched his head. The knot digging into the back of his head and neck, holding his gag in place, loosened and fell away. Spitting the cloth out with it, Boris tried to draw in a much-needed deep breath. It only succeeded in sending a stabbing pain through his shoulders and into his chest. He gritted his teeth against the whimper that was wrung from him.

"Let's start off simple, shall we? Something both you and I know already. Who are you here with?"

"You already know," Boris said through clenched teeth.

"Yes, I do. But I think you should tell me. Don't you?" The man accompanied his words with another pull on the rope, wrenching Boris' arms ever higher. "You know how this works, Boris. You haven't forgotten, I'm sure, that none of this ends until I get what I want. Until you've broken."

Oh, Boris knew. He would never forget. He could never forget. He was still broken.

"My brother. I'm here with my brother."

The room was silent for a long minute. When a faint crackling sound broke the silence, Boris twisted against his bonds, trying to turn his head enough to look behind him. An orange light glowed from behind his back. He bit down on his lip, but panic was rising inside of his chest, threatening to burst out. The temptation to plead for mercy, for all of this to end flooded his mind, stealing away every other thought.

"I see you still remember how much you disliked fire. I personally find it very motivating as I think you did. Perhaps you should be a little more forthcoming. You and I both know that your brother isn't the only one you're traveling with, and I must insist on complete honesty. It might make all the difference. So, let's try again. Who are you here with?"

"My brother and his slave girl."

"She's not that anymore, is she?"

"No. He let her go. I don't know why." Boris let his head droop in defeat.

"That wasn't so hard, was it? Why are you here?"

Boris shook his head. "I can't tell you that."

"Of course, you can. I'm just going to have to make you want to. And we both know that I can do that."

"No. Please, no," the words slipped out unbidden, and Boris shook his head, denying the plea in them even as he spoke them. Pleading didn't do any good.

Footsteps approached him from behind, and then walked around. Boris didn't dare look up at the man he knew was now standing directly in front of him. He saw his booted feet on the floor in front of him. The man knelt down, and Boris saw the small knife in his hand, the blade glowing a soft red with heat. The man set it down on the floor and began pulling open Boris' shirt.

"No, no, no. Don't do this. Please," Boris moaned, trying to pull back away from him.

"You could always just answer my question." The man's voice was devoid of any sympathy or remorse as he picked the knife up again and brought it up to Boris' bare skin. "Why are you here?"

Boris bit off the scream that rose in his throat as the heat of the blade touched his body. The man drew it across his chest, leaving a cauterized, blistering cut behind it. He pulled it back and moved to a different spot. It was his indifference, his complete lack of emotion that was the hardest to bear. Boris stifled another scream as the heat tore into his flesh. Then it was moving to a different spot.

"No, no, no, no. Stop. I'll tell you," Boris cried out. "I'll tell you."

He pulled it away, his impassive eyes studying Boris' face. "Go on."

"He's here for his sister." Boris' voice broke with shame. "He's trying to find his sister."

"Very good. That was easy, wasn't it, Boris? And what will he do after he finds his sister?"

"Don't. Don't ask me that."

Again, the knife came up. Again, Boris tried to smother the inevitable cry of pain. Tears sprung to his eyes.

It was no good.

He couldn't fight this man.

He couldn't resist. He'd tried. He'd spent more than a month trying and it had just left him crazy and broken. A whimper escaped his closed lips.

"He'll look for his mother." Boris already knew what the next question would be.

"Where?"

Boris shut his eyes. Sasha would kill him if he told. This man might kill him if he didn't. Chances were good that he wasn't going to see Sasha again, anyway. Still, he kept his mouth closed. He shook his head. Once, twice, three times the man cut into him with the hot knife. By the third time Boris was trembling with the effort to remain quiet, his jaw quivering at the enormous strength it took to keep it closed. Searing pain sprouted up from the places on his chest and stomach where the knife had done its work.

"You know you can't keep this up forever. You'll tire of the pain eventually. You always do. Why put yourself through so much? Do you think Sasha will think more of you for it? He already hates you. You're nothing but a burden to him. You gain nothing by hiding this for him."

The knife was gone and for a second Boris gasped in relief, he let the tension in his muscles release. It was short lived. The tension on the rope increased again and there was no amount of willpower that could hold back the scream of agony as his shoulders were twisted to the breaking point.

Maybe the man was right. Maybe there wasn't any point in refusing him. Sasha did despise him. He despised what Boris had become. He despised the burden of caring for him. Boris knew all that.

"Where?"

"Karu," Boris whispered. It didn't matter what Sasha would think of him. All that mattered was the pain. The pain that gave him nightmares and stole his mind. He had to stop the pain. He couldn't' live with the pain.

The man let the rope ease up a little, and Boris let out a shaky breath. It was worth it. Getting rid of even a fraction of the pain was worth anything.

The man had more questions for him, but Boris could no longer refuse him. His willpower was gone. His defiance spent. With each answer, he sank further and further into a black hole of despair. The man wrung information freely from him until there was no more to be had.

"Well, this has been a very productive time, Boris. Far better than our times in Dorsten, although I do miss the variety of motivations we had available to us there, don't you? Now, would you like to go back to your brother?"

"Yes."

"Ask me," the man said, his tone mocking, reminding Boris of the untold humiliations he'd put him through before. It had taken him a while in Dorsten to get Boris to the point where he'd ask for something.

Boris hesitated only a second this time. "Can I go back to Sasha now? Please?"

"Not so much pride or stubbornness left in you now, is there? Pity, really. You were so full of it when I first met you. Who would have thought you would become this?" The man's icy chuckle filled the room. "I will take you back where he can find you, if he is bothering to look for you. But there is something you must do for me."

"What? I'll do anything, just take me back to him."

"Your father still wants to use you, Boris." Boris' blood ran cold at the mention of Father. "He and I are both very interested in your brother. Help us, and I will set you free for now."

Boris stared across the black expanse of water. The waves beat a peaceful rhythm on the sides of the boat, but it was insufficient to drown out the sound of Boris' own thoughts. The solace of nothingness beckoned to him. He could slip away, lose himself in it, and no one would think anything of it. It was so easy. And he was so tired. Fighting the numbness was exhausting.

"Can I sit?" Boris jumped a little at Dagmar's voice behind him. She lowered herself next to him. "I'm sorry, I didn't mean to startle you."

The temptation to withdraw was almost overwhelming. He stared at her, torn between saying something or nothing.

"Don't. You don't have to hide. Not from me," Dagmar said, tilting her head a little as she watched him. "You know, I'm worried she's not going to make it."

Dagmar's deliberate attempt to talk about something other than him made Boris' mind up.

"Sasha's mother?"

Dagmar nodded. "She doesn't want to live. But I can't tell him that. He has his heart set on getting her home and making her better. There's just some things that can't be made better and he doesn't know that yet."

Boris stared down at his hands. Dagmar wasn't the only one who had something they couldn't tell Sasha. If Dagmar noticed the sudden change in his demeanor, she made no mention of it. In fact, she didn't say anything at all, just leaned against the deck rail watching the moon on the water. It was her silence that finally prompted Boris to speak.

"There's something he should know. But I can't tell him, either."

"What do you mean?" Dagmar pulled her eyes away from the sea long enough to study him.

"No. I can't. If he finds out, he'll kill me."

"I don't think he'd do that," Dagmar said slowly.

"You don't know what I did."

"Boris, what are you talking about?"

Again, the temptation to retreat came. He could shut down, go silent, stare vacantly at nothing, and Dagmar would eventually go away. He shook his head, trying to rid it of the thought.

"It's something that happened in Kaldura, isn't it?" Her voice was gentle, coaxing. It carried none of the harshness or judgment that was always in Sasha's when he asked about it.

Boris nodded, holding his head between his hands.

"Boris, Sasha might get angry with you, but he won't hurt you and he won't even stay angry. He never does."

"He hates me already. If he found out that I'm the one who told..."

"Told what?"

Boris groaned and moved his hands to cover his face entirely. "Everything. I had to. I had to make the pain stop."

"Boris," Dagmar grabbed his hands and pulled them away, compelling him look at her, "what did you tell and who?"

"I told him where we were going and why. I just wanted the pain to stop. I didn't want to hurt anyone. I didn't want to get Sasha in trouble. I just had to make it stop. I couldn't take it. But he'll never believe that. He'll... he'll..." Boris stammered over the words, "he'll want to kill me. And I'll deserve it."

"The man following us? Sasha said he was in Karu too." Boris nodded, and Dagmar continued, "But nothing happened. We're all fine and we're going to be home soon. I'm sure if you told Sasha what happened, he would understand. He really doesn't hate you."

"I can't. You can, if you want. But I can't. I can't even look at him knowing what I did. He ought to hate me. I wasn't strong enough."

"It's not my secret to tell. And you don't think it would really make it any better coming from me, do you? You're going to go back and live with him. That's going to be kind of hard if you just keep it secret, don't you think?"

"I guess, but I still can't. I betrayed us. I was weak. He won't see anything but that."

"Maybe. But I don't think so. I mean, he does know what it's like to be tortured. You know that, don't you?"

They sat in silence for some time, Boris considering Dagmar's words. She was right about one thing. The Sasha who had beaten him at

Father's bidding wasn't the same one he knew now. There had been plenty of times since Boris' arrival into Sasha's life in Dival that his brother had cause to be angry and annoyed with him. But never, not even once, had Sasha acted on that anger. Sasha had never hit him, had never even threatened to. The most he'd done was raise his voice or disappear for hours, inevitably returning in a better mood. For someone steeped in the violence of Aruuk, it was remarkable.

But Boris hadn't told Dagmar the worst of what he'd done - what he was doing. And there would be no forgiving that, he knew. He might be able to work up the courage to confess some of his betrayal to Sasha, but never all of it. Never what he still had to do. It was unforgivable, and he hated himself for being too weak to not be a part of it.

Eventually Dagmar got up and left him to his thoughts. The sky was softening to gray when he noticed that Sasha was sitting on the deck at the other end of the ship. Lawrence was with him and the two were clearly talking. Boris watched, trying to make up his mind. He wanted to believe Dagmar. More than that, he wanted to do what she thought he ought to. Lawrence was straightening up now and getting ready to move away. Boris watched in curiosity and growing apprehension as the captain rested his hand on his brother's shoulder for a moment before walking away.

Boris twisted his hands together as he watched his brother. Dagmar made it sound so easy. Was it really possible that Sasha wouldn't hate him? He couldn't make himself believe it.

Getting up stiffly after having spent the entire night in the same position, he crossed the deck toward Sasha. His brother did not appear to hear him come up and Boris stood unsure for several seconds.

Taking a deep breath, he spoke, "Sasha, there's something I need to talk to you about."

"Not now, Boris. Not now."

Boris recoiled, not from the anger in Sasha's voice, but at the sorrow in it. He had seen Sasha be many things - grieving wasn't one of them. He retreated once more.

Chapter 33

FAILED. THE WORD POUNDED through Sasha's head as he watched her body disappear beneath the waves. Everything he'd set out to do had ended in failure. The only thing he had to show for his entire journey was a very bitter, frightened girl who had tried to kill him and who he wasn't remotely interested in keeping around. Agathe chose to stay, and Mother was dead. And the failure left him so empty and tired that Sasha could not even work up the sadness he knew he ought to feel. He hated the looks of sympathy the others thought they owed him. He hated the way everyone moved around him, careful not to disturb his grief. But more than anything, he hated himself.

For the failure.

For the emptiness.

For the desperate, consuming desire to just get home and put all of it behind him.

He was making his way back to his cabin when he noticed Boris sitting alone. Boris had wanted to talk to him, he remembered. He hesitated by his door, debating. He did not want to talk to Boris. He did not want to talk to anyone. He'd already told Dagmar that he just wanted to be left alone. Turning away from his brother he went inside. The darkness was welcoming. The quiet, a relief.

Laying back on his bed, staring up at the low wooden ceiling, Sasha tried to rest. The day went wearily by, and night came. Then it was day again, and Sasha was no more rested than when he first lay down. A knock on his door finally roused him from his stupor.

"Who is it?" Even his voice was empty as he called out.

"Dagmar. I brought something for you to eat."

"I'm not really hungry."

"But you haven't eaten anything in two days."

More to get Dagmar to leave him alone than anything else, Sasha relented and opened the door. She stepped inside and put the bowl of food into his hands.

"Are you alright?"

"I'm fine," Sasha answered shortly. And he was. He didn't feel anything at all. It was like someone carved everything out of him leaving him hollow.

"I'm so sorry. I wish there was something I could have done."

Which Sasha thought was a ridiculous thing for her to say because she had done more than he could have imagined her doing, but he couldn't say that. He couldn't say much of anything, because every time he tried a lump would choke him up and he couldn't get past the first few words. So, all he said was, "I know."

When she left again, Sasha set the food aside and went back to his bed. After about an hour or so, the smell of the food finally enticed him to eat some of it.

For days, Sasha spent most of his time in the cabin. The few times he went out, he tried to avoid the others that he shared the ship with. But there was one day when the shout of land in sight drove him from his isolation and he joined the others on deck. It was near evening and the outline of Bren was just visible on the horizon, wreathed in a light mist.

"We'll put in tonight and unload in the morning," Lawrence announced to everyone standing on the rail.

The idea of waiting an entire night was suddenly unbearable to Sasha. He wanted to get home. He needed the familiarity of it. He craved the lowly structure with a desperation he hadn't thought possible. He remained on the deck, watching as the shore lamps drew ever closer, guiding the ship in as the sun went down. After some time, he realized that he was not alone.

Only a couple feet away, Boris stood as well. He wasn't watching the approaching coastline, though. Sasha looked over to see his brother staring at him. Boris looked like he wanted to speak, and Sasha almost turned and walked away. He didn't feel like talking to anyone. There was some pleading in his brother's eyes that he could not ignore, though. He watched as Boris wrung his hands together, trying to force himself to speak.

"I'm sorry about what happened to your mother," Boris finally managed to get out.

Sasha nodded his acknowledgement of the condolence. He'd run out of things to say in response. Words just weren't adequate for a lot of things.

"What was it you needed to tell me that night?" Sasha asked after a few minutes had gone by.

Boris hesitated. "Nothing. I forgot it," he mumbled.

Sasha studied Boris in the fading light. There was something Boris wasn't telling him. But all at once, Sasha knew it didn't matter. He'd failed at everything he'd set out to do, but he still had his brother. And at the moment there was nothing more Sasha wanted then to keep his mad wreck of a brother. If he was to be the only person Sasha had in the world then he needed to make the best of it.

"You know, I don't really care what happened in Kaldura. I'm just glad we got you back safely."

"Really?"

"Really. I mean, it's hard enough going home like this. I can't imagine if I had to go home without you too." Sasha sighed. "I don't know how I'm going to answer everyone's questions when we do get home. They'll want to know everything that happened."

"They'll understand."

"I know. I just failed so badly. Kezi's the only thing we're bringing home, and she tried to kill me. I don't even know what we're going to do with her, to be honest. And I don't know what Hamo will say when he finds out I bought a slave girl."

Morning came and Kezi solved their problem of what to do with her by herself. They no sooner came ashore when she took off, sprinting down a crowded street and disappearing around a corner. Sasha watched her go but didn't give chase. He just couldn't make himself care enough. Besides, she was probably safer out on the streets here in Bren then she was in Karu, Sasha thought.

Walking through the town was a small comfort of its own. Bren did not have the glamorous heights of Kaldura nor the lawless rabble of Karu.

"Maybe we could see Meri while we're here?" Dagmar suggested.

Sasha shook his head. He was ready to be home, but he was not ready to tell anyone what happened. He would happily put that off for another day or two if he possibly could. And of all the people to tell first, Meredith would have been his last choice. Hamo probably, or Ophelia maybe, but not Meredith.

Chapter 34

THE EVENING AIR WAS CRISP with the lateness of the season. Lights still showed out of the windows of the house as they approached. Now that they were this close, Sasha decided that he could wait at least another day to talk to anyone. When they reached the front steps, he stopped.

"Aren't you coming in?" Dagmar asked when she noticed that neither he nor Boris followed her.

"I think I just want to get home. I'll come by tomorrow, probably."

Dagmar nodded and opened the door. Sasha heard the chorus of greetings as he walked away, certain he'd made the right choice. There was no way he could face all that right now. They would ask questions, they'd want stories, they'd offer sympathy. None of those were things he could even contemplate bearing.

The little cabin was dark and cold, the air inside musty after standing unused for so many weeks. Sasha set his things down inside and went outside to get an armload of firewood. The pile was getting low, he noticed. For once, the idea of chopping wood wasn't dreaded. He looked forward to having

something to occupy his time. With that thought
came the realization that he had absolutely no other
plans. What he was going to do with himself now
that he was home was entirely undecided. Maybe it
was time for him to throw himself into learning a
trade. It certainly had its appeal.

Dew lay heavy on the ground when Sasha stepped
outside early the next morning. Boris was actually
asleep, and Sasha shut the door quietly behind him
so as not to disturb his brother. He ought to be
heading over to Hamo's and getting it over with, but
instead his steps led him toward the creek. The
summer heat had shrunk it to a trickle. He followed
it, all the way up to the little falls. The water still
gurgled merrily over the rocks and splashed against
them as it ran down. Sasha found a rock that was
mostly dry and covered with moss and sat down on
it. In the silence, he tried to collect his thoughts, but
they refused to cooperate. He had to do something.
He couldn't spend his days listlessly staring at
nothing the way Boris did.

A branch snapped behind him and Sasha turned
to see Ophelia standing behind him. Sasha realized
he'd been hoping all along that she would show up
here. Somehow, it was easier to talk out here, alone
with her, surrounded by the shelter of the forest.
Without a word, she came and sat down next to him.

"I didn't bring them back."

"I know."

"Dagmar?"

Phelie nodded. "Are you alright?"

"I'm fine." Sasha sighed. "I just hate that I
failed."

"But you didn't."

"I was going to bring them home. I didn't do that.
I couldn't do that. Agathe still belongs to that man
and Mother's gone."

"You gave your sister a choice, Sasha. You can't
be mad at her if she didn't choose what you wanted."

"It's a wasted choice. She'll never have any say in her son's life. He'll grow up exactly the way her master wants him to."

"But he'll live." Ophelia leaned forward, cupping her chin in the palm of her hand. "I don't know, Sasha. I might have decided the same."

"Really? Even if it meant giving up your only chance at being free?"

"I might. If it was my own child. Love's weird like that. I mean, just think of what Father was willing to risk trying to get us back."

"I guess." Sasha peeled a piece of moss off the rock and began picking it apart. "I just wish she would have let me try to get them both out. It would have been really fun to have a nephew, you know? I've never had a family like that before."

"Did you actually have a plan for getting them out?"

"A great plan." Sasha smiled a little for the first time in days and it eased the ache inside him. "But I'm not going to tell you because you'll call it terrible."

"Only because it is. So, tell me all about it."

"My plan, or the whole trip?"

"The whole trip. Unless it's too hard for you."

"You already know the hardest parts." Sasha sighed, staring out over the creek and into the deep woods beyond it. "You know, I don't even miss her the way I think I should. She was taken away when I was little, and I really never even got a chance to know her. And the few days we had after I bought her, she wasn't really with it. I thought she was getting better. She started to. And then she wasn't."

"Dagmar said she liked it when you were with her."

Sasha nodded, remembering how peacefully she had passed in his arms. There was some comfort in that at least. Pulling up another piece of moss to ruthlessly shred, he started telling her about their trip. Ophelia listened quietly until he told of their mysterious follower.

"Wait. So, you had someone you didn't know following you through a strange city and you didn't leave?"

"Why would we have left?"

"Um...I don't know. Maybe because it was dangerous." Ophelia stared at him, eyebrows raised in disbelief.

"Not that dangerous. Nothing happened. Quit looking at me like that. We were fine."

"Nothing? But you just told me that Boris disappeared for an entire day and was completely incoherent for days after you found him again. That's not nothing, Sasha. Did you ever figure out what happened to him?"

"No. I've asked him but he won't talk about it. He's been better though, ever since we got to Karu." Sasha went on to tell the rest of his story. By the end, Ophelia was shaking her head. "What?"

"So, this person followed you both places you went and that doesn't bother you? Don't you wonder how he found out where you were going? You're crazy."

"Yes, I guess. I hadn't really thought about how he knew about us at all. I have no idea who it could even be or how they found out where we were going to be. Whoever it is, we left them behind in Karu. I have Lawrence to thank for that."

"But you thought you'd left them behind in Kaldura too."

"I suppose, but I saw him standing on the docks as we pulled away." Sasha brushed away the bits of moss covering his trousers. "What did I miss here?"

"Aunt Taliea is going to have a baby and Meredith is coming home to visit soon and she's bringing someone with her."

"Who?" Sasha had a feeling he already knew the answer before Ophelia spoke, and he didn't particularly like it.

"Karl. He's the one who ran away with us."

"I know who he is. I met him when we were in Bren getting ready to leave."

"Well, technically, you met him before that. Anyway, Father's bringing them home as soon as he's done with Council meetings."

"He's not here?"

"No. Hasn't been for two weeks."

"Oh. I didn't know that." Sasha's face fell a little. He'd just about made up his mind to ask Hamo today if he could start learning iron work. He needed something to keep him busy and take his mind off of everything.

"He'll be back in a day or two probably." Ophelia noticed the change that came over him. She added with a grin, "And then we have to put up with Karl until he goes back."

"You don't like him?"

"He's a little bit annoying. He was when we ran away too. Only Meri could see it then and she doesn't now. She's crazy about him now."

They sat in comfortable silence for a few minutes.

"So, what are you going to do now?" Ophelia quietly asked at last.

"Learn a trade. Figure out how to get along with Boris, I guess. At least, until I get another better idea."

"I think that might be the best plan you've had yet. There's nothing wrong with just living, you know. Not doing anything big or important. Just living."

"It's kind of boring."

"Boring is nice and safe." Phelie laughed. "I should really get back before Mother misses me. You know, you can come by and visit anytime. And you can bring your brother. You don't have to hide him from us."

"I know." Sasha got to his feet and held out a hand to help Ophelia up.

"We're all really sorry about what happened with your mother, but if you don't want to talk about it, I'll tell the others."

"I'd like that. Thank you."

They walked together until the path diverged. Sasha watched as Ophelia disappeared into the woods. A shiver of apprehension came over as he sensed the presence of another person in the woods with him. He opened his mouth to call out to Ophelia to wait for him, but she was gone already.

Scanning the trees around him, he noticed nothing out of the ordinary. The birds were still twittering. The leaves were still rustling in the cool breeze. The scurrying squirrels still scampered up and down trees. Sasha stood a moment longer then smiled to himself. All this talk of someone following them had made him paranoid. He'd be as bad as Boris if he wasn't careful.

Returning home again, Sasha surveyed the dwindled pile of wood along the side of the cabin. He didn't want to spend the next few hours chopping wood, but he needed to spend them doing something and the wood needed to be split. Boris was, amazingly, still asleep when he stuck his head inside to check and Sasha decided it was best to leave him that way. He couldn't remember the last time his brother slept so long.

Gripping the smooth wooden handle of the ax, he selected a large log and set it up on the old tree stump. The ax whistled as it sliced through the air and bit into the log. As many times as he'd done this now, Sasha would have thought he'd gotten better. Jerking on the ax to free it, he stepped back. Out of the corner of his eye, he caught sight of a movement.

"You're up finally," he said, turning to see Boris standing at the corner of the cabin. "Don't suppose you want to take a turn at this?"

Sasha said it half joking, but Boris shrugged and came over. He held out his hand and Sasha happily relinquished the ax to him. Sitting back against the cabin, he watched as Boris swung the tool with a good deal more competency than he had ever been able to manage.

"When did you get so good at that?"

"During my sentence. I got good at a lot of things." Boris paused to catch his breath. "You were gone this morning."

"Yes. I thought you were still asleep, and I wanted to get out."

"You've been out. We only just got back." Boris shook his head in bewilderment as he went back to work. "You should be careful."

"Of what, exactly?" Sasha thought back to the moment in the woods when something was off. There was no way Boris could know about that. Besides, he'd already decided it was nothing.

"I," Boris paused as he brought the ax up, "can't say. You should just be careful."

"There you go again with your senseless warnings." Sasha gave him a quizzical smile. "Whatever was going on back there in Kaldura and Karu, it's past. It's over. I saw the man standing on the docks as we pulled away, I know we left him behind."

Boris didn't answer, he just nodded. But the troubled shadow over his face didn't leave. For the next hour neither spoke. Boris continued his task and Sasha moved to stack the freshly cut wood.

"Are you going over to your friends today?" Boris said as he set the ax down and started back toward the cabin door.

"Not today. Hamo's not even there right now. Probably tomorrow or the day after."

"You're planning on leaving me behind, aren't you? You still don't want me around them."

Sasha winced at the accusation of his brother's question. He couldn't say what he was thinking. He couldn't say that he didn't want Boris around his friends because his brother wasn't in control of himself and watching him slip away into whatever hole he lived in was painful and embarrassing.

"I'll take you with me, if you want," he said at last.

"You will?"

"I will." Sasha turned away. The look of gratitude on his brother's face was almost painful.

"Thank you," Boris whispered as Sasha walked away.

Chapter 35

SASHA LAY AWAKE IN THE darkness. Boris had been asleep, again. Sasha couldn't remember the last time his brother had slept two nights in a row. Of course, the only reason Sasha was awake now was because Boris' sleep had been interrupted by a nightmare. His brother was now sitting out on the front steps. For a few more minutes, he tried to go back to sleep but finally gave it up and tossed his blankets off.

A few minutes later, a bright fire came to life in the hearth and Sasha sat back on his heels watching it. He looked around the single room that they shared, and his eyes fell on his bow and quiver of arrows in the corner. Picking them up, he pulled the door open and sat down next to his brother.

"Hey," he whispered, but Boris didn't turn to him. "I was just thinking. Maybe we could go hunting today. You know, like old times. If you want to, of course."

Sasha almost gave up waiting for Boris to answer. He could see his brother's hand opening and closing into a fist again and again.

"I would like that," he said at last, slowly.

"Of course, I only have one bow. But we could take turns and it would be fun."

Boris nodded.

"I'll go get ready," Sasha said, turning to go back inside.

Boris sat for another moment, his hand clenched tightly around a small, crumpled square of paper. With a groan, he brought his hands up to his face. He couldn't do what they were asking of him. Not now. Not when Sasha was trying so hard. But failure, failure wasn't an option, was it? Failure meant more pain, and Boris couldn't bear the thought of more pain.

Nestled hidden inside a thicket of bushes surrounding an old, fallen tree, they sat waiting. The creek ran by only a few yards away, its noise masking any slight sound they might have made. In the predawn gray, it was difficult to make anything out, but it wasn't long before the nighttime sounds of the woods gave way to the cheerier noise of the day. Sasha brushed his fingers along the fletching of the arrow knocked on his bowstring.

Sitting here with his brother, he could almost forget the events that had pulled them so far apart in the first place. It was almost like being back in Aruuk, hiding in their favorite hunting spot. It was comfortable.

As the sun rose and dried the heavy layer of dew that covered the ground, Sasha kept his eyes on the creek, waiting for an animal to cross his path.

"You know, you were the reason they hurt me," Boris said softly, taking Sasha by surprise and destroying any chance of an animal coming close.

"I know. I'm sorry."

"No. You don't understand. I wasn't done. You're the reason they kept me alive, too."

Sasha turned a curious eye to his brother, but Boris wasn't looking at him. He was staring down, his left hand fiddling with the iron band on his arm, clearly troubled.

"When I was captured, it wasn't so bad at first. There were quite a few of us. They didn't do anything to us other than disarm us. For two, three days nothing happened. And then," Boris swallowed hard, his hand twisting the band around and around, and paused a moment before going on, "then, he came."

Sasha did not bother asking who his brother was talking about. There was only one man responsible for what Boris had been put through.

"He went from one man to another, talking to them. Most of them he had killed right then and there - it was awful, but a few, a few he left alive. When he came to me, he asked why he should let me live. And I was scared. I didn't want to die. I told him the only thing I thought he might want to hear - that I was your brother and that I had saved your life. I thought you were with them, that you were on their side, that they were your friends. And I thought it worked. He didn't kill me. He just looked really happy about it, actually."

Sasha shifted uncomfortably, a sick feeling creeping over him. He could imagine the look on Lord Bayner's face when Boris made his plea. He could imagine the smug, satisfied smile on his thin lips, the cold gleam of hatred in his eyes. Knowing that Boris was tortured because of him was bad enough. Knowing that he had revealed his connection to Sasha in the hopes of being saved made it worse.

"For the first few days they didn't do anything with me, just locked me up by myself in the dungeon. No one came to see me. No one spoke to me. And then, one day, it started." Boris let out a deep, shuddering breath. "They asked me questions at first, and I didn't answer them. But the pain just got worse and worse, and I couldn't take it anymore. I told them what they wanted to know. I thought it would make them stop. I thought it would end. But it didn't. After that, he just did it because he wanted to, because of you."

"I'm sorry," Sasha repeated, sensing the inadequacy of the words as he spoke them.

"For more than a month, he kept at it. He came up with new things to do, new ways to hurt me. And he always reminded me that it should have been you, that it was really you he wanted to hurt. And then it was over. They stopped coming for me. They stopped doing anything at all with me. And I thought maybe he had finally decided to let me die, and I was glad. That's when they brought me here."

Sasha waited, but Boris had no more to say.

"Why are you telling me all this now? I mean, I'm glad you did. But I've asked you before and you wouldn't talk about it."

"Sasha," for the first time, Boris looked up and held Sasha's gaze, "If something happens..."

"Boris, nothing is going to happen. We've already talked about this." Sasha's voice held a hint of frustration at his brother's fears. They were bordering on insanity. Then again, so was his brother.

"Please, just let me finish," Boris pleaded. Sasha acknowledged his request with a nod. "If something happens, and it...well, it might, I don't want you to hate me. I don't want you to think I was weak. I tried. I want you to know that I tried as hard as I could. I tried for as long as I could. And whatever might happen, I don't want to die at his hand."

"Lord Bayner?" Sasha's confusion was growing with every word Boris spoke. "Why would he be trying to kill you? He doesn't even know where you are. I doubt he'd be very welcome here in Dival, anyway."

Boris started to speak but changed his mind. He stared out into the trees. By the agitation still on his face, Sasha guessed his own words hadn't helped. He wasn't sure what would. Either way, Boris' fear had robbed the morning of its comfortable nostalgia.

Sasha tried to turn his focus back to watching for game, but his mind refused to let go of Boris' words.

"I don't know what you're afraid of happening, but I won't hate you. I couldn't. I know what it's like to be tortured. I didn't hold out very well either, and they only had me for a week. But I'm not going to let anything happen. I promise." Sasha realized as he spoke just how much he meant the words. Whatever had happened between them, Boris was his brother. The only real family he had left.

Nearly a week later, Sasha still couldn't shake the premonition that Boris' words had caused. In need of a distraction, he decided it was time to go over to Hamo's. And since he'd promised him, Boris was coming too.

"Are you sure they want me to come? They're not going to be upset that you're bringing me?" Boris asked once again.

Sasha bit back the sharp answer that was on the tip of his tongue. It had been days now, and Boris hadn't drifted off into one of his trances. In fact, it was the longest Sasha had seen him go without one. Sasha didn't want to push him into one now. For the first time since he'd seen Boris in Bren, Sasha could hope that his brother would one day go back to the way he used to.

"They don't mind. Honestly."

"Do you?"

"No. Besides, even if I did, Phelie told me to bring you sometimes, so now she can't say I don't."

"Do you always listen to her?"

"No." Sasha shook his head, laughing.

The house came into view and put an end to a discussion Sasha really didn't have any interest in continuing.

"I should warn you, though," Sasha stopped before they got to the door, "there is someone here who can't stand me, and probably not you either."

Boris turned to him, bewildered.

"He's one of the ones taken on the raid, and well, he blames us."

"We did help." Boris shrugged.

"We did. And that's why he doesn't like us. He does like Meri, though. That's why he's here."

"The way you like Phelie?"

"What? No, nothing like. Phelie's just a friend."

Boris shrugged again and Sasha hurried to the door. He paused before knocking. He hadn't been here since he'd left in the spring. The weight of his failure came rushing back. Hopefully, Ophelia had done what she said and told them that he did not want to talk about it.

At the sight of Sasha standing in the doorway, little Drogo squealed with delight and toddled over as fast as his little legs could carry him.

"Sasa!" Sasha smiled.

In his months away Drogo still hadn't learned how to say his name correctly. Prying him off his legs and swinging him into the air brought a pang of remembrance. If only he had convinced Agathe to escape with her son, he might be doing this with his real nephew. Although now that he thought about it, he had no idea how old the boy was and hadn't thought to ask at the time. Not that it mattered. Agathe made her choice, even if it was a choice he didn't understand.

As the initial excitement of their arrival wore off, Sasha glanced around the room, searching for Hamo but failing to see him.

"Wait here." He told Boris and went back out toward the barn.

He found Hamo filling a feed trough for the horses.

"We're back," Sasha announced needlessly.

"Really? I would never have guessed." Hamo glanced up long enough to smile. "I'm sorry about what happened."

"They told you already?"

"Dagmar and Phelie did. Said you didn't really want to talk about it."

"I don't. I just wish I could have made things turn out differently." He kicked a loosened board on a stall. "You know, I shouldn't have given Agathe the choice. I should've, I don't know, bought her or something and then she would have had to come with me. And Mother. If I could have been there sooner, maybe she wouldn't have wanted to die. Lawrence said that was what was wrong with her. That she was tired of living."

"She died free."

"Does that matter?"

"Dagmar said she died peacefully in your arms. Do you think she could have had a better end somewhere else?"

"I guess not. I just wanted so badly to bring her here and to show her that it could be different, that I could be different."

"Sure you don't want to talk about it?"

Sasha laughed a little. "Just this. I don't want everyone asking questions."

"Well, I think tonight, most of the questions will be for Karl. Do you remember him?" They started back toward the house together.

"Oh, I remember. So does he. We already met again."

"And get along well?" Hamo asked, smiling again.

"Not really." Sasha smiled as well. "I brought Boris with me tonight. He didn't want to be left alone."

"How is he?"

"Better. I think." Sasha's smile faded as he remembered their talk in the woods. Although Boris had not been lost for hours at a time staring into empty space, he had clearly remained bothered even after Sasha's assurances. "He's got some crazy idea that Lord Bayner's going to come and do something to him, but other than that, he's better. I think it might actually have helped taking him with us."

240

"Lord Bayner retired to his estate on the far side of Dorsten. I don't think he'll be coming after anyone."

"That's what I've told him. I think it's just because of all his nightmares."

When they reached the house, Sasha stopped.

"There is something I wanted to talk to you about."

"Oh?"

"I want to start learning a trade. I want something to keep busy with."

"And you want me to teach you?"

"You said you would when I was strong enough. I'm pretty sure I'm as recovered as I'll ever be."

"You're sure iron work's the trade you want to learn? There are easier ones, although I'm probably a little prejudiced against it."

Sasha bit his lip, considering for a moment.

"Yes. It's what I want to learn."

Coming back into the house, Sasha looked around for Boris and was relieved to find him sitting at least close to everyone else and apparently following the conversation.

"If you want Meri to do something, you just have to tell her it's not allowed." Ophelia was laughing as she spoke, addressing her words to Karl, "Then she'll be sure to do it."

"That's not fair! I haven't done that since we were little," Meredith protested.

Ophelia looked over as Sasha moved to sit next to his brother. Rolling her eyes, she laughed again.

"When we were little? Like just the year before last. That got us into a lot of trouble, wouldn't you say?"

"It all worked out," Karl said. "If you hadn't been caught, none of us would have gotten away."

Ophelia considered his words for a minute. "I suppose that's one way to look at it. Although, I don't remember you feeling quite that way when we were running. I remember you complaining because we hadn't thought of a way to get food."

"Which was a good point. You hadn't. If your father hadn't already been there, we would probably have starved to death."

"If you go back far enough, technically, you could say it was the snake that rescued us," Meredith put in. "If it hadn't been for that, Father would never have found us."

"What snake?" Karl and Sasha asked together.

"You know, the snake." Meredith turned to Sasha. "The one I screamed over. And sort of sent you to the bottom of the ravine. You didn't know it was a snake?"

Sasha laughed, shaking his head. "You mean, my entire life got turned upside down because of a snake?"

"Well, it was a good thing in the end, even for you. You would never have ended up here if it hadn't been for that snake," Meredith said. "So, really, I think you should thank me for being afraid of the snake."

"Should I thank you for the broken ribs and the dislocated shoulder and the headaches too?" Sasha asked, half smiling. He hadn't intended to take any part in the conversation, but the way Karl was glaring at him now made him want to.

"Probably not," Meredith said, her face growing serious. "Were you actually hurt that bad?"

"Yes, I was."

"Oh. Sorry. I really didn't know that."

"I survived." Sasha shrugged and leaned back, content to have annoyed Karl for the moment.

Boris turned to him and whispered, "They talk a lot."

Sasha nodded.

They did talk a lot, and he was glad of it. It carried away the pain of his failure and distracted him. And tomorrow, he would start working in earnest. He'd fill up his days so that he didn't have to think about Mother or Agathe or Boris' strange worries. He'd finally settle down to making a life for himself here. Ophelia was right. There was something nice and comforting about a boring life. After the chaos of the last two years, Sasha was more than ready for the mundane.

Chapter 36

SASHA STRAIGHTENED UP AND RAN a hand across his stiff neck with a grimace. The hand came away wet and sticky with sweat.

"I'm never going to get this." He tossed away the misshapen lump of metal.

"It's been a month. No one gets it in a month," Hamo answered. "We're done for the day anyway."

Sasha didn't argue with that. The cool autumn air that awaited them outside offered relief from the sweltering heat of the forge. The leaves were a brilliant collage of warm colors and were beginning to carpet the ground in preparation for winter. His second winter away from Aruuk, he realized.

"Can I come home with you for a bit?"

"You know you can. Boris might wonder where you're at though."

Sasha didn't say anything. Boris was the reason he wanted to delay going back to his own cabin.

"What's going on?" Hamo stood watching him.

"Nothing," Sasha lied, and then thought better of it. "I'm not ready to go back just yet. I made him scared of me again this morning."

"How?"

"I yelled at him." After a month of getting along with his brother, Sasha's patience had snapped that morning. "He just doesn't really help with anything. Well, he does. He'll chop wood if I ask him to. But things like keeping the fire going, he just won't. And I told him all that this morning."

"I see."

"I know, you don't have to say it. I shouldn't have. And I'll make it up to him, just not right now."

Hamo nodded, as he finished smothering the flames, reducing the fire to nothing more than glowing embers. Sasha wiped away the sweat that was running down his face. The heat in this place was almost unbearable at times, he thought.

It was a short, but chilly ride to the house as the sun started to go down. Sasha guessed that the first heavy frost would be on the ground within the next couple of weeks. Without any great plans for the coming spring and summer, Sasha found himself looking forward to a quiet winter. Maybe by spring he would be at least somewhat proficient at his chosen trade. Right now, it felt like his progress was almost nonexistent.

Inside the house, the smell of dinner reminded Sasha of the other reason he wanted to come. He hated his own cooking, and Boris wouldn't get close enough to a fire to do any. Little Drogo crawled up onto his lap almost as soon as he was sitting.

"You know, you're never going to be allowed to leave again." Edith came in and smiled at the sight of the toddler. "He asked for you every day that you were gone."

"I don't even know why he likes me so much."

"Who knows? Children do strange things like that."

"Where's Phelie at?" Sasha glanced around the room but saw no sign of her.

"Taliea wanted to make some things for the baby and Ophelia and Dagmar went over to help her. She was planning on spending a couple of nights, I think."

"Oh." Sasha tried to keep the disappointment out of his voice. He'd been looking forward to talking to her. It was a guaranteed method of raising his own spirits.

Sasha couldn't quite enjoy supper as much as he would have liked. Knowing that Boris was home and most likely sitting in the dark since he wouldn't keep a fire going on his own dampened his own appetite. Even little Drogo's childish antics couldn't keep the weight of guilt off of him. After lingering as long as his conscience would let him, Sasha took his leave, dreading what he would have to do when he got home. Boris had been staring out at nothing again when he'd left that morning. As far as Sasha could guess, that was what his brother would be doing when he returned.

Night had already fallen on the short autumn day as Sasha guided his horse through the woods on the little path that led to home, rehearsing his apology in his head. He really hadn't meant to say what he did to Boris. He hadn't meant to call him worthless, or a burden. He hadn't meant to say that his life would have been so much easier without him. But he had said all that and there was no taking it back. The best he could do now was apologize and hope to draw Boris back out.

Sasha pulled his horse to an abrupt stop. He stared at the cabin ahead. He stared at the bright light flooding out of its windows into the dark forest around it. And he smiled with relief. Something he said must have gotten through to Boris. Boris had kept the fire going.

Kicking his horse on, he hurried up the last stretch of the path. It took only a few minutes to put his horse up and then he made his way to the door and pushed it open.

"Boris, I'm really..." Sasha's words turned to nothing, and his heart skipped a beat then beat wildly out of control.

"Hello, Sasha. It's been a long time."

"No. No, no. How?" Sasha cried, backing instinctively toward the open door.

"You're not wanting to leave already, Sasha? We've only just been reunited - father and son. You're not in that big of a hurry to get away from me, are you?" As his father spoke, Sasha felt the prick of a knife on the back of his neck, felt a firm hand on his arm pushing him forward again.

Twisting around just enough to catch sight of the person wielding it, Sasha paled.

"You? I don't understand."

"It's a simple matter of politics, Sasha. A lesson I would have taught you eventually, when the time was right. You see, a common cause can unite even the greatest foes. But you already know that, don't you? You already know the benefit of an alliance to face a common threat. That's what you did when you convinced these people to set aside their own disputes to fight me. Come, sit," Father motioned to a chair that had been moved to the middle of the floor. With the knife still pressed against his neck, Sasha obeyed.

His eyes left Father for the first time, and he saw Boris.

"What have you done to him?" Sasha stared in open horror at the bloody mess his brother was. If he didn't know that it had to be Boris, he would not have recognized him.

"Never mind that. We'll get to your brother soon enough." Father paused, his fingers drumming lightly on his leg. "Do you have any idea, Sasha, what happens to a country whose armies have been decimated, whose main source of income has been stripped from it? Do you? No? I will tell you. It grows weak. Revolts and riots happen. Uprisings. A once strong country brought to its knees, its people starving, freezing, destitute. Was that what you intended when you set your country up for defeat? When you betrayed everything you'd known for a handful of strangers?"

Sasha shut his eyes. The burned down palisades, the missing guards, the buildings in disrepair. It all made sense now.

"How did you know?"

"Come now, Sasha." Father's voice lingered over his name, turning it into a condescending sneer. "You're smarter than that, I hope. Lord Bayner and I discovered we had many things in common after my defeat in the mountains and his defeat in government. Both brought about by one person. So many things in common, Sasha. Common enemies, common ambitions, common suffering, and," Father paused, his eyes fixed pointedly on Sasha, "Common targets. He needed a refuge and I needed information. We both needed revenge."

Sasha squirmed in his chair. Of course, it was Lord Bayner. He alone, aside from Sasha's friends, knew of his betrayal. And the voice he'd heard that night in his father's house was none other than his.

"But if you knew..."

"Why didn't I act sooner? Oh, I could have. I knew the night you were in my house. I knew why you were there. I knew what you took. I could have sent men to kill you before you had gone ten steps from my house. But that would have been so boring, so ordinary. No. I needed a better way to punish you. And besides, it was so much more amusing to watch you. Lord Bayner made sure we always knew where you were, although you did go through great lengths to evade him from time to time." Sasha went cold as Father's words sank into him, their meaning fully realized and merging with the memories of Kaldura and Karu. "And you did such a good job of disappointing yourself that I didn't wish to intervene. I couldn't have planned it any better myself. You failed yourself."

248

"What do you want?"

"For now, we're going to talk. I'm going to help your brothers," Father gestured to two boys standing behind him that Sasha had not noticed before, "understand what it means to disobey and betray. These lessons always mean so much more when there are worthy examples to accompany them, don't you think? And when we are done talking, I'm going to give you a choice."

Sasha took a deep breath. This was a nightmare. A horrible, terrifying nightmare. And he was trapped in it. Trapped, like he had been when he lay dying, and the nightmares had come. But this one couldn't be awakened from. The sick knot in his stomach swelled and his heart hammered in his throat.

"I had such high hopes for you, Sasha," Father was talking again. "Did you ever wonder why I took so much time with you? I never spent that much time with Boris. Boris wasn't worth it. But you? I spent hours teaching you, guiding you, molding you into what you could be. You were the one I planned on one day taking my place. Oh, your other brothers would have fought you for it. But you were the right one. The one born to lead. The one fit to take my place."

Sasha wondered if the words were meant to stoke some long dead desire for his father's title. If they were, he wasn't sure what the point was. There wasn't the slightest chance that Father would let him walk away alive now. One way or another, Sasha was dying.

"I had another son like you, once. Intelligent, capable of making decisions based off of something other than mere anger, cunning. He was everything I'd ever wanted in a son. Anton. Is his name familiar to you?"

Sasha shook his head, although a spark of memory as to who Father was speaking of stirred in the back of his mind.

"You were young." Father smiled, which was far more frightening than when he remained impassive. "He was brilliant, Anton was. I truly thought he would be my successor. I poured myself into teaching him. And I gave him a gift. One of the most beautiful slave girls I have ever seen. I gave him a rule. The same one I gave you. You remember, don't you?"

"I remember," Sasha murmured.

He tried to shut out Father's voice and turned his focus on Boris instead. There was little about him to recognize him aside from his eyes. Vacant, lifeless but still living, they bored into Sasha accusingly. Sasha may not have been the one to reduce him to this bloody mess, but he'd been the one to restore the vacant glaze to his eyes just that morning. Guilt washed over him. He'd left his brother like that. Father's voice droned on and Sasha, all the years of submission resurfacing, was compelled to listen to it.

"It still pains me to think of what happened to Anton. So much potential wasted. And for what? A child he never knew. You see, he grew fond of that girl. So fond that when she became pregnant with his child, he refused to kill it. He hid her from me for months. Lied to me. Kept it a secret from me." Father paused, plucking at an invisible speck of dirt on his trousers. "Of course, secrets have a way of being found out. Especially such treacherous ones. The baby was only a few days old when it's crying was brought to my attention and Anton's disobedience discovered. Naturally, I could not overlook his crime. He was the first son of mine to openly defy me. It broke my heart, but it required punishment. His was a slow death, one that was remembered for many years after."

The spark of memory turned itself into a picture in Sasha's mind. He was seven or eight. They were gathered in the market square. Screams filling the air. The stench of blood filling his nose. A brother he did not know being slowly dismembered. If

Father's purpose was to remind Sasha of just how gruesome his own fate could be, he was succeeding. Sasha felt the cold, clammy sweat of fear on his palms and his nausea grew.

"Then there was the girl to deal with. Such a beautiful girl. And so young. I gave her a choice. You know, I always find it interesting and entertaining to see what people will choose when given the opportunity. I told her I would only take one more life for their crime. Hers or her son's. Do you know who she chose?"

"Her son," Sasha whispered. Like Agathe had. Like Ophelia said she would.

"Yes, her son. She died well, if that matters. And I kept my word. Her son lives to this day. Every breath he takes is bought at the price of his parents' blood." He paused and Sasha let his eyes wander to the two sons standing behind him. Neither was more than twelve. Probably close the way he and Boris had been close at that age. That was why Father dragged them into this. "Now you're probably wondering why I've wasted so much time telling you this story."

Sasha nodded, although the sick feeling in the pit of his stomach told him he knew exactly where Father was going with this. A choice, Father had said. He was to be given a choice.

"Choices. They're so interesting. They show you what really matters to a person." Father leaned forward, his gaze intent upon Sasha, watching his every expression and reaction. "Anton chose a slave girl over me. She chose her son's life over her own. You chose your new friends over your own countrymen. I told you that story because I am going to give you a choice."

"Let him go. Do whatever you want with me, just let him go," Sasha blurted the words out before Father was even finished, without thinking, but he did not regret them. He looked down at Boris, still slumped over in a pool of his own blood and knew it was the only choice he could make. His brother deserved to live. After everything that had been done to him, he deserved a chance to live a real life, free of all the shadows that clung to it now. "The treason wasn't his, it was mine. Only mine. He had nothing to do with it."

"But, Sasha, that's not an interesting choice." Father smiled once more and Sasha found his heart was pounding, and despair gripped him. "That's not even difficult for you. See how quickly you made it. No, that is not the choice I give you."

"Then what?"

Father did not answer right away. He regarded Sasha for a moment, his mirthless smile burning into him, before moving toward the back corner of the room out of Sasha's immediate sight. Sasha's eyes remained on Boris. The pool of blood formed beneath his brother was larger than Sasha thought possible. And all the while, Boris just stared, his eyes empty pools of hopelessness. The sound of something being dragged across the wooden floor drew his attention from his brother and all the horror of the previous minutes paled against the realization of just how far Father was going to go.

"No," Sasha gasped.

She hung limp in Father's grasp, a streak of deep red running down her face and staining her shirt, her hands bound behind her.

"Phelie?"

A gag prevented any response from Ophelia, but her dark eyes, wide with fright, sought his.

"No. You can't do this. Don't do this, Father. No."

"Your choice is this - only one of them will leave here alive in the morning. Tell me which."

"No. I can't. Just kill me and be done with it. Please. Just let them go. Don't do anything to them."

"Oh, you are going to die, Sasha. Make no mistake. And your death will be such that it will

252

always be remembered. Now, who will it be?"
Father allowed one hand to run up her body as
Ophelia stiffened and pulled away from him,
stopping at the collar of her shirt. "See, this is what
happens when you let yourself care for people.
Compassion is weakness. Now you must decide
which one goes. Of course, Boris did betray what he
knew of your plans in Kaldura. But then, he is your
brother and he refused to obey me and kill you. Such
a difficult decision. I don't envy you. But while you
make that decision, I'm sure you'll understand if I
want to enjoy her."

With a single motion, Father's hands ripped her
shirt open and started pulling it off her shoulders.
Ophelia struggled against him, and his arm shifted
from her waist to her throat and tightened, forcing
her to struggle for breath.

"Wait. Stop. Don't do that, please. No." Sasha
started up from his chair before Lord Bayner's hand
caught him and forced him down again, shifting the
knife to the front of his throat and pressing it against
the skin. His eyes met Ophelia's once more. Tears
slid silently down her face. "Phelie, I'm so sorry. So
sorry. For all of this."

"Have you made your choice?"

"I can't."

"You must or they both die."

"Please, just stop."

Father ignored him, his hands still working at
Ophelia's clothes. Sasha wanted to turn away, to
close his eyes, but he couldn't. He watched in
helpless horror.

Ophelia screamed through her gag and her eyes
widened in terror.

Father's arm loosened from around her throat
sending her stumbling forward. He brought both
hands up to clasp his own chest as blood gurgled up
in his throat and out of his mouth. Shock flooded his
face as he looked down at the deep red stain
spreading across his torso.

The knife pressed against Sasha's neck pulled away slightly as Lord Bayner stepped back in stunned disbelief. With a speed driven by desperation, Sasha did not wait to see what the cause of the sudden turn of events was. He spun around and yanked the knife free of Lord Bayner's hands. For one second, his eyes met the man's and he read the plea in them. In the second that it took Sasha to raise the knife, he recalled all the hours of torment he'd suffered at that man's hands and even more, how many hours of torment Boris had suffered.

Sasha plunged the knife in.

Lord Bayner staggered backward, staring down at the knife protruding from his own heart. Sasha relinquished his hold on its hilt and let him fall back. With a heavy thud, the man collapsed. Sasha watched a second more as his eyes turned lifeless.

Turning around, he caught Phelie as she stumbled into his arms. His hands trembled as he loosened the knots that bound and gagged her and felt her arms wrap around him, her hands gripping his shirt ferociously. Sobs wracked her entire body as he held her.

"It's alright. You're alright. You're safe," he said the words as much to reassure himself as her. "It's over. It's all over. We're safe now."

He looked up, over her shoulder to where Boris stood still. The bloody knife in his brother's hands was the only explanation needed. Whatever stupor their torture had driven him to, Boris had managed to break free from long enough to end Father's life. Boris swayed a moment longer before the knife slipped from his grasp and his body sank to the floor.

"Boris!" Sasha released his own grip on Ophelia and stumbled over his father's body to his brother. "Boris."

"You should have picked me to die," Boris' voice was weak as his eyes fluttered open.

"No. You're not going to die."

"Too late. Too much blood."

"No. I'll go get help. I'll get Taliea, someone. You can't die. You can't."

"Don't hate me, Sasha. Please," Boris struggled to get each word out. "I didn't mean..."

"I don't hate you. I couldn't."

"It's my fault." Boris gasped for breath.

"No. No. Hang on. I'm going to go. I'm going to get help. You just have to hang on for a little while. You'll be alright." Sasha slid his hand under his brother's head and lifted it up to his chest, feeling his brother's labored breathing against his own. "I'm sorry. I told you I wouldn't let this happen."

"You're the oldest one now." Boris' voice dropped to a barely audible whisper and Sasha leaned close to catch his words. "Don't waste it."

"What are you talking about?"

"Sasha, I don't..." Boris' eyes widened and his breath rattled in his throat then his heaving chest stilled, and silence replaced the noise.

"NO." The single word tore out of Sasha's chest, filling the room with its anguish.

"No," he repeated, softly, his eyes blurring as he held his brother's body close to his own. "You can't go. You can't leave me."

Chapter 37

HOW LONG SASHA MIGHT HAVE gone on sitting there remained unseen. As the minutes slid away, the silence in the room deepened. A whisper broke through Sasha's grief, and he looked up to see its source. The boy standing only a few feet in front of him went white when his eyes met Sasha's. Fury, both sudden and unstoppable in its force, consumed Sasha. Releasing Boris' body, he rose and snatched the boy as he tried to back away.

"You should be the one dead. You should be dead," Sasha screamed, the words coming from somewhere deep inside him that was beyond his control.

His hands moved of their own volition, throwing the boy down on the ground, closing one tightly around his throat, pummeling his face with the other. Through the red haze of his wrath, a voice called his name, but Sasha could not reach it. He could not think of anything except that someone must pay the price for his brother's life.

The boy underneath him struggled and tried to cry out but Sasha only squeezed his throat tighter, feeling his breath struggle and fail against his grip.

He struck him harder, the sensation of soft flesh giving way before his fist filling him with a savage pleasure. The boy's face was nothing more than a bloody blur swimming before his eyes. The boy's arms, lifted to shield himself, fell limp beside him.

Again, a voice called his name, but Sasha was further from it than before. His eyes lighted on the knife Boris had dropped and it was in his own hand the next second. He brought it up.

A pair of hands stopped its descent abruptly.

"Sasha, Sasha." The voice was closer, insistent, reeling him in from his fury. "Don't do it. Don't."

He pressed down on the knife, panting, heaving, but it refused to budge.

"He should be dead." Sasha could not even recognize his own voice in his ears. It belonged to another being. He pushed down on the knife harder. "They should all be dead. They killed him. They. Killed. My. Brother." He bit each word off as his anger rose and then fell, beaten.

"Sasha. Don't. Please."

Slowly, he released the pressure he was placing on the knife. His breath came heavy and fast. Blood pounded in his ears. The room slowed its spinning. The red haze that filled his vision faded.

"Sasha. There're enough people dead here tonight." Finally, he dragged his eyes away from the now bloody face that was his own handiwork and met the source of resistance. Ophelia knelt before him, her eyes were red rimmed from crying, her face blotchy, but her gaze was steady and held his. "Please, Sasha. Don't do this. It won't bring Boris back."

Sasha's fingers uncurled, releasing their grip on the knife and letting it slide into her hands. He stared down at the mangled face then back up at Ophelia. There was fear in her eyes still, too, he noticed. Her arms were around him again, and deep, heaving sobs shook her. He held her. He pulled her closer. He clung to her, as much as she clung to him.

Through the darkest hours of the night, neither moved. Ophelia, having cried until she could cry no more, still clung to him. And Sasha, envious of Ophelia's tears and how easily they came for her, wished that there was some release for the awful, burning pain inside. But now even his anger was bottled up inside him.

At last, stiff and with a swollen face, Ophelia pulled herself away from him.

"Sasha, I need to get home. And we need to let Father know what happened."

Incapable of words, Sasha nodded numbly.

"I don't want to go back alone. Please."

Again, Sasha nodded. He got to his feet and stared at the room as if seeing it for the first time. Father, Lord Bayner, Boris - all dead. And maybe the boy. He hadn't stirred all night. Sasha took in the other boy, still standing where he had been, too afraid to move.

"Wait." He stumbled like a drunk man to the far wall and retrieved a length of rope. He turned to the standing boy, motioning to a chair. "Sit."

Ophelia watched with some concern as he secured him to the chair, her arms wrapped about herself, holding the torn remnants of her shirt together as best she could. Sasha pulled one of his own shirts out and handed it to her.

"Thank you," she whispered, refusing to meet his eyes now.

The morning was still very early, the air damp and chill with the approach of winter. The host of birds that inhabited the woods still sang their morning tunes. Sasha hated them. Their happy sounds were a mockery of the pain trapped inside him.

It was still dark when they reached the house in silence. Sasha knew as soon as he saw it that he would never be able to go in with Ophelia. He couldn't bear the idea of bringing her back to them like this. It was his fault. It was all his fault. They would be right to blame him for her humiliation and suffering. He stopped halfway across the clearing.

"Sasha?"

He just shook his head, backing away.

"We need to tell them what happened."

"I can't. I can't. I have to go."

Without waiting for her to say anything else, Sasha turned and fled back into the refuge of the woods. He hurried on, not daring to look back when he caught Edith's exclamation of shock and horror. This was his fault. Father did all of this because of him.

His hasty retreat brought him within sight of his own cabin faster than he imagined it would. From the outside, nothing seemed amiss. Nothing about its log walls spoke of the carnage within. Even the light flooding out of the windows was nothing out of the ordinary. Sasha could almost believe himself to be coming home from an early morning hunt. He could almost believe that Boris sat inside waiting, alive and whole. It wasn't until he was pulling open the door that the stench of death and blood gave away what had befallen in that room.

Sasha entered quietly. The room was exactly as he had left it. The bodies lay exactly where they had fallen. The boy sat bound to his chair exactly as Sasha had tied him. Sasha paused, taking in the guilt that flashed across the boy's face at his entrance. Sasha stood a moment longer, just staring at it all.

He wanted them out of his sight.

He needed them out of his sight.

His eyes fell on his captive once more and Sasha's face hardened with decision. He crossed the room quickly and stood behind the chair. He'd done a poor job tying the knots and it took only a brief glance to show that the boy had been struggling to loosen and break free of them. They came undone with ease and Sasha grabbed a fistful of the boy's shirt, yanking him to his feet.

"What are you going to do with me?" the boy spoke for the first time, but Sasha ignored him.

Grabbing a shovel from the lean-to that sheltered his horse, Sasha continued dragging the boy along until they reached a small clearing amongst the trees. Here he relinquished his hold on both the boy and the shovel, letting them fall to the ground.

"Dig."

For a second, the boy stared up at him, eyes wide and uncomprehending, and Sasha's anger came rushing back to the surface, wild and fierce.

"I said, dig," he yelled, giving the shovel a kick that sent it flying into the boy.

He winced and picked it up. With a final, furtive glance at Sasha he pushed the tip of the shovel into the ground and began.

He was only a few shovelfuls in when he turned to Sasha once more. "What am I digging?"

Sasha, leaning back against a tree, almost didn't bother to answer. He watched as the boy went back to digging. After a few minutes, he sighed and answered, "A grave."

It took the boy hours to dig anything near big enough to bury anyone in. He was awkward with the shovel and clumsy in his fear. The sun had reached its height and was halfway down the sky again. Sasha left his spot against the tree. He stared down at the gaping brown hole in the ground.

"Come."

The boy stopped digging and struggled to climb out again. Sasha, his hand once more clamping a fistful of the boy's shirt, led them back to the cabin. Once again, it struck Sasha that the exterior of his home was deceptive. They entered and Sasha pointed to the first body on the floor - Lord Bayner's. His eyes still stared lifelessly up at nothing. The hilt of the knife still stuck out of his chest. Blood stained the entire front of him and formed a crimson pool beneath him. Sasha stared at him. There wasn't even a hint of remorse inside him for ending Lord Bayner's life. The man had been a monster.

"Bring him."

The boy grimaced as his hands took hold of Lord Bayner's already stiff arms and started to pull him towards the open door. Several times, he fell completely over trying to drag the much heavier body but at last they made it to the grave. With a final heave, the body rolled in, and Sasha led them back to the cabin again. This time it was Father's body he pointed to, and that the boy hauled out the door. Father was a much bigger man than Lord Bayner had been. Sasha watched indifferently as the boy struggled but made no effort to help.

There was little daylight left by the time Father's body joined the other. Sasha stared down at it, conscious of the fact that he felt neither remorse nor sorrow for the man and that he ought to. Children were supposed to mourn a parent's loss. But there was nothing, nothing but the anger and bitter hatred that throbbed just beneath the surface of his detachment. He turned to where the boy sat, collapsed on the ground and clearly exhausted.

"Fill it in."

The boy went to work, but his movements were even more sluggish than before. It was well after dark when he lifted the final shovelful of dirt and tossed it onto the mound. In silence, they made their way back through the trees and to the cabin. The fire had burned down entirely, and it was cold and dark inside. Sasha, still with a firm hold on his captive, found his way to the chair he'd secured the boy to earlier and forced him into it once more. Binding him to it more carefully than he had before, Sasha turned his attention to the fire.

Sasha sat down next to Boris' body. He had to bury him still, too. But he couldn't. Not yet. And not with them. Boris deserved his own grave. He deserved a place that would be marked and remembered. As his eyes ran over his brother's lifeless form, they fell on the iron band still resting on his wrist. He deserved to be buried without that. Hamo had told Sasha it could not be removed without a King's Pardon. Sasha wasn't sure if that meant in death, too, but it did not matter. He would go to the forge and get a file. He would remove it no matter how many hours it took working at it. His brother was not going to be buried as a criminal.

A moan from near him disturbed Sasha's thoughts. He turned to see the boy he had nearly killed stirring.

So, he was still alive. Sasha didn't care. Ophelia may have stopped him from killing, but that did not mean he had any plans of taking care of the boy. He could die, and Sasha wouldn't mind. A feeble plea for water did nothing to change his mind. He sat unmoving, ignoring the cry until it finally stopped. Sasha almost hoped it was because he was dead. Then he would be absolved of any responsibility towards him.

Sasha wasn't aware of falling asleep as he sat on the floor beside Boris. It wasn't until his head fell forward that he jerked awake again. He hadn't meant to fall asleep. He rubbed his eyes, forcing himself fully awake. However long he'd been asleep, it hadn't helped. Nothing had changed. Beneath the layer of outward numbness, lay the same anger and guilt, and far below all that was a deep, painful, paralyzing sorrow.

Rising to his feet, he left the cabin behind him and set out into the night to satisfy the only clear thought he could put together. He needed to get the band off of Boris. Then, maybe, he would have whatever it took to lay his brother to rest.

It was a much longer walk than he remembered. Either that, or he'd been asleep for longer than he realized, because by the time he returned home the sun was coming up. Without bothering to shut the door behind him, he went straight to Boris and took hold of his arm.

It was already stiff with death, making it difficult for Sasha but he started anyway. The file bit into the metal slowly. Sasha pressed down harder, his eyes blurring with tears of anger and frustration. The file slipped and cut across his own hand leaving a trail of blood behind it. Sasha didn't notice the pain as he kept going. He didn't notice the footsteps coming up behind him. His own hand worked faster and faster but without any precision. It slipped and slid, never filing the same spot twice. He just wanted the thing off.

A hand came over his own, stopping it, stopping him. Only then did he notice the trembling in his hands.

"Give it here, Sasha," Hamo's voice was gentle as it cut through the haze of his own wretched determination.

"No. I want it off. I want it off. I don't care if I get in trouble. He's not going to be buried with it. I can't...I can't do that."

"Let me do it." Hamo's hand forced the file from his own and Sasha sat back unresisting. "No one's going to get you in trouble for taking it off."

Sasha watched as Hamo's work was almost instantly more effective than his own had been. Maybe it was for the best that Hamo did it, but Sasha did not want to be around Hamo. He couldn't. There had to be some part of Hamo that blamed Sasha for what happened to his daughter.

If only he had listened more to Boris' warnings. If only he had not been content to believe that they had left all their troubles behind them. If only he'd questioned Boris more about what happened in Kaldura. A hundred ways he could have made things go differently floated around in his head. He had to get out of here. He had to get away from Hamo before Hamo started talking about it.

Without another word to Hamo, he got up and freed the boy sitting in the chair. They had one more grave to dig. The boy was half asleep, having somehow managed to doze while sitting tied to a chair. He allowed himself to be pulled along by Sasha out into the woods again.

It took much longer for Sasha to settle on a place this time. He wandered about the woods, the boy in tow, searching for a spot that would be suitable. Boris wasn't going to be buried anywhere near the two men who had tormented him to death. At last, he found a spot that was both memorable and out of the way. It was one of the few groves of pine trees that grew down here off the mountains, and the evergreens seemed fitting keepers for his brother's grave. He threw the shovel once more to the boy.

"Dig."

His captive struggled to stay on his own feet as they started back from the house. It was only Sasha's grip on him that kept him from falling over. The sound of water flowing nearby brought about the boy's first resistance to Sasha's leading. He pulled away from him a little.

"Can I get some water, Chief Sasha? Please?"

Sasha froze. "What did you just call me?"

"Chief? You're the oldest son. You're his heir."

"Don't call me that," Sasha said. Boris' last words came to mind. Boris had known that somehow.

"Yes, Sasha." The boy hesitated over his name the same way Dagmar had when he'd first set her free. His eyes traveled longingly toward the direction of the creek although he did not dare repeat his plea.

Sasha ignored his request, and the disheartened little sigh that followed, and continued on.

It was late in the day by the time they reached the cabin and Sasha hoped that Hamo was no longer there. The door stood ajar as he'd left it earlier. And Hamo was definitely still there. Sasha stood in the doorway, staring at the room.

"You moved him," he said at last, nodding toward the bed that now held the other boy. The fact that he was still alive annoyed Sasha a little.

"I did. It's off him, so you can bury him whenever you want."

Sasha nodded, looking down at where Boris lay. The iron band was gone, although a scar remained in its place. Staring at him now, Sasha could not bear the great longing that filled him. He wanted to talk to Boris. He wanted to hear his voice again. He wanted to go back and undo all the harsh words he'd spoken. But it was too late. No matter how much he willed the body to sit up and be alive, it wasn't.

"Sasha?" Hamo spoke. "Are you alright?"

It was such a ridiculous question, such an impossible question. How could he be alright? How could anything be alright when something he hadn't even known existed had split wide open inside of him and nothing could bring it back together? How could he ever be alright again?

"I'm fine. I'm just tired," he answered.

"You don't have to be, you know," Hamo said softly. "Who are they? Your brothers?"

"His sons," Sasha said, refusing to acknowledge their relation to him.

"What are you going to do with them?"

"Nothing."

"That one might die if you do nothing." Hamo glanced at the one lying on a bed.

"I don't care. Let him."

Hamo opened his mouth to say something, and Sasha could already guess what it would be. Hamo would argue with him. He would tell Sasha that he couldn't just let him die. That it wasn't right. And Sasha didn't care. He couldn't make himself care. But Hamo did not speak. He looked at Sasha then to the injured boy before nodding slightly.

"Would you like me to stay?" he asked at last.

Sasha shook his head. Words weren't strong enough to express how much he wanted to be alone. He couldn't even force himself to meet Hamo's eyes, let alone talk to him about what had happened.

"I could ask Taliea to come and help take care of him?"

"No. I don't want anyone coming." Sasha knew he shouldn't refuse but the words leaped out before he could stop them. "I just want to be left alone."

The silence that filled the room after Hamo left was heavy. For a long time, Sasha just sat on the floor next to Boris. He needed to bury him. He did not want to bury him. There was a finality to that act that Sasha was not ready to accept.

"I'm sorry for everything," he whispered to ears that would never hear again. "I'm so sorry. I should have listened to you. I just wish I could have had a chance to tell you I was sorry for yelling at you. I didn't mean it. I didn't mean any of it."

Sasha waited a moment as if to give Boris one last chance to be alive.

"Come on." He turned to his captive at last and spoke. "Help me carry him."

Boris wasn't going to be dragged across the ground. He would be carried to his final resting place. Carried, and laid in it with great care. It was a good distance to the grave he'd had dug, but that didn't matter. They carried him, wrapped in a sheet, to the spot beneath the firs. The subtle scent of pine brought back waves of memory of the life they'd shared in the mountains. Carefully, they lowered him into the hole and Sasha watched as the dirt slowly covered him, one shovelful at a time, until there was nothing left but a mound of brown earth to mark his brother's burial place.

It was dark again by the time they made it back, the second night since Boris' death. After securing his captive once more, he sat back and watched the boy try to sleep. The memories of that fateful night came flooding back unwelcomed and uninvited. Sasha shut his eyes, but that only made it worse. He replayed every word, every movement, every feeling, lingering over Boris' last words. The last words he would ever hear from his brother. There was a puzzle in those final words. A puzzle Sasha hadn't not bothered to try to figure out up to now. But now, staring at the boy in front of him, Sasha's mind wandered over it. If what he thought Boris and the boy had said was true, then there was action he had to take. He rose and moved his own chair directly in front of the boy's. A swift kick aimed at his shins woke him.

"What did you mean when you said I was the oldest son?" Sasha ignored the grimace of pain that flashed across the boy's face.

"Just that you were his oldest son now."

"How? There were a lot of brothers older than me."

"Not anymore."

"How?" Sasha repeated, his voice hardening and causing the boy's face to go a shade paler.

"Most of them died in the battle. The ones that came home Father executed for treason."

"All of them?"

The boy nodded.

Sasha leaned back against his chair, his arms across his chest. He knew Aruuk had suffered great losses during the battle in the mountains. Never in his wildest dreams did he imagine it claimed the lives of so many of his brothers. And of course, Father executed the remaining ones. He must have known that someone had turned traitor and in his usual bloodthirsty manner had dealt with all of them.

Sasha was not bothered by the fact that they were all dead. But the idea that some of them had been killed because of his treason added another weight to his guilt. More people dead - all because of him.

Aside from the guilt, the information posed a problem. A dead Chief meant an empty seat of power. And an empty seat of power meant a grab for that power. It was supposed to fall to the eldest son, but when murder could change who the eldest was, there was no telling who would win eventually. In

Aruuk, it meant a bloodbath between the Chief's surviving sons. Sasha was well aware of the fact that Gundar had murdered all of his brothers, both older and younger, to ascend.

If Sasha was truly the oldest one left, then his life would never be safe. As eldest, he had the strongest claim to that power and if at any time word got out about his existence, he would be their first target. Unless he eliminated his brothers first. The two in front of them would be the first to deal with, and possibly the only ones who knew of him.

"Who else knows about me?" Sasha asked.

"Just us, and Halle."

"Who's Halle?" The name was familiar to Sasha.

"He's the second oldest to you. Father didn't bring him."

Sasha remembered him now. Halle was a few years behind him, but he'd seen the boy often enough before he'd left home. He was the son of Mara, the wife who'd replaced his own mother as Gundar's favorite.

Sasha puzzled over his dilemma. The one on the bed, he fully intended to just let die. He could kill the other one and be done with it. The second the thought crossed his mind, Sasha knew he could not do it. No one here would understand that he acted out of self-preservation.

There was one other way to eliminate the threat these brothers posed to him. Gundar hadn't used it, as it was considered the more merciful means of dealing with unwanted brothers and generally only reserved for the younger ones who were too young to be too ambitious yet. But Renalt had. He'd offered all of his younger brothers the choice. A eunuch couldn't be Chief, but they could at least live. It was the more compassionate choice. He could emasculate the boy in front of him and remove the threat he posed. It'd be doing both of them a favor.

Sasha's face must have betrayed some hint of his thoughts because the boy sitting across from him shifted against his bonds and his face went ashen. For a long time, Sasha toyed with the idea. In his present state of mind, and aided considerably by his lack of sleep, there was merit to that decision. A few minutes and it would be done. No one here would ever have to know.

He slid his knife out and ran a finger across its sharp edge. No one here would have to know. And he would not only be protecting himself, but he would also, in a sense, be protecting them as well. They would not be sought out by other brothers for death.

But beneath all the good reasons he had for it lay the very simple fact that he wanted someone to hurt for what had happened to Boris. And the boy fidgeting in front of him would fill that void easily.

He tapped the knife against the open palm of his free hand, and stared at the boy, his face hardening in decision. And the boy, seeing that decision on Sasha's face, began to struggle in earnest.

"Don't do it, Sasha," he cried out, fighting to break free. It was a ridiculous effort. Even if he managed to free himself from the ropes that bound him to the chair, Sasha was sitting right in front of him, ready. "Please, please don't. I'll do anything you want, I promise, anything. I'll be good. I'll listen to everything you say to do. I'll never disobey you. Just please don't hurt me. You don't have to do this to me."

"It's for your own good. It saves your life, too."

"But it will be for the rest of my life. And it will hurt. Please, Sasha? I'll do anything, anything."

"I have to."

"No. No, you don't. Please, Sasha. I'm your brother too."

It was the worst plea he could have made for it sent Sasha into a rage. Grabbing him by the front of his shirt and pulling him as far forward as his bonds allowed him, Sasha's voice rose in a yell.

"Don't you ever say that again. You are nothing to me. Nothing." His voice dropped to an icy whisper as he continued, "I hate you. And if killing you would bring him back, I would do it in a second."

The boy, his face contorted and red with crying, flinched and tried to pull away. "But he said you were different."

Sasha, taken aback by the words, let go of him. He stared down at him in disgust, but the disgust was for himself. He wasn't different. If he were, he would not have nearly killed the other one. He would not have been so unkind to Boris.

Getting up and setting his knife down, he tore a strip of cloth off the bottom of the boy's shirt and balled it up.

"Please don't, Sasha," the boy whispered. "Please?"

Sasha ignored him and crammed the cloth into his unresisting mouth, tying it in place with a length of rope. He picked his knife up again and hesitated. The boy, realizing he could not escape his bonds, slumped defeated against the back of the chair. Tears ran tracks down his little brother's dirty face. His mouth was silent, but his eyes continued to beg.

Sasha thought about Boris, and all that had been done to him in the end. He thought about Ophelia, and what Father was going to do with her.

But thinking of Ophelia then was a mistake. Thinking about her made him think of the way she stopped him. It made him think of the horror in her eyes when he was about to kill. It made him think about her words that night. His hand tightened around the knife, his knuckles turning white with the strain. If she were standing in the room now, she would look at him the same way. The same fear, the same horror at the action he was about to take. But it was better this way, he argued with himself. The boy deserved it for being a part in Boris' death.

Sasha's face contorted in frustration at his own indecision and weakness. Giving vent to a strangled yell, he slammed the point of the knife down into the empty space of the chair between his brother's legs, causing him to squeal and buck against his bonds in fright.

Sasha crossed the room, heedless of anything but the confusion and anger that tore through him. The door slammed behind him as he left the single room of the cabin that had witnessed so much pain and death.

Chapter 38

SITTING OUTSIDE ON THE STEPS, Sasha could still hear his little brother's frantic efforts to free himself. The cold air bit into Sasha but he ignored it, like he ignored the sounds coming from inside the cabin. Sounds that were caused by him.

Sasha buried his face in his hands. How had it come to this? How had he? He'd almost mutilated his own brother. He still considered the idea. And sitting out here, in the sharp cold, the thought of what he'd almost done, what he might still do, turned his insides sick. It was something Father would have done. And that was what bothered him the most. All this time, he'd thought he was different, that he could make himself different. Yet, now, he was just the same. Just like Father. All his efforts evaporated and the truth of what he was stared him in the face.

Forcing himself off the steps, Sasha wandered away from the cabin. He had no set path, no destination in mind, only that he had to get away. It was little surprise, though, when his steps brought him to a grove of pine trees standing guard over a single mound of freshly dug soil.

Sasha sat next to his brother's grave and for the first time since that awful night, his grief pushed through the anger and numbness and rose to the surface. Tears that refused to come when he watched his brother die now refused to stop.

"This is all my fault," Sasha whispered into the silence of the night. "I should have been better to you, Boris. I should have... I don't know what to do."

The quiet darkness swallowed up his words. They were meaningless now anyway. Any chance he had of being a better brother to Boris was lost forever. But it wasn't his only chance, a voice in his head whispered. Sasha thought about Boris' last words.

"You're the oldest one now. Don't waste it," he'd said, although Sasha wasn't sure how Boris thought he could waste it. Sasha didn't want to be the oldest. He didn't want to be the one responsible. And he certainly did not want to live in fear of his life forever.

The sun's rising found Sasha stiff with cold, his eyes red and sore from another sleepless night and the tears he'd shed. Conscious of the cold that ate through him, Sasha finally got up and started back to the cabin.

He climbed up the three steps that led to the door and pushed it open. It swung open without sound. He stood in the doorway. The sun was not high enough to chase away the nightly shadows but even through the gloom he could see the look of horror and despair on his little brother's face.

His little brother.

The words crashed through him leaving him reeling with their force. For a moment he just stood there, waiting for the impact of those words to fade. He didn't care about the boy in front of him. Couldn't care. But he also couldn't go through with his plan.

Sasha came close to him. He pulled the knife free from where it had sat embedded all night. Fresh tears spilled out of his little brother's eyes as they followed every move Sasha made. He renewed his efforts to break free, but they were feeble and futile, more of a reflex than an actual attempt.

"Hold still," Sasha said quietly as he brought the knife up close to his trembling face and slid it beneath the rope that held his gag in place. With one swipe the rope came apart and fell away. "You can stop crying. I'm not going to hurt you."

With the gag gone and Sasha's order to stop crying, the boy struggled to bring his own sobs under control. With enormous effort, his breathing evened out. Sasha sat down in the chair opposite him and slid the knife back into its scabbard at his side. The gesture did more to calm the boy's fright than Sasha's words.

"Just so we're clear, I still hate you. And if you ever give me any reason to think you're dangerous, I will kill you and I won't feel bad about it. Understand?"

The boy nodded, trying to twist enough to wipe his face on his shoulders.

"What's your name?" Sasha asked after several minutes of silence had gone by.

"Lars." His voice still quivered when he spoke.

"His?" Sasha jerked his head toward the injured one.

"Aki."

Again, they lapsed into silence. Sasha stared at Lars, lost in thought. If he wasn't going to kill them, what was he going to do with them? Not take care of them, that was certain. He didn't need anyone to take care of. All he'd done when he'd had Boris to care for was mess it up. His eyes narrowed, and his hand darted toward Lars, making him flinch. He pulled it back again with the wolf's tooth talisman held between his fingers. He'd lost his own when he was first captured in Dorsten, but the memory of Boris and him going out on their first wolf hunt was still very clear.

Rubbing it between his thumb and forefinger, he asked, "How many times did you have to go out for this?"

"Three times, Sasha."

"You went with him?" Again, he nodded to where Aki lay.

"Yes. Only he got his on the second time."

"So, he's better than you?" Sasha had gotten his first too, a fact that had angered Boris. The way Lars' face fell at his words reminded him of just how much it meant to be better than anyone else. He'd forgotten a little just how harsh the competition was.

"Just at that."

The ghost of a smile crossed Sasha's face. He could almost hear Boris saying the same thing when they were younger. The smile was gone as an empty ache took its place. He leaned forward, resting his forehead in the palms of his hands. He was tired.

"Are you really not going to hurt me?" Lars asked.

"Not unless you give me reason to."

"I won't. I promise, I won't. I'll be good and I'll listen to you."

Aki started whimpering a few feet away and Sasha turned toward him. Aside from waking up every now and then and crying for water, he'd remained inert. A moment later his whimpers turned to the now familiar plea for water. Sasha still didn't care if he died. It would be one less thing to figure out. But he couldn't ignore him anymore, either. With reluctance, he got up and took a cup of water over to him.

It was the first time Sasha had really looked at what he'd done. The cup of water still in his hands, he took in the swollen, battered face and the dark bruises that were forming around his neck. Most of the blood had been wiped away, and Sasha assumed Hamo had done that. Although Aki was awake, his eyes were so swollen that he could not open them enough to make anything out.

"Is he going to die, Sasha?"

Lars' question reminded Sasha that he had actually come over to give Aki a drink, not to inspect his injuries. But staring at him now, seeing what he had done to him, Sasha suddenly realized that if he allowed him to die it would be no one but Sasha's fault. Aki's blood would rest solely on his hands. And he knew he could never live with the burden of that.

Shaking his head, he answered, "No, he's not going to die."

He held the cup to the boy's lips and helped him drink. Aki managed to swallow only a very little bit before he was sick. Coughing and retching and crying all at once, he lay back against the bed. Sasha watched in alarm as Aki vomited up everything he'd just swallowed. If he didn't want Aki dying, he'd have to help him.

But Sasha had never taken care of anyone who was injured. He hadn't even watched it done. He needed help himself, but he'd already told Hamo he didn't want any. Aki began to cry harder, reaching both hands up to his head as tears squeezed their way out between his swollen eyelids. That decided it for Sasha. He couldn't sit here and watch and listen to the pain he'd caused. Without another word he left.

Standing outside of Aldrid and Taliea's home, Sasha had a moment to hope that Hamo had not relayed his words to them. It would make asking for help harder. It was bad enough that this was all his fault. Despite the early hour, he did not have to wait long for an answer to his knock. The sympathy on Taliea's face was enough to tell him that they knew.

"I know I told Hamo that I didn't want anyone," Sasha started in before she could speak. He wasn't sure how well he could handle any sort of condolences at the moment. "But I need help. I don't want him to die, and I don't know what to do for him. Will you come?"

"You know I will. Do you want to come in while I get some things together?"

"I'll just wait out here."

Taliea was not long in coming and when she exited the house, Aldrid came out with her. Sasha wasn't sure he wanted both of them to come, but he couldn't very well refuse.

Reaching his own home again, he led the way inside. Taliea ignored the bloodstained mess and went straight to the bed Aki lay in. He was crying again, and the sound of it tore at Sasha. He watched Taliea for a moment before noticing that Lars was once again trying to sleep in his chair. With the presence of Aldrid and Taliea in the room, it seemed cruel to make him sleep that way. His fingers worked at the knots and Lars looked up at him, confused and half asleep. Once the ropes fell away, Sasha lifted him out of the chair and helped him toward the other bed.

"Sasha, what happened to him?" Taliea said from across the room.

Sasha looked up, surprised at the tone of her voice. He thought it was pretty obvious what happened to him. But when he looked over, it was clear she wasn't talking about Aki's face. She and Aldrid were pulling off his blood and vomit covered shirt and Taliea was staring at his back. Even from across the room, Sasha could see the scars.

"Lars, what happened to him?" he questioned in Aruuken.

Lars rubbed his eyes and frowned. "He got in trouble with Father. He spilled something hot on Father's arm, so Father had him beaten with hot metal rods."

"Father did that to him?" Sasha stared at him in horror. Lars' words made him feel far worse than he already was.

"He would have done less if Aki hadn't cried." Lars shrugged.

"That doesn't seem like an awful harsh punishment for an accident to you?" Sasha had almost forgotten how callous they were. Lars' nonchalance reminded him.

"Maybe," Lars conceded, mostly so that Sasha wouldn't be angry with him, "Aki's different, though. He's slave born."

"What did you just say?"

"That he's slave born?"

"That can't be true. Father didn't keep any slave born sons."

"But Aki's not really his son." Lars looked up at him as if it were the most obvious thing in the world. "Aki is Anton's son."

"Anton's son?" Sasha felt sick. He'd almost killed the boy who was only alive because of his parents' deaths. In that moment of rage, he'd almost undone the sacrifice they'd made.

"I'm sorry. I didn't mean to make you angry." Lars' demeanor changed at once and his voice quivered.

"You didn't. Just go to sleep."

The sleepless night caught up with Sasha as he sat waiting. Neither Taliea nor Aldrid tried to keep him talking, which he was glad of. Even Aki grew quiet again. While Taliea worked quietly, Sasha found it impossible to keep his eyes open. Leaning his head back against the wall, he gave in.

"Sasha?" Taliea's voice woke him up.

"What's wrong?" He sat up, startled by how deeply asleep he had been.

"Nothing. He's resting now."

"Oh. That's good, right?"

Taliea bit her lip and hesitated.

"It could be," Aldrid spoke for her. "He needs to rest."

"But?"

"He won't die, Sasha. It's just that there's really no way to know just how he will recover," Taliea said. "He could be completely fine when he recovers, as if nothing ever happened. Or, he could have some ongoing problems. Memory loss. Things like that."

"I did this to him," Sasha murmured. "I can't believe I did this. It's my fault."

"You're doing what you can to make it better," Aldrid said. "That's all you can do. Besides, I don't think anyone holds it against you. I'm sorry about what happened to Boris. I wish there was something we could have done."

"Thank you."

"Now, I'm leaving some things for him," Taliea said, and Sasha noticed for the first time that her hands were full. She held the items up one at a time as she spoke, "This will help bring the swelling down. Just put it on him every day. And this is for the pain. Make a tea with it whenever the pain gets to be too much. Most importantly, he needs water. He hasn't had anywhere near enough in the last couple of days." Sasha dropped his gaze. That was his fault too. "You'll need to wake him often and make him drink. But don't be surprised if he gets sick a lot. That's one of the things that can happen with injuries like that. Just keep making him drink."

Sasha's head was swimming when she finished her direction and once again he thought of how much he did not want to be responsible for anyone else. The burden of it was too great. What if he messed up as badly as he did with Boris? There were so many times he wished he could take back with Boris, times when he'd lost his temper, or ignored his brother for hours.

"I'll come by to check on him when I can, but he should start mending soon."

"How are you doing?" Aldrid asked the question Sasha had been dreading the most. Why was it that people asked that when the answer was so obvious?

"I'm fine."

"It's alright if you're not," Taliea said almost the same thing Hamo had. "Your brother was worth your grief."

"I just can't believe he's gone."

"I imagine it will feel that way for a very long time and that there is nothing anyone can say or do to change that," Taliea said.

Sasha looked up at her in curiosity. For someone who was so happy every time he saw her, she sounded like she understood something of the pain lodged inside him.

"You know, if you need anything, you just have to ask," Aldrid said.

Sasha nodded his thanks, overwhelmed by the sudden need to be alone again. He'd managed to go a few hours distracting himself from Boris' death, but now it was back at the forefront of his mind. Taking care of Aki and showing mercy to Lars couldn't bring his brother back any more than his anger could.

Chapter 39

AFTER THEY LEFT, SASHA MOVED a chair to Aki's bedside and sat down, appreciating the quiet in the room. Lars was still asleep, probably making up for the days he'd gone without. Aki was resting.

He stared out the window, watching nothing but the time pass. If he shut his eyes, he could picture a normal day. He could picture Boris sitting in his corner, as far from the fire as he could get. Remembering the horrific burns on his body that had been put there in his final hours, Sasha finally understood his brother's fear of fire. It was why he could never keep one going. And Sasha had yelled at him for that fear.

A knock on the door disturbed his thoughts. Sasha stared at the door, wondering who was behind it. Not that it mattered. He had no intention of answering. Asking Taliea to come had been more than enough.

"Sasha, I know you just want to be left alone, but we need to talk," Hamo said, his voice muffled by the door.

Sasha considered answering. But whatever Hamo needed to talk to him about most certainly had to do with what happened that night, and Sasha was not ready for such a conversation. Chances were, he thought, he'd never be ready for that conversation. He remained where he was, staring at the door and ignoring the person on the other side of it.

After a few minutes of silence went by, Sasha was sure Hamo had left again. An unexpected curiosity came over him and he wished he knew what it was Hamo needed to say. He puzzled over it for a while, unable to come up with a completely satisfying answer. At least it gave him some distraction for those few minutes.

Aki moaned next to him, and he turned his attention to the boy. Gripping his head between his hands, Aki tried to sit up. Sasha could see that he was trying to open his eyes despite the swelling. With a gentle hand, he pushed the boy back down onto the pillow.

"Lay still, Aki."

"What happened?" Aki croaked.

"You don't remember?" Sasha answered, a spark of hope rising in him.

"No."

Sasha glanced over to where Lars still lay asleep. "There was an accident. You were hurt."

There was no harm in telling him that, Sasha thought. Then maybe, when he recovered, he wouldn't look at Sasha in the same fear that Lars did, or Boris had. Even Ophelia had looked at him in fear. Aki would not, not if he had anything to do with it.

"Here, drink this." Sasha reached for the cup of water and lifted Aki's head up to meet it.

"It hurts to swallow."

"I know." Sasha looked away. Of all the marks he'd left on him, the bruises around his throat were the most condemning. There was no accident that could have left those. They were clearly the work of a human hand. He could see where his own fingers had pressed in, stealing Aki's breath from him, strangling him. "Go back to sleep. You'll feel better when you wake up."

For the next two days, nothing much changed. Aki slept almost constantly, and more often than not Sasha had to wake him to get him to eat or drink. Despite the deep discolorations that were showing through the skin on his face, Aki was beginning to mend as Taliea said he would. The swelling was receding. And as much as Sasha hated to admit it, Aki's recovery was a relief. He would not have to bear the weight of his death.

It was on the third morning that Sasha realized that there was no food left in the cabin. His own appetite was lacking, but even so, it was all gone. Gone, and the only way to get more was to leave the safe confines of the cabin. Here in the cabin, he could, and did, ignore when someone knocked on his door. He could ignore the daunting task of moving forward.

He glanced toward where Lars sat crouched in the corner. Sasha had grown weary of tying him up all the time and had allowed him to remain loose so long as he didn't cause trouble. It worked well for Sasha, too. Lars did everything Sasha told him to, including much of Aki's care. As if he could sense Sasha watching him, Lars looked up and met his gaze. He was terrified. Sasha saw it every time he saw the boy's eyes.

"Come here."

Lars was quick getting to his feet. Sasha could thank Father's cruelty for such constant, prompt obedience. At the moment, it served him well.

"I'm going out for a few hours to get food. You stay here, look after Aki." Lars wasn't quick enough to hide the gleam of hope in his eyes and Sasha didn't miss it. "I don't really care if you run away, you know. It's not like I actually want you around. It's less trouble for me if you are gone."

"Yes, Sasha," Lars said, his face betraying his hurt as quickly as it had betrayed his hope.

Sasha watched his face for a moment, wondering if Lars knew how much he gave away in his expressions. He would not have lasted very long like that with Father.

Saddling his horse for the first time in a week, Sasha set off in the direction of town, hoping that he did not run into anyone he knew. Hallann was small, and not very good for staying out of sight in. His only comfort was that he hadn't made any friends in town. He only ever went when he needed to and never engaged in the small talk that people here liked.

The sky was gray with dense snow clouds and the air was icy. Sasha rode into Hallann just as the first few flakes started to fall. Pulling his hood up over his head as much to keep the snow off as to keep his face hidden, he hurried through the few stops he had to make. Watching the people around him, Sasha was a little hurt by how ordinary their day seemed to be going. Clearly, no one was aware of the events that had shaken Sasha's own world and left him devastated.

Mounting up for the last time to ride home, Sasha kicked his horse into a trot. The snow was falling thicker now, the first snow of the winter, and the brown of the road was quickly turning white. He was nearly past the last of the houses clustered along the main road when he caught sight of them. Ophelia and Dagmar. There was no one he wished to avoid more. Ophelia had seen him kill one man, and almost kill another. She had been degraded by his father because of him. Whatever friendship they had shared was gone for sure. Without waiting to see if she had noticed him as well, he gave his horse another kick and left the town behind him.

Sasha sighed as he took in the cabin whose sole occupant at the moment was Aki. Lars was nowhere to be found inside. Not that it came as a surprise. Or a disappointment. Shrugging, he carried in the supplies he'd brought and went to Aki's bedside.

"Hey, Aki." He laid his hand on the boy's shoulder and gently nudged him. He was rewarded a moment later when Aki's eyes, both ringed black with bruises, squinted open. "Where's Lars? Where's your brother?"

Aki winced and brought a hand up to his head. "He left." Sasha noticed his voice was getting stronger. "He said you didn't care if he did."

"I don't. But he might have picked a better day to run," Sasha said more to himself than Aki. "It's been snowing all morning."

Aki winced again and groaned as he tried to sit up a little. Sasha pushed him back down on the bed.

"Just lay still. Is it pretty bad again?"

Aki nodded.

"I'll make you something for the pain." Sasha started to get up, but Aki's hand reached out and grabbed his sleeve, stopping him.

"Please don't. It just makes me sick and then it hurts worse."

Sasha frowned. Although Aki had been sick a disturbing number of times since Taliea had been by, he hadn't noticed a particular connection with the tea.

"Are you sure?"

Again, Aki nodded.

"Alright. Try to get some sleep then, I guess." Sasha stood up.

"Sasha?"

"What?"

"You're not angry with Lars, are you?"

"No. I really don't care if he wants to run away. I'm not chasing him."

Aki relaxed at Sasha's reassurance. Sasha was sure that was why Father chose to bring these two along. They were close, the way he and Boris had been close, and he desired to teach them the cost of such closeness. Compassion was weakness, Father would have told them. And Sasha and Boris were to be examples of that weakness. Only Boris had taken the chance away from him.

More than once through the afternoon, Sasha caught himself looking out the window, half expecting to see Lars return in defeat. Although the snow stopped falling after only a couple of inches covered the ground, the wind was picking up and it was simply a miserable day to be out in the weather. A quick search of the cabin was enough to show that he hadn't even bothered to steal anything worthwhile for his trip - no clothes, no blankets, and, of course, no food. Not that he cared, Sasha reminded himself. Lars lost in a snowstorm was not his problem.

He sat near the fire and tried to shut out the image of his little brother lost in the cold. The wind howling outside and rattling the shutters reminded Sasha of his own, almost disastrous trip during the winter. He'd been so afraid of freezing to death, of Dagmar freezing to death. The only reason he'd persisted was because he couldn't bear the thought of what would happen if he didn't. He couldn't live with failure. But that wasn't why Lars was running.

Lars was running scared.

And it was Sasha he was scared of.

A particularly loud gust of wind shook the small cabin and Sasha jumped up. The suddenness of his action woke Aki.

"What happened?"

"Nothing." Sasha reached for his warm outer clothes. "I'm going to go out and see if I can find Lars. Will you be alright by yourself for a bit?"

"I thought you weren't going to do that?" Aki's face twisted up with pain and confusion.

"I wasn't. But he'll freeze to death out there. Go back to sleep. I'll be back in a bit."

Aki didn't argue and Sasha finished bundling up before heading outside for his horse.

It didn't take much skill at all to find where his brother was headed. His tracks were plainly visible in the powdery white snow. Sasha was a little surprised to find that they headed off deeper into the woods rather than towards the path that led to the road. If he was trying to make it back to Aruuk, he was heading the wrong way. With the last light of day, Sasha guided his horse along the tracks. The trail reached the creek and ran alongside it. As he continued following it, he was surprised by how far Lars had gone.

Sasha pulled his horse to a stop when he caught sight of a figure huddled against the base of a large tree. Swinging down, he stood for a moment, undecided. He'd found Lars, but maybe he should just let him go. He didn't really want to bring him back and have to take care of him.

The snow muffled his footsteps as he started forward and he was soon standing unnoticed just behind the boy.

"Lars."

The boy jumped at the sound of his voice and when his eyes found Sasha they went wild with fear. Sasha crouched down, his own eyes taking in his little brother's convulsive shivering and blue tinged skin. He wore nothing more than his ordinary clothes and those were of very little use against the cold.

"What are you doing?" he asked.

"Going home."

"You're going the wrong way. And you're going to freeze to death."

"I'm not cold," Lars answered through chattering teeth.

Sasha almost smiled. "You know, if you could have stopped shivering long enough to say that I might have believed you."

Lars' head hung and he turned away from Sasha.

"You said you weren't coming after me. You said you don't want me."

"I did." Sasha sighed. "Look, if you really prefer to run off in the cold and take your chances out here rather than come home with me, I don't care, and I won't stop you. But at least" - Sasha reached for the clasp of his cloak and undid it - "take this so you won't die of cold."

Lars looked from Sasha to the proffered cloak then back to Sasha, confusion and indecision replacing the fear on his face. He reached out a tentative, trembling hand and took the cloak from Sasha, his eyes never leaving Sasha's face. Sasha shrugged and stood up to go.

He'd only made it a few steps before Lars called after him. "Wait. You're really not going to make me go back with you?"

Sasha turned and saw Lars was standing now, and not wasting any time in getting the warm outer garment over his shoulders. He pulled it close around him.

"I'm really not."

"If I go back with you, what happens?"

"What do you mean?"

"Are you going to punish me?"

"No. If you come back with me, I guess I'll just be stuck taking care of you." Which I don't really want to do, Sasha reminded himself.

Lars stood undecided for another moment before starting towards Sasha. "I'll come."

"Come on then, I'm starting to get cold." Sasha tried to ignore his own relief at Lars' words as he mounted his horse again and helped Lars up in front of him.

Chapter 40

"CAN I GET UP TODAY? PLEASE, Sasha?" Aki pushed himself up on his elbow to ask. "I'm almost all better. It doesn't hurt nearly as bad as before. And I'm tired of lying here."

Sasha frowned. He'd been hoping Taliea would come back before this and tell him whether or not Aki was ready to leave bed. She'd been by once, a few days ago, and Sasha expected her again any day. So far, she was the only knock he'd answered, although there had been others. Avoiding people was the only way he could see to avoiding conversations about what happened. As long as he could manage that, he could push away the grief that ate away at him. He could pretend it wasn't there.

"I guess you can try. But if it makes your head hurt worse, lay back down," he said at last. "Lars, come with me."

Lars obeyed, following him out the door and around the side where the wood pile was. Sasha had gotten into the habit of sending him out alone to bring in firewood, but today he needed more than wood. Lars didn't wait for Sasha to tell him what to do. He started filling his arms with logs.

"Wait. I brought you out here to talk to you."

Lars stopped and looked up at Sasha, his eyes questioning and timid. He hadn't been quite as frightened of him since Sasha brought him back, but the fear was still there and quick to reassert itself in moments like these.

"I don't want you saying anything to Aki about what happened to him. As far as he knows, it was an accident, and I want it to stay that way. Understand?"

"Yes, Sasha."

"Good, because if you tell him anything other than that, you'll regret it." Sasha's voice was stern, and Lars stepped back, his face whitening a little.

"I understand, Sasha. I won't tell."

"Now finish getting some wood."

Sasha watched as Lars finished his task, noting how low the pile had once again gotten. Boris had been the last one to add to it, and Sasha had yet to be able to bring himself to move the ax from where his brother had set it. Maybe he could just have Lars do it since he was having Lars do pretty much everything else.

Inside, Aki had managed to make it from his bed to a chair at the table, but now sat with his head resting in his hands.

"Is it worse?" Sasha asked, sitting down across from him.

"No." Aki looked up quickly, and grimaced. "It's fine."

Sasha shook his head. There was a very tiny part of him that harbored guilt for the lie he'd told Aki, but for the most part, it was nice to have someone in the home who wasn't terrified of him and that made the lie worth it. To Aki, Sasha was the one who'd nursed him back to health, not the one who'd nearly killed him. Sasha didn't see any reason to change that.

Sasha was about to open his mouth and tell Aki that he should go back to bed when a knock sounded on the door. Even though he knew it would only be

Taliea, Sasha was reluctant to answer it. At least with Aki up and about, this was probably the last time she would need to come.

He pulled the door open and froze.

"Phelie?"

"I came to bring this back to you," Ophelia said, her hands holding out the shirt he'd given her to wear that night, her eyes looking everywhere but at him.

Everything he'd spent the last two weeks refusing to think about came rushing back. Seeing Ophelia in Father's hands, being given a choice between her life and Boris', watching Father undress her, the fear in her eyes when she held his knife back. He'd buried all of that away, and he intended to keep it that way. He started to close the door again, but Ophelia's hand was quick to stop it.

"Don't," she said. "Can we talk?"

"I don't think that's a good idea." Sasha choked over his words, totally unprepared for the onslaught of memory and emotion that assaulted him now.

"Please?" She finally met his eyes and no matter how much Sasha wanted to, he couldn't refuse.

He stepped away to let her in, but she shook her head.

"Can we go somewhere else, maybe?"

"I guess." Sasha glanced back to where Aki and Lars were both staring curiously at the open door and decided that elsewhere was definitely a better idea. "Just a minute." Bundling up against the cold, he turned to the boys, "I'm going out for a bit. Aki, don't stay out of bed too long."

They walked in silence for some distance, the snow crunching softly beneath their feet. Although he hadn't intended to, Sasha was not at all surprised when they reached the small waterfall. He knew he should say something, but words weren't his friend at the moment. Sitting down on a fallen tree, he plucked a piece of bark from it and began tearing it apart with his fingers. Ophelia was apparently at a loss for words as well, since she had said nothing since leaving the cabin. Sasha risked a glance in her direction and saw that she was staring at the falls.

"I saw you, in town," Ophelia said without looking at him.

"I know. I saw you, too."

"You rode past us."

Sasha winced at the hurt accusation in her voice. "I didn't think you'd want to talk to me."

"Because of what happened?"

"Because what happened was my fault. You were almost raped because of me. Boris is dead because of me. And because you watched me almost kill someone."

"You cannot blame yourself for what your father chose to do. Those were his decisions, not yours."

"Does it matter? The only reason he even came here was because of me. Besides, I thought you would still be afraid of me."

"I'm not scared of you. I've not been afraid of you since you came here."

"You were." Sasha could not keep the bitterness out of his voice, "I saw you, when you stopped me. You were afraid of me."

Ophelia turned to face him for the first time. "Why are you being like this? I have never lied to you. Not once, Sasha. And you know that. I was afraid for you, not of you. You were about to do something that could not be undone and however much you thought you wanted to kill him, I knew you didn't really."

"Well, he didn't die, if that's what you came to ask about. He's just fine, in fact," Sasha said, kicking a clump of snow away angrily. The worst part was that he wasn't even sure why he was angry. It was just there, and completely unreasonable and out of his control.

"I already knew that," Ophelia said softly. "It's not why I came."

"Then why did you?"

"Because you've locked yourself away for the better part of two weeks. You won't see or speak to anyone but Taliea, and the only reason you see her is because of your brother. Because you are my friend, and you shouldn't have to face all of this alone." Ophelia paused and wiped away a tear. "And because I need you. Everyone else feels sorry for what happened to me, but you're the only one who was actually there with me."

Sasha did not have any idea what to say to that and so he picked the simplest thing. "He's not actually my brother, you know."

"What? Who's not?" Ophelia studied him in confusion.

"The one I almost killed. He's my nephew. But it's kind of a complicated, sick story."

"I'd rather not hear it right now, then. I'm glad he's still alive, though. They really didn't do anything, Sasha. It was all your father and Lord Bayner."

"I know, I know. See, you're still afraid I'll kill them."

Ophelia tossed her hands up, "How many times do I have to say that I'm not? Is it really so hard for you to understand that?"

Sasha kicked at another clump of snow and shoved his hands down into his pockets. He knew Ophelia was staring at him, waiting for him to answer. But anything that came out of his mouth right now would be laced with this unreasonable anger. He shouldn't be angry at her. Nothing she'd said was wrong.

"It's not even me you're angry at, is it?" Ophelia said, her voice softening. "You really blame yourself for everything that happened."

"Boris knew. And he tried to tell me. I just wouldn't listen. I should have. You don't know how much I wish I had," Sasha said, his voice breaking. "And now he's gone, and I never even got the chance to tell him I was sorry. I was horrible to him. And do you know what he said, when he was dying?"

"I don't know what anyone said, Sasha."

"Father was going to make me choose between you and him - which one of you I wanted to live," Sasha went on, barely acknowledging her words. "And he said that I should have picked him to die. He thought I could actually do that. Then he begged me not to hate him. He saved all of us, and still thought I would hate him. How could I have done that? How could I have ever made him think that? I hate myself more than I could ever hate him."

"I don't think he'd want you to do that, either. If he were alive..."

"But he's not. And it's my fault he's not. If I'd just listened. If I'd just died in that battle, none of this would have happened."

"If you had died, a lot of other things wouldn't have happened either. If you had died, Boris would have had no one to go to here. What would have happened to him then? Go back to your father? You can't go back and undo the past, Sasha, and you can't carry the weight of everyone else's choices, either."

"I don't know what to do."

"You're already doing it." Ophelia looked at him curiously.

"What do you mean?"

"You're taking care of your brothers, or brother and nephew, I guess. And you're talking to me."

"Is that something I needed to do?"

"It's something I needed you to do. I've missed you. What were you going to do? Just hide for the rest of your life."

"It was working just fine." Sasha was reluctant to admit that he'd missed her too. Missed the friendship they shared. He thought there wasn't a chance of getting it back and wasn't planning on trying.

"No, it wasn't. You're not a hermit, no matter how much you try to be."

"And is that the only reason you came - to save me from being a hermit?"

"I already told you why I came. If I talk about what happened to anyone else, they don't really understand." Ophelia stood up. "And I want you to take me to wherever you buried him. I would like to see his grave."

"I don't know," Sasha started.

"He saved me too, Sasha. It's only right. Dagmar wants to know where it is, too."

Of course, she did, Sasha thought. Dagmar was the one to see what Sasha had been blind to - the fact that his brother was more than a broken wreck and a burden. She'd been his friend, which was a lot more than Sasha could say for himself.

"I'll take you," he said, getting to his feet.

Neither said a word while they walked, but Sasha didn't mind. It wasn't the same stiff silence they had shared earlier.

The grave was not so far from where they'd been sitting. After two weeks, the mound of brown dirt was now white with snow. The only splash of color against the bleak gray, white and brown of the wintery forest, was the verdant evergreens that stood in a cluster.

"This is a good place." Ophelia made no effort to conceal the tears that gathered in her eyes. "In the spring, you should plant something over the grave to mark it permanently."

"Is that how you do it here?"

Ophelia nodded. "It's our way of making a memorial to someone we lost. And a reminder that life goes on despite the loss."

"I don't know if I'm ready for that reminder."

"But if it doesn't go on, then his death is wasted, isn't it?"

Although Ophelia had not understood anything that was said in the final moments between Sasha and Boris, Sasha could not help but remember Boris' last words. *Don't waste it.* Boris had been speaking of Sasha's position as the eldest son, at least that's what Sasha assumed he was talking about. But what did Boris think he could do about that? How was there a way he could not waste it? He glanced at Ophelia. If there was one person he could talk to about it, it was her. Ophelia didn't give him the chance, though.

"Father's tried talking to you."

"I know. I wasn't ready to talk to anyone, him especially."

"Why him?" Ophelia looked at him questioningly.

"He ought to be angry with me, for you."

"He was angry. Actually, I've never seen him so angry as when I told him what happened, but it wasn't at you." Ophelia paused, looking away and Sasha knew there was something more she meant to tell him. "He needed to talk to you. There had to be an inquiry."

"An inquiry?"

"Three people died in one night. One of them a nobleman. The Magistrate had to know what happened."

"They blame me?"

"No." Ophelia shook her head. "They just had to determine who was to blame. It's all taken care of now, though."

"How?"

"Father made the report. They just needed a witness. They had one."

"You?"

Ophelia nodded, still not looking at him.

"I'm sorry. You shouldn't have had to do that. Not alone."

Ophelia gave him a weak smile that did little to make him feel less ashamed. He couldn't imagine having to tell strangers what happened that night, but it had to have been worse for Ophelia, and he'd left her to do that.

"He left your brothers out of it. He said if you wanted to bring charges against them as accomplices, that was up to you."

"I guess I should probably go talk to him, shouldn't I?"

"You should. He's not angry with you, I promise."

"I should get back," Sasha said, not wanting to make any commitment right now. "I shouldn't leave them alone for so long."

Ophelia nodded. "Do you mind if I show Dagmar where this is?"

"No, I don't. She deserves to know. She was better with him than I ever was."

Aki was asleep on his bed again when Sasha finally said goodbye to Ophelia and reentered the cabin. Lars, sitting in his customary corner out of the way, looked up at Sasha's entrance. His face underwent a series of quick transformations as Sasha came toward him and sat down next to him.

"Relax, I'm not going to hurt you." Sasha sighed as he watched his brother stiffen. "I just need to talk to you."

"What do you need to talk about?"

"Home. Your home. What's it like?"

"I don't understand, Sasha. You already know what it's like."

"No. I know what it used to be. Father spoke of uprisings and revolts. What's happened since their defeat in the mountains?"

"Father didn't want us talking about it."

"Father's dead," Sasha said harshly. "And you could be too if I decide to exert that particular right as his eldest son and heir."

"No, please don't. I'm sorry. I didn't mean to anger you."

"Then answer me," Sasha said shortly. "What is it like now?"

"What he said is true. After the battle, the defeat," Lars didn't hesitate this time, "So few warriors returned. Only three of his sons came back and he had them executed."

"I already know that."

"He didn't stop there. He sort of went mad," Lars whispered the words as if half expecting Father to resurrect in the room and punish him for his disloyalty. "He also executed most of the clansmen that survived for the same reason. After that, he didn't have enough men to guard anything or to raid."

"So, no Spring Market?" Sasha couldn't exactly say he was sorry to hear that.

"No Market. He had nothing to sell."

"What about the revolts?"

"It started with the free people. No one had enough food. No one had enough money to buy food. They blamed Father."

"Who blamed me," Sasha said more to himself. "Go on."

"Then the slaves turned on us. At first, they just refused to work. And there weren't enough men left to make them. Then some of them started burning down houses, killing their owners."

"So, what's it like now that all that has happened?"

"There're almost no slaves left. After the first month or so, they just started leaving and we couldn't stop them. Father tried putting together a few raiding parties, but that didn't really work. Now, people just scrounge for whatever they can. A lot of people starved to death last winter, and probably will again this winter."

"But Father still hated me enough to come down here to get revenge rather than deal with his country."

"I think it was easier for him to do that than to face the real problems," Lars said, his face turning thoughtful.

Sasha studied his little brother for a moment. "I think you're probably right. So, what were his plans? Who'd he leave in charge?"

"He left Faramund in charge until spring. He did not expect to return until spring. We were going to stay at the lord's estate when he was," Lars eyed Sasha warily, "finished here."

Sasha nodded his understanding. "Probably wanted to skip out on the whole starving part. Faramund, the clansman from Jarle?"

"Yes."

That made sense. Faramund was an older man, far too old to have great ambitions of overthrowing a current chief. He'd been the clansman of Jarle, a sizable town on their coast, for as long as Sasha could remember. More than being old and unthreatening to Gundar, he was one of the few clansmen capable of organizing anything other than a raid. Jarle was a trading port that brought in more money year-round than any other town in Aruuk. And he was the one who had made it that. It made sense to have a man like that in charge during such upheaval.

"So, no one's expecting him back until spring. No one will miss him until then."

"Yes, Sasha. I haven't lied to you, I promise."

"I believe you." A wry smile tugged at his mouth as he watched relief sweep over his little brother.

He leaned his head back against the wall and shut his eyes. There were at least three months of deep winter left, four if it was going to be a particularly harsh one. Three months to decide what Boris had meant, and how he was going to fulfill it. Did Boris seriously expect him to go back and take up the position of Chief? Sasha didn't want it. It would be fraught with difficulties, especially now. Pushing all thoughts of it away, he glanced sideways at Lars.

"Do you miss being home?"

"I," Lars looked confused, "I don't know."

"It's alright. Whether you miss it or not, I'm not going to be mad."

"I really don't know. It's all I've ever known."

Sasha shrugged and started to get up.

"Sasha, what are you going to do with me?" Lars asked and Sasha turned around to meet his wide, questioning eyes.

Sasha shrugged again. "Haven't really decided yet. I don't know what I'm going to do with either of you."

"If you decide to only keep one of us, it will be Aki, won't it?"

"Why would you say that?"

"You like him better than me." Lars stared down at the ground while he spoke.

"I don't," Sasha said, but it was a weak protest. He couldn't deny that there was some truth to Lars' words. He preferred the fact that Aki saw him as a rescuer and not someone to be feared. Lars saw him as quite the opposite. Sasha sighed. "Look, I'm not picking between the two of you. Whatever I decide, it will be for both."

The words didn't seem to dispel Lars' worries nearly as much as Sasha hoped they would, but there was nothing he could do about that. He had no idea what he was going to do with them. Or what he was going to do about Aruuk and the absence of its Chief.

Chapter 41

SASHA CROSSED THE ROOM AS quietly as he could, careful to avoid the spots of the floor that creaked beneath his weight. It was still dark out, but his eyes had adjusted to the darkness. Sitting down at the table, he started putting on his boots.

"Where are you going?" Aki's voice startled Sasha. He'd thought they were both still asleep.

"Out hunting. I'll be back in a bit. Go back to sleep."

"Can I go with you?"

"No." Hunting was one of his few unblemished memories with Boris, and Sasha was not prepared to invite anyone into that.

"I can help. I'm really good at helping. I can dress and carry whatever you get," Aki whispered. Sasha straightened and turned to see him half sitting up in the bed he and Lars shared. It didn't take any light to know the eagerness and desire that was on Aki's face at the moment. "I mean, I'm sorry. I wasn't trying to argue with you. I'll stay if you don't want me to come."

Sasha smiled a little. "It's alright. I guess you can come." Aki's enthusiasm was hard to dismiss. "Just be quiet about it."

Aki's version of being quiet wasn't exactly the same as Sasha's. His movements were still a little clumsy from what Sasha had done to his head. Lars was a heavy sleeper, though, and they made it out the door without waking him. Sasha pulled his cloak tighter around him as the bitter cold air hit him. Their breath hung in little clouds before them, and a fresh layer of snow crunched beneath their feet as they headed into the woods. It wasn't until they had reached a good spot to sit and wait that Sasha realized Aki was wearing only his everyday clothes and nothing to protect against the cold.

"Why didn't you put something else on?" Sasha leaned close and whispered so that he wouldn't disturb the wildlife nearby.

"Didn't have anything else," Aki whispered back. "It's alright, though. I'm used to it."

Sasha frowned and shook his head. Now that he thought about it, neither of the boys had anything more than what they wore.

"Didn't you bring anything with you when you came here?"

"Yes. But we left all our things with our horses. We expected to go back to them."

Sasha sighed. "And where are these horses?"

"At a stable in town." Aki blew on his hands in between each word.

Nodding, Sasha leaned back and turned his attention to the woods that were coming to life with the gray dawn. Settled in so near the creek, they did not have long to wait. Sasha slid an arrow free of the quiver and laid it on his bowstring. He fingered the fletching absently as he watched the small deer approach. Although it no longer bore the white spots of a fawn, it was still young. Drawing back slowly, he had to wait only a moment before the animal stopped and lowered its head to drink. With a hiss, the arrow shot free and sped toward its mark. Sasha held his breath until the sick thud of the arrow piercing flesh told him that he had not missed. The bleating cry of an animal in pain followed. The deer staggered for a few steps before collapsing.

Sliding his knife free, Sasha moved out of their hiding place and Aki followed.

"I can do it for you, if you want," Aki offered when Sasha had finished the deer off and was preparing to dress it.

Sasha shrugged and handed him the knife. Cleaning animal carcasses wasn't something he'd been taught to do at home. Nor was it something he particularly liked to do. It was always the slaves' job. He watched with curiosity as Aki knelt in the snow and went to work. His nephew was better at it than he was.

"When'd you learn to do that?"

"When I was eight. It was one of my jobs. Sometimes they'd send me out after they made the kill and sometimes, they would take me with them. I liked it better when they took me with them because then I'd have hours when I didn't have to do anything but be quiet."

Sasha smiled a little as he listened. In the last couple of weeks, Sasha had noticed his nephew's tendency to share far more than what was actually asked of him. It made him wonder how he had stayed alive for a full twelve years.

"That wouldn't have been your job," Sasha said, his face betraying his bewilderment. "That's something slaves did."

"That's what I was." Aki paused what he was doing and looked up at Sasha.

"But you were one of the Chief's sons." Sasha was careful not to say anything about Aki's real father. Lars had told him he didn't know, and Sasha wasn't sure if he'd remembered even that much of the night he'd almost died.

"I didn't know that then. And I never really was anyway. He just told me I was."

"So how did you end up, you know, here?"

Aki took a deep breath. "I knew my mother had been a slave and that she'd died but I never knew how. I always just assumed my father was too. I was raised as a slave. And then, when I was ten, I was waiting with the other ten-year-olds. We were supposed to be branded that day. And I was waiting my turn when a man came and told me that Chief Gundar had summoned me."

"That must have been terrifying," Sasha muttered.

"I've never been so scared. I thought I'd done something terribly wrong if it had come to his attention. But instead of punishing me, he told me that he was really my father and that he'd decided he wanted me as a son." Aki paused, filling their game bag with the fresh meat. "So then, I got to move into the Chief's house. And I didn't have to get branded, which was nice because I really didn't want to be branded. It would have hurt really bad. And I had my own room, and I didn't have to do the same work anymore, although I still had to work."

"Was it better then, being his son?"

Aki cocked his head, considering the question. "I don't actually know. I still had to do everything I was told to, and I got into more trouble as his son since he actually noticed me - a lot more trouble."

"Is that where the scars on your back come from?"

"Yes. Just a few months ago." Aki stood and staggered a little as he shouldered the heavy game bag.

"Here," Sasha took it from him, "you don't have to carry that."

They started back and hadn't gone far when Sasha changed his mind and their direction. If their horses and gear had all been left behind, then it was about time he recovered them. The boys needed more than the clothes on their backs.

"It was all a lie, anyway, wasn't it?" Aki said suddenly, his face somber.

"I'm afraid so."

"He wasn't really my father. He killed my father and my mother. I'm not sure why he even pretended I was his son."

"You remember that part then?"

"I didn't. Not until a few days ago. Do you think they actually loved me?"

"Your real parents? I think, Aki, that's why they chose to die for you."

"It's my fault they're dead, though. If I'd never been born, they'd still be alive."

Sasha thought about Aki's words for a moment before answering. "Honestly, probably not. If Anton was willing to defy Father over that, then sooner or later he would have defied him over something else. And girls like your mother don't tend to survive that long. Besides," Sasha remembered Ophelia's words and understood them better in light of Aki's statement, "you can't blame yourself for what someone else chose to do. It was Father's choice to murder them, not yours."

Reaching town took some time and it was late morning by the time they reached the inn Aki said the horses were stabled at. Sasha didn't need to ask which ones they were. This far into winter, there were few people traveling and the only horses in the stable were Father's. A hasty search of Father's things revealed a pouch full of money that Sasha used to pay for the month of care the horses had received.

"Where are we taking them?" Aki asked when they had loaded all of the party's possessions onto three of the horses and saddled the other two.

"I can't take them back with me. I don't have room for this many." Sasha thought for a minute. "We'll take them to a friend of mine. He'll have something he can do with them."

Seeing Stephan wasn't exactly what Sasha wanted to do, but it made the most sense. He had no need or space for five more horses, and Stephan always did. They were good horses, too. Father never had anything less than the best in his stables.

Stephan wasn't outside when they rode up to the large barn. Motioning for Aki to wait, Sasha dismounted and started for the open barn doors. Voices drifted out to meet him and he almost turned back. He didn't want to bother Stephan if he was already busy. It was the fact that he had nothing else he could do with them that kept him there. After all, it was probably just a courier passing through. Stepping into the barn, Sasha froze.

"Sasha?" Hamo and Stephan both turned toward him, and Sasha studied the ground at his feet.

He hadn't seen Hamo since the day Hamo had removed the band, and he hadn't exactly been nice that day. He'd meant to, ever since he and Ophelia had talked. But that was two weeks ago, and in those two weeks, Sasha had not been able to muster the courage to do so.

"I...," Sasha swallowed hard. "I brought something for you, Stephan, if you want them."

He turned and exited the barn as fast as he could, not really caring whether or not Stephan would follow him. He reached the first horse and started undoing the straps that held the packs in place.

"Where are they from?" Stephan, standing directly behind him, asked.

"My father. But he can't use them anymore and I have no use or space for them." Sasha's fingers were slow and clumsy, his thoughts everywhere but on the horse in front of him.

"Why don't you let me take care of them?" Stephan laid a hand on his shoulder and pulled him away. Sasha didn't argue. He wasn't accomplishing much anyway. "You and Hamo need to talk."

Sasha ignored his last words and turned to Aki. "Get down."

Aki slid to the ground, holding onto the horse for a second to catch his balance. Aside from the fact that he couldn't remember what had caused his injuries, there were almost no other symptoms remaining. Losing his balance was one of the few and only showed itself sometimes. Sasha watched with anxiety as a grimace of pain flashed across his nephew's face. Maybe he should have insisted on leaving him home.

The pained look passed in a second and Aki turned to Sasha. "Do you want me to help? I'm really good at taking care of horses. I did it a lot before. It was one of my jobs too. It was actually one of my favorite ones."

Sasha shrugged. "If you want."

With Stephan and Aki taking care of the horses, Sasha couldn't make up another excuse to avoid Hamo. He glanced over to where he stood waiting by the barn door and, heaving a heavy sigh, made his way over. Shoving his hands down into his pockets and kicking at the snow, he tried to come up with something to say.

"I'm so...," Sasha started.

"I know. It's alright, I understand," Hamo interrupted. "Which one is that?"

Sasha followed his eyes to Aki. "That's the one I almost killed."

"Phelie told me he was better. What changed your mind?"

"I don't know. I just couldn't actually let him die. Not after everything else I messed up." Sasha went back to studying the ground. "You were going to take him that day, weren't you? After I said that I didn't care if he died."

"I was."

"Why didn't you?"

"You weren't really going to let your brother die. I knew that. You were angry and hurt. But not cruel. You've never been cruel."

"I really am sorry, Hamo. For what happened to Phelie. She told me about the inquiry, too. I shouldn't have made her do that. And I probably shouldn't have ignored you all those times. I just thought it would make it easier, but I don't think there really is a way to make it any easier. He's just gone, and I miss him no matter what I do."

"I'd love to tell you there's an end to that, but there isn't. He'll always be gone, and you'll always miss him. But that doesn't mean you just stop living. That's a poor way to repay the life he gave you."

"I know. There's something more." Sasha hesitated. He'd almost told Ophelia this, and he'd spent the last weeks thinking about it. "My father's death has left Aruuk without a leader."

"What does that have to do with you? I assume his eldest is his heir."

"That's me. I'm his eldest."

Hamo looked confused.

"Between the defeat in the mountains and Father's killing spree afterwards, all of my older brothers are dead."

"And you're seriously considering going back?"

"I don't know. Something Boris said," Sasha began, but a shout from Stephan interrupted him. He turned to see Stephan coming out of the barn. "What is it?"

"Whoever that was you brought with you, your brother I guess, he's not well."

Sasha didn't bother to correct Stephan on his relationship to Aki as he hurried into the barn. It was easy to see what Stephan meant. Aki lay curled up on the ground, his head between his hands, moaning.

"Aki," Sasha knelt next to him and rested his hand on his nephew's shoulder. "What happened?"

"I'm sorry, Sasha," Aki murmured. "It hurts so bad."

"What's wrong with him?" Stephan, leaning over Sasha's shoulder, asked. Sasha had a moment of relief and gratitude when he realized that Stephan genuinely did not know about what he'd done to Aki. He'd just assumed Hamo and Ophelia would have told everyone.

"He hurt his head. It's gotten better, most of the time." Sasha silently berated himself for dragging Aki around so much throughout the day. He should have made him stay home. "I should get him home."

"You can't take him anywhere like that," Stephan said.

"I need to. He needs to lay down and I've already left Lars alone for most of the day."

Stephan shook his head. "Leave him."

"What?"

"Leave him here, with me. It'll be better for him, and you can come back and get him when he's feeling better." Stephan laid his hand on Sasha's shoulder for the second time. "It's alright, Sasha. Let me help."

Sasha took a deep breath, considering Stephan's offer. It was generous. It was Stephan's way of showing how sorry he was for what had transpired. Sasha couldn't refuse, especially when Aki was clearly not in any condition to travel anywhere.

"You're sure you don't mind? He won't understand anything you say to him."

"I don't mind. I think we can manage for a bit without that. He's not exactly talkative right now anyway. I've got a bed he's free to use."

Sasha slid an arm under Aki's shoulders and sat him up. Aki kept his eyes shut and his head cradled in his hands.

"Aki, I'm going to get you up now, alright?"

Aki moaned again as he tried to lift himself up.

"I don't want to move."

"I know. We're not going to move far. There's a place here where you can rest." Sasha pulled him all the way up and started toward the house.

Chapter 42

"WHERE'S AKI?" LARS SEARCHED the empty doorway behind Sasha with growing alarm on his face. "What did you do with him?"

"He's fine." Sasha set down the bundle of things he'd carried back. "He went out with me this morning and got one of his headaches. I left him with a friend. Here, these are your things."

Lars joined Sasha at the table. His eyes widened as he saw what it was Sasha had brought.

"He told you about the horses?"

"He did." Sasha was already untying the thongs that held the parcel closed.

"Is he coming back?"

"Of course, he's coming back."

"And he's not in trouble?"

Sasha sighed and rolled his eyes. "He's not in any trouble. Why can't you just believe me? He's fine. He just wasn't able to come back with me."

Lars looked down at the bundle and started pulling a set of clothes out. By the nervous glances he kept directing toward him, Sasha could tell his words meant nothing to Lars. And why should they? Sasha frowned as the thought came to him, but there was no denying its truth. He'd been the one to lie to Aki and demand that Lars go along with the lie. He'd threatened Lars into going along with it. Just like Father would have done.

Sasha sat down in a chair, resting his elbows on the table while he watched Lars sort through the belongings. He wanted Aki to keep believing the lie. He needed him to. He didn't want Aki looking at him the way Lars did, jumping every time he walked in the room, flinching every time he came close.

"Will you believe me if I take you with me to get him tomorrow morning?" he asked.

"You would take me with you?"

"Yes. I would." Sasha bit back his exasperation. It wouldn't help. "You know what, I'll take you with me somewhere now, if you want."

"To Aki?"

"No. Somewhere else. Another friend's."

Hamo had asked him to come over before they'd left Stephan's but up until this moment, Sasha had no intention of doing so. The prospect of spending the evening solely with Lars changed his mind. And he wanted to talk to Ophelia. There was more he wanted to say to her. Now that he thought about it, going seemed like the only reasonable option. And with his decision came a reprieve from the loneliness that haunted him.

"Come on." Sasha stood up and reached for his cloak, not waiting for Lars to respond.

Lars followed him out the door, his face a picture of uncertainty as he fell into step beside Sasha. They were not yet out of sight of the cabin when Lars timidly broke the silence.

"Sasha?"

"What is it?"

"What do you think will happen in the spring?"

Sasha stopped and faced Lars. "I think when they find out Father isn't coming home, a lot of people are going to be killed. That's how it goes. You don't have anything to worry about, though. You get to sit out the bloodbath here."

"It's not me I was thinking about."

"Oh?" Sasha started on again.

"It's my brothers and sister and mother. Do you suppose they'll all be killed?"

"Faramund would be a fool to let any heir of Father's live if he wanted to claim the position himself. He's old though. He might not even want it. But if he doesn't, someone else will. So, yes, I think they would be. How many brothers do you have?"

"Two full ones and a sister."

"Younger than you?"

Lars nodded. "What happens if you go back as Chief?"

"I'm not. I don't want to."

"But if you did, would you kill them?"

The fact that Sasha considered Lars' words before answering bothered him a little. It shouldn't even have been a question. If Hamo or Stephan had asked him, he wouldn't have had to think about it. Sasha shook his head slightly, driving away the images that wanted to force their way in. Images of all the things he'd done and wished he hadn't.

"No," he said at last, weighing each word carefully as he spoke. "I do not think that I would. I hope I would not. It would not be right."

Lars' eyebrows drew together in deep thought, and he walked on without saying a word. Sasha was tempted to say more on the subject but, considering how little faith Lars put in his words, decided against it. And they were out of time anyway. Patches of light glistened across the snow beneath each window of the house, warm and welcoming.

Sasha slowed his pace, questioning the mad optimism that had convinced him to come tonight. Maybe he should give it more time before he faced the world again. It was the fact that Lars was watching him out of the corner of his eye and pretending hard not to that prevented him from changing his mind.

"Come on," Sasha said aloud, though he meant the words as much for himself as for Lars.

"So, you decided to come after all?" Hamo met them coming out of the barn. "That's good."

Sasha wanted to disagree with him. The smell of food and the sound of talk and laughter that drifted through the door as they approached assured him that he'd made no mistake in coming. He'd missed this without knowing it.

Smiling at Lars' apprehension and suspicion, he followed Hamo inside. He felt his little brother press closer to him as they came into the sitting room. Remembering his own experience, and how strange and shocking it had been, he put his arm around Lars' shoulders and leaned down to whisper to him.

"They don't bite, you know." When Lars looked up at him questioningly, Sasha smiled and shook his head. "It's just a joke, Lars. They're my friends."

As the rest of the family noticed their presence, Sasha braced himself for the looks of pity and sympathy that he was sure would come. That was the part he wasn't ready to face. But, after a few minutes went by without them, Sasha began to suspect that Hamo had warned them against it. Edith was the only one who made any mention of his loss. And that was done quietly.

Sitting at the table, Sasha remembered how much he missed good food. Lars did as well, he noticed. The boy ate with a relish that was lacking when Sasha cooked.

Little Drogo, having finished his own food, now scrambled up onto Sasha's lap. Sasha, glad of the innocent distraction, smiled as the toddler hid his face behind his pudgy hands only to pull them away a second later giggling. Sasha played with him for several minutes before he felt someone watching him. Turning, he saw Lars staring at him - eyes agog and hurt at Sasha's interactions with the little one.

Sasha tried to ignore him, but it was hard to do now that he'd seen the longing in his little brother's eyes.

When, just a few minutes later, Lars spilled the cup of milk Edith had given him, Sasha couldn't ignore his brother any longer. The terror in his eyes and the way the blood drained from his face as he looked from the mess to Sasha was painful and Sasha didn't have the heart to scold him.

"I didn't mean to, Sasha. I'm sorry."

Sasha caught Ophelia's eyes briefly before answering his brother. She shook her head a little and smiled as she pushed away from the table and retrieved a cloth to clean it up with.

"It's fine, Lars. I know you didn't."

Lars wasn't expecting to hear that from Sasha and relief washed over his anxious face. Sasha turned away from him again. He shouldn't have brought him along. It was just making Sasha feel worse and worse.

Chapter 43

SASHA WATCHED AS LARS CARRIED in an armload of wood and set it down by the hearth with a loud clatter. Snowflakes clung to his little brother's clothes, melting slowly in the warmth of the cabin, as he laid two fresh logs on the fire. Winter was in no hurry to loosen its grip on the world yet.

"Sasha?" Lars turned to face him. "That's almost the last of it."

"It'll last for tonight. We'll chop more tomorrow." Or, rather, Lars would chop more tomorrow, Sasha thought. By the glum look on Lars' face, his brother understood the same. He sat down on the bed next to Aki, his mouth pulled down into a frown.

"It's your turn to be a slave now," Aki leaned forward and said in what was meant to be a whisper. Sasha, his back to both of them, stiffened with guilt as the words reached his ears.

"Shut up, Aki," Lars said, glowering at him but Aki only grinned.

Sasha turned around in time to see Lars' face go red and his hands clench into tight fists at his sides. Another second, and Lars would lash out at Aki.

Sasha had seen Boris look like that enough times to know.

"Stop, both of you."

Two faces, one sullen and the other amused, turned at the sound of his words. Sasha considered them for a moment, giving vent to a particularly heavy sigh. It's my own fault, he thought, and I guess that means I'm the only one who can fix it. He crossed the room to them, sitting on the edge of the bed. Both boys continued to watch him, their expressions shifting to wary curiosity. Sasha took a deep breath.

"Lars, you're not my slave and it is wrong of me to treat you as such. You're my brother, as much as Boris was" - Lars' eyes widened with shock as he remembered how adamant Sasha had been about that - "and I should have been acting like it. I'm sorry. It's not going to be like that from now on. From now on, we'll share the work. We'll get through the winter here and in the spring," Sasha paused. He remembered Boris' words, and Lars' fears for his family. It was time he made a decision. "In the spring, we will go home together."

Lars gasped. "But you said..."

"I know. I was wrong. And I've changed my mind. If I don't go back, many people are going to die - including your family. I can try to stop that. And, even if I fail at that, we can at least try to get your family out. Do you want to do that?"

"Yes."

"Well, then, it's settled." Sasha glanced over at Aki. His nephew's face did not mirror Lars' tentative hopefulness. Sasha didn't bother to try to figure out why. There was something else he needed to do. Something he'd put off far too long. Something that made him just like Father. "Aki, I want you to come outside with me."

Aki's face paled and he dropped his eyes as he shuffled across the room. Before Sasha followed him out the door he turned to Lars.

"You remember what I asked you to lie about?" Lars nodded. "You don't have to worry about that anymore. I'm going to tell him the truth."

"Why?"

"Because it's the right thing to do. I should never have asked you to lie for me anymore than I should have treated you like my slave. Lars, I really am sorry about that. You have no idea how much I wish I could go back and undo that."

Lars nodded again, considering Sasha's words. Whether he accepted them or not, a great weight was lifted from Sasha's shoulders.

Aki stood outside, shifted from one foot to the other, his arms wrapped tightly around himself, waiting. He looked up when Sasha opened the door and joined him, lines of worry creasing his forehead.

"Am I in trouble, Sasha?" Aki's voice quivered a little over the words. "I didn't mean anything by what I said to Lars. I just said it as a joke."

"Come on."

Sasha led the way to the lean-to that sheltered his horse. When Aki wasn't begging to go over to Stephan's to help with the horses, he was out here with Sasha's black mare, brushing her until her coat shone. Inside, the wind was not so bad, and the warmth of the horse made the place bearable. Sasha ran an appraising hand along the mare's neck while she, in turn, nuzzled Aki's shoulder.

"I think she likes all the attention you give her."

"Do you not want me to do that?" Aki asked, trying to decipher Sasha's purpose in bringing him out here. "I'll stop if you don't want me to do that."

"No. If you want to brush her for hours, I don't care," Sasha answered. He knew what he had to say, but now that they were out here, saying it was a monumental task. Aki would hate and fear him within just a few minutes. But Sasha was done acting like Father. Sasha blew his breath out slowly. "Aki, there's something I should have told you a while ago but didn't."

Aki's hand stopped mid stroke on the horse's nose. He stepped back away as if to distance himself from whatever Sasha was about to say.

"Do you remember, when you first really woke up and you asked me what happened to you?"

"Yes," Aki answered carefully. "You said it was an accident. That there had been an accident and I was hurt."

"I lied." Sasha was a little surprised at how easily those words came out now. "I didn't want you to know the truth, because I didn't want you to be afraid of me the way Boris had been, and the way Lars was."

"Why would I have been afraid of you?" Aki's voice was weighted with suspicion.

"Because I was the one who hurt you." Aki took another step back. "I was angry at what happened to Boris and to Phelie. I was angry and I took that anger out on you. I nearly killed you. I would have killed you if I hadn't been stopped."

"But I don't understand. You were the one who was there. When I woke up, you were the one taking care of me. If you wanted to kill me, you wouldn't have done that. Why?"

"You weren't the one who'd tortured Boris. It wasn't your fault. You didn't deserve to die. I just couldn't see it at the time. When you woke up, I didn't want you to be afraid of me, so I lied, and I made Lars lie too. But that wasn't right." Sasha ran his hand across the mare's back one last time before turning to face Aki. "I know you probably hate me for what I did to you, and I completely understand that, but I'm sorry for it and I will never hurt you again."

Aki was quiet for so long that Sasha was beginning to think he wasn't going to say anything at all. He just stood in front of the horse, his fingers fiddling with her forelock, his face unreadable.

"A lot of people have hurt me," Aki started in a whisper, avoiding Sasha's eyes and Sasha remembered the scars on his back. "But no one has ever helped me before." Aki finally looked up at Sasha. "No one's ever been sorry for hurting me. You really are different."

Those were the last words Sasha expected to hear. They were the best words he could have heard.

Chapter 44

CAN I ASK YOU SOMETHING?" Sasha leaned forward, placing his elbows on his knees, and studied his folded hands as he spoke. "Suppose I was to go back and take my father's place. What would you think?"

Looking up he met three pairs of stunned eyes.

"I didn't know you were actually thinking of going back," Hamo started.

"That would be very dangerous, don't you think?" Edith added.

"It could be. And I wasn't. Not really." He risked a glance in Ophelia's direction. The fact that she wasn't the first to speak was worrisome. Her refusing to meet his eyes now was worse. He turned back to Hamo and Edith. "Look, I know it sounds crazy, and maybe it is. But Lars has two younger brothers, full brothers, and a sister. He's worried sick about them. And he ought to be. Besides, I think it's what Boris wanted."

"Well, if you put a stop to every crazy idea you had, you wouldn't have ended up here," Hamo said. "But, Sasha, have you really thought about this? I know not everything has worked out the way you wanted it to here, but you have a life here."

"Not to mention, your chances of having someone try to kill you here are considerably less than they would be there," Edith added.

"I know." Sasha hesitated, glancing at Ophelia once more but she was still avoiding him. It didn't matter. He already had his mind made up. But it bothered him. He didn't want anyone thinking badly of him for leaving, especially not Ophelia. "Boris knew I was the oldest. He knew I was the heir. And one of the last things he said to me was to not waste it. I think if I just stayed here, I'd be wasting it."

"What would you do if you went back?" Hamo asked.

"I'd like to think I could show them that there's a better way to live. They're starving, they've lost almost everything, they might be ready to change."

"Honestly, Sasha, that sounds like a disaster," Hamo said.

"I guess," Sasha said, his confidence ebbing. "But they are my people, and I think I owe it to them to try."

"I'm just worried they might not be grateful for the effort."

"If I go, I'll go straight to the clansmen. With Father's signet ring, they can't deny that I have the most valid claim." Sasha had only just recently remembered that ring and its importance. Unfortunately, it was buried with Father which meant they were going to have to dig him back up. Sasha decided not to mention that part. "If they'll swear to me, then I won't have too much to worry about."

"And your brothers?"

"The oldest one left alive is thirteen or fourteen. Not much of a threat at the moment. I'd have to figure out something with them, I guess. But there has to be a better way than slaughtering or maiming all of them."

Sasha leaned back and waited. For the last two months he'd thought about it. Toyed with the idea.

Tossed around plans to accomplish it. Debated its possibilities. Questioned his own motives about it. And all of that led him back to Boris' words. Words that Lars had only driven in deeper when he spoke of the despair and destitution of the people. In some indirect way, he was responsible for all of it. And now it was his to make right. He'd promised the boys that he would.

"You know I won't stop you," Hamo finally said.

"But do you want to?"

"Yes. And no. But I think my motives for stopping you would be selfish. You're safe here. But, then again, safety isn't the most important thing. You know that whatever you decide to do I would be proud of you. You've come a long way from the first time I met you."

"I could barely stand when you first met me." Sasha smiled. Never in a million years would he be able to tell Hamo what his words really meant. "It's nice to know I've fully recovered from that."

"You'd have to leave soon, wouldn't you?"

"As soon as the weather breaks. I can't afford to wait too long," Sasha said. "The longer they're left wondering where the Chief is, the more unrest there will be."

A sudden movement caught his attention from the corner of his eyes. He turned in time to see Ophelia getting up and leaving the room for outside. Sasha watched her go, trying to suppress the disappointment that came unexpectedly. He wasn't sure what he'd wanted her to say. He hadn't even known how much he wanted her to say something. But the fact that she'd remained silent and was now no longer even in the room hurt and confused him. He was so sure he was doing the right thing; he'd thought she'd be happy.

"Did I say something wrong?" Sasha turned back to Hamo and Edith.

While Hamo shrugged, Edith answered, "Maybe you should go ask her."

"Right. I should do that, I guess."

The moon reflecting off the blanket of white snow lit the night up enough that Sasha's eyes needed no time to adjust, and it only took him a few moments to locate Ophelia by the paddock fence. Her back was to him, and she didn't seem to hear him come up behind her although Sasha wasn't making any particular effort to be quiet.

"Are you angry with me?"

"No," Ophelia answered too quickly, turning her head so that he couldn't see her face. "I'm fine."

"You're sure? I mean, you don't usually walk out like that."

"I'm sure." Ophelia sighed. "I guess you'll be getting ready to go then soon, won't you?"

"I guess. Probably the next couple of weeks."

"I don't want you to go, Sasha," Ophelia said flatly, finally turning to face him.

"I thought you would. It's the right thing for me to do. I thought you'd be happy I was doing it without everyone else telling me I should."

"No. I mean, I don't *want* you to go."

"It won't be forever. Just until I can get things figured out there."

"It could be. You might be killed. Or you might decide you like it better than here. And I don't want you to go."

"I think I can promise you I won't decide I like it better. There's nothing about Aruuk that I like better than here. Besides, there's too many people I like here. I don't want to lose them forever. This is my home now."

"Homes can change, Sasha. You know that better than anyone. And you're choosing to go back."

"I'm confused. Are you angry?"

"No. Yes. Why can't you just stay? You have your brothers to take care of. Isn't that enough?"

"I would have thought you'd be the first to say it's not. I'm sorry, Phelie. I didn't want this. I never thought it would bother you so much." Sasha sighed, leaning forward on the fence and staring out at the moonlit forest. He would miss this. He would miss everyone. He would miss Ophelia. "I will come back. I promise, Phelie."

"Don't. You shouldn't promise something like that. You have no idea what will happen." Ophelia brought a hand up and swiped away a tear that was running down her face.

"Are you crying? Why?" Sasha said in discomfort.

"Just because I want to." Now she sounded truly upset.

Sasha shoved his hands down into his pockets and stared at his feet. "I should probably get back." He wasn't sure what else to say. "I'm going to have a lot to do in the next couple of weeks."

He waited for Ophelia to say something, but aside from a brief, stiff nod, she remained silent.

Chapter 45

IT WAS STILL VERY EARLY WHEN the trio set out, leaving the small cabin behind in the predawn haze. Sasha glanced behind him and met Lars' eyes, bright with excitement. He smiled a little. Lars had spoken of little else in the last three weeks. Most mornings found him looking anxiously out the window to see if the snow was melting. Aki was considerably less enthusiastic, refusing now to even look at Sasha. By the swift, angry motion of his hand that he brought to his eyes over and over again Sasha had no doubt he was crying and trying his best not to.

Although the air was still cold, the snow was gone leaving behind many shades of brown. The mud squelched beneath their horses' hooves, turning an otherwise silent ride noisy. Spring was still too much of a newcomer to have welcomed back all the summer songbirds. Sasha took in the now familiar woods around him. The trees had seemed so strange with their wide sprawling limbs and brilliant autumn foliage, so different from everything he'd grown up. Now they were welcoming. And he was leaving them behind. Sasha found himself torn somewhere between Lars' excitement and Aki's reluctance - especially when he thought of the goodbyes he'd yet to say.

"Will Stephan be there?" Aki asked, and the hitch in his voice confirmed Sasha's suspicions. It hardly came as a surprise that Aki wanted to see Stephan one last time. He'd practically lived in Stephan's barn, as much as Sasha would allow him to at least.

"If he's not, we'll ride by his place. I don't think we'll have time for you to say goodbye to each horse, though," Sasha teased, trying to coax at least a smile from him. It didn't work.

The somber faces that met them when they reached Hamo's did little to help the lump in Sasha's throat. He pulled his horse to a stop and, taking a steadying breath, swung down. He glanced toward Ophelia standing in the back, but she refused to look at him. He hated that more than he thought possible.

"I guess it's time, then," Sasha said as he approached Hamo, extending his hand.

Hamo clasped his hand. "There's still time to change your mind."

"You know I can't. I will come back though. They may be my people, but this is my home."

"You're always welcome here, you know that."

When he turned to Edith, Sasha was a little startled by her embrace. "Be safe," she whispered before letting him go.

Sasha moved to the little ones. They were easier to say goodbye to, especially little Drogo. Without a real understanding of what Sasha was undertaking, he wrapped his chubby arms happily around Sasha's neck.

The sound of someone approaching on horseback made Sasha turn toward the drive in time to see Stephan approaching.

"You weren't going to leave without saying anything to me, were you?" Stephan dismounted.

Shaking his head, Sasha answered, "We were going there next."

"Can I talk to you for a minute?"

"Sure." Sasha followed Stephan out of earshot of the others. "Is something wrong?"

"He doesn't want to go."

"You're talking about Aki, I assume."

Stephan nodded.

"I know. His life wasn't great there before, and he's afraid it'll be worse with the headaches he gets now." Those headaches still came frequently, and Aki was completely incapacitated by them. "There's nothing I can do about it, though."

"There's something I can do about it." Stephan held up a hand to stop Sasha's questions. "Leave him. Alina and I have talked about it a lot. He's starting to really learn the language here, he's better with the horses than most men I've ever met, and I could use the help. I'm not getting any younger. I'd pay him fairly and help get him set up in whatever he wants to do when he's old enough if you're not back by then. What do you say?"

Sasha smiled slowly. "You know, Stephan, if I didn't know any better, I'd say you actually care about him."

"Maybe I do." Stephan returned the smile. "Or maybe I'm getting old enough to realize I need help and want to snatch it up when I find it. He's good help."

"It's his choice. If he wants to stay, I don't mind. I'll ask him."

Aki's eyes were suspiciously red when Sasha laid a hand on his knee to get his attention. In a few words, Sasha explained Stephan's offer, watching as his nephew's face went from forlorn to ecstatic in a matter of seconds.

"Well, I guess I know your answer then, don't I?"

"Did he really say that? He really wants me? I'll work hard and I'll do everything he tells me to. I won't cause him any trouble. He really wants me to stay with him?"

"He does, or he wouldn't have asked. So, I'll let him know you want to?"

"You'll let me?" Aki asked.

"It's your choice." Sasha shrugged. Before he could say anything else, Aki slid down from his horse and wrapped his arms tightly around him. Startled, Sasha stepped back, laughing a little.

"Thank you," Aki's voice was muffled, "For letting me choose."

Aki relinquished his hold and backed away, embarrassed.

"Don't make Stephan regret this," Sasha said and Aki shook his head, smiling at last.

There was only one person to say goodbye to now. And Sasha wasn't sure she would even say anything to him. They'd hardly spoken since he'd announced his plan three weeks before.

"Phelie?" He stepped closer to her, half expecting her to walk away.

For the third time in just a few minutes, Sasha found himself once again held in an embrace. Ophelia's arms tightened around him and for a moment his own determination wavered.

"Don't let them change you," Ophelia whispered in his ear, "And you'd better come back."

"You know I will." Sasha let out a shaky laugh, "If you're here, I'll come back. Always."

Epilogue

FATHER'S HOME!" LITTLE DROGO'S face was red from being pressed against the window. "And he's got someone with him."

Edith stepped out of the kitchen at Drogo's cry. "Who is it?"

Drogo shrugged, turning back to the window.

"Maybe that's why it took him so long to come home this time," Edith said, more to herself than to Drogo, as she joined her son at the window. Whoever was with Hamo would remain a mystery for the moment. Hamo was walking to the house alone.

"You were gone longer than you expected," Edith said after the initial excitement and chaos caused by his arrival abated.

"We had a little more to take care of this year." Hamo smiled. "And I hope you don't mind if I brought someone with me."

"That probably depends on who it is. Care to enlighten us?"

Hamo turned toward the barn door where someone was coming out. Before he could say anything, though, Drogo broke away from the cluster and started running.

"It's Sasha!" The words were only just out of his mouth before he hurled himself against Sasha's legs.

"It's good to see you too, Drogo." Sasha laughed, prying himself free.

"Are you really the Chief now?" Drogo looked up, his eyes wide with awe.

"I was. I'm not anymore, though."

There was one thing about summer that he loved more than anything else, Sasha thought, and that was the length of the days. With supper finished, questions asked and answered, and stories told, there was still at least a couple of hours of daylight left. The forest was a patchwork of shadows and late sunlight as he trudged through it. Three years away was not enough to erase the memory of where he was going.

The song of the creek running over its rocky bed reached his ears and Sasha smiled to himself. The falls in the mountains were breathtaking, magnificent, and powerful but they were nothing compared to the gentle cascade of clear water that ran through these familiar woods.

"You remembered it." Ophelia's presence was hardly a surprise to Sasha. Quite the opposite, in fact. He'd seen her slip away only an hour before and had been counting on finding her here.

"Did you think I could forget?"

"Three years is a long time."

"A very long time." Sasha led the way to the rock that jutted out above the water and sat down.

"Was it hard?"

"It was. Really hard." Sasha shut his eyes. There was so much he wanted to say and none of it wished to be said. He reached an idle hand into his pocket, fingering its contents. "What did I miss here?"

"Karl and Meredith's wedding, and Karl was very upset about that."

"Oh, I'm sure." Sasha rolled his eyes.

"Aki's doing well."

"I know. I saw him in town with Stephan." Sasha's hand tightened around the object in his pocket. "Did anything happen with you?"

"You've been gone three years, Sasha. Of course, things have happened. But nothing that big. Are you really here to stay?"

Sasha nodded. "I officially renounced my title and claim. Aruuk no longer has a Chief. I left them with a ruling counsel and, hopefully, they'll keep it that way."

The two lapsed into silence for a while. Sasha pulled his hand free of his pocket. There was more that he needed to say, so much more, but his tongue was like chalk. The sun sank down, turning the sky orange and purple. Sasha took a deep breath, collecting his thoughts and willing the knot of anxiety that gnawed on him to go away.

"I, um," he started, then cleared his throat and began again. "I really missed you."

Ophelia tilted her head, looking at him.

"I, uh, made... well, that is, I helped make something for you. If, that is, you want it." Sasha held out his hand, clasped tightly around something. "I hope you... well, here."

Ophelia's eyes went from his face to his hand as she held out her own to take it. Sasha uncurled his fingers, wishing that his heart would stop beating so wildly. He'd dreamed of this moment. He'd lived for this moment.

Ophelia gasped softly at the sight of the gold medallion on a thin chain resting in the palm of his hand. Her fingers brushed against it, running over the blood red stone nestled in its center.

"Oh, Sasha," Ophelia murmured, lifting her eyes to meet his.

"You're crying?" Sasha said in alarm.

"They're good tears, Sasha." She smiled.

"You like it, then? You'll take it?" Sasha let out a quivering breath. "Phelie, I...I'm not very good at this. I had to ask your father how this was even supposed to go because I didn't have any idea. I don't know much about how to be a good husband. But I know this, I love you, Phelie. I've loved you for a long time. And even when things were really hard over there, I loved you and thought about you all the time. You've been my best friend, and I know I want to spend the rest of my life with you, if you'll put up with me. I know I don't have much to offer you and I know there are things that I've done that I wish I hadn't, so I would understand if..."

"Yes," Ophelia cut him off.

"Yes?"

"Yes. I'll take it, I'll take you." Ophelia smiled, tears still shining in her eyes, "I'll marry you."

Sasha lowered his head with a great sigh. "I was so worried you wouldn't. Are you sure?"

"I'm sure. I thought you'd never ask." She laughed.

"Your father said that it's the custom for the man to put this on the girl." Sasha held the chain up letting the medallion swing back and forth catching the last rays of the summer sun. "May I?"

Other titles by S. T. Hobbs

The Divalian Chronicles –

Prequel ~ The Thief and the Slave

Book 1 ~ The Traitor's Alliance

Book 2 ~ The Last Chief

Book 3 ~ The Courier's Apprentice

Book 4 ~ The King's Successor

The Oracle's Odyssey –

Book 1 ~ The Forgotten Curse

Book 2 ~ The Fallen Gates

Book 3 ~ (Coming soon) The Fates' Finale

S. T. Hobbs